Heat Waves

Berkley Heat titles by Susan Lyons

SEX ON THE BEACH

SEX ON THE SLOPES

HEAT WAVES

heat WAVES

SUSAN LYONS

Heat | New York

THE BERKLEY PUBLISHING GROUP
Published by the Penguin Group
Penguin Group (USA) Inc.
375 Hudson Street, New York, New York 10014, USA
Penguin Group (Canada), 90 Eglinton Avenue East, Suite 700, Toronto, Ontario M4P 2Y3, Canada
(a division of Pearson Penguin Canada Inc.)
Penguin Books Ltd., 80 Strand, London WC2R 0RL, England
Penguin Group Ireland, 25 St. Stephen's Green, Dublin 2, Ireland (a division of Penguin Books Ltd.)
Penguin Group (Australia), 250 Camberwell Road, Camberwell, Victoria 3124, Australia
(a division of Pearson Australia Group Pty. Ltd.)
Penguin Books India Pvt. Ltd., 11 Community Centre, Panchsheel Park, New Delhi—110 017, India
Penguin Group (NZ), 67 Apollo Drive, Rosedale, Auckland 0632, New Zealand
(a division of Pearson New Zealand Ltd.)
Penguin Books (South Africa) (Pty.) Ltd., 24 Sturdee Avenue, Rosebank, Johannesburg 2196, South Africa

Penguin Books Ltd., Registered Offices: 80 Strand, London WC2R 0RL, England

This book is an original publication of The Berkley Publishing Group.

This is a work of fiction. Names, characters, places, and incidents either are the product of the author's imagination or are used fictitiously, and any resemblance to actual persons, living or dead, business establishments, events, or locales is entirely coincidental. The publisher does not have any control over and does not assume any responsibility for author or third-party websites or their content.

The recipes contained in this book are to be followed exactly as written. The publisher is not responsible for your specific health or allergy needs that may require medical supervision. The publisher is not responsible for any adverse reactions to the recipes contained in this book.

PRINTING HISTORY
Heat trade paperback edition / July 2011

Library of Congress Cataloging-in-Publication Data

Lyons, Susan.
 Heat waves / Susan Lyons. — Heat trade paperback ed.
  p. cm.
 ISBN 978-0-425-24124-0
 1. Cruise ships—Fiction. I. Title.
 PR9199.4.L97H43 2011
 813'.6—dc22
                                2010043028

PRINTED IN THE UNITED STATES OF AMERICA

10 9 8 7 6 5 4 3 2 1

AUTHOR'S NOTE

I've had so much fun writing a book set in Greece, one of my favorite places in the world. I hope you'll enjoy the cruise as much as I have.

As in my previous two Berkley Heat books (*Sex on the Beach*, set in Belize, and *Sex on the Slopes*, set in Whistler), I've used a destination wedding as the setting for my story. There's something sexy about an exotic location, and something romantic about a wedding. Put the two together and they're a recipe for some very spicy romance.

If you haven't read my previous books, you'll notice that in *Heat Waves*, wedding planner Gwen Austin mentions her two bosses at Happily Ever After, Sarah and Andi. You can read Sarah's romance in *Sex on the Beach* and Andi's in *Sex on the Slopes*.

I'd like to thank the people who made this book possible: my fabulous editor, Wendy McCurdy; her amazing assistant, Katherine Pelz; and my wonderful agent, Emily Sylvan Kim of Prospect Agency. My heartfelt gratitude goes to my critique partners, who provided invaluable input at various stages: Michelle Hancock, Elizabeth Allan, Nazima Ali, Delilah Marvelle, and Christina Crooks. For research assistance, thanks go to Nick Franson and Skye White.

I love to hear from readers. You can e-mail me at susan@susanlyons. ca or write c/o PO Box 73523, Downtown Postal Outlet, 1014 Robson Street, Vancouver, BC, Canada V6E 4L9. Please drop by my website, www.susanlyons.ca, where I have excerpts, behind-the-scenes notes, discussion guides, reviews, contests, a newsletter, recipes, articles, photos, and all sorts of good stuff.

Now, make yourself a Heat Wave (the recipe's included in the book), and settle down to enjoy a sexy, romantic cruise among the Greek islands.

CONTENTS

Rock the Boat   1

Making Waves   181

Heat Wave

INGREDIENTS

1½ oz. coconut rum
1 oz. peach schnapps
3 oz. orange juice
3 oz. pineapple juice
½ oz. grenadine
fruit for garnish (optional)

INSTRUCTIONS

Mix all ingredients except the grenadine in a parfait glass, with ice cubes or crushed ice. Top with grenadine. If desired, garnish with a maraschino cherry and/or a slice of orange, pineapple, or peach.

Rock the Boat

Chapter 1

AFTER seventeen hours of travel from Vancouver, Gwen should have been tired, but an equal measure of excitement and nervousness drove her to hurry from customs and the baggage claim. She tightened her grip on her purse and the carry-on bag that held her laptop and files—crucial items she'd never have entrusted to her checked luggage—as she burst into the arrivals area of the Athens airport. She was in Greece!

The place was bright, noisy, and bustling. An airport, yet a totally foreign one, with signs in Greek and strangers talking in languages she didn't understand. And she was here alone.

She caught herself running her thumb over the now-bare spot on her left hand, a habit she'd thought she had finally kicked. "Oh, Jonathan," she whispered under her breath, "we were supposed to come to Greece together."

When he had slid the wedding ring onto her finger, he'd

promised to look after her forever. Six years ago they'd begun to plan their big trip for his sabbatical year: Italy and Greece, with all the ancient sites and museums to please her philosophy prof husband, and all the scenery, restaurants, and shopping that she craved. Like everything else in their lives, the holiday would be the perfect blend of both their interests and tastes.

Instead, they'd spent his sabbatical year and the two after it fighting a losing battle with his cancer.

In some ways, it didn't seem right that the first exotic destination wedding she was in charge of as a wedding planner with Happily Ever After would be in Greece. But maybe it was good. Organizing and imposing control over the myriad details that went into putting together the perfect wedding would distract her from the melancholy that descended whenever she found herself wishing Jonathan was at her side.

Right now, though, it was less melancholy than anxiety that made her heart race as she scanned the crowd of strangers. With relief, she spotted a sign bearing her name and the Dionysus Cruises sailing ship logo. It was held by a pretty, young Greek woman in a short-sleeved white blouse, teal blue skirt, and sandals. Gwen hoped she'd make as good a first impression in her lightweight taupe pants and jacket worn over a silk tee the color of her flaxen hair.

Gwen waved a hand and towed her wheeled bag toward the woman. "*Kalimera.* I'm Gwen Austin. Are you Elpida Drakos?" Elpida was the rep who'd dealt patiently with dozens of e-mails, phone calls, and faxes.

"*Kalimera*, Gwen." The woman shook her hand, smiling as she returned the greeting for *good morning* in Greek, then continued in perfect, lightly accented English, "Welcome to Greece. Yes, I am Elpida."

"Thanks for coming to meet me."

"It is my pleasure." Elpida took the handle of Gwen's wheeled bag. "Come. Our van is in the parking lot."

Carry-on and purse slung over her shoulders, Gwen followed her outside. The dazzling sunshine, the wall of heat, brought her to an abrupt stop. *Greece, oh my God, I'm actually in Greece!* It was the first time she'd been anywhere outside Canada and the U.S. She and Jonathan had taken a few short holidays, but mostly they'd been saving for their big European trip.

She lifted her face to the sun's kiss and greedily sucked in air that hadn't been climate controlled and recycled. Though research had told her the temperature would be only a few degrees hotter than back home, the air felt drier on her skin and the light was more blinding. She slipped sunglasses from her purse and peeled off her jacket, savoring the warmth on her lightly tanned arms and shoulders.

Elpida waited patiently. "Nice to be off the plane?"

"Yes, and nice to be in Greece." Though, as she glanced around, she had to admit that an airport was pretty much the same anywhere in the world, and not the most scenic of sights.

"Wait until you're on the ocean." Elpida led her past bright yellow taxis toward a parking garage. "It is a short drive to Zea Marina at the port of Piraeus."

Liz Tippett and Peter Kirk had chosen to charter a small motor sailer to cruise the Cyclades Islands, including stops on Mykonos and Santorini. The trip would end in Crete where, a week from tomorrow, they'd be married on a pink sand beach. When Gwen thought about the entirety of what she'd be handling, she tended to hyperventilate. However, over the past eight months of working with Sarah and Andi at Happily Ever After, she'd developed an approach that worked for her. She broke each project into its individual tasks and details and developed a plan for each, plus a contingency plan. So what if she was a control freak? In this business—in life—it was the safest way to be.

"I wish I could go with you on the cruise," Elpida said. "It sounds so exciting and romantic."

"It will be if I do my job right." She believed that every bride and groom deserved a romantic, utterly fabulous start to their married life, just as she'd had when she married Jonathan at age nineteen. Her childhood had been unstable, with a dad who was charming but a total jerk, and a mom who both loved and hated him. In her teens Gwen had gone a little crazy, until that one tragic night. The next year, Jonathan had come along and she'd found love, happiness, and her place in life. At least until he'd fallen ill, and life had spiraled out of control again.

Elpida stowed Gwen's luggage in a small white van bearing the Dionysus name and logo, then they both climbed in. "I am sorry to not have better scenery to offer you on your first day in Greece, but development is such that"—Elpida shrugged as she pulled away— "really it is almost one city from Athens to Piraeus."

"That's okay. I'm eager to get to the *Aphrodite*."

"You will enjoy our Greek love boat."

When Gwen had first spoken to Elpida, the Greek woman had mentioned that Aphrodite was the goddess of love, beauty, and sexuality. When Gwen had relayed that information to the bride and groom, Liz had laughed with delight. "A love boat," she said, in the English accent that was still pronounced after two years of living in Vancouver. "Brilliant."

"You understand, though," Elpida now went on, "that the *Aphrodite* has just returned from a weeklong cruise and at this moment passengers are disembarking? They'll be gone by the time we get there and the new crew will have boarded, but the cleaners and maintenance people will be busy giving her a spit and polish."

Gwen smiled at hearing that expression come from Greek lips.

"I'll stay out of the way. I just want a quiet corner to meet with the captain, chef, and cruise director." She'd been e-mailing with them as well as with Elpida, and had arranged her schedule so as to arrive at the ship several hours before everyone else to run through everything in person.

With any luck, she'd even have time for a nap. Then, when Liz, Peter, and their guests arrived at two, she'd feel calm and in control. Or at least that was the plan.

"Of course," Elpida said.

"I'm particularly looking forward to meeting Giorgos, the cruise director." He had worked with Sarah and Andi before, and his knowledge of the islands had been invaluable in planning this trip. She'd be relying on him for so much over the next week. "Am I pronouncing his name correctly?"

"Er, yes, but—" Elpida broke off, blasting the horn and cursing in Greek at a taxi driver who'd swung in front of her. "Bad drivers and no scenery. A fine introduction for you."

"It's okay."

"It is a pity you couldn't come earlier and see Athens, but I'm glad you're planning a couple of days at the end of the trip. There are so many wonderful sights, from the shops of the Plaka to the National Archeological Museum. And of course the Acropolis."

"I'm looking forward to it. But later is better. Now I wouldn't be able to relax. I'm so focused on the cruise and the wedding." Besides, she'd get emotional seeing the Acropolis without Jonathan. It had been one of the spots he'd most looked forward to. Best to leave that experience for the end of her trip, when she could afford to indulge in sentimentality and—

Elpida cleared her throat, breaking into her thoughts. "I must tell you, Gwen, there has been a small change. Giorgos will not be on the *Aphrodite*. He had—"

"What?" No cruise director? Panic swelled quickly, her breath speeding up so she could barely force out words. "That's impossible." Giorgos was supposed to lead the shore excursions, provide details of Greek history, give language lessons, and do a hundred other things she couldn't possibly handle on her own. "I need him. I can't do this by myself." It had never occurred to her that she'd need a contingency plan for his absence; he'd seemed one hundred percent reliable.

Damn, she was having trouble catching her breath and her heart was racing. Realizing she was starting to hyperventilate, she forced herself to breathe slowly and deeply. She hated this feeling, reminiscent of the days when Jonathan's cancer treatments had failed, and the days after his death when she was terrified of facing the future alone.

"No, no," Elpida said quickly, "we have another cruise director filling in. Santos Michaelides."

"Whew." Gwen sank back, heart still pumping madly. *Breathe. Everything's going to be fine.* "You scared me." *Okay, I can handle this.* It was only a small change in plan. What a pity, though, because she and Giorgos had worked well together, at least by e-mail. "I assume Mr. Michaelides is equally experienced?"

"Er, well, he does have Giorgos's notes."

"His notes? What do you mean? Hasn't Mr. Michaelides handled these cruises before?"

"Not actually. He's brand-new to Dionysus. But I'm sure it will be fine."

"Oh my God." She was new at her job and so was the cruise director. And, though she wasn't superstitious, she couldn't help but remember that this was Friday the thirteenth. "How did this happen?"

"Giorgos's grandmother is in ill health and he had to go visit her on Corfu."

"Poor Giorgos. I hope she'll be okay. But doesn't Dionysus have other experienced cruise directors?"

"Yes, of course." Elpida glanced in the mirrors before changing into the right-hand lane, and Gwen glimpsed a frown furrowing her brow. "It is up to the manager of the company to allocate crew. He assigned Mr. Michaelides to the *Aphrodite*, so I am sure he's confident of his ability."

"Have you even met Mr. Michaelides?"

The other woman glanced her way, the frown now replaced by a knowing smile. "Oh yes, he has been in the office. I must say, in some ways he's an improvement on Giorgos."

"In what ways?"

"Let me say"—she winked—"the single ladies will enjoy the excellent . . . is the expression *eye candy*?"

"That's the expression." And it wasn't one bit reassuring. "This man will be professional, won't he?" Gwen needed him to do his job, not play the shipboard Lothario and seduce the wedding guests. She knew that type very well. Her dad, who she rarely saw, had always been a player—superficially charming and completely unreliable.

"Look, here is Zea Marina."

Distracted from her concerns, Gwen gazed ahead, seeing that the ocean beckoned from between thickly clustered buildings. She leaned forward eagerly as Elpida drove closer. This was more like it, and much better than the traffic-clogged industrial strip.

Zea Marina was a large bay with several docks, ringed with light-colored buildings that seemed to include apartments, restaurants, bars, and shops. Sunlight reflected off the walls of the buildings, the surface of the ocean, and the white hulls of numerous luxury yachts, making her glad she wore sunglasses. Though the place was spectacular, what Gwen really longed for was a more rustically picturesque Greece with small villages and ports, tavernas by the ocean, ancient ruins, and shops full of local crafts and jewelry.

Elpida parked, hoisted Gwen's bag out of the van easily, then led her to the dock. They boarded a Zodiac that could hold a dozen or more people.

Gwen commented, "I remember you saying that Dionysus chooses not to dock their ships here, but anchors them out in the bay."

"Yes, it's more exciting for the guests to approach from the water." Elpida started the engine, cast off the lines, and steered away from the dock.

A fresh breeze tossed Gwen's straight, shoulder-length blond hair and she scented the tangy air. "This is invigorating after the heat and traffic."

Elpida nodded, then pointed. "There she is. The *Aphrodite.*"

"Oh my, she's beautiful." The ship was close to 150 feet long, tiny compared to the massive cruise ships that could run to 1000 feet or more. All the same, she loomed large as they approached and was dramatically lovely with her indigo hull and shiny wood cabin. Gwen clicked a few pictures, imagining the ship with her sails raised, flying with the wind. On deck, Liz and Peter would be hoisting drinks, laughing with their family and friends, creating wonderful memories.

"Your home for the next week." Elpida slowed the Zodiac. "She will be good for you, I'm sure, our love boat."

Gwen hoped so. This was a huge career step. While the captain and crew would be responsible for the guests' safety, it would fall to her—assisted by the brand-new cruise director—to ensure that everyone had a fabulous time. She had plans and more plans, and contingency plans, but each day would bring a dozen new challenges. Sarah and Andi had taken a chance on her, a woman who'd been out of the workforce for four years. She didn't want to let them down.

Nervousness fluttered through her and she focused on her deep breathing. It didn't help that she now realized Elpida had never actually answered her question about Santos Michaelides being professional. It was too late to ask again, though, because a stocky, middle-aged Greek with a neat beard and a white cap with gold braid and insignia was smiling down from the deck. Pleasant looking, but not eye candy, so probably not Mr. Michaelides.

She climbed up the ladder and he helped her on board, his grip firm and warm. "Welcome aboard, Ms. Austin. I'm Captain Aristides Papadopoulos. But as I said in e-mail, everyone calls me Captain Ari."

He was only two or three inches taller than her five foot seven, and he looked fit and strong in his uniform of white pants and short-sleeved shirt with the Dionysus logo.

She thanked him in Greek. "*Efkharisto*, Captain Ari. I'm Gwen."

Elpida swung aboard. "*Yassas*, Captain Ari." Gwen recognized the casual word for *hello* or *hi*.

"*Yassas*, Elpida."

"Everything on track?" the Greek woman asked.

"*Ne*." It sounded like *no*, but Gwen knew it was Greek for *yes*. "Gwen, your cabin is all ready for you. We thought you might want to unpack and change out of your travel clothes. Then perhaps a snack?"

"That sounds wonderful." A shower, too, would be heaven. "As soon as I've changed, could I meet with you, Chef Ilyas, and the new cruise director, Mr. Michaelides?"

"If Michaelides has arrived by then."

"He's not aboard already?" Anxiety pinched her again. She glanced around the wooden deck, noting a couple of people at work washing windows and polishing brass, somehow expecting the new cruise director to materialize. "I thought the three of you were going to be here. That's what I arranged with Giorgos."

Captain Ari exchanged uneasy glances with Elpida. "We are, uh, expecting him any moment."

It didn't sound as if Giorgos's replacement was reliable, and that was definitely not a good thing. Minor glitches Gwen could cope with, but the cruise director was critical to the success of this week.

She hated when things got out of control. It took her back to the worst days of her life, to the panicky feeling that nothing would ever be right again.

As she struggled to take a deep breath of ocean air, Captain Ari glanced past her and said, with some relief, "Ah, there he is now."

Gwen let out her breath in a low *whoosh* and swung around to size up the man she hoped she'd be able to count on.

A small water taxi was approaching the *Aphrodite*, a young Greek at the wheel and a slightly older one sitting beside him, his longish black hair whipping in the wind. Sunglasses hid his eyes, then he took them off and studied the threesome on board.

A smile flashed, even brighter than Elpida's. Before the boat had stopped, he stood, balancing with the natural grace of a sailor. His black T-shirt and pale, much-washed jeans weren't tight, but the breeze plastered them against a lean, muscled body.

Well, how about that? Reliable or not, he was the sexiest thing she'd seen in . . . maybe ever. Disconcertingly, she felt a twinge of lust in female parts that hadn't twinged in years.

That feeling gave her a new awareness of herself as a woman—an awareness that made her wish she'd had a chance to freshen up. Not that she cared one bit whether this man found her attractive, but a girl did have some pride.

She straightened her shoulders and resisted the urge to tidy her windblown hair.

The water taxi bumped up against the *Aphrodite*. The man paid the driver, slung a duffel bag over his shoulder, and stepped onto the bottom rung of the ladder.

His bearing was confident, almost arrogant. His eyes, so dark they might be black, sparkled with something that hinted at devilry, and a gold earring winked. There was a rakish air about him, and for a moment she envisioned him in pirate's garb.

She stepped back as he came aboard. "*Yassas*," he said casually. "Elpida, Captain Ari." He rattled off something quickly in Greek that turned their rather skeptical looks to grins.

In that moment, disconcertingly, he reminded her of her father, a man who was handsome, confident, and had lots of charm but virtually no substance. Then she shook her head. No, there was no reason to jump to that conclusion. Maybe he had a legitimate reason for his lateness.

He turned that sparkling gaze on her. "And Ms. Austin? It's a pleasure." His voice was husky, a little rough to match up with his hair and earring, and he used it like a caress. "I'm Santos Michaelides." He held out his hand. "Sorry to be late. My taxi had a flat tire." He was obviously Greek, yet his English was colloquial and only slightly—charmingly—accented.

A flat tire. Yes, it was a reasonable excuse from what she'd seen of the road to Zea Marina. "Call me Gwen." She took his hand, intending to shake briskly, but an odd sensation rippled through her: heat, dizziness, and an inappropriate and disconcerting arousal. Realizing she was clinging to his hand, she quickly drew hers away and rubbed her forehead. "Sorry, I must be a little jet-lagged."

"I'm sure that's it." His black eyes danced, indicating he was used to women reacting this way. She had the fanciful thought that if he'd really been a pirate, he wouldn't have to take women captive; they'd throw themselves at his feet.

As for her, she was here to work. She turned away from those far too seductive eyes and said to Captain Ari, "Could you point me toward my cabin? I really could use a shower and a change of clothes, then that snack you promised." Without risking another look at Santos, she said, "Could we all get together in twenty minutes to go over the details of the cruise?"

Everyone murmured agreement, then the captain hefted her bag easily. "Right this way. As you requested, you're on the lower deck. We have lots of singles sharing cabins, so those folks have the twin-bed rooms and you've got a double."

A double bed. Where she'd sleep neatly on one side, the way she always did now. As for Santos Michaelides, she only hoped his considerable charm proved a useful addition rather than a disruption to her carefully planned cruise.

Chapter 2

A double bed. Damned if those words didn't send a surge of lust straight to Santos Michaelides's groin. So did the rear view of the wedding planner as she walked away: a spill of pale gold hair, straight back, narrow waist, curvy butt, long legs. He couldn't wait to see the woman in a bikini.

"She's pretty, isn't she?"

"Huh?" He turned to Elpida, who was studying him with amusement. "The Canadian? Yeah, I guess." So was Elpida, but it was Gwen Austin who got to him.

Elpida tossed the thick black hair that curled around her face and said knowingly, "Greek men always go for blondes."

"Like Greek women don't?" he shot back. Not that he cared about the color of a woman's hair. He'd dated blondes, brunettes, and redheads in equal numbers. With Gwen, it wasn't so much the blond hair as the way it combined with lightly tanned skin, huge eyes the rich caramel of Metaxa brandy accented by lashes and brows a shade or two darker, and a full, mobile mouth that was the stuff of wet dreams. It was her manner, too. He was used to women flirting with him but Gwen, who clearly felt the same attraction he did, was doing her best to deny it. It only made her more intriguing.

No wedding ring—he'd checked that out—so probably she was just being professional. The folders of notes he'd been given by Giorgos and the manager of Dionysus Cruises told him she was compulsive about her job, to the point of being anal.

And he, too, should be thinking about work, not whether Gwen's mouth tasted as lush as it looked. He was here to do a job—or, rather, two jobs: his real one as an insurance fraud investigator, and his cover job of cruise director.

Elpida wound up a commentary on the merits of guys of different nationalities, then studied him appraisingly. "Your taxi really had a flat tire? That wasn't just an excuse for being late?"

"No, it did. And that's after the hotel messed up my bill and I had to stand in line forever to get it fixed." He'd wanted to board the *Aphrodite* with Captain Ari and the rest of the crew so he'd blend in as if he were one of them.

"Friday the thirteenth," she said.

"Here's hoping it improves." Arriving late had set him off on the wrong foot with Gwen, a woman he had to work with, and had to deceive. A woman who stirred inconvenient lust. And that was bizarre, because only three days ago, in Toronto, he'd shared a night of steamy sex with his "friend with benefits."

Now he was as horny for the wedding planner as if he hadn't had sex in a year. *Gamoto*, he cursed silently. As if the coming week wouldn't be complicated enough already. Though he loved under-cover work and was happy to be back in Greece, he usually had more prep time to get his head around an investigation, do research himself rather than rely on an intern, and develop his cover.

"Where's my cabin?" he asked Elpida. "I should stow my gear and get into uniform before the meeting."

"I'll take you to crew quarters. You're sharing with the cook."

"Thanks." He'd known he'd be sharing a cabin and would have little privacy. All his confidential files were on his laptop, well password-protected.

He followed as she led him belowdecks.

Last week, his employer, Insurance Assured, had turned up information that Flynn Kavanagh was flying to Greece to attend the wedding of a friend, Liz Tippett. Kavanagh, a Vancouver IT consultant, had been charged with using his technological wizardry to steal five million dollars from a client, but was acquitted at trial a few months ago. Insurance Assured had paid out but kept an eye on the man. The female undercover agent who'd gotten friendly with Kavanagh's mother at her fitness club had found out about the trip to Greece, and that had raised enough of a flag to put an investigator aboard the *Aphrodite*. Santos, a Greek who lived in Toronto but had grown up on one of the Greek islands, was the logical choice, and he'd just wound up an assignment where he'd nailed an auto insurance fraud ring.

Elpida showed him to a small cabin with two twin beds, one with jeans and a shirt tossed across it, and a small desk that doubled as a bureau. "You've done this before?" she asked. "Been a cruise director?"

"You bet." He told the lie with a flash of smile, the persuasive one he'd perfected in his work. "Don't worry." He slung his duffel on the vacant bed. "I have the files, contact names, all the information I need."

The manager of Dionysus Cruises had also given him an intensive briefing. Sworn to—and paid for—secrecy, the man had treated it as a cloak-and-dagger adventure. When Giorgos, the real cruise director, had returned from his last cruise, he'd been ordered to pretend he'd had a family emergency and take a week's vacation, the bill footed by Insurance Assured.

"A lot of work has gone into planning this cruise," Elpida warned. She moved to the door. "Change into uniform and bring your files when you come up. You'll want to refer to them. Gwen's meticulous about details." She gave a lopsided grin. "Have a fun week."

He groaned. Yeah, that was the impression the files had given of the wedding planner. Himself, he was more the intuitive type. If you concentrated too hard on the details, you could miss the broad picture. Santos looked at patterns, the odd things that didn't quite fit.

Unzipping his duffel, he thought wryly that today, on the *Aphrodite*, the piece that was out of place was he himself. Lucky that most people took things at surface value and that he was good at his job.

Though he hated uniforms, donning the white pants, Dionysus-logoed white shirt, and rubber-soled sandals helped him get into character. He studied his reflection in the small mirror. He'd asked the manager of Dionysus whether he should cut the hair he'd grown for his last assignment and the man had said no, the company's image was contemporary, not overly formal.

Lugging Giorgos's bulging file folders, he headed up to the main deck. Captain Ari was in the dining room, seated at the head of a rectangular wooden table, with Elpida on his right. The two were absorbed in conversation and didn't notice him, so Santos had a chance to survey the room. It had a Greek simplicity and attractiveness: wooden furniture with cushions in that vivid, particularly Greek shade of blue, white walls with wood trim, brass accents, and a well-equipped bar in one corner.

At the table, a portly, balding man set out fresh fruit, rolls, and orange juice, together with two classic Greek breakfast items: a bowl of thick, creamy yogurt and a pitcher of dark, liquid honey. When Santos went over, the man gave a genial smile and introduced himself as Ilyas, the chef, Santos's roommate.

Ilyas poured everyone small cups of strong coffee from a *bikri*, the traditional pot for making Greek coffee.

As Santos took a sip, Gwen stepped into the dining room and walked toward them. Damp hair, falling long and straight to her shoulders, told him she'd had a shower and not bothered with a hair dryer. A shower. Naked. Water streaming over the curves now hugged by tan capris and a sleeveless knit top in a pretty coral shade.

His body tightened at the thought of her naked. Focusing on her face didn't help either. A touch of makeup made her eyes even larger, and the coral on her lips had the same effect. Those lips could drive a man insane.

They widened in a delighted smile—not at the sight of him, but at the spread on the table. "This looks delicious." She took the chair at the foot of the table, opposite the captain, and slung her huge shoulder bag over the back.

A scent drifted on the air, something tropical and flowery. Spicy. Sexy.

She reached for the glass of orange juice and took a long swallow, tilting her head back in an unconsciously seductive motion that made him want to trail kisses down her exposed neck. "Mmm, I needed that."

At the moment, what he needed was way more intimate.

Next she reached for the coffee.

"I could make you a cappuccino or caffe latte if you prefer," the chef offered.

She shook her head. "Greek coffee is perfect."

Chef Ilyas beamed. "You know Greek coffee?" He took a seat across from Santos.

After taking a sip, she gave an appreciative smile. "I've been doing my homework. Online, and also in Greek coffee shops and restaurants. My hometown, Vancouver, Canada, has some great ones. I'm guessing you're Chef Ilyas Petrakis?"

"A pleasure to meet you, after all those e-mails."

She wrinkled her nose charmingly. "Sorry if I was a bit obsessive, but I really want things to go well."

"And they will," Captain Ari broke in with a reassuring smile. "We have done this before, you know."

"Of course." Finally, she turned to Santos. "Although I understand you're new, Mr. Michaelides." She pronounced his name well for an English speaker.

He tapped his files and gave her his persuasive grin. "Call me Santos. I'm new, but prepared. I aim to please. Just let me know what you need."

Her eyes widened, and delicate color tinged her cheeks.

He realized his words had come out with a double meaning that he hadn't intended—at least consciously. Even when he tried to focus on work, he was affected by her. Damn, he had no business being affected. No business gazing into intoxicating brandy eyes or thinking about kissing full, coral lips. Much less lifting the hem of her top and reaching under it to cup a sweet, firm—

"Help yourselves to breakfast." The captain's voice broke into his thoughts. "We can talk while we eat."

Santos had already had room service at the hotel, and the thing he most wanted to nibble on was Gwen's lush mouth. But he couldn't resist yogurt and honey. The Greeks made the best in the world.

Gwen served herself some of everything and dug in.

He liked a woman who wasn't afraid to eat, especially if she was fit and curvy like this one.

And he liked the way her white teeth nipped into the flesh of an orange segment, neatly separating it from the rind; the way she chewed slowly, eyes half closed as if she was concentrating entirely on the flavor.

He raised a piece of orange to his own mouth so he could taste what she was tasting. Flavor burst on his tongue, sweet and tangy. The inside of her mouth would taste the same.

She swirled a little honey into her yogurt, then lifted the spoon and slowly sucked the yogurt into her mouth. If she'd been another woman, he'd think she was teasing him, but Gwen didn't cast sly glances from under her lashes; she focused on her breakfast.

Her sensual gusto made him guess she was like that in bed, too. His cock pulsed at the thought of her wide mouth wrapping around him, her pink tongue licking him as thoroughly as she was licking that spoon.

He shifted, feeling growing pressure beneath his fly.

Pity they weren't both here on holiday. They could have a lot of fun. Maybe she wasn't into holiday flings, though. A wedding planner with a company called Happily Ever After might well be looking for one of her own. In which case, she sure as hell shouldn't look in his direction. As his grandparents had told him with bitter disappointment, he took after his parents. For him, life was about adventure, not stability. He always made that clear before hooking up with a woman. He hated when people got unrealistic expectations and then were hurt when he didn't live up to them.

While they all ate, Captain Ari reviewed their itinerary and the weather forecast, which promised sunshine and light breezes. "We'll have the sails up much of the time," he told them. "Passengers like that."

"Wonderful," Gwen said. She'd polished off the last of her yogurt, thank God, and now took another sip of coffee. "There should be no problem staying on schedule?"

"None at all."

"Great." She cleared space on the table in front of her, then took a file folder from her bag. From it, she extracted a paper-clipped bundle with a spreadsheet on top. "Elpida, is everything on track for picking people up at the airport and from the hotels?"

"Hotels?" Santos asked.

"Some guests arrived a few days early, to explore Athens," Gwen explained.

"We have airport and hotel pickup under control," Elpida said.

"I brought you a copy of the spreadsheet." Gwen peeled off the paper clip.

Elpida waved a hand. "I have a more recent one." She handed Gwen a folded sheet. "I brought you a copy. One flight was delayed, but it will still arrive on time for our two o'clock departure." She glanced at her watch and rose. "I must go now."

"Thanks." Gwen skimmed the paper, then put it down and picked up another paper-clipped bundle. "Chef Ilyas, let's confirm menus."

Unobtrusively, Santos took the sheet of paper Elpida had given Gwen and quickly scanned it. Yes, Flynn Kavanagh was still on the list, his flight and arrival time unchanged from the information Insurance Assured had supplied. He replaced the sheet and listened while Gwen and the chef reviewed their plans.

He concentrated not on the details but on impressions. Gwen struck him as a control freak who had to organize every tiny detail. It was an interesting contrast to the sensual, uninhibited way she'd dug into her breakfast and the excitement on her face when she gazed out at the ocean.

The Dionysus Cruises people seemed efficient as well, but far more relaxed. He sensed that, while they respected Gwen, they were humoring her a little.

He certainly hoped things ran smoothly, because it would give him more time to mingle with the passengers, particularly his suspect.

What he really wanted to do was mingle with Gwen, between the sheets.

He spooned up the last of the delicious concoction in his bowl. If he painted his cock with yogurt and honey . . . Would she be gentle, or a little rough? Would she suck him between those full lips, take him deep into her mouth?

And why was he indulging in lustful fantasies when he—and

she—had a job to do? Over the years he'd learned there was no explaining attraction, but the way Gwen got to him was . . . unique.

Now, there was a disconcerting notion, one that didn't make the least bit of sense.

"Santos?" Her voice made him raise his head from rapt contemplation of that last spoonful of yogurt.

"Yeah?" He put the spoon into his mouth.

Her throat muscles rippled as if she was swallowing, too, then she cleared her throat. "I've gone over everything I need to with Captain Ari and Chef Ilyas. In fact"—she gazed at the two other men—"feel free to get back to work, if you want."

They both departed, then she fixed those captivating brown eyes on Santos. "Those are Giorgos's files? You're familiar with everything in them?"

He opened the top folder and riffled through a pile of papers that outlined this afternoon's and evening's activities. Though he'd only had a day and a half to get up to speed, he was a quick study, plus he'd grown up on the Cyclades Islands. He grinned at her. "It's not exactly rocket science."

The corner of her mouth curved. "Is that a Greek expression, too?"

"Uh . . ." He hadn't lived in Greece since he was seventeen, when he'd pissed his grandparents off by going to London to work. After that, he'd attended college in the States. Currently, he lived in Toronto, where Insurance Assured's head office was located. "Greece has picked up most of the Americanisms," he hedged.

"Small world." Her smile faded and her arched brows drew together, creating a furrow up the center of her forehead.

"What's wrong?"

The lips he'd been fantasizing about, still pink though she'd eaten off most of her lipstick, pressed together. "It may not be rocket science, but I need you to take this seriously."

"No problem," he tossed off. At the moment, his most pressing concern was the pressure in his groin.

Her frown deepened. She glanced around as if ensuring no one was nearby, and lowered her voice. "Santos, I'm sure you've done this kind of thing many times, even if not with Dionysus Cruises. But for me, this is a big deal. This is the first time I've been in charge of an exotic destination wedding."

"Yeah?" The word exotic was perfect for her scent—like sultry, spicy flowers.

"I've never been to Greece, never handled a wedding where the guests were all together for a week before the ceremony, never even been on a cruise. This is all new to me." Her breathing had sped up and there was a pleading look in her soft brown eyes.

Then she took a deep breath and firmed her jaw. "I've organized every last detail and I'm prepared for anything, but I was counting on Giorgos's experience. I need to know I can rely on you."

Despite the lust that clouded his brain, he was paying attention. Her frankness had a certain appeal. Him, he was more of the "baffle them with bullshit" school, but then his undercover job had made him adept at deception.

Playing his role, he held a file folder. "Of course you can. Here's all the information."

Those brandy eyes didn't even glance at the file, they remained fixed on his own eyes. "Having the information is different from being committed to doing the job well."

"Gwen, when I commit to doing something, I can be relied on." It was when people wanted things he wasn't prepared to give—like staying in Greece to take over his grandparents' restaurant, or being a husband or dad—that he couldn't be relied on any more than his parents. In his work, he lied all the time to get the job done. In his personal life, he was up front with people so no one would expect more than he was prepared to give.

Her gaze remained fixed on him, telling him without words that he hadn't reassured her.

He sighed. "You and I may not have Giorgos's experience, but we can do this together. I hear how important this is to you and I won't let you down." And damned if, when he said those last words, the promise didn't seem more like a genuine one, a personal one, not just role-playing. What was it about this woman?

This time, she seemed to believe him, because she gave a warm smile. "Thanks, Santos." She touched him, just a gentle press of warm fingers against the back of his hand, but it resonated all the way through him. Sexually, of course, and it made him realize that staying away from her would take willpower he likely didn't possess. But there was something more, something he couldn't define.

Her eyes were warm with gratitude and trust. She trusted him, the man who was deceiving her.

He studied her face. Lovely, a little stressed, and with a maturity he hadn't noticed at first. She was likely two or three years older than his own twenty-seven, not that it lessened her attractiveness.

Deception was his job. Rarely did he think twice about the dishonesty of playing an undercover role. Again, he asked himself what it was about this woman. The combination of vulnerability and strength? The trust she placed in him? Normally, he'd have been annoyed if a woman wanted to rely on him, and yet, bizarrely, he wanted to deserve Gwen's trust.

All she was asking was that he partner with her the way Giorgos would have. He could do that—had intended to do it—and still deceive her about his real identity.

He drummed the fingers of his other hand on the table, deliberating. It was within his discretion to tell her about his real mission. In the past few days, since Insurance Assured had learned about Kavanagh's trip to Greece, one of the law student interns at his office had run basic background checks on all the passengers and crew.

The criminal record checks had turned up a few minor infractions that the intern had investigated in more depth. Santos had that information and also a list of the people who'd come up squeaky clean, Gwen included.

He turned his hand over and captured hers, which made her give a soft gasp and made his own flesh tingle disconcertingly. "Gwen, let's go to your cabin."

She jerked her hand free, her huge eyes widened further, and color tinged her cheeks. "What?"

"No, sorry, that's not what I meant." Though his erection sure as hell liked the idea. "I need to talk to you privately."

"Talk?" she asked skeptically.

"Yeah, just talk." An irresistible demon made him say, "Unless, of course, you have something else in mind."

Her mouth opened, lips quivering, and the color on her cheeks deepened. "Of course I don't."

"Never play poker."

"What?"

"Your body gives you away."

"Oh! How dare you . . . ?" she sputtered. "A gentleman would never say—"

The old-fashioned term made him grin. "You seriously think I'm a gentleman?"

Her chin stuck out. "No, probably not. When I first saw you, *pirate* was more the word that came to mind."

He gave a surprised laugh. "I'm kind of flattered." A life of adventure? Yeah, that was what he'd always sought.

Her eyes narrowed. "Did I say it was a compliment?" There was an edge to her voice.

"Oh, okay." Weren't women supposed to like pirates? Johnny Depp and all that? But her comment made him think past the superficial. "Yeah, I guess there's not a lot to admire about pirates."

"Not at all," she said stiffly. She studied him a long moment, then her face softened. "Well, the earring's kind of cool."

He touched the small gold hoop, its band engraved with a Greek key design. He'd worn it since he was seventeen—the one thing he'd taken as a reminder of home when he left—unless he was on an undercover job where he had to remove it. "I may not be a gentleman, Gwen, and I like adventure, but I'm no pirate. I take my job seriously." He took her trust seriously, too, a fact that was disconcerting enough that he wouldn't share it with her. "It's my job I need to talk to you about."

"In private?" she asked skeptically.

He leaned closer and indulged himself by hooking silky blond hair behind a delicate ear, then he whispered, "It's about the real reason I'm here. It has to be our secret."

Chapter 3

THIS man was *not* easy to be around, Gwen thought as she gathered her things and followed Santos. Easy on the eyes, yes. She appreciated the way the slim-fitting white uniform highlighted his broad shoulders, narrow waist, taut butt, and long legs. The short sleeves showed off strong brown arms, and even his feet, bare in sandals, were sexy. She'd never spent much time noticing men's looks, but Santos had such a physical presence, it was impossible not to.

That must be why her body felt flushed with sexual awareness as she followed him down the stairs that led belowdecks.

What on earth did he mean about the real reason he was on the *Aphrodite*? Was this some ploy to get her alone and . . . She smothered a chuckle. The words *have his way with her* had actually popped into her mind. During Jonathan's illness, she'd obviously spent too much time dipping into her mom's supply of old romance novels, where the dashing pirate took the beautiful lady captive and ravished her until she screamed in ecstasy.

Though Gwen had only ever made love with one man, she figured she enjoyed sex as much as the next woman and *she* had certainly never yelled in pleasure. Since Jonathan's death, even though she'd recently begun to date and had even kissed one man, she hadn't felt even a twinge of arousal. It was kind of reassuring to react this way to Santos. Her sexuality had only been on sabbatical, it hadn't died along with her husband.

This wasn't the best time for it to reawaken, though. She was here to do a job, not have the stereotypical cruise ship romance with a sexy crew member. Besides, despite his assurance that he could be trusted, his easy, confident charm reminded her too much of her father. A man like that raised red flags with her for fear he was another snake oil salesman. She wasn't as gullible as her mom.

She stared at the back of his head with those virile, black curls. Curls that made a woman's fingers itch to— "Oh!" Her foot missed a step and she lurched forward, the heavy bag with her files slipping from her shoulder and throwing her even more off balance.

Santos swung around instantly, in time to throw out his arms and catch her as she tumbled into them. Her bag thwacked against her thigh but she barely noticed as he gripped her tighter, then swung her down the last couple of steps to the level hallway.

Male touch, powerful and assured.

He didn't release her.

She didn't step back. Her heart thudded, but this time it wasn't from an incipient panic attack; it was pure excitement at the hardness of his chest against her breasts, the firm warmth of his arms circling her, the solid strength of his thighs and—oh, God—an erection that grew against her belly.

Stunned from the near fall and the arousal racing through her, she gaped up at him.

His black eyes looked a little dazed, too. "Are you okay?" he asked softly.

She nodded. "I, uh . . ."

"It knocked the breath out of you?"

No. You *knock the breath out of me*. She struggled to find words. "I slipped. Thanks for catching me. I'm, uh, fine." If *fine* included burning cheeks, nipples that ached to be caressed, and hot dampness between her legs. She should pull away, but she was using every ounce of willpower to resist rubbing against that erection. It had been years since she'd felt one. Was that the reason for her supercharged reaction?

"You're more than fine." His voice was even huskier than usual. "Jesus, Gwen, you feel good." He gave a soft chuckle. "Guess it's obvious how much you turn me on."

"This is a bad idea." Only a couple of minutes ago, she'd had all sorts of reasons to resist Santos. What were they again?

"Feels like a good one to me." He shifted his hips, pressing a little harder, and it was all she could do to hold back a whimper of need.

Then, with the force of a cold shower, she remembered the last man who'd held her, aroused her, satisfied her. Jonathan. He was gone, yet she felt disloyal. They'd planned to come to Greece together, and now here she was, behaving like a slut with a man she'd barely met.

She had frozen in Santos's arms, and now took a step back, breaking away.

He ran a hand through his hair, dragging it back from his face. "We need to talk."

She heaved her bag back on her shoulder. "I'm not sure that's a good idea. At least not in my cabin."

"Christ, Gwen, I'm not going to assault you." He sounded so frustrated and aggrieved, she believed him.

"Fine." On shaky legs, she led him to her cabin, and he followed her in.

When he shut the door behind them, she felt a moment's panic.

He was so big and masculine and the room was tiny, with little floor space between the double bed and a small desk that doubled as a bureau. She hadn't unpacked earlier, and her wheeled bag lay open on the bed, clothes tumbling over the sides. Including a skimpy, black lace bra and a white thong.

Her instinct was to hide them—going from slut to shy virgin—but she resisted. Santos had no doubt seen more lingerie in his life than she had. Striving for casualness, she slung her shoulder bag onto the desk, perched on the bed, and gestured toward the desk chair. "Have a seat and say what you came to say."

He turned the chair to face her and sat, his crisp white uniform a striking contrast to his brown skin, the overly long black hair that framed his striking face, and the gold earring.

With a knowing smile, he glanced from her to the bra and thong then back again, his gaze drifting casually, confidently down her body.

She believed that he wouldn't assault her, but he hadn't promised not to try to seduce her. The idea both thrilled and appalled her.

When he crossed one leg over the other—the guy way, with one ankle just above the other knee—her gaze automatically flew to his crotch. His erection had yet to subside. Her sex-starved body melted and moistened at the thought of feeling him thrust hard and fast, deep inside her.

No! She forced her eyes back to his face. She wasn't ready for a sexual relationship. Besides, her sole purpose for being aboard the *Aphrodite* was to give Liz, Peter, and their families and friends a wonderful pre-wedding cruise and a fabulous wedding in Crete at the end of the week. She had to remain in control and couldn't allow herself to be distracted by this experienced, sexy stranger who happened to be extremely well endowed.

Striving to sound businesslike, she asked, "What's this secret we had to discuss in private?"

He took a deep breath and let it out audibly. "Right. I think you should know that I'm not really a cruise director."

"What?" She leaped to her feet, realizing too late that the action almost catapulted her into his lap. Hurriedly she stepped aside to pace the tiny strip of floor between the bed and the wall, wringing her hands. "You got the job under false pretenses? Oh no, this is terrible. I really, really need a cruise director." Panicked and furious, she glared at him. Her heart and her breath both raced.

He uncrossed his legs and leaned forward, studying her with a concerned expression. "I can do the job. Giorgos has everything organized. It's just a matter of following his notes."

Notes that, she now realized, he'd carelessly left lying on the table in the dining room. "Oh no, it's not." She dragged her hands across her temples and into her hair. The man didn't have a clue. "What if something goes wrong? This is a disaster!"

He scowled. "It's not a disaster. If I say I can do the job, then I can damn well do it."

She struggled for breath, fighting to get the words out, to make him understand. "You have to have a Plan B, you have to be flexible, and to do that, you need to know the places, the people. That's the information *I* don't have, that I was relying on *you* to know." She hated, hated, *hated* it when things were out of her control.

She spiraled back to the days of disease, chemo that didn't work, agony. When things spun out of control, people got hurt. Jonathan had died.

A wave of dizziness hit her and she couldn't force air into her lungs.

Santos's scowl turned to worry. "Gwen?" He rose. "Are you okay?" His hands caught her shoulders and held her firmly. He eased her down to sit on the bed. "Breathe, Gwen. Calm down, slow your breath."

"I—I—can't," she gasped.

"Yes, you can," he said with calm certainty. He sat beside her, an arm around her shoulders, holding her securely. "Close your eyes, I've got you. Focus on your breath. Don't think of anything else, just your breath. You can control it."

Control it. Yes. Yes, she could. This she could control. She'd learned how. Deliberately, she shut out everything and focused on pulling air in and out, more slowly, more deeply. Her heart began to settle and the panic faded.

As it did, she became aware that he was murmuring, "Everything will be all right. I can do this job, you can count on me, I won't let you down."

Rely on him? Could she? Her dad had always let her down. Even Jonathan, the most reliable man in the world, had, through no fault of his own, broken one promise: to look after her forever. There'd been times, crazy times, when she hated him for it. And hated herself for being so stupid and mean.

Forcing the memories away, she felt the panic attack fading. She raised her hands to fan out over her cheeks. "I'm so embarrassed."

"Don't be. It's okay." He tugged her closer and she went, burying her face against his chest as he stroked her back, soothing her.

Jonathan used to hold her this way when she was upset about something. Though he couldn't make her troubles go away, he had let her share them and he'd supported her. Now Santos's touch offered the same comfort, but this kind of intimacy with a man she barely knew was unsettling.

The crisp cotton of his uniform shirt was smooth against her flushed cheek, and a scent that was both ocean and earthy male rose from the skin beneath. This kind of intimacy with sexy Santos was arousing.

And all of this was distracting her from what he'd said about not really being a cruise director. She pushed herself out of his arms. "Thanks, I'm fine now." It would be easier to control her body and her feelings if she wasn't so close to him. She stood and moved over to the wall, standing with her back against it. "What are you doing here if you're not a cruise director?"

He studied her a long moment, then said gruffly, "Don't worry about it. Just think of me as a substitute cruise director, and I'll do the job you need done."

If he was trying to prevent another panic attack, keeping secrets wasn't the way to do it. "Oh, no." She shook her head vigorously. "You can't leave it there. You have to tell me. I need *all* the information so I'll know what to do."

"Do?" He rose now, too, looming a good five inches over her. "Don't think you're going to report me to the captain."

He was crowding her space and, with the wall behind her, she couldn't back up. His body was so close she could feel the heat coming off him. Maybe she should have been intimidated, but she was too aroused. Santos was so physical. Jonathan had had presence, but it had been a calm, intellectual one, not a virile, overwhelmingly masculine one. The comparison made her feel disloyal again.

She forced herself to stand still rather than obey her body's urge to step forward and plaster itself against the man. "Why the hell shouldn't I report you if you got the job under false pretenses?"

"Keep your voice down. And no, I didn't. The manager of Dionysus Cruises knows exactly who I am."

She jammed fisted hands on her hips and glared up at him. "And who, *exactly*, are you?"

He was breathing hard; she could see the rise and fall of his chest against the slim-fitting shirt. Even with both of them pissed off, she could literally feel how sexy he was. Her body was flushed and tingly. Primitive instincts she'd never felt before urged her to slap his face or rip his clothes off, or maybe do both.

Voice low, he said, "I'm an insurance fraud investigator."

She didn't know what she'd been expecting him to say, but it wasn't that. Stunned, she sank onto the edge of the bed, hands clasped in her lap. "Seriously?" But what on earth was he doing on the *Aphrodite*?

He sat on the chair again, feet flat on the floor, his knees almost touching hers, and leaned forward to take her hands. "Yes. Giorgos's family emergency is made up. In fact, he's on a paid holiday."

"The manager of Dionysus put you on the *Aphrodite* to investigate something? The crew? Are there, uh, insurance policy violations or something?" Oh damn, another thing that could mess up this trip.

"I can't tell you who or what I'm investigating."

She gaped at him, not having a clue what to do or say. Why did this have to happen on her first destination wedding? How was a control freak supposed to cope when everything was spiraling out of control? A horrible thought dawned. "It's not a wedding guest, is it?"

"Gwen, I can't tell you."

"Santos! You have to. I can't deal with this unless I know exactly what's going on." She tried to suck in air, imagining the worst-case scenario. "Is someone on this ship a criminal? Could they be a danger to the others?"

"It's white-collar crime, and I honestly don't believe there's danger involved."

"But you don't know! You have to tell me who it is, so I can . . ." She shook her head, not having a clue what she could do, only knowing that being left in the dark made her feel powerless, and that she was again having trouble finding air.

He squeezed her hands again. "I'm sorry. But breathe, Gwen. You're going to have to trust me with this. I can't tell you any more."

"Why did you even tell me this much?"

He frowned slightly, as if he wasn't entirely sure. "There's something about you. I didn't want to deceive you."

That was kind of sweet, if he meant it. "So, you're, uh, under-cover? Have you done this kind of work before?"

"Lots of it." The frown had gone. His mouth kinked up on one side and he added suggestively, "I'm very good at what I do."

It was such blatant flirtation, he likely expected a laugh, or at least to distract her. Instead, she persisted. "You're sure you can't tell me anything more?"

He shook his head. "You're not trained to do this and you'd give it away." He chuckled. "Damn, woman, your face gives everything away."

That was the second time he'd said something like that. Self-consciously, she tugged her hands free of his and raised them to her cheeks, fingers spread. "Just what do you think you've read on my face?"

He sat back on the chair and tilted his head, studying her. "That you're responsible to the point of being anal and you get panicky when you think things might go wrong. That you've given tentative approval and trust to the Dionysus people you've met so far, and you don't know what to make of me."

Either her face was an open book or he was unusually perceptive. Of course, in his job he probably had to be. She took a deep breath. Okay, maybe this wasn't such a catastrophe. He'd gone undercover before, and the insurance company wouldn't have sent him again if he wasn't good at his work.

Life would be much easier, though, if she didn't have these dis-concerting feelings of arousal.

He was still gazing at her, a sparkle lighting his eyes. "I can also read that you're as hot for me as I am for you."

"Oh!" Behind her hands, she knew she was flushing again. "I, uh . . ." She swallowed. "You're trying to distract me."

His white smile flashed. "No, it's you who distracts me. Since the moment I saw you." Even though he was no longer touching her, she could feel sexual energy flowing between them. With Jonathan, their attraction had been steady and loving. These weird sexual sparks were something new. Superficial, of course, but she couldn't remember ever feeling so turned on. Even now, when she was worried about Santos's investigation and its effect on the cruise, her travel-weary body felt more alive and aware than she could ever remember it being. "I, uh . . ."

"Inconvenient, isn't it?" Mischief glittered in his eyes. "But undeniable. Question is, what are we going to do about it?"

"Nothing," she almost yelped. "I mean, we can't. We both have jobs to do."

"Yeah, we do."

Ridiculous to feel let down that he'd given up so easily.

"So," he went on, "since you are so diligent, what is it you need to do before the guests arrive this afternoon? You've gone over all the details with the captain and the chef."

Maybe he hadn't given up. Was he asking a genuine question or suggesting that she had an hour or two to spare? The glint in his eyes indicated the latter. "You and I need to review Giorgos's notes," she reminded him.

"I reviewed the notes this morning when I was having breakfast in my hotel room. And you reviewed your copy on the plane, *ne*?"

How had he known that? Oh yeah, he thought she was anal. "We should talk, though. We need to be on the same page, work efficiently as a team."

"I agree entirely."

"Oh." Refusing to acknowledge disappointment, she said, "Then if you'll just hand me my bag, I'll get out my notes and we can—"

"That's not what I had in mind." He made no move to reach for the bag that sat atop the desk. "If we're going to be a team, you and I need to get to know each other. It's hard to be an efficient team when you're strangers."

That made sense. Didn't it? How could she tell if anything made sense when he was staring at her intently, black eyes gleaming with a heat that was indisputably sexual? Her breasts felt sensitive, and her nipples ached to be touched. Between her legs, a needy pulse beat against the moist crotch of her thong. "Get to know each other?" she breathed. By talking, right? That was what he meant. That was what *she* meant. That was how people got to know each other.

"For example . . ." He leaned forward again, raised his hand, and stroked hair back from her temple, letting it sift through his fingers. "Since I first saw you, I wondered if your hair felt like pale morning sunlight. And it does."

What did he mean? Did that even make sense? And did she care? It was poetic and charming, and he was still playing with her hair, brushing her temple, her scalp, her ear with soft, seductive caresses that sent hot shivers through a body that hadn't felt an intimate touch in years.

But this wasn't her husband; it was a stranger. Her hands clutched the edge of the bed on either side of her knees, and her arms trembled slightly. "When I first saw you," she said dryly, reminding herself as well as telling him she was on to him, "I knew you were a ladies' man." A player like her father, not the steadfast kind of man she respected.

He didn't deny it. "And I knew you were a beautiful woman. But this isn't about what we already know. It's about what we want to learn about each other. Such as"—he leaned closer and she couldn't make herself pull back—"whether your hair smells of sunshine or flowers." He buried his face in her hair and nuzzled the tender skin behind her ear.

Oh my, that was an erogenous zone she'd never known about. More sweet prickles of arousal shot through her. She felt him inhale, then exhale warm breath, and she quivered with pleasure.

This was wrong. They should be reviewing notes. Besides, responding to Santos was, in a way, being disloyal to Jonathan, who'd been the opposite of a flirtatious player. And yet, whatever arguments might clamor in her head, she didn't have the willpower to reject this bliss. Just a few minutes longer, then she'd insist they get back to business.

"Flowers," he said, "exotic flowers. Sensual, spicy, not too sweet."

"Wild ginger."

Jonathan had liked it, too, that small touch of the exotic in their traditional lives. It was probably the only thing the two men had in common. When she'd married Jonathan, he was thirty-five to her nineteen. He taught philosophy at university. A serious, cerebral man, respectable and totally reliable, the opposite of her father and the bad boys she'd dated before him.

The Greek with the gold earring—a man who she guessed was younger than she was—was clever, but seemed far more physical than cerebral. A man of action, not introspection. He was full of vitality, from the springy black curls that tumbled every which way to the strong brown feet in sandals. And he was charming. A bad boy, she was pretty sure, just a much more sophisticated, irresistible one than those she'd dated in her teens.

"Your turn," he said. "What do you want to know about me?"

Things she shouldn't care about. Like whether his glossy hair felt as silky as it looked.

She dug her fingers into the simple woven bedspread on either side of her, and did not reach over to find out.

Whether the parts of his body concealed by his uniform looked as good as they felt. How long it would take him to give her her first orgasm in three years.

Instead, she said, "I want to know how old you are."

"Twenty-seven," he answered, letting his lips brush that deliciously sensitive spot behind her ear.

Six years younger. Jonathan had encouraged her, as a young

woman, to be more mature and responsible. Santos made her want to be the opposite: to abandon responsibility and indulge in pure pleasure.

"My turn." He lifted his head. She guessed he might ask her age, too, but instead he said, "I want to know if your mouth tastes like oranges and honey."

She gave a soft gasp. Since she was seventeen, only two men had ever kissed her: her husband and a recent date whose touch had left her feeling cold, lonely, unaroused.

His gaze fixed on her parted lips and he began to lean toward her, then pulled back a couple of inches. "But first, there's something you need to know. I'm not a guy who does commitment."

Surprised, she said, "I figured."

"You need to know I don't believe in those happily ever afters your company's selling. Or rather, I do for other people. Not me. I'm not that kind of guy." His expression, for once, was dead serious.

"Okay, I appreciate your honesty."

He tilted his head. "That bother you? You looking for commitment?"

She shook her head, her skin so sensitized now that even the soft brush of her hair against her bare shoulders felt sexy. "No, I'm not. Not for the foreseeable future, anyhow." Maybe one day, but that would be years down the road. Her entire adult life, until Jonathan died, had been intertwined with his. There were so many things she needed to learn about herself before she even thought about getting serious with another man. And speaking of which . . . "Don't you think you're getting ahead of yourself? I haven't even agreed to a kiss."

Now the charm he wore so naturally, so attractively, lightened his face again. "Ah, but you will."

Chapter 4

RELIEVED that Gwen wouldn't want more than he could give, Santos moved closer again until his lips almost grazed hers.

Flecks of gold sparkled in her brandy-colored eyes, and her lips parted to say, "You're very sure of yourself." Her tone was dry, but she didn't draw away.

He out-and-out wanted this woman; she wanted him, too, and it'd be crazy to resist. They could share some sexy play without anyone else knowing, and without it affecting their jobs. "Of us. And sure that, once we do kiss, it won't stop there."

She gave a tiny, startled gasp and stared at him wide-eyed. "Don't talk like that. A kiss. Just one kiss. That's all I can think about."

He'd expected a teasing response, but she had surprised him again. For a beautiful, smart woman who wasn't into commitment, she seemed almost inexperienced with flirtation. "One kiss," he agreed, knowing the chemistry between them would never let them stop with that.

He touched his lips to hers, featherlight, a tease and a promise.

Just a sideways brush, and then another, a bit firmer. Another brush, and she returned the pressure tentatively. He reached up under the fall of light golden hair to cup the back of her head, holding her steady as he slanted his mouth more firmly against hers.

She sighed, warm breath caressed his lips, and he flicked her lower lip with the tip of his tongue.

Her long, silky lashes fluttered down and her eyes closed as she surrendered to the kiss, and her tongue darted out to meet his.

The arousal he'd felt since he first saw her flared quickly into passionate heat that tightened his body, but he kept the kiss a slow and easy exploration, again sensing inexperience, maybe innocence, in her response. He didn't want to rush her or scare her off. Besides, there was something about her that made him want to savor.

She made an *mmm* sound that was part pleasure and part need, and it fired his blood. He stroked her bare shoulder, her arm, feeling smooth, supple skin. His hand drifted over to the curve of her hip in the slim-fitting capris, to her waist, firm under a thin layer of coral fabric, and finally to the fullness of her breast. Her nipple was as hard as his cock. When he caressed its taut peak through her top, she thrust her breast more firmly into his hand.

Finally, one of her hands left its resting spot on the bed and lifted. Her fingers threaded through his hair and she gave another *mmm*.

As his tongue dipped into her mouth, he guided her backward and she cooperated, shoving herself up the bed until she was stretched out prone beside her overflowing suitcase.

He went with her, still kissing her, until he lay between her spread legs, the hard press of his erection rubbing the juncture of her thighs.

She whimpered against his mouth and her lower body twisted against him. The friction, through their clothing, made him groan with need. Her body language told him what she wanted, and he was more than ready to give it to her. One kiss, oh yeah. A kiss that could take them all the way to climax.

Her top had ridden up and he reached between their bodies to caress the silky skin above the waistband of her capris, then he slipped a hand inside them, against her smooth, warm tummy, and eased the button free.

As he fumbled to slide the zipper down, she suddenly jerked away, breaking the kiss and struggling to get out from under him.

He lifted his weight, freeing her. "Gwen?"

She scooted against the headboard, drawing her knees up and hugging them to her. Shaking her head wildly, she said, "I can't."

"Sorry. I didn't mean to push you." But she'd been into it; her body language had been crystal clear. What had gone wrong? He sat on the edge of the bed, not too close to her, and tried to ignore his swollen cock straining for stimulation and release.

"No, it's not you. I mean, I wanted . . . But Santos, this is . . ." Another head shake, sending pale gold hair swirling. "It's too much, too fast, and it's been a long time for me."

"Huh?" His lust-hazed brain processed that comment. "You haven't been dating?" Why not? She was pretty, intelligent, and she was definitely sexually responsive.

"I've gone out a couple of times in the last few months, but we didn't . . . I wasn't, uh, into them." She released her knees, raised her hands to her face, and hid behind them. Voice muffled, she said, "Sorry about freaking out, but here's the thing. I was married and he died—it's going on two years now—and I haven't been with anyone since."

"Oh, man, I'm sorry." She was so young. It had never occurred to him she might be a widow. He reached out tentatively to touch her knee. "Hell, Gwen, that's terrible."

"It is." She lowered her hands so her eyes peeped over the tops of her fingers. "So I'm feeling guilty and disloyal, which I know is crazy, but this has happened so fast."

"I didn't know."

"Of course not. You didn't do anything wrong, and I wanted . . . But I . . ." She shook her head. "And we should be working. What was I thinking?"

That their attraction was more powerful than her obsessiveness about her work. He was flattered. And, at the moment, concerned about her. "We'll do our jobs, but right now this is more important. Tell me why you're so upset."

She gazed at him for a long moment. "Okay, you might as well hear the rest. I met Jonathan when I was eighteen and married him the next year. I'd been pretty wild in my teens, but I'd never actually, uh, had intercourse." She swallowed. "I've never been with anyone except Jonathan, and this is so sudden, so unexpected. Yes, I'm attracted to you, and I do want to, uh, get back to having a sex life, but I . . . I guess I don't know how, or if I'm ready."

She'd only been with one man? He could hardly get his head around that. Trying to lighten the mood, he teased gently, "Isn't it like riding a bicycle?"

She dropped her hands and gave a wobbly smile. "I've only ridden one bike, and it's been a few years. Jonathan was sick. Really sick. Fighting cancer. We were together all the time, but after a while, sex wasn't on the agenda."

"Oh, man," he said again. "I can't even imagine how awful that must have been. I mean," he amended quickly, "not the part about not having sex." Though he couldn't imagine that either. "But, you know, being with someone who . . . *Gamoto*, I don't mean to bring back sad memories."

"It's okay," she said softly. "No one ever knows what to say. Truth is, there's nothing anyone can say that would help. All I can do is get on with life." She tilted her head. "What does that mean? *Gamoto*?"

"Sorry. It's a Greek curse, like, uh, *shit*. We use it a lot."

She flushed slightly. "Jonathan didn't like me to swear, but believe me, I *thought* those words a lot of times in the three years between his diagnosis and his death. And after."

"I bet."

"But look." She shook her hair back, chin up. "I'm okay now. After he died, I had a rough time for a while, then I pulled myself out of it and rejoined the world of the living. I went looking for a job and found this great one."

"You hadn't been working?" She'd married when she was nineteen and never had a job?

"Not for three years. I'd had a job as a conference planner, but when Jonathan was diagnosed we knew it would be a tough battle. I'd already booked off an extended holiday for his sabbatical year, and after that, when he wasn't getting better, I quit. I wanted to look after him myself, and just be with him. We knew our time together could be limited."

She was one hell of a woman. The opposite of his parents, who'd always been on-again, off-again with each other, not to mention with him. Their priority was fun and adventure, not family or responsibility.

Gwen put her hand over his where it still rested on her knee. "This is another secret, okay?"

He was flattered she'd trusted him with information she rarely shared, but he didn't understand. "Why?"

"It's a downer if I talk about Jonathan and me, especially at a wedding."

He nodded slowly. "I can see that. What do you say if people ask if you're married or dating?"

"I say I'm happily single, that I think a good marriage is a wonderful thing, and that maybe one day I'll get married myself. It's all true."

"Isn't it hard, planning other people's weddings when yours ended the way it did?"

"The opposite, actually. I love the romance of seeing two people who are deeply in love planning a future together. I'm always optimistic that things will work out for them. It lets me live vicariously, I guess. Right now, I need to heal and figure out who I am as a single woman. One day, maybe I'll want that romance, that dream, that kind of partnership again for myself. It's what Jonathan wanted for me. But for now, all the joy and hope I see every day at work kind of rubs off on me."

"You're quite something, Gwen."

"You're not bad yourself. You're easy to talk to." A grin flickered and she reached up to tug gently on his earring. "For a pirate." She leaned back, propping pillows behind her. "Sorry for freaking out—again. But it's probably for the best. The focus this week needs to be on Liz and Peter and their family and friends. You and I are here to work. And you even have two jobs to do."

She was right. Not to mention hooking up with her would be complicated by the baggage she was toting. All the same, there was something about her. Much more than the brandy eyes, pale gold hair, luscious lips, and sweet curves. She was special. A woman he could like, and a woman he had to respect. A woman who'd stuck by her man when the going got rough.

A better person than him. She would never let anyone down.

Not the kind of woman he normally slept with. Yet she attracted him more than anyone he'd met in a long time. In the long run, she'd find another man who loved her and they'd build a life together, because she was that kind of woman. She was like his grandmother rather than his mom. But in the short run, she was inexperienced and insecure, and he knew that, with him, she'd rediscover her sensual side and have some fun.

And there he was, being analytical, which definitely wasn't his style.

"Santos, what are you thinking?"

"That you're right, and you're being very logical. But you know, I'm not much for logic. I rely more on intuition."

"And what's it telling you?"

He studied her, sitting propped against pillows on her bed, and wanted to tug her into his arms. "The attraction between us isn't going to go away."

Her gaze flicked over him and her lips curved ruefully. "Probably not." Then they straightened. "So we'll just have to ignore it and control the situation."

He snorted. "If you can do that, you have more self-control than I."

"I'm very good at control."

Oh no, she wasn't getting away with that. "Are you, now?" He trailed his fingers up the bare skin of her calf below the hem of her capris.

She shivered. "I didn't say it'd be easy." Then she glared at him. "You're not making it easy."

"What's the fun in *easy*?"

A reluctant smile twitched her lips. "What are you suggesting?"

"That we stay open to the possibilities. Let's get to know each other and see where it goes."

"I'm not going to . . . flirt with you in front of the guests. It's unprofessional."

"Okay." He swung off the bed. With his hand on the doorknob, he turned to her, grinning at her surprised, disappointed expression. "We'll do our flirting in private."

"Oh!"

Grinning wider at her startled gasp, he went out the door and closed it behind him.

GWEN stayed in her cabin for the next hour, unpacking and settling in, reviewing her notes for the umpteenth time, and worrying about Santos. How on earth had she let herself get carried away like that? She should have insisted that the two of them review their notes—up on deck, not alone down here.

His presence had, to use a particularly apt expression, rocked her boat. How could she rely on a cruise director who was really an undercover investigator? And how could she deal with her attraction for a man who made her feel more female, alive, and sexy than she could ever remember feeling—a thought that, in itself, felt like a betrayal of her wonderful husband? How could she work with a man who made her forget about the most important thing in her life this week: Liz and Peter's wedding?

By being in total control. By having her spreadsheets, notes, and contingency plans, and focusing on her job. What else could she do?

Also, she needed to report to her bosses. She had no intention of running to them for help every time she ran into a problem, but this situation was significant enough that they should be informed. It would be the middle of the night for Sarah and Andi, so she didn't use her GSM cell phone. Instead, she sent an e-mail. They'd pick it up in the morning and get back to her. Internet would be spotty during the next week, but Elpida had assured her it would kick in here and there, particularly at the big ports.

Shortly before the first guests were expected to arrive, she went back on deck, her skin almost twitching with nerves. Of course the first person she saw when she stepped outside was Santos, leaning against the ship's rail and talking to a crew member.

She had only a moment to admire his virile grace before he turned, as if sensing her presence, and came toward her. "Gwen." He took her arm in a gesture that looked casual but sent tingles through her. "I've met the rest of the crew. Let me introduce you."

"That's a good idea." And so was easing away from his grip, and those disturbing tingles, so she did it, and pretended to ignore his amused glance.

As he guided her around the ship making introductions, he was on his best behavior, yet she was totally aware of him. Did he feel the same way? He had a natural charm and ease with people, but she sensed a deeper warmth in his eyes, a secret message, when he turned his gaze on her. Every time even their clothing brushed, she had to stop from jumping.

She felt hypersensitive not just to him but to everything around her: the cornflower blue of the clear sky and the deeper navy of the ocean, the bite of the sun on her bare shoulders, the tang of salt on the breeze, the friendliness on the faces of the crew.

One of the crew she and Santos were talking to at the stern of the *Aphrodite* pointed behind her. "There is the first group of guests. I'll tell Captain Ari."

She spun, eager and nervous, and saw the Zodiac approaching with a full load. Elpida was at the wheel, and beside her sat Liz and Peter. The bride waved madly when she saw Gwen. After a quick wave back, Gwen raised her camera and began clicking. "That's Liz Tippett, the bride. The man beside her is her fiancé, Peter Kirk."

Liz, a slender, strawberry blonde, and Peter, all dark and rugged, complemented each other beautifully. He got his looks from his mother, who'd been Greek Canadian and had died when he was a child. Though his Greek relatives had preferred not to come on the cruise, the bride and groom would spend some time with them during their honeymoon on Crete.

As the captain and more crew came to the stern, Gwen said, "Don't forget to hand out cameras." There was no official photographer for the cruise. Instead each guest would either use their own camera or be given a disposable. Gwen would collect all the images at the end and put together a photo album.

A few minutes later, the Zodiac docked and guests came aboard. Gwen glanced at Santos, wondering if one of these people was his suspect, but his smiling face gave nothing away.

Liz, dressed in white capris and a cute blue top, came over with Peter and gave Gwen a big hug. "This is brilliant!" she said in her lovely English accent. "I'm so excited. Our love boat is gorgeous, isn't she?"

"She is. Did you have a good trip?"

"Long and tiring," Peter said, "but we're here and that's what matters."

Liz hugged his arm. "I can't wait to shower and change into shorts, and I'm dying to see my parents."

"They'll be here in half an hour." Gwen saw that Elpida had already headed back to land to pick up more guests, who would be arriving at Zea Marina in Dionysus vans.

Gwen introduced the bride and groom to Santos and Captain Ari, and the captain volunteered to escort them to their cabin. She then turned her attention to the rest of the guests.

Most of this group were from Vancouver and had traveled on the same connecting flights. She exchanged quick hugs with Peter's two dads, William Kirk and Phil Barton, who'd helped out with some of the planning. A few years after his wife died, William, Peter's biological dad, had met Phil, and they'd been together ever since, raising Peter and getting married when gay marriage became legal. Whenever Gwen saw them with Peter, it was obvious how close they all were.

There were a few other relatives of Peter's, too, and several of his and Liz's friends. With assistance from Santos and the crew, she got the guests directed to their cabins and their luggage under control.

When everyone, including Santos, had disappeared belowdecks, Gwen let out a long breath. So far, so good.

The next boatload would have many of Liz's family and friends from England. The third run would be an assorted group, some folks who'd arrived early in Greece and others from various locations and flights.

Gwen studied the updated schedule of arrivals Elpida had provided, even though she'd already memorized it. The neat list, and the other woman's conscientiousness in double-checking the details, gave her a sense of security.

She liked everything to be laid out tidily, with a Plan B for every possible contingency.

As for Santos saying he and she should see where things went . . . No, that just wasn't the way she operated.

DURING cocktail hour, Santos had little time to dwell on his attraction to the sexy wedding planner. His cruise director role in itself would have been enough to keep him busy: matching names to faces, answering countless questions, coping with flirtatious comments from a few of the single, and one of the married, guests. On top of that, he did his best to keep an eye on Flynn Kavanagh.

The man had arrived with the final group of guests. Though he lived in Vancouver, he had RSVP'd too late for Gwen to get him on the same flights as the rest of the Vancouver contingent.

Kavanagh had auburn hair, clear green eyes, and a slight accent to match up with his Irish name. About Santos's height of six foot two, the former IT consultant had a leaner build but definitely wasn't skinny. He was very fit for a computer geek, and, though he seemed a bit reserved when he first came on deck, he was soon drawn into conversation with several guests and spoke like a real person, not a propeller-head. In fact, he had a charming way about him, which he seemed as happy applying to elderly women as to pretty young ones.

Santos watched him head into the bar and return with drinks for himself and a couple of the women. Soon after, he went in again. When he hadn't come out after several minutes, Santos sauntered in that direction himself, joining up with a few other people who were going in.

Kavanagh was in a far corner of the bar, talking to Kendra Kirk, a tall, striking woman with short black hair who Santos had yet to talk to. She was the groom's cousin and had been part of the Vancouver group of arrivals. The file showed that she'd paid extra for a single room, so it seemed she didn't have a date or close friend here.

While participating in a conversation about tropical drinks—no, he'd never tasted a Heat Wave—Santos eyed the pair. Did they know each other? Their body language conveyed tension, not of a friendly sort. Though he couldn't hear what they were saying, he caught Kavanagh's tone. He seemed annoyed, and she looked edgy and uncomfortable. Her voice was lower, maybe urging her companion not to make a scene. Interesting. Was there some prior connection between these two? The insurance company's intern had verified Kavanagh's friendship with the bride, but hadn't looked for any connections with the groom's family. Of course, possibly they'd just met. Maybe one had hit on the other and been rejected.

The guests at the bar got their drinks and left, but Santos remained, making trivial chitchat with the bartender until Kendra sauntered over alone. Leaning against the bar beside Santos, she said to the bartender, "I'm back for my drink."

He handed her a glass of white wine.

Quietly, Santos said, "Is everything all right? Is there perhaps a, er, delicate situation you need help with?"

She tossed a glance over her shoulder toward Kavanagh, who remained in the corner, his gaze fixed on them. "No," she said rather loudly, perhaps to send a message to the other man. "Everything's fine. I can handle him without help."

Together, they walked outside. "He's not your boyfriend?" Santos asked.

"No, not at all. We just met." She flashed a superficial smile. "Thanks for your concern."

He watched her stroll to the table where the parents of the bride and groom sat together. Then he ducked back into the bar, where the bartender was handing Kavanagh two drinks: one of those fruity Heat Waves a few of the other guests had tried and a bottle of Mythos, a Greek beer.

"Girlfriend troubles?" Santos asked sympathetically.

"What?" The man's head jerked. "Oh, her? No, I don't even know her. Excuse me, a lady at my table's waiting for her drink." He stalked away.

The incident was probably nothing, but Santos decided that as soon as he could get down to his cabin, he'd e-mail the office and ask the intern to look more deeply into Kendra Kirk and any possible connection with Flynn Kavanagh.

Tomorrow, when things had settled down a bit, he'd look for an opportunity to search Kavanagh's cabin. Maybe the man's reason for being on this cruise was an innocent one, but Santos would love to find evidence to prove him guilty of the five-million-dollar theft— and to locate the stolen money. Kavanagh's lifestyle hadn't improved since the theft, which meant chances were he had the money salted away and was biding his time, waiting for the heat to die down.

Yes, it would be great to tidy this file up in the first couple of days, so as to have more time to devote to the attractive wedding planner.

Chapter 5

AT eight thirty that night, Gwen stared in wonder at the most glorious sunset she'd ever seen. It was all she could do to remember to lift her camera every few minutes and click a shot.

She rubbed her thumb over the bare place on her finger where once she'd worn Jonathan's rings. How he would have loved being here. She longed for the touch of his shoulder against hers, the clasp of his hand, the opportunity to share an experience they'd dreamed of and planned for.

Their entire group gazed in silent awe at an ocean sunset viewed through the columns of the ruined Temple of Poseidon. They were at the *Aphrodite*'s first stop, Cape Sounion, a short and glorious sail down the coast from Zea Marina.

The group from the *Aphrodite* didn't have the place to themselves. Other tourists had arrived on tour buses, accompanied by guides who provided monotone commentaries they'd obviously recited hundreds of times before. Santos had given the wedding party a much more dynamic presentation, telling them about the temple's history and even pointing out where Lord Byron had carved his name into a marble column. Though most of his information had likely come from Giorgos's notes, he'd delivered it smoothly, only faltering a time or two in answering questions.

As the sun set, though, everyone had fallen silent. Nature's spectacular display, in saturated shades of orange and violet over an indigo ocean, combined with the timeless grandeur of the ancient temple to render them awestruck.

Something nudged Gwen's sweater-clad shoulder, and for the briefest moment, lost in a reverie, she thought it was Jonathan. Then she realized Santos had come to stand beside her.

At first she'd felt awkward with him after their kiss and her two freak-outs. Also, she'd been obsessed with wondering who on earth, among the passengers and crew, he was investigating. But over the afternoon and evening, she'd relaxed and the two of them had fallen into an easy pattern, working well as a team. No one could possibly guess he wasn't a real cruise director, and she hoped her own inexperience didn't show too much either.

Even though they both behaved professionally, and Santos sprinkled his easy charm over all the guests, she'd felt a different kind of energy flowing between her and him. Awareness, chemistry, sexual tension.

Now, though his shoulder touched hers only lightly, she felt his heat and the warm zing of possibilities as they watched, unspeaking, while the sun dipped lower and began to sink into the ocean. Was this wrong? Sharing this moment with him, having these feelings for him?

After the sun had finally disappeared, people began to stir. She stepped away from Santos as the wedding guests wandered in their direction, as if drawn to him.

No wonder. He looked almost as impressive as the temple, standing tall in his white uniform, brown forearms bare, shunning the sweaters and jackets the rest of them wore. His features were as classic as a Greek statue, and his black hair blew wildly in the breeze.

A few hours earlier, the two of them had been kissing passionately on her bed. If she wanted, they would do it again—and more. She'd never thought she was the kind of woman to attract a sexy, charismatic foreign lover. And yet she had.

When she was eighteen, she hadn't thought she was the kind of girl to attract an intelligent, attractive university professor, yet she had.

In the final months, when she and Jonathan had known the disease was winning, they'd talked about the future. Her future. He'd told her she was a wonderful woman with a loving heart, and she needed, one day, to find another man to build a life with. He'd meant marriage to a responsible, reliable man like him.

If he knew she was—let's face it—lusting after a stranger who didn't believe in commitment, would he say she was crazy to waste her time this way? Yes, probably. But she wasn't ready for a serious relationship, definitely not ready to give her heart to another man. Would it be wrong to simply have a little fun?

Silently, the guests clustered around Santos as if waiting for a pronouncement.

He raised both arms to the sky, to the temple, maybe to the god Poseidon himself and said, simply, "Welcome to Greece."

The words sank in with a sense of rightness. She'd always wanted to travel, and tonight was one reason why. Coming from such a new world herself, it was a powerful experience to set foot in an ancient land, to walk where perhaps gods themselves had walked. How lucky she was to have found a job that allowed her this opportunity.

Santos touched her arm and leaned over to murmur, "You okay? We should head back. The temple's closing and it's getting dark."

She nodded. "Yes, of course." Then more loudly, to the guests, "Time to head back to the *Aphrodite*. Chef Ilyas will have dinner ready." On the sail from Zea Marina to Cape Sounion, the chef had laid out delicious appetizers of spanakopita, calamari, and tiny meat-balls called keftedes, as well as pita bread, hummus, and tsatziki. For dinner, he and Gwen had decided to keep it simple: souvlaki skewers of chicken, lamb, and prawns, served with Greek salad, rice, and po-tatoes. People would be tired, jet-lagged, and ready to turn in early. The opulent Greek feasts would be left to other nights.

Atop the temple, the wind blew briskly and the air had chilled since the sun had set. Waiting while the wedding guests started down the hill, Gwen hugged her sweater around her shoulders.

Santos, standing beside her, said softly, "Things are going well, yes?"

Did he mean with the wedding trip, or between the two of them? "Very well."

Peter and Liz, arms tight around each other's waists, strolled past them and down the steps, such a perfect couple.

Peter's two dads sauntered along next, holding hands. They were slim, elegant, and dressed in the height of fashion. Another few people went by, then came the bride's parents, clutching each other's arms tightly for balance. They were both short, plump, and gray-haired in their practical, if unstylish, travel clothes.

"Funny how couples often grow to look alike," Gwen whispered to Santos. It had even happened with her and Jonathan. After a year of hassling each other about their clothing choices, they'd begun to shop at the same stores.

"The future in-laws look at each other like they're different spe-cies," Santos said.

She nodded. The Tippetts, who lived in a tiny village in England, and the Kirk-Bartons had been polite to each other, but weren't yet comfortable together. "It's early. They'll get to know each other and loosen up. I hope."

The last of their group straggled down the steps, among them

Flynn Kavanagh, a friend of Liz's. He walked alone, hands thrust deep in his pockets, frowning.

She worried about him as she and Santos fell in behind the last of the guests, hanging back a few steps so they could talk without being overheard.

Santos moved closer, arm brushing hers, and it felt so good that she couldn't make herself pull away. "Did you see that guy near the end, with the big frown?" he asked. "He's not having fun."

So he'd noticed it, too. "That's Flynn Kavanagh. It's odd because he seemed fine at first, then—snap!—when we were having appies, he just changed. All evening he's barely spoken to a soul. I hope it's just jet lag."

"I saw him in a corner of the bar with that tall brunette, Kendra, the groom's cousin. There was a lot of tension in the air."

"Uh-oh."

"They don't have history, do they? Like maybe they're exes?"

"Peter and Liz didn't say anything about that. I hope it's not true, because it could make for some nastiness." And another thing to worry about.

"Or maybe he was hitting on her and she wasn't interested."

"Maybe." Though, from what she'd seen before Flynn's mood changed, he was a charming guy and not the kind to push himself on a woman. But he'd clearly looked upset . . .

"Stop worrying. Whatever's going on, you'll handle it."

Was the man a mind reader or did he already know her that well?

Santos captured her hand and held it, warming her chilled skin not just with the heat of his own but with the spark of attraction. "You've been doing great, Gwen. You're obsessive about details and you're genuine. People see that you like them and want them to have a good time, and they respond."

"Thanks." She should free her hand from his, but the guests were ahead, intent on their own conversations. Even if someone turned back, it was dusk so they wouldn't see anything.

What message was she giving, letting him hold her hand? What message did she want to give?

An irresistible charmer like him might be like her dad, delightful on the surface but not trustworthy. Yet Santos had said he wouldn't let her down, and so far he was taking his cover role seriously. "You're doing a wonderful job, too. I'd never have guessed you weren't really a cruise director." Lowering her voice even more, she asked, "Have you seen anything yet? I mean, in your other job? It's driving me crazy, wondering who you're watching. It's not Flynn, is it? Or Kendra?"

He chuckled. "Great. Now every time I mention one of the guests, you're going to assume it's them."

She laughed ruefully. "Sorry. I'll try to stop jumping to conclusions."

They strolled in silence for a few minutes, then she said, "Where are you from anyhow? Your English is perfect."

"I grew up mostly on Naxos, one of the Cyclades Islands. I've lived in England and the States and I'm currently in Toronto. The head office of the insurance company is there."

"I'd assumed you lived in Athens. So, if it's a Canadian company, then it is one of the guests you're investigating, not the crew?"

"Right now, there's only one person I'm interested in." His thumb caressed her wrist—apparently another erogenous zone she'd never known about, from the way arousal pulsed through her veins. "And that's you, Gwen. What are we going to do about it?"

They were nearing the bottom of the hill. Reluctantly, she tugged her hand away. "Sleep on it. And I mean alone. I'm in no shape to think straight tonight."

"While you're sleeping alone, *glyka mou*, dream about how much fun we could be having."

"Santos, what does that mean? *Glyka mou?*"

"I'll tell you when we're in bed together."

THE next morning, Santos woke early, sexually frustrated and determined to win Gwen over. He respected her feelings for her husband, but she couldn't stay stuck in the past. He also respected her commitment to her work, and he had every intention of doing both of his jobs well, but that was no reason they couldn't have some fun in their off hours.

Besides, they were aboard the *Aphrodite*. The goddess of sex would be mightily disappointed if the two of them resisted their mutual attraction.

His chef roommate, Ilyas, had already left the cabin, so Santos turned on his computer, hoping for an Internet connection. He was in luck. When he read a message from the law student intern in Toronto, he let out a whistle. After apologizing for not having taken the initiative to dig deeper with his research, the intern said that Kendra Kirk was the Crown Counsel who had prosecuted Flynn Kavanagh.

That would certainly explain the tension between them. She was no doubt furious that, rather than being behind bars, the man she'd failed to convict was holidaying in Greece—and, to add insult to injury, on the same ship as her. And no way could Kavanagh be happy to see the woman who'd gone after him in court.

Why had he and Kendra both denied knowing each other? Maybe the explanation was as simple as wanting to keep the trial in the past and not let it intrude on Liz and Peter's wedding celebration.

Or maybe it wasn't.

And thinking about Liz and Peter . . . Kendra was Peter's cousin, and it was a small, close family. Kavanagh was Liz's friend as of two years ago when she, a psych major, had begun tutoring his Asper ger's brother in social skills. Santos barely knew Liz, but she struck him as a smart, caring woman, not the type who'd associate with a criminal. Surely she knew about the charge against Kavanagh and the trial, so she must have chosen to believe her friend. Had she told her fiancé about him?

Did either of them know Kendra Kirk was the Crown Counsel who'd prosecuted Flynn Kavanagh? Surely not, or they wouldn't have invited both of them here.

This file was getting more interesting by the moment. Santos would definitely keep an eye on the lawyer as well as on Kavanagh.

His curiosity piqued, and eager to see Gwen, he hurried up to the main deck.

During the night, the ship had cruised to the small island of Kythnos, a place he'd never visited before, and dropped anchor. He was greeted by sunshine, azure waters, and the sight of a golden sand beach fringed by trees.

Gwen was conferring with Chef Ilyas, who, with an assistant, was setting out an American-style buffet breakfast. He gave both Gwen and Ilyas a smiling *"Yassas,"* and was pleased at the gleam of awareness in her eyes.

Glancing around, he saw that Kavanagh was already there, at a table by himself, though other guests soon joined him.

When the man's roommate came on deck, Santos risked whipping down to make a quick search of their cabin. Thankfully, the custom aboard the *Aphrodite* was to leave doors unlocked. He didn't have time to deal with Kavanagh's computer, and found nothing of interest in the rest of the luggage. Hurrying back to join the guests, Santos thought that his cover role—chosen so he'd have lots of opportunity to mingle with the guests—had a downside: He was too busy and too visible.

He'd have liked to check Kendra Kirk's cabin, too, but even if he'd had time, she never made an appearance on deck. Casually, he approached the groom's dads, who he knew were Kendra's uncles.

"Is your niece okay?" he asked. "Perhaps a touch of motion sickness? Is there anything I can get for her?"

Phil Barton huffed. "She'll be working. She takes her job far too seriously."

"Well, it is an important job," William Kirk, Peter's biological dad, said mildly. "But yes, she's too obsessed with it."

Another one like Gwen, Santos wondered, who verged on anal in her compulsion to do her job well? Seeing how things played out between her and Kavanagh would be interesting.

"She's not going to get away with spending the whole trip down in her cabin with her computer," Phil said.

William put an arm around his husband's shoulder. "Damn right. When it's time to go ashore, we'll roust her and make her come."

Gwen called for everyone's attention. "We have an hour until the *Aphrodite* gets underway. You can laze on deck, or crew members will take you to shore in the Zodiac if you want to walk on the beach. Or you can swim off the back of the ship." She glanced at Santos, cheeks slightly flushed. "Can you keep an eye on the swimmers?"

"Sure." He went to change into board shorts, then, shunning the ladder, dove off the deck into sparkling blue-green water.

The cool Aegean was invigorating. This was one of the most enjoyable assignments he'd had in a long time.

After the swim, he assisted everyone out of the water, then came up the steps onto the deck, wet bathing suit plastered to his body. Gwen was, for the first time this morning, alone. He had the impression she'd been walking across the deck and had frozen when she saw him. She was definitely looking.

He walked over, liking the way her eyes widened as he approached, half-naked and dripping. He also liked how she looked, summery and casual in a turquoise halter top and short white shorts that rode low on her hips. "You should have come in. The water's great." Playfully, he flicked a few drops from his bare arm to hers.

She shivered, but he didn't believe for a moment it was from the cold. "Another time. Today, I'm trying to have a brief chat with each of the guests so they'll feel they know me and be comfortable coming to me if they need anything."

Comfortable wasn't the word he'd use for how she made him feel. The expanse of skin between the bottom of her halter and the top of her shorts cried out to be licked, and those long, shapely legs made him fantasize about what it would feel like to have them wrapped around him. In fact, he'd spent a good part of the night dreaming about their bodies twining together.

"Sleep well last night?" he asked in a suggestive tone. "Pleasant dreams? I had a couple of very nice ones myself."

Her cheeks colored. "Actually, I slept like a rock. Travel, jet lag, fresh air . . . They knocked me out."

"I know another way to ensure a good night's sleep."

She cast a quick glance around. "I have no doubt. But I don't even know you."

He winked. "We can fix that."

"I didn't mean *that* way."

When one of the guests came over to ask Gwen something, Santos sauntered away to shower and dress for the shore expedition.

The *Aphrodite* cruised a short distance to dock, then a bus took the passengers inland to the village of Chora, the capital of the island of Kythnos. As Santos steered people to points of interest Giorgos had outlined in his notes, cameras clicked busily. Guests gushed about the typical postcard sights: whitewashed buildings that were blindingly bright in the sunlight, narrow cobblestone streets, battered pots bursting with red geraniums and purple bougainvillea, and old men drinking coffee at the *kafenio* beside the town square.

Kavanagh wandered around on his own, an expensive Nikon raised much of the time, but Santos was kept too busy to approach him. Kendra's uncles had succeeded in rousting her, as they'd put it, and she was hanging out with Liz and Peter, taking a few shots with the disposable camera she'd been given. She and Kavanagh cast occasional glances in each other's direction, then quickly looked away. At one point, she went over to the man; they exchanged a few words, then parted on what didn't look like good terms. There were no raised voices this time, though, and their body language wasn't actively hostile. Maybe they'd declared an uneasy truce for the sake of Liz and Peter.

When it was time to head back to the *Aphrodite* for lunch, Santos helped Gwen round everyone up, then fell in step beside her, bringing up the rear. "How do you like Greece so far?"

"It's beautiful. I love it." The brandy-colored eyes she raised to him sparkled with golden flecks, more intoxicating than the Metaxa they reminded him of. Softly, she said, "Jonathan and I were supposed to come here. Italy, too. For his sabbatical."

"Oh, man, I'm sorry. This must be really tough for you." And here he was, acting like a jerk, hitting on her. Except, she'd responded.

"In some ways. But I'm glad I came." She glanced around. "I can't imagine growing up someplace like this. You said your home was on Naxos? That's not one of the islands we're stopping at."

"No." After this assignment, he should go and visit his grandparents. He loved them, but they'd never accepted who he was, which made things difficult for all of them. They'd finally given up on him and let his second cousin—who loved Naxos and was raising his family there—take over their restaurant, but they never let Santos forget that they'd brought him up to be the one who took over from them. A replacement for his mom—yet in the end he'd been as much of a disappointment.

"What's it like there? Was it a good place to grow up?"

"It's pretty. It has a great nude beach I'd love to take you to." He made a halfhearted effort at a suggestive look, but she responded with a level gaze that somehow made him tell her the truth. "The pace of life is slow. I wanted more excitement and couldn't wait to leave."

"Excitement." She glanced around, then said quietly. "You find that in Toronto? In your job?"

He verified that no one was in earshot. "Toronto's a hundred times more lively than Naxos. And my work lets me travel, learn different things for different jobs. It's a challenge, going undercover and playing different roles."

"Dangerous?"

"Sometimes."

A smile flickered on her lips. "I'd like the travel aspect, but that's it. I don't do well with uncertainty, and definitely not with risk."

"I bet you're better at it than you think." He let his arm brush hers—a touch that would look casual, though it was anything but. She didn't draw away, and the soft friction of warm skin against warm skin ignited sparks within him.

"I guess that remains to be seen," she said.

When everyone was back on the *Aphrodite*, the ship got under-way, sailing to the island of Syros, where they'd spend the rest of the day. Guests constructed lunch from a buffet of Greek salad and make-your-own pita wrap sandwiches, then spread out. Some sat in the dining room, others chose the shaded lounge area on deck, and a number went for the bright sun. Kavanagh joined a group of Liz's friends, and Kendra had disappeared belowdecks again.

After lunch, most of the guests assembled in the dining room so Santos could fill them in on plans for the rest of the day. "We'll be going ashore to explore Syros in an hour or so," he said. He gave them a short history of the island, including the mythology, then he handed out maps of the capital city. "Here's the lay of the land, with the highlights marked." He told them about the walking tour he would lead, and the optional bus trip to a medieval settlement. "But if you want to wander off on your own to shop, have a drink, or explore, feel free. Make your way back to the ship and we'll head off for dinner at eight. We're going to a taverna on the waterfront."

He loved the way undercover work let him play so many different roles. Standing at one end of the room speaking to a crowd of seated tourists and pretending to be a cruise director didn't give him the slightest twinge of anxiety.

His only problem was forcing himself to glance around and meet everyone's eyes rather than focus on Gwen, who looked like dynamite in a bright yellow top over white capris. A number of the women on the cruise had flirted with him. A striking redhead had made it clear she was available and a pair of bubbly blondes from England had proposed a three-way. Under other circumstances, he'd have been tempted, but he didn't feel that same gut-deep pull of attraction with any of them that he did with Gwen.

"Any questions?" he asked the group.

One woman said, "I love that vivid turquoisy blue you see all over the place. Why's it used so much? Do they get a deal on blue paint?"

A few people chuckled and Santos said, "The theory is that blue is a protection against evil."

He remembered asking his grandmother the same question when he'd been a little boy. She bought into the superstition, and not only his grandparents' home but also their restaurant had blue doors and shutters. Those blue doors had given him the only home he'd ever known—yet, he'd rejected it as soon as he could move away.

Refocusing, he said, "All right, you can relax until we dock, or join me for Greek lessons."

Gwen said she couldn't join in; she still had more guests to chat with. Kavanagh let himself be persuaded, though, and seemed to enjoy the mental challenge. He was the best in the group.

"You have a knack for this," Santos said. "You haven't learned any Greek before?" He had no specific purpose in asking; he just wanted to get the man talking, see if anything of interest turned up.

"No, beyond a few words from restaurant menus."

"Other languages?"

Exaggerating his Irish accent, Kavanagh said, "Well now, there's a wee smattering of Irish Gaelic, from spending my youth in Ireland. Then French, because my ma believed I should be fluent in both languages of my new country."

"Don't you just love an accent?" one of the middle-aged women said dreamily. She glanced between Kavanagh and Santos. "The two of you have such wonderful ones."

"We only put them on to charm the ladies," Kavanagh said with a wink. "Right, Santos?"

Santos couldn't help but grin. The man would be likable if he wasn't, in all probability, a big-time thief. "You're not supposed to let them in on our secrets." Then, probing for a reaction, he added, "A man's entitled to his secrets, after all."

"That's the truth," Kavanagh said, the humor dying from his face. "We should get back to the lesson."

As Santos reviewed the basic greetings, he thought that there was definitely more to the man than met the eye. It was almost as if there were two Flynn Kavanaghs. One was lighthearted and charming. The other was darker, distracted, and definitely not cheerful. If he'd stolen the five mil, the theft clearly hadn't solved all his problems.

Chapter 6

AS the clock hands moved toward eight and guests assembled on deck, ready for dinner, Santos gazed over to the railing, where the pair of English blondes were turning their charms on Kavanagh. The man laughed with them, yet didn't seem to be giving them his full attention. Then his gaze sharpened, fixing on something behind Santos.

Santos turned, to see Kendra Kirk. The woman had an innate elegance, even in a simple T-shirt over a long skirt, yet, when he stepped over to talk to her, it was duty rather than attraction that drew him. He caught her shooting a glance in Kavanagh's direction, but then she turned abruptly away, stumbling into Santos. He caught her arm to steady her. "Are you okay?"

She gave him a smile that didn't touch her eyes. "Great, except for being hungry."

"We'll soon solve that problem." Teasing, flirting a bit to loosen her up, he added, "Everyone knows Greek food is the best in the world."

This time her smile seemed more genuine. "Spoken like a loyal Greek. I admit I haven't eaten much of it."

"Do you like lamb?"

When she nodded, he said, "You must try the roast lamb tonight. Be adventurous, Kendra."

"Maybe if it just extends to roast lamb," she said dryly. "Other than that, I'm not the adventurous type."

Another woman like Gwen. He winked. "Never know until you try." Now that she seemed more comfortable with him, he edged the conversation toward a topic that interested him more than her taste in food. "I heard someone say you're a lawyer?"

"True."

"Perhaps not the most adventurous career?" He hoped she'd talk about her work so he could get a sense of how she felt about it—and how she felt about criminals she failed to convict. "Or is it?"

"It has its moments."

"Tell me more."

Her brow creased in a frown and he realized she was watching Kavanagh again. Maybe that was his answer and, as he'd suspected, it pissed her off to see the man free and enjoying himself. "Kendra?"

Her eyes, a striking greenish gray, refocused on him. "Sorry, I think Gwen's trying to get everyone organized to go for dinner."

A sigh of frustration escaped him, and he covered up with a wry smile. "A cruise director's job is never done. I'll look forward to talking to you again." So much for getting any more out of the prosecutor.

Still, it was no hardship to head over and assist Gwen. All day, he'd let his attraction show with secret gazes and seemingly casual brushes against her. Her flushes and covert glances had told him he was getting to her, but she'd given no clear indication he'd won her over. Later, when the stars came out, he'd find a way to get her alone and ramp up his efforts. No way was that woman going to bed alone again tonight.

THE dinner at Diogenis Taverna had worked out well, Gwen thought with satisfaction as waiters in traditional costume brought out platters of baklava and cups of Greek coffee.

Their group had booked half the restaurant and arranged for a menu of traditional dishes including seafood, moussaka, roasted lamb, and roasted chicken. Most guests had stuck with red or white Greek wine, but the bolder ones had ordered retsina.

The night was mild and clear and the guests were equally split between outside tables and inside ones with a waterfront view. Her bosses recommended having seating plans for dinner, shuffling the guests around so people didn't always sit with the same friends and relatives and instead got to know each other. She was happy to see the guests chatting so comfortably with folks they'd just met.

In one corner of the restaurant, three local men ranging in age from teenaged to gray haired played sweet, catchy music on bouzoukis, stringed instruments similar to a mandolin.

Shot glasses of ouzo arrived. Gwen tasted hers, enjoying the licorice flavor, but only had a few sips. Pleasant as the evening was, she was on duty. Besides, liquor would cloud her judgment. She needed to be in full possession of her faculties to resist the allure of Santos.

All day he'd behaved circumspectly, but she'd seen a gleam in his eye, read double meanings into what he said, and enjoyed each casual brush of his body against hers. Just being near the man was a serious test of her self-control, and never for a moment did he let her forget it.

Before this trip, she had been easing back into the dating world slowly, going out occasionally and only very casually. When she'd kissed the last man she'd dated, it hadn't been because she'd been attracted; it was an experiment. Yet she'd been aroused by Santos from the moment she saw him and had kissed him passionately within an hour of meeting him.

Yesterday, she'd e-mailed Sarah and Andi, and earlier today she'd heard back from them. Sarah had e-mailed from Inuvik, where she was organizing an eco-themed wedding, accompanied by her photographer husband. She'd said she and Andi both had full confidence in Gwen and she should trust her instincts. The feedback was flattering but made her feel a little anxious because, as a control freak, instinct was the last thing she relied on.

Andi had phoned from the Vancouver office, where she was holding down the fort as well as running two local weddings and adjusting to life as a newly engaged woman. She seconded what Sarah had said, then went on. "We sure can't institute a company policy against fraternization." It was a reference to the fact that both she and Sarah had met their guys at destination weddings. Then she'd teased, "Hey, maybe the company policy is to fall in love when you're organizing a wedding."

Gwen had snorted. "Fall in love? No way. If I ever do that again, it's going to be way down the road." And with a solid, reliable man like Jonathan, not one who shunned commitment. No way would she repeat her mother's mistake and fall for a man like her father.

"Famous last words. But hey, if you're not into the love thing, remember the advice you gave me when I met Jared in Whistler."

"Which advice?"

"Being a slut isn't necessarily bad." Chuckling, Andi had hung up on her.

As Gwen recalled that conversation, she glanced over to the next table, where Santos was entertaining Liz's gray-haired mother. He'd charmed all the women, splitting his attention equally among them even though a couple of Liz's single, attractive girlfriends had blatantly hit on him. He'd have no trouble finding another woman to warm his bed.

Damn, she hated that idea.

But having sex with him herself . . . No, she didn't think it would be slutty; single people should be free to enjoy their sex lives so long as no one got hurt. But it would be a big step. She'd only ever had one lover, and the first time she'd made love had been on her wedding night.

She and Jonathan had agreed on that—him because he'd had other lovers and wanted things to be special with her, and her because she was determined to no longer be the wild child. Well, at the age of thirty-three, she was grown up, anything but wild, and she might or might not ever get married again. One thing she was sure of: She wasn't going to wait for another wedding night before she had sex again!

This wasn't the most sensible time to test-drive her newly re-awakened sexuality, not when she was in charge of her first destination wedding. But how long would it take to find another man she wanted to get naked with?

Frustrated, she focused back on her job. The guests seemed to have finished their dessert, and if they wanted more coffee and ouzo they could get it on the *Aphrodite*. She spread the word that it was time to head back to the ship.

As a straggly group, they strolled along the waterfront to where the *Aphrodite* was docked. Once aboard, a number of people lingered on deck, gazing at the stars.

Santos pointed out a few constellations in the clear night sky, and people oohed and aahed. Gwen found a spot at the railing a little apart from the others and gazed upward, too. How easily she'd fallen under the spell of the Greek islands. Sunshine and breezes during the day, velvety stillness at night, tavernas and ruins, white walls accented by blue trim, bright flowers overflowing colorful pots. Not to mention the delicious food. Jonathan would have enjoyed this so much. They'd thought they were being sensible, planning for the big sabbatical trip rather than taking a two-week holiday when they were younger. By not seizing the day, they'd lost the opportunity to see Greece together.

She didn't want to lose out on any more opportunities.

Gazing at sparkling stars, she listened to Santos tell the Greek legend of how the Big Dipper and Little Dipper got their proper names. A mother and son had been turned into bears in the sky: Ursa Major and Ursa Minor.

He came to join her. "See them?"

"I do." But she turned from the sky to study the even more enticing sight of his face, all planes and angles under the light of the stars. "Thanks for the story." Lowering her voice, she asked, "From Giorgos's notes?"

"No." He paused. "From *Yiayia* Maria, my mother's mother. *Yiayia* means *grandmother.*"

"Nice. It's been a good day, Santos. *Efkharisto.*" Somehow it seemed right to thank him in Greek.

"*Parakalo.* My pleasure. Especially if it means I can be with you."

"Shh." She glanced around, relieved that no one was near them.

He took her arm, his touch searing even through her cotton sweater, and guided her farther away from the others. "*Se thelo poly.*"

"What?"

He rested his hand atop hers on the wooden railing and squeezed gently. "I want you."

"Santos!" His touch, the gleam in his eyes, and his words made her tremble. Again she looked around, noticing that most of the others had gone below.

"Do you want me, Gwen?" With his thumb, he stroked her wrist, and her pulse leaped.

"Yes," she admitted, as if that wild beat under his thumb hadn't already told him. "But—"

"No. No *but*. Let's try *and* instead. Yes, *and* we will go to your cabin together and make love now, *glyka mou*."

"Oh," she said on a sigh, "that's so tempting, but I don't think it's a good idea."

"No one need know, if you're concerned about us looking professional."

The stroke of his thumb was mesmerizing. It made her nipples throb, and her sex, too, imagining that gentle, persistent caress. "True, but I still don't think it would be right."

"Are you afraid your employer would be angry? Your duties for the day are over, and your time should be your own."

"It is. And my bosses, Sarah and Andi, would have no problem with it because they both got together with guys at weddings they organized."

"Then there's a tradition to be honored." He circled her wrist, clasping it between thumb and fingers. "What better country than Greece to do it in?"

She chuckled, thinking of Andi's joke about company policy. What would Santos say if she told him Sarah had married Free Lafontaine and Andi was engaged to Jared Stone? That was a tradition neither she nor Santos had the slightest interest in honoring.

Sex, though . . . Steamy, delicious, uncomplicated sex. Santos was a charmer, and when it came to serious relationships he was like her dad, not her. Yet in his role as cruise director, he hadn't let her down. All she needed from him—aside from great sex—was one thing. She glanced around to make sure no one was paying attention to them. "Santos, if we do this, it has to be our secret. Agreed?"

"Sure, if it's important to you."

"I can trust you?"

"You doubt me?" He sounded offended.

"Sorry, but I don't know you. On the one hand, you said you

don't believe in commitment, but you also said that when you commit to something, you can be relied on."

"Ah. What I mean is that I don't make promises"—his voice roughened—"or let people put expectations on me unless I agree. But when I do, yes, you can rely on me."

"Thank you. In that case, I suppose if I took an hour of *personal* time . . ."

"No, that's no good."

She gaped at him in the starlight. "It isn't? I, uh, wasn't that what we were talking about?"

"Personal time, yes." He smiled down at her. "But an hour isn't nearly enough for the pleasure I want to show you."

Her pulse thudded. More than an hour? She and Jonathan had had a good sex life before he fell ill, but she couldn't remember ever spending that long making love.

"Gwen?"

She stared out at the ocean, where starlight reflected off the dark surface. In that moment, she realized this was a transition point in her life, the second major one since she was widowed.

"After Jonathan died," she said, so quietly it was almost like she was talking to herself, "I was grieving, afraid, life was overwhelming. I was pretty much a shut-in for a year. Then one morning, when I was huddled at the kitchen table with a blanket wrapped around me"—her husband's blanket—"a friend phoned and asked me for lunch. I said no, the same as I'd said to all invitations for months and months."

Santos's fingers circled her wrist, holding her lightly but comfortingly.

What was she doing, responding to his seduction by telling him this stuff? And yet she was working toward something, and she wanted to share the process with him. Maybe it was a test. If he couldn't relate, if he made a silly joke or blew her off, then he wasn't the right man to trust—even short term—with her sexual being.

She went on. "My girlfriend said, rather sharply, 'Don't forget there's a world out here.' Of course I knew that; it was what I'd been hiding from. Then it struck me that the world wasn't cold and cruel. The bad things had happened in my house, where disease had eaten at Jonathan bit by bit. Outside, I had friends and I'd once had interests and job skills. In that moment, I knew it was time to find the guts to get back out there. So I did. I called her back—and I granted myself a fresh start."

His fingers tightened. "I'm glad."

"Me, too. And I've come a long way in eight months. But there's a part of me that's still been hibernating."

Again his thumb strummed her pulse. "Your sexuality."

She nodded. Jonathan had owned her sexuality. Now Santos stirred it to life again. He wanted her and she wanted him.

"Now it's wide awake," he said. "It's time, Gwen." He spoke the words with quiet certainty, giving her the understanding she'd been looking for.

She'd come to Greece with memories of Jonathan for company, and now a different man stood at her side. Under a black velvet sky glittering with stars, with the scent of a foreign ocean in her nostrils, there was only one answer. She faced Santos, tipping her head up to him. "You said you'll show me pleasure and I believe you. That's an offer I won't refuse."

His smile flashed white. "Good. Now, how shall we do this?"

An imp made her say, "How many ways are there?"

He laughed softly. "I look forward to finding out. But I meant, we should probably split up now and meet in your cabin."

"Absolutely. I'll go down first. Make sure no one sees you. Or, if you do bump into someone, tell them there's some detail you forgot to check for tomorrow."

"Yes, boss." He gave a mock salute. "I'm anxious to check *all* your details."

Smiling, she raised her voice. "Good night, Santos. Thanks for everything. See you in the morning."

"*Kalinikta*, Gwen. Sweet dreams."

She left the deck, which seemed deserted but for one couple entwined in a kiss. Long blond hair gleamed in the moonlight and she smiled, knowing that Liz and Peter were enjoying their pre-wedding cruise.

In the lounge attached to the dining area, a dozen or so of the bride and groom's friends were sitting with bottles of Mythos beer and shot glasses of ouzo. Other than that, the *Aphrodite* was quiet.

When Gwen slipped into her cabin, she pulled off her cardigan and went into the en suite, so different from bathrooms back home. The shower was an uncurtained, handheld one. Very Greek, she'd been told, which in her eyes made it charming, even though she'd yet to master the knack of showering without spraying the towels and toilet paper. That wasn't an issue tonight, though, because she'd showered before dinner.

Quickly, nerves thrumming, she freshened up, then perched on the side of the bed. Should she change into a sleep shirt? Strip down to her underwear? Climb into bed? The cabin was bare-bones and she didn't even have candles to make it more romantic.

Her first time with Jonathan had been so different. For their wedding night, he'd booked a luxurious waterfront suite at the Pan Pacific Hotel. She'd worn a gorgeous silk-and-lace negligee and he'd ordered champagne and strawberries. After dating rough-and-tumble high school boys, it had seemed like the height of sophisticated romance. She was nervous, but trusted Jonathan to make her first time special. He'd come through for her, too, as he always had.

Stop! This is not the time to be missing your husband! She had a hot young lover on his way, a thought that excited her and also made her anxious. Santos was so experienced, and she'd only been with one man. Would she disappoint him?

The door opened with the slightest of creaks and he slipped inside, still wearing his uniform and now carrying a bulging briefcase.

"Did you see anyone?" she whispered.

Shaking his head, he put the briefcase on the desk, then came over to her and held out his hands. When she took them, he tugged her gently to her feet. His voice a low rumble, he said, "Nervous?"

"A little. Like I said, it's been a while."

"We'll take it slow. You'll have a good time." He stated it with certainty and she believed him.

Standing a few inches apart, hands linked, she cautioned, "Since my cabin's at the end of the corridor, there's no one on one side, but the bride's aunt and uncle are on the other side. I haven't heard them, so I think the walls are pretty soundproof, but we should be quiet."

"This will help." He released her hands and stepped over to the desk, opened his briefcase, and took out a portable CD player. A moment later, a woman began to sing in Greek. He kept the volume low, just enough to disguise the sound of them talking—and, hopefully, any other sounds they might make. Not that she'd ever been noisy in bed, but Santos didn't seem like a man who'd hold back on expressing himself.

Gwen stayed on her feet, though her legs were trembling from nerves, as he brought out a bottle of ouzo and two shot glasses. As he poured, he said, "At dinner, I noticed you enjoyed ouzo but didn't drink much. Because you were on duty?"

She nodded and took the glass he handed her. Maybe alcohol would relax her.

He raised his own glass. *"Yassou."*

She repeated the toast back, then took a small sip, savoring the pungent bite of licorice.

Santos swallowed his in one gulp.

Body tingling with anticipation and nerves, she took another hasty sip.

He put his shot glass down on the tiny table by the bed, rested both hands lightly on her shoulders, and pressed a lingering kiss to her forehead. "All day I've been thinking about kissing you."

"Me, too," she admitted. Not to mention getting him out of that tailored uniform so she could take a better look at the fine body she'd ogled when he went swimming. And now the moment was here, and she was suffering an attack of nerves.

"Santos, why me?" She definitely hadn't been the only woman ogling, and a few had come on to him. "I saw two or three other women pretty much throwing themselves at you." Yes, she was insecure. She needed Santos to do what he did so well: make her feel special.

He paused in tracing the line of her nose with his lips, and shrugged. "It happens. But you're the one I'm attracted to." Now his mouth drifted across her cheek, distracting her.

"But why?" she persisted. For her, the answer was easy. He was the most handsome, sexy, dashing man she'd ever seen. The last man in the world for a long-term relationship, but when it came to sex, he was a much hotter pirate than Johnny Depp.

He brushed hair back from her face and kissed the soft skin in front of her ear, then worked his way around the lobe to end up sucking gently on the sensitive spot behind it.

Erotic sensations quivered through her, weakening her knees, but she managed to pull away. Before her legs gave out, she sat on the edge of the bed. Drinking a bit more ouzo for courage, she persisted. "I really want to know. Why me?"

He reached for the bottle, poured himself another shot, but this time only sipped it. Standing in front of her, an erection tenting the front of his white pants, he studied her in the cabin's muted light.

"The first thing I noticed was your beauty. Your hair, your eyes, the shape of your face. That wonderful mouth. But there's so much more to you, Gwen. I like your commitment, your loyalty, your generosity."

He'd given her exactly what she'd craved. Knowing that he really saw her and thought she was special was almost more arousing than his sexy caresses.

He put his glass down again, this time almost full, and sank to his knees in front of her. "*Se thelo poly, latreia mou.* I want to make you happy. I want to make love to you." With both hands, he grasped the hem of her yellow top.

She didn't resist as he slowly pulled the top over her head and tossed it onto the desk. Under her thin, silky bra, her breasts were sensitive, her nipples already puckering in anticipation of his touch.

"Beautiful," he murmured, but he didn't caress them. Instead he went for the button at the waist of her capris. In the space of a few seconds, he'd stripped them off, leaving her wearing only a bra and a white thong that was growing damp between her legs. "Oh yeah, beautiful. I knew you would be."

Self-conscious, she wanted to cover herself but managed to resist.

With one quick gesture, he flipped the bedcovers aside, revealing the crisp white bottom sheet. "Lie down."

She started to hike herself farther up on the bed, but when he began to undo his shirt buttons, aroused curiosity overcame her nerves and she scooted back to the edge. "No, wait. Let me."

A grin flashed. "Now you're talking." He dropped his hands.

Chapter 7

SITTING only inches from the sexiest man she'd ever seen, Gwen reached up to free the next button, her trembling fingers brushing taut, warm skin, feeling the tickle of chest hair. One by one, she pulled the buttons through the holes, easing the sides of the shirt apart, revealing more and more of the torso she'd admired when he was in board shorts.

Jonathan had been broad shouldered and slim, but his body had been a professor's. In comparison, Santos was so muscular, so brown and virile. She loved his firm pecs, six-pack abs, and the scattering of curly black hair that arrowed down the center of his body, drawing her eyes again to his erection, which was, temptingly, right in front of her face.

Her mind might be jittery with nerves but her sex knew what it wanted. It ached and moistened with the desire to feel him fill her. She fumbled with his belt buckle, finally undoing it and then working on the button of his pants.

He stood quietly, leaving it all to her, but the rapid breaths that fluttered his stomach in and out betrayed his impatience.

She forced his zipper down, hooked her hands into the sides of his pants, and began to slide them down. Under them he wore slim-fitting white cotton boxers that strained to contain the swollen full-ness of his package.

He moved away slightly to kick off his sandals and pull off his pants and shirt, both of which he tossed on the chair. Clad only in brown skin and white underwear, he faced her.

The boxers revealed so much more than the long, loose board shorts had, and every inch of it was mouthwatering.

In high school, she'd fooled around with a few guys, approaching intercourse but never crossing that line, but ever since she was seventeen she'd only seen one man's penis. Now she was desperately curious to see Santos's.

But he took her firmly by the shoulders, pulled her to her feet, and before she could even squeak he'd picked her up and was laying her on the bed, head on a pillow.

As he'd done yesterday, he stretched out atop her, his legs be-tween her spread ones. The rigid length of his penis pressed against her most sensitive flesh, with now only two thin layers of cotton separating them, and instinctively she squirmed against it.

His mouth claimed hers in a sweet licorice kiss, a tangle of lips and tongues and teeth nipping. Of sighs, breath caught in quick gasps, soft giggles, moans. Her hips thrust convulsively and she wished the barrier of their clothing would magically disappear.

"Hey," he murmured, mouth separating from hers. "There's no hurry."

Maybe not for him, and until a few minutes ago she'd have said slower was better. But now, surprising and almost shocking her, her body clamored with need. Damn it, she hadn't had an orgasm in years. She'd had so little interest in sex that, after a couple of failed attempts to masturbate, she'd wondered if she'd ever have one again.

Now the delicious tension mounted quickly, irresistibly. "So long," she muttered, "it's been so long. I want . . ." No, she was too shy to beg that he make her come.

"*Latreia mou.*"

She had no idea what it meant, but his tone made it an endearment. He lifted his weight off her and she sighed with disappointment. Grabbing a pillow on the way, he slid down the bed. Deftly he lifted her lower body and shoved the pillow under her to raise her pelvis. In one quick move, he yanked her thong down and off.

Then, sprawling on the bed, he nudged her legs farther apart and buried his face between them.

"Oh!" She quivered as he blew hot breath against her damp skin. Then he licked, a hard stroke with the flat of his tongue against her swollen sex. "Yes, Santos, oh yes."

He licked again and again, each hot, firm stroke a delicious pressure against her sensitive, needy flesh. His tongue flicked her clit and she gasped, tensed, yearned for more.

Her hands gripped the sheet below, clenching and fisting as she thrust herself against his face, letting her body say what she was too shy to as she reached for the climax that was building.

He murmured something in Greek, the movement of his lips resonating against her. He licked again, firmly stroking her sex and ending with her clit, which he sucked gently into his mouth.

"Oh my God." She couldn't stand it, so much tension gathering, so much need and anticipation.

When he did it again, she held her breath, straining toward him in search of that one final . . . *Oh, God, yes!* Pleasure crashed through her in waves, a release so sharp it almost hurt.

It swept her away, then gradually ebbed, leaving her floating, somehow depleted and filled at the same time. She realized she'd squeezed her eyes shut, and now opened them to see Santos kneeling between her spread, bent legs, one hand gently capping each knee.

Her cheeks, warm from climax, heated even more with embarrassment. She'd been so uninhibited, so totally selfish as he drove
her to pleasure. "Sorry," she whispered. "I, uh, guess I really needed
that."

His smile was warm. "Never apologize for your sexuality. It's
beautiful, Gwen. You're beautiful." A teasing sparkle lit his dark
eyes. "Next time, you might be a bit quieter, though."

"Oh!" Her hand flew to her mouth. "Did I . . . What did I do?"
She was quiet during sex. Wasn't she?

"Just said, 'Oh, God, yes,' but you didn't exactly whisper it."

She'd cried out. Had the music—some kind of catchy Greek pop
song—covered the sound? "If my neighbors say anything, I'll tell
them I had a nightmare."

He gave a soft laugh. "I am your nightmare?"

"More like the sexiest dream I've ever had." She gazed appreciatively at him, all brown muscles and glossy black hair, his boxers
still bulging with an enticing erection. "Now, what were you saying
about *next time*?"

SANTOS studied the woman spread beneath him. Her body was
slim and firm, gently curved in all the right places. The bra had ridden up, revealing the soft bottom curves of her breasts, and other
than that she was entirely naked. Her golden hair lay every which
way on the pillow, her brown eyes glowed, and a flush bloomed on
her cheeks and chest. She looked much more relaxed than earlier, as
if that orgasm had freed her from the tension and uncertainty she'd
been carrying.

"Next time," he repeated, bending forward to plant a hand on either side of her shoulders. "Next time is right now." Then he kissed
her slowly and thoroughly. She tasted like ouzo and her scent was
wild ginger, both intoxicating.

At first she responded lazily, her body still drugged from climax, then her breath quickened and her tongue and lips became more demanding.

His body craved release, but he tried to ignore its urging, wanting more than quick satisfaction. He was only Gwen's second lover and she'd waited a long time to be with a man. She'd said her sexuality had been hibernating, and he'd awakened it. That made him proud, and determined to bring her the kind of pleasure she hadn't known in years.

Her mouth was as lush, as sexy as it looked, but he eased away. "So many other parts of you I want to taste."

"Mmm, help yourself."

He slipped kisses across her chin, then, as she arched to give him access, down the slender curve of her neck. She was sensitive, responsive, constantly moving in tiny ways to show him where it felt good, where she next wanted him to kiss. Her hands twined in his hair, playing with the strands, occasionally gripping his head when her breath caught or she wanted to guide him.

He caressed her breasts through her bra, then sucked one budded nipple into his mouth. No, he didn't want to taste silk, he wanted bare skin. Rather than reach under her for the back clasp, he peeled the bra higher to reveal small, firm, lovely breasts. When the bra was bunched above her breasts, she pulled her hands out of his hair, fumbled behind herself to undo it, then tossed it away.

Humming approval in the back of his throat, he studied creamy skin and dusky areolas with brighter pink nipples. Cupping one breast, he lowered his head, the black hair he hadn't cut in months brushing her pale skin, and took both nipple and areola into his mouth. Testing her reactions, he licked, sucked, then increased the pressure as she murmured, "Oh yes, so good."

Eventually he moved to the other breast, then slowly down her body. She panted, hips twisting, sweat sheening on her skin.

His skin was damp, too, his heart pounding and his breath coming fast. His cock, rubbing against the bed as he moved, was so hard it felt like it might burst.

He took pride in his ability to please a woman, to defer his own pleasure, but with Gwen it was growing increasingly difficult. Maybe it was seeing a woman who was usually so in control letting go so openly, so trustingly, with him. Or was it because she tasted so sweet, smelled so exotic, was so damned beautiful? Or perhaps it was the knowledge that she'd chosen him as only the second man to know her intimately.

The rich, womanly scent of her arousal grew stronger as he circled her navel with his tongue and moved lower. She'd had a bikini wax but wasn't completely bare, and he found the curls of blond hair womanly and arousing. They were a silky caress against his lips as he kissed his way through them. When he dipped lower, she spread her legs, offering herself, and he paused a moment to admire the damp, rosy folds between her legs.

"Santos?" Her breathy whisper was needy, impatient.

Now he thrust his hands under her curvy butt, held her up, and admired her with his tongue. He tasted her delicious salty musk, captured fresh drops with his tongue, and spread them, making her even slicker.

His loins ached with the effort to hold back when all his body wanted was to pump mindlessly into her. Gwen deserved lovemaking, not fucking.

Her clit was a swollen pearl and he circled it with his tongue, again testing to see what she liked. When he closed his lips around that sensitive bundle of nerves and applied the gentlest of suction, she writhed and gasped, "Yes, yes."

He flicked with his tongue, felt her body push harder against him and tense, as if everything in her had focused on that one tiny center and she was waiting. Waiting for him to give her what she needed.

His tongue circled her clit, then again he flicked over the top and sucked gently, and with a gasp of pleasure she surged against him. Waves of release pulsed against his lips and he stayed with her through them, though his own body was rigid as he clung to self-control.

When the spasms eased, he jerked off the bed to struggle out of his boxers, find one of the condoms he'd stashed in his pants pocket, and sheathe himself in record time. She sprawled loose-limbed, eyes closed, chest heaving gently. "Gwen?" he said urgently.

Her eyes opened, glazed with satiation. Then her gaze sharpened and her eyes widened as she took him in. "Santos, oh, God, I'm so selfish."

"You're beautiful. But now it's time for both of us, together. Yes?"

"Oh, yes." She held out her arms.

He sank down gratefully as her arms folded around him and her legs lifted to wrap his hips. The head of his cock nudged her where she was slick with the juices of arousal. Using all his willpower, he eased between her folds slowly, knowing she'd be tight after years without sex.

She opened gradually, her sheath hugging him so snugly, he groaned with pleasure. "I can't believe how good you feel."

"You, too." Her hips tilted, urging him deeper.

He thrust, groaning again. "Jesus, I'm not going to last long."

"Don't hold back. Let me feel you."

Her words banished the last thin thread of his self-control and he plunged into her, fast and deep. Had anything ever felt this good? He pulled back, thrust forward, and did it again. In and out in a driving rhythm, the pressure inside him mounting until it almost made him scream, his balls tightening and drawing up and then, impossible to stop, orgasm ripped through him. He barely managed to muffle his shout in the pillow as his body let go.

Gwen's nails dug into his shoulders, her hips jerked, and her internal muscles spasmed around him as she, too, reached climax.

For long moments, they clasped each other tight and hard, bodies hot and sweaty, then their muscles relaxed and they slid apart. After he dealt with the condom, he lay on his back, an arm around her shoulders, and she curved into him, head tucked between his neck and shoulder. "Wow," she said.

"Are you okay? Hope I didn't hurt you, but I kind of lost control there at the end."

"So did I. It felt incredible. I've never—" She bit back whatever she'd been going to say and pressed a kiss to his shoulder. "I feel so sexy, thanks to you."

"You're special, Gwen. I wanted to show you that."

"Thank you."

He thought about something she'd asked earlier. "You wanted to know why I'd chosen you. So, how about you? Why me? Why did you come all the way to Greece to find a man to break your dry spell?"

She shifted over, her head on the other pillow, and looked him straight in the eyes. "I wasn't ready. Not until I met you." Her lips squeezed together for a moment, then she gave a rueful grin. "Okay, I admit at first it was about your looks and that whole pirate thing. That attracted me, but if that's all there'd been, I would have stopped after our first kiss. But today, the way you worked with me, helped me make this trip a success . . ."

"I know how important it is to you. I want to make you happy." Lying there with her, there was no place he'd rather be.

"You do. Out of bed and in." She gave a soft sigh. "Whatever I need, I can rely on you to give it to me."

He stiffened slightly. "You do know . . . I mean, this is great, terrific, but it's—" What was the polite way of saying, *This is just sex, so don't go thinking I'm some responsible guy you can rely on, because I don't do commitment?*

"Oh," she said in a kind of squeak, her body tensing, too. "Santos, that wasn't what I meant. I know you don't want anything serious, and I'm not looking for that either. I just meant that you're great to work with, and it's wonderful how you read my needs in bed."

Relieved, he relaxed again. "Just don't want there to be any misunderstanding."

"Believe me, I appreciate your honesty." She paused. "I understand what you said, about you deciding when you're going to promise something, and not wanting people to put their expectations on you. And I wondered . . . Someone—some woman?—did that to you, and it didn't turn out well? But," she made a quick, dismissive gesture, "I'm probably being too nosy. I don't know the, uh, rules of this kind of relationship."

"You can ask, and I'll decide if I answer. And vice versa." Did he want to share this with her? He hadn't, not with anyone else, but Gwen had shared more of her own vulnerabilities with him than most women did. He liked her openness and wanted to give her the same in return. Problem was, she likely wouldn't get it. She'd think he was a shit.

"It's really okay—" she started.

"Don't be so meek and mild," he growled. "It doesn't suit you." Had her husband wanted her to be that way? He stroked her arm where it lay across his chest. "I'll tell you. You may not like me very much, though."

Her expression turned wary. "I want to know."

The woman really did have an issue with trust. Had some man—clearly not her husband—done a number on her?

"When I was a kid, I spent a lot of time with my grandparents on Naxos. They had a restaurant in the tourist area. My mom, their only child, hadn't liked the island and couldn't wait to leave. With me, they were determined I'd be different, that I'd love island life, love the restaurant, and want nothing more than to work with them and eventually take it over. But I didn't. I was like my mom, bored and seeking excitement. I couldn't wait to get away. They've never understood, or really forgiven me. I feel like a shit, because they were so good to me, but I wasn't the guy they wanted me to be."

She captured his hand where it lay on her arm and threaded her fingers through his. "That's too bad for all of you. But you didn't let them think you'd take over the restaurant, did you? You didn't mislead them?"

"No, of course not. I loved—love—them." They'd given him a home when his parents hadn't, loved him as if he were their own child. That was why their disappointment cut so deep. "But maybe I didn't protest enough. I didn't make them listen."

"That's why you're so up front with people now."

"Yeah." He squeezed her fingers. "Thanks. So, this is good with you? You and me? I want to do it again. Tomorrow night, if we get a chance."

"Me, too. As long as no one suspects."

"You're not much of a risk-taker, are you?"

"Of course not. I grew out of that habit long ago."

Grew out of? It wasn't immature to take the occasional risk. Hell, he'd built an exciting, rewarding career around it. "Some risks are pretty harmless. You have to have some fun in life. Some adventure."

"Being in Greece is an adventure for me," she said defensively. "And being with you is a risk."

"There you go," he teased. "Risk-taker."

"Taking risks can get you in trouble," she said a little starchily.

"Speaking from experience?"

"As a matter of fact." Her voice was solemn and she ducked her head, burying it against his shoulder again. "A very bad experience."

He snuggled her closer. "Tell me."

Her shoulders moved up and down as she took a deep breath, and he thought she'd refuse. Then she said slowly, "When I was a teenager, I dated a college boy who was definitely a risk-taker. He was fun, exciting, charming. In fact, he was a lot like my dad, but I didn't see that at the time."

"Your dad?"

She waved a hand. "My dad's a whole other story. Anyhow, this boy, Brad, and a group of his friends were into organizing raves."

He was curious about her father, but even more so about her last words. "You went to raves?" That didn't match up with the Gwen he was getting to know.

"Yeah, I liked excitement, the way you did." The way her father did. "Anyhow, at the end of the summer—I was seventeen, going into grade twelve—there was one in this huge barn out in the Fraser Valley." She shivered and he tightened his grip. "It had been a hot, dry summer. People were dancing, drinking, taking ecstasy, smoking pot and cigarettes." A shudder rippled through her whole body. "I hate remembering this."

"You don't have to tell me." But he hoped she would, rather than shut him out.

"No, it's okay. It's in my mind now. Talking will help put it back in its place." She swallowed, then went on. "There was a fire."

"Oh, man." His arms tightened again.

"It was horrible." Her voice trembled when she said, "Three kids died. Several others had bad burns."

"*Gamoto*. But you were all right?"

"Yes. I'd gone outside for some fresh air. But . . ." Another swallow. "Brad died. And the girl he was dancing with had third-degree burns and was scarred for life. They were right by the bales of hay where the fire started."

He sucked in a breath. "That could have been you."

She nodded against his chest. "I'd been dancing with him right before. But I was a little dizzy, so I went out for air. If I hadn't, yes, it would have been me."

What could he possibly say? "I'm sure glad it wasn't."

"Me, too. Anyhow, it shocked the wild child out of me. I became the kid my mom had always wanted," she added wryly. "I stopped dating, just hung out with other kids in groups. One night, a few of us were at this one boy's house working on a school assignment and his older brother dropped by. Jonathan. We just . . . hit it off. He was so different from anyone I'd dated. He was older, a lot older. Mature, reliable, responsible. Everything I wanted and needed."

"A lot older?"

"Yeah. Sixteen years. He taught university."

"You were in grade twelve and he was a university professor? That's, uh, unusual. What did your parents say?"

"Mom was so happy I'd settled down, and she knew Jonathan was a good influence, a man who'd take care of me. Dad"—she shrugged—"who cared what he thought?"

"Tell me about your father."

She shook her head, her hair brushing softly against his skin. "Not tonight. You need to go."

"Guess you're right." He hated to leave, though, and not just because of her curvy body and the great sex. He was interested in Gwen. He actually wanted to hear her life story. Yet that was crazy. Safer to keep this all about sex so she wouldn't start thinking funny thoughts.

Despite what she said, it was in the back of his mind that the first time she'd slept with a man, she'd married him. Of course, her husband had been the complete opposite of Santos: conservative, responsible, reliable. The kind of man who likely would have taken over the family business had his grandparents wanted him to.

"Being with you like this is all the risk I'm willing to take," she said, reinforcing the fact that he and she were very different.

He eased away from her and dropped a soft kiss on her lips. "Fair enough."

Anxiously, she gazed up at him as he slid out of bed. "You'll be careful, leaving?"

"I will." Teasingly, he said, "It's going to be hard to behave when I see you tomorrow."

"Santos, you have to—"

He raised a hand, stopping her. "I know, I know."

She pulled the covers up to her shoulders and watched as he drew on his clothing, which he did with deliberate slowness.

"If you're nice to me," he drawled, "I'll let you take my clothes off again."

Chapter 8

SANTOS woke to the sound of the anchor chain being wound up and sprang out of bed to get ready for the day. Whistling cheerfully, he made his way on deck. Things were going great with Gwen. Now all he needed was a break in his investigation.

Gwen hadn't arrived yet, nor had Kavanagh or Kendra, so he hung around the breakfast area chatting with whoever came along. When Kendra came in, wearing a T-shirt, capris, and sunglasses, she went straight to the buffet and fixed herself a bowl of yogurt with fruit and honey. As she was pouring coffee, he went over and said, "Lovely morning, isn't it?"

"Lovely." She smiled, but it looked forced.

Close up, her face looked tired, a little strained, and he wished she'd take off the sunglasses. "Looking forward to Mykonos?" he asked.

She had just started to answer when, glancing past her, he saw Kavanagh enter the room.

Kendra's gaze followed his and her smile faded. "Please excuse me. There's some work I need to do." She hurried away, carrying her yogurt and coffee.

So much for learning anything from her right now. Instead, Santos strolled over to Kavanagh. "That one doesn't seem to know the meaning of the word *holiday*."

He scowled. "Wouldn't know. I've barely met her."

What would happen if Santos called him on the lie? Instead, he tried a more subtle approach. "You don't seem in the best mood this morning. Anything I can do?"

Kavanagh shook his head, looking grumpy. "Just need my morning coffee. Excuse me." He strode past Santos and over to the buffet, where he began to dish out food, almost flinging it onto his plate.

Great. Blown off by the two people he was most interested in. Why were they both in such a foul mood this morning? Surely by this time, even if they didn't like being together on this cruise, they'd have gotten used to it.

He watched as Kavanagh went to sit with the bride's parents, and he wondered where Gwen was. Had she slept in? He imagined her curled up in the sheets where they'd made love. For a moment he fantasized about sneaking into her cabin and waking her with morning lovemaking, then, as his cock stirred to life, he struggled to refocus his thoughts.

How long was Kavanagh going to spend on deck? Would there be time to sneak below and try to hack into his computer? No, it wouldn't be safe; passengers were wandering around. Santos poured another cup of coffee and, body under control now, went to join a group of guests. But even as he answered their questions about Mykonos, half his concentration was on the door as he waited for his first sight of Gwen.

GWEN woke and stretched lazily. The gentle motion of the ship told her they were underway. Sunday morning, and the *Aphrodite* would dock in Mykonos, the most glamorous of the Greek islands.

And she felt glamorous. Or at least utterly female and very sexy. Thanks to Santos, she felt like a real, complete woman for the first time in years. She hugged the covers closer, remembering the wonderful things they'd done in this bed.

Finally, she forced herself to get up and take a shower. Adjusting the water temperature, she remembered his last words, about letting her take his clothes off. He'd meant them as a tease, and they'd definitely worked. Her fingers itched to take him up on that offer.

In the meantime . . . She stroked her hand down her belly, slicking soap gently over flesh that ached a little, in a very good way.

When she returned to Vancouver, surely her dating life would get on track now that she'd rediscovered her sexy side and gotten over her feelings of disloyalty to Jonathan. Though it was hard to imagine finding a man as attractive, charming, and irresistibly sexy as Santos. He'd made her come *three times*. She'd never been multiorgasmic, never believed she was that sexy. Only with him . . .

No, there'd be other men she was attracted to, others who would satisfy her, even if not multiorgasmically.

Damn, she'd managed to spray shower water on the toilet paper roll again. Quickly, she rinsed herself free of soap and got ready for the day.

When she arrived on the main deck, many of the guests were already there, eating breakfast outside. Invigorated by sex, she loaded her plate and headed out.

At a table in the sun, Santos sat with five or six guests. Her whole body flushed at the sight of him. Her lover.

He glanced up and they exchanged quick, warm smiles, but she thought it better not to join his group, at least until she got better control over her reaction to him. Besides, whenever she overheard one of his conversations, she wondered if the person he was talking to was the subject of his investigation.

She looked around, deciding where to sit. Hmm, Flynn Kavanagh, seated with Liz's parents, was smiling, which was good to see. She'd talked to the man a few times and concluded he was a moody guy, sometimes almost as charming as Santos and other times a real grouch. Apparently, it wasn't anything about the cruise that bothered him, he just had an odd personality. Though she was tempted to join their table and see what had them all looking so amiable, she decided to leave well enough alone.

She sat down at a different table and chatted and answered questions as she ate breakfast. Then a cry went up from a few guests who stood by the ship's railing, telling everyone that Mykonos was in sight. More passengers headed for the railing, cameras in hand.

Gwen went, too, sliding in beside Liz, who just happened to be standing next to Santos. Unable to resist letting her bare arm casually brush his, she clicked photos of the guests along the rail and of the scenery. Fishing boats bobbed on a gentle swell, and a giant cruise ship moved majestically toward its next port of call, almost dwarfing the *Aphrodite*.

As they approached the harbor and Santos talked a bit about the island, she admired Mykonos Town. A dazzling expanse of cube-shaped white buildings rose up a low hill, broken here and there by the vivid blue domes of churches and by windmills. She'd read about the windmills, and it was a thrill to see the picturesque structures. Phallic symbols, she thought, hiding a smirk, with their round white walls and conical thatched tops. But for Santos, the notion would never have occurred to her.

It also reminded her that, despite or perhaps because of having three orgasms, she'd never gotten a really good, up-close-and-personal look at his package.

"You'll definitely want to see the windmills," Santos said to the group of guests who were listening to his travelogue.

She barely managed to hold back a chuckle. "Impressive, are they?" she asked, tongue in cheek.

He shot her a puzzled look, no doubt seeing the twinkle in her eye and wondering what on earth she was thinking about.

"The island is famous for them," he said, "though few function as windmills any longer. They've been converted to homes, tourist attractions, an archaeological museum."

His was definitely functional, and she was extremely glad of that fact.

"Ooh, I can't wait to dock so we can explore," Liz said. She hugged the arm of Peter, who was on her other side. "And shop!"

"Mykonos is also famous for its stores," Santos said. "You'll find a great selection here, and generally high quality. On Santorini, too. The other islands have cheaper prices, but not as much selection."

Lowering her voice, Liz said, "We need to buy gifts for the wedding party. Gwen suggested we do it in Greece so they'd be souvenirs of the trip as well."

"You'll have lots of choices," he said. "A couple of designs are very popular. The leaping dolphin and the Greek key." He fingered his earring. "This is an example of the key. It's a geometric design with a number of variations and—"

"Liz, Gwen, what am I going to do?" A high, sobbing cry cut across what he was saying as Esther, a middle-aged aunt of Liz's, came rushing over, panic written clearly on her face.

"What's wrong?" Gwen felt a quick rush of anxiety herself and caught the woman by the shoulders to steady her.

"It's my best friend, Mary," she wailed. "She's slipped and fallen, broken her hip. I just got a phone call from the hospital because she's got no family and I'm her 'notify in case of an emergency' person."

Liz hugged her. "Auntie Esther, I'm so sorry. Will she be all right?"

"Yes, dear, but she's having an operation, and she'll have no one there for her, will she? And besides, she was looking after Conrad, and he can't be alone."

"Conrad?" Gwen asked.

"My old tabby," the woman answered, tears sliding down her cheeks. "I don't know what to do."

"Okay, folks," Santos said quietly to the others, "let's give them a little privacy." He steered the clustered guests away, and Gwen gave a sigh of gratitude.

She wondered if she should hunt down Liz's parents, but the bride seemed to be dealing with this.

"Now, Auntie," Liz said, peering into the woman's eyes, "do you want to go home?"

"I don't want to miss your wedding, dear. But Mary . . . and Conrad . . ."

"Is there anyone else who could look after them?" Gwen asked.

Esther shook her head. "I'm the only person she has. Conrad, too." She glanced at Liz. "If your parents weren't here, or my sister and her husband, I'd ask them to help, but all our family is on this cruise."

"Then perhaps you do need to go home," Gwen said tentatively, casting a questioning look at Liz. Could she or her parents come up with a better solution?

"I think you do, Auntie," Liz said. "Gwen, you can arrange that, can't you?"

A sudden departure wasn't something she'd planned for. "I . . ." She swallowed. Mykonos, they were on Mykonos. A tourist island. It had to have an airport. There was no reason to get anxious; she could deal with this. "Esther, can you go find your tickets and passport?" Gwen would call Elpida at Dionysus Cruises and ask about switching Esther's flight.

"I'll help you," Liz told her aunt, "then I'll tell my parents and Auntie Madge and Uncle Frederick."

"Thanks," Gwen said gratefully. When both women had hurried away, she leaned on the railing for a moment, allowing herself a deep, steadying breath of sea air.

Santos came over. "Did things get sorted out?"

"She has to leave. I'll call Elpida and see what she can do."

"That's too bad."

His frown sent a strange thought flashing into her mind. "It's not her, is it?" she demanded, keeping her voice quiet so none of the guests standing a few yards away could hear. "She can't be the one you're investigating."

His lips tightened as if he was holding back . . . what? A grin? "You know I can't tell you."

"I hate not knowing." Tension from Esther's dilemma spilled over, making her imagine other things that could go wrong. "Santos, there could be implications for the cruise, even the wedding. I need to know so I can prepare." She needed a plan and a contingency plan.

His eyes narrowed. "Sorry, but that's how it has to be."

Damn. "You're not going to arrest anyone, right?"

"I'm not a police officer."

"You could call one, though, if you got whatever proof you need."

His gaze was guarded. "I can't make any promises. We're talking about a criminal."

What? Santos really might do something to ruin the wedding? But he'd promised to help her . . . Her breath quickened with the onset of panic. "No, you can't call the police. That would spoil everything!" She struggled to catch her breath.

"Gwen, calm down. I may not have to. I wasn't sent here to have anyone arrested, only to do surveillance."

Trying to slow her breathing, she muttered. "That's not exactly reassuring."

"It's the best I can give you. Now, don't you need to call Elpida?"

"Oh, God, yes."

RELIEVED, Gwen stepped out of Captain Ari's cabin with a printed e-ticket and handed it to Esther. Thanks to Elpida's amazing efficiency at the Dionysus Cruises office back in Athens, travel arrangements had been made. Gwen had helped Esther pack, and now Captain Ari himself hefted her bag to escort her to a waiting taxi.

Liz came scurrying up the steps. "Auntie, there you are. I was hoping you hadn't already gone." She gave her a hug and a kiss. "Hugs to Mary and Conrad, and have a safe trip."

"And you have a wonderful, wonderful wedding, dear." There were tears in the older woman's eyes as she took the arm Captain Ari offered.

Liz leaned against Gwen and sighed as Gwen tucked a comforting arm around her. Then she pulled herself straight again. "I meant to tell you, Kendra has allergies. We've given her some meds, and hopefully that'll fix her up. But I thought you should know. Just in case."

"Thanks." Was this the day that trouble would hit, one thing after another? She hoped Kendra's problem really was only allergies and not something more serious. Fortunately, Captain Ari had paramedic training, and of course there'd be doctors on Mykonos.

When Kendra came up on deck ten minutes later, Gwen hurried over. "Liz tells me you're suffering from allergies. Is there anything I can do?"

"Thanks, but I've taken some stuff. I'm sure I'll be fine." The words were reassuring, but her face, partly hidden behind sunglasses, looked strained.

Really, since the woman had arrived on the *Aphrodite*, Gwen couldn't remember seeing her smile. Trying to cheer her up, she said, "I hope so. We have such a wonderful day planned, exploring Mykonos Town, taking an island tour, then going over to Delos, the sacred island."

"Sounds like fun." Her tone was anything but enthusiastic.

Gwen was relieved when Santos called out, "Okay, everyone's here. Let's go see Mykonos."

A number of guests let out a cheer, which lifted Gwen's spirits. As Santos, Liz, and Peter led the procession to disembark, Gwen told Kendra to go ahead. She'd stay behind to make sure no stragglers got lost.

Moving across the deck, rounding people up, she kept one eye on Kendra. Flynn Kavanagh stopped to talk to her, and Gwen remembered what Santos had said about there being tension between the two of them. She'd noticed it, too, and seen that usually they avoided each other. This time, at least, they didn't seem to be fighting, but their conversation didn't last long and Kendra joined up with Mr. and Mrs. Tippett.

Crossing her fingers that Kendra's allergies and mood would improve, that Flynn would retain his own good mood, that Liz's aunt's flight would leave without a hitch, and that there'd be no more emergencies, Gwen rounded up the rest of the guests and herded them toward the waterfront of Mykonos Town.

Despite the fact that it was Sunday, the town was humming. Santos led their group to the shopping area, then took some people to an archaeological museum while the others stayed to shop.

Gwen chose to be alone, not with the guests, nor Santos, nor the memory of Jonathan. For this little amount of time, she'd enjoy being a sexy, independent woman. Poking up and down the labyrinth of alleylike cobblestone streets, she was dazzled by not only the picturesque charm of the cubist white buildings and the profusion of bougainvillea, but the local crafts, stunning artwork, and expensive jewelry. She succumbed and bought herself gold earrings and a pendant with leaping dolphins before stopping to join a few of the guests for coffee and delicious almond pastries.

Everyone gathered again for a bus tour of the island, including lunch at one of the popular beaches. Then the bus took them back to the harbor, where they headed off on a boat excursion to an archaeological site on the sacred island of Delos. She caught herself rubbing her bare ring finger. Impossible not to think of her husband. How she wished Jonathan could have explored what had once been a great city, where now wildflowers bloomed and tiny lizards sunned themselves. She admired mosaics, temples, and the classic stone theatre that had been built to seat more than five thousand people.

At the theatre, she drifted off alone to sit on a sun-warmed stone seat. Closing her eyes, she imagined summer nights in the second century B.C., actors on stage, the same herbal scent in the air. She couldn't believe she was actually being paid to be here.

Of course, not only did she have to deal with things like Esther's emergency, but she was the person others turned to when they needed to find a drugstore, wanted someone to take a picture of them, realized they'd left their shopping bags on the bus, or had blistered heels. She dispensed assistance and, when she was out of her depth, turned to Santos, who always sorted things out.

They made as good a team out of bed as in. But it was torture, working efficiently as a team all day and pretending that was all they were to each other. The man had been inside her.

Opening her eyes, she located him unerringly where he was providing a firm arm to Liz's mom as she negotiated the stone steps.

He made such a great cruise director that sometimes she almost forgot he was actually an investigator. But then she'd suddenly remember, and focus far too intently on everyone he talked to, wondering if they could be a criminal. Worrying that something would happen to disrupt the wedding.

Life would be so much easier if he really was a cruise director. If her priorities were his as well. But she couldn't expect that. What she did expect—and was pretty sure she could rely on him to provide—was amazing sex. Just looking at him was enough to make her hot, and when he was nearby, she had to clench her fingers to keep herself from touching him.

By early evening, when the group returned to the ship to rest and then get ready for a night on the town, Gwen was sun-kissed, dazed by everything she'd taken in, and totally in love with Greece.

She was also seriously in lust with Santos and frustrated from not being able to do anything about it. As she went down to her cabin, she wondered what kind of spell he'd cast on her last night. She'd actually shared a bed with that totally hot man, and all she'd done was lie back and let him pleasure her. She'd never explored those firm muscles, never caressed a package that put all those Greek statues to shame. Next time the two of them got naked, things were going to be very different.

She only hoped it would be soon because she craved him so badly she was afraid one of the guests—or, even worse, the bride or groom—would catch her mooning after him like a hormonal adolescent.

As she stepped into the shower to freshen up, she thought she really should turn the temperature to cold. Instead, she luxuriated in the warm gush of water over her shoulders, down her breasts, and between her thighs. Why had she never before noticed how sensual a shower could be? She hooked the shower head into the bracket on the wall, lathered soap between both hands, then slowly, caressingly slicked her soapy hands across her skin. Her nipples pricked to alertness, her hips felt curvy and feminine, and when she slid a hand between her legs—where she was sensitive, but no longer sore—she imagined Santos touching her there.

Last night his lips had been on that naked flesh. Pressing, teasing, stimulating her.

Her breath quickened and her body heated. Closing her eyes, she leaned back against the wall, letting her hand linger and toy with the folds of her sex where a tingly ache pulsed. Leisurely, she stroked, found the engorged bud of her clit, and flicked it gently.

She imagined Santos, naked, the way he'd been in her cabin. His erection proud and strong, glistening with pre-come.

She stroked her labia, up and down, faster and harder, pausing each time to lightly rub her clit, feeling arousal mount. Remembering the way she'd felt when the head of his penis nudged her, then he pushed inside and began to pump, slowly at first.

Yes, Santos had started out slow, but his breathing had been labored, his dark face flushed. He'd held back, given her two orgasms, and then he'd clearly needed to come. She'd wanted him to come; it was his turn. And it had felt so incredible, him plunging deep and hard inside her, moving faster and faster . . .

Her fingers rubbed hard, slicking shower water and her own juices across her flesh as she gasped for breath.

When he'd jerked and begun to come, he had triggered her, too, and she . . .

"Oh, God," she sighed as her body clutched and spasmed in climax.

Nice, she thought when she finally turned off the shower and reached for a towel, but nowhere near as good as the real thing. Maybe she was crazy, risking a shipboard fling, yet it felt so right.

Now, when could she and Santos find private time to do it again?

She paused in drying herself. And what would happen after the cruise, when she was back in Vancouver and he was only a pleasant holiday memory?

Briskly she began to towel herself again. Now that she'd rediscovered the joy of sex and male company, surely she'd find great guys to date. Maybe one day she'd find a special one like Jonathan to settle down with, but she was in no hurry. She had lots to learn about herself as a single woman, and Santos had shown her how much fun it was to simply play.

Tonight, their whole group would play in the party town of the Cyclades. First they'd have dinner in an elegant restaurant, then they'd hit the club scene. She and Santos couldn't flirt in public, but she could definitely dress to tempt him.

Thank heavens for her bosses, who'd insisted she needed a classy but sexy cocktail dress and dragged her out shopping. She slipped into the figure-hugging black dress, cut low at the front and back and high on her thighs. Under it, she wore a black thong and nothing else. To accent the dress, she added a long rope of artificial pearls, looped twice around her neck.

She picked up a black silk shawl embroidered with gold and silver flowers and, studying her reflection, draped it this way and that. The dress and the flower embroidery on the shawl made her sun-darkened skin and sun-lightened hair look even more dramatic. Oh yes, she looked as great as she felt.

When she'd been married, she'd felt older than her age and had tried to act that way, to measure up to Jonathan—and because it annoyed her when people judged them over the disparity in their ages. Now she felt young and carefree. She only hoped the evening went smoothly work-wise, with no crises either large or small. She had deliberated whether to e-mail her bosses about Liz's aunt's change of plans, then decided not to; she'd handled it and there was no reason to bother them.

A touch of makeup, her purse, a pair of shoes, and she was ready to go. Despite the uneven cobblestone streets, high-heeled sandals were a necessity tonight, but out of respect for the *Aphrodite*'s wooden deck, she carried them rather than put them on now.

Along the corridor, she heard voices and doors opening and closing, and she hurried out to join the others. Most of the guests, at least the ones who planned to go clubbing, had dressed up, and there was a buzz of excitement in the air as people showed off new clothes and jewelry and tossed compliments back and forth.

On deck, the view took her breath away. Dusk had fallen and the town looked magical, the white walls lit by yellow, white, and blue lights. It was a Greek postcard come to life. And she was here, breathing sea air and—she glanced around—oh, my. Gazing across the deck at the most handsome man she'd ever seen.

Santos had forgone his usual uniform and tonight wore black pants and a short-sleeved shirt the color of the golden sand beaches they'd seen earlier in the day. As terrific as he looked in tailored white, the colors and more relaxed fit of these clothes, together with his long hair and earring, made him even more dashing.

Though he was listening to one of Peter's friends talk, his gaze remained on Gwen, and he tipped his head to her with an appreciative smile that told her her outfit had had the desired effect.

Soon everyone was assembled, and Santos led them to the restaurant they'd booked, situated a little way up the hill.

When they had arrived and gotten settled on the rooftop patio, Gwen knew this was the perfect choice for glitzy Mykonos: elegant décor, a gourmet continental menu, and an incredible view of the attractively lit harbor and town.

Resisting temptation when she prepared tonight's seating chart, she'd placed herself and Santos at different tables. It proved a wise decision because the ambience was so romantic she'd have been hard-pressed to maintain her self-control.

Maybe they'd get a chance to dance together later, and that would be a real test . . .

Chapter 9

SANTOS wasn't surprised that Gwen's seating plan put him at a dinner table across the patio from hers, but he chose a seat that let him keep her in view. She looked so damned hot in that revealing black dress.

He couldn't let her distract him from his real job. Tonight, for the first time, her chart put him, Flynn Kavanagh, and Kendra Kirk all at the same table.

Santos had searched Kendra's cabin. He'd cracked the combination lock on her briefcase in seconds and found work files that were unrelated to Kavanagh. Her computer password protection was also easy to circumvent. Her laptop held more office files, many from Kavanagh's trial, and a few personal ones, such as financial files for herself and her mother. Her e-mail showed no correspondence between her and the man. His best guess, from what he saw, was that she'd come aboard the *Aphrodite*, recognized Kavanagh, and taken a second look through the files on his case.

Santos had also snuck into Kavanagh's cabin again, but, though he had training and experience hacking people's passwords and security settings, he hadn't been able to breach Kavanagh's. The man had been a skilled IT consultant, so that wasn't surprising or suspicious.

So far, when Santos looked at the broad picture—the pattern that was Flynn Kavanagh—the only piece that didn't fit neatly was his relationship with Kendra Kirk. Santos's theory was logical: They'd both been unpleasantly surprised to see each other aboard the *Aphrodite* and were trying to hide their personal animosity so as not to disrupt the cruise. Yet intuition told him there might be something more going on.

Interestingly, though the two hadn't spoken to each other tonight, they weren't glaring either. Kavanagh waited for Kendra to seat herself, then sat down beside Liz's aunt Madge, who was directly across from Kendra. Santos would have expected the two to choose opposite ends of the table rather than being in each other's line of sight.

Once everyone was seated, Santos suggested they go around the table and introduce themselves, and say how they knew the bride or groom. It was only the third day of the cruise, and people wouldn't all know each other yet. Hopefully, it would loosen people up and he could use it as a springboard to get a better read on Kavanagh and Kendra.

When they finished, he said, "As I'm sure you all know by now, I'm Santos Michaelides, cruise director on the *Aphrodite*."

"What a perfect job," Madge said enviously.

Thinking of Gwen, he chuckled. "It has its benefits." Glancing around the table, he seized the opportunity she'd unwittingly offered. "How about everyone else? What do you do back home?"

They started on his left, with a friend of Liz's who said she was an interior decorator. Santos was impatient to get to Kavanagh, but wanted to set a pattern of back-and-forth chatter, so he asked the woman if she was finding Greece inspiring. She gushed on about that for a few minutes, and then Santos moved on to the man on her left, Liz's uncle Frederick.

His wife, seated across from him, chimed in, too, which broke the formal pattern of going around in a circle. Capitalizing on that, and hoping to catch Kavanagh somewhat off guard, Santos turned to him next. "How about you, Flynn? What kind of work do you do?"

Speaking rather stiffly, with none of the charm he sometimes displayed, he said, "Computer programming. I won't bore you with the details."

In fact, the man had handled all the IT work for a number of high-powered law and accounting firms and corporations. *Had* handled. Though he'd been acquitted, he'd lost his clients' trust. As far as Insurance Assured had been able to find out, he was currently unemployed. Perhaps he was living off that stolen five mil. Money Santos's employer had had to pay out to their client.

"Programming's intriguing," Santos said, "and I imagine it pays well, doesn't it?"

He shrugged. "Decently."

"Do you build software or video games?" Santos persisted. "Or programs for clients who need specialized applications?"

Kavanagh shifted uncomfortably. "Er, actually at the moment—"

"Sorry, and no offense, Flynn"—it was Kendra Kirk, shooting the man a chilly look—"but here we are on a lovely night in Mykonos. We want to leave our boring jobs behind."

Santos checked Kavanagh for reaction. Expecting annoyance and dislike, he was surprised to see gratitude in his green eyes. Her interruption, though verging on rude, had gotten him off the hook so he didn't have to answer Santos's question.

Kendra was still talking. "Santos, tell us about the nightclubs. Where are you going to take us?" She leaned forward eagerly, but there was something forced about her expression.

An odd thought struck him. Was she deliberately seeking to divert people's attention from Kavanagh? But why would she come to the rescue of the man she'd prosecuted? No, probably she just disliked the guy and didn't want to hear him talk, and was genuinely looking forward to a night on the town. Still, intuition told him to keep a close eye on these two.

"Santos?" she prompted impatiently.

"Sorry, just doing a mental review of my notes." Getting back into his role, he said, "Not everyone will want to go clubbing. People can stay here for another drink, wander the waterfront, or head back to the *Aphrodite*. For those who do want to check out the night scene, there are three clubs we recommend." He went on to describe them, knowing that the group would likely split up depending on their preferences.

As appetizers and drinks were served, he was tempted to again steer the conversation in a direction that would be uncomfortable for Kavanagh and see what happened. But, if the man really was a criminal, that might make him suspicious and even more guarded than he was now.

So Santos joined in the general conversation, noting that neither Kavanagh nor Kendra participated much. They did send subtle glances in each other's direction, though. Glances that, to his astonishment, looked a lot like the ones he and Gwen exchanged.

Could they be lovers? Lovers who'd perhaps had a falling out, which would explain their initial tension, then made up? But she'd prosecuted him.

And she'd lost. Perhaps her office had laid charges against Kavanagh, then somehow she'd met him and they'd become lovers. Perhaps she couldn't drop the prosecution without arousing too much suspicion, so she'd slacked off enough that the jury was sure to acquit. It was a theory. Another possibility to explore.

Dinner was winding down, the last cups of coffee being drained.

Could he follow Kavanagh and Kendra after dinner? Would they split up, as they'd always done before? Casually, he asked, "What has everyone decided? Kendra, did any of those clubs sound good to you?"

Her gaze flicked to Kavanagh before she controlled her face and stared at Santos. "They did, but I'm pretty tired. Jet lag, allergies, maybe just fresh air and good food. I think I'll head back to the *Aphrodite*."

Others chimed in, more than half opting for the clubs and the rest, including Kavanagh, saying they'd wander back to the ship and maybe get a drink along the way.

Kendra had a single cabin, like Gwen. Would Kavanagh sneak into it? It would be tough to pull off without being seen, because passengers would be club hopping and likely would trickle back anywhere between midnight and dawn. That would make watching Kavanagh difficult, too. And, on the personal side, Santos would have a hard time slipping into Gwen's cabin.

But damn, how could he wait another day? Every time he looked at her, he wanted to get naked with her. And each time one of the male passengers came on to her, even though she seemed oblivious and didn't flirt back, Santos felt a hot rush of territoriality. For this week, she was his.

Tonight, somehow, she had to be his.

The guests were rising, beginning to leave. He went over to Gwen.

She flicked the light shawl into place over her shoulders, which only made him want to slide it off and bare the smooth skin underneath.

In a public voice, he said, "So, Gwen, what's the plan for tonight?"

When her eyes flared wide in panic, he added, "Which club are you going to?" Then, with a twinkle in his eye, "Is there anything *special* you want me to do tonight?"

Color tinged her cheeks. "Oh, um, let me think."

As people filed by them, heading for the stairs, he took her arm to shift her aside. Now that he had a hand on her, he didn't want to let go, but forced himself to. Still, he stood close enough that their shoulders brushed lightly, and she didn't move away.

"The bride and groom are always top priority," she said softly. "So I'm going where they go."

That seductive gingery scent of hers drifted toward him. He wanted to bury his face in the curve of her neck, breathe her in, lick her until she whimpered with need. Having rationalized himself out of trying to watch Kavanagh and Kendra tonight, he leaned closer to her and said, "Any reason we need to go to different clubs? Everyone's an adult and they can find their way back to the *Aphrodite* when they're ready to pack it in."

"You're right." She gazed up at him, eyes golden in the restaurant's subtle outdoor lighting. With a teasing lilt, she said, "Guess that means you can do whatever you like."

"Anything I like?"

Her only answer was a catlike smile.

"Then I'll come along with you and"—he winked—"help you keep an eye on Liz and Peter."

"I'm always glad of your help, Santos," she said in a louder tone as the last pair of guests drifted past, then she returned the wink. So sweet, so sexy, so damned irresistible.

He took a quick look around, making sure all of their charges had gone, then caught Gwen's face in both hands and kissed her.

His lips had barely settled on hers when she jerked back. "Santos! We can't."

"Everyone's gone. Come on, just one quick kiss."

Her parted lips said she wanted to, but her brandy eyes were indecisive. All the same, when he lowered his head again, she rose on her toes to meet him.

He honored his promise and kept it quick, but the kiss was deep, hard, and steamy, and it left both of them gasping for breath. A passing waiter applauded, then a female voice called up the stairs, "Gwen? Are you still up there?"

"Coming right down," she called breathlessly. Then, to Santos, "You're a bad influence."

"I do my best." Smugly he went down the stairs after her.

Out on the street, he gave directions to the nightclubs, as well as back to the harbor and the *Aphrodite*. After ensuring that Kavanagh and Kendra, who were pretending to ignore each other, had joined the group that was heading to the harbor, he led his own group to a trendy club.

The place pulsated with throbbing music and flashing lights. En masse, they took to the dance floor, mostly dancing as a group rather than with partners. Other dancers jostled them, patterns shifted, sometimes he found himself in front of Liz, then one of the other young women. But whenever he could manage it without being obvious, the woman across from him was Gwen.

Everyone was close enough together, relaxed and uninhibited, so that arms brushed and people casually caught each other's hands or put an arm around a waist. If he and Gwen had been alone, the music of the stand-and-sway variety, he could have wrapped her in his arms and pressed their bodies close, but this was a kind of foreplay. Secret foreplay, teasing and intimate, with no one around them guessing that their touches, their glances, had special meaning.

Her hair gleamed almost white, shimmering as she tossed her head, begging his fingers to slide through its silky strands. Her body, shown off so beautifully in that sleek black dress, moved sinuously with the music, and he imagined her writhing naked in his arms. She wore a double strand of pearls, hanging low enough that the creamy beads bounced against the upper curves of her breasts, which were revealed by the sexy black dress.

His cock stirred and swelled and he was relieved the music was so fast, the crowd so boisterous, or he'd have had a full-fledged hard-on. They'd only been at the club ten or fifteen minutes and already he wondered if he could persuade Gwen to leave.

"Santos, come dance with us," a teasing voice demanded, and firm female hands tugged both his arms. Next thing he knew, he had two of Liz's old friends—a pair of rosy-cheeked, honey-haired girls who'd grown up in the same small village as Liz but now lived in London—twining around him, making sure that their hips and breasts bumped against him.

Over the past couple of days they'd made it clear he could have either one, both, or a three-way. They were pretty and vivacious, but Gwen was far more appealing. Even now, with two curvy bodies getting pretty damned fresh with his, he was more attuned to Gwen.

She'd left the group of dancers to head over to the bar.

"Need a cold drink," he shouted above the music to the English girls, and went after her. Sliding in on an angle beside her, using the crowd as an excuse to press his body against hers, he said, "Having fun?"

She stepped away. "Not as much as you're having," she said snippily.

Jealous? The thought made him grin.

When her brows rose and she glared, he lost the grin. "They started it, and I walked away." Glancing around to make sure no one they knew was in earshot, he said, "*Thelo na se paro, latreia mou.* Only you."

"What?"

"I want to make love with you. Only you."

Her glare softened. "Really?"

Perhaps not jealous so much as insecure. "No question." He hoped she could see the sincerity in his eyes. Perhaps so, because this time when he pressed his hip against hers, she didn't move away. "You and me, alone, Gwen. Tell me you want that, too."

A smile flickered on her lips. "I've wanted it all day."

"Then let's slip out."

"But . . ." She glanced toward the dance floor.

He noticed that the two blondes were now dancing with a friend of Peter's. "Don't tell me you're hanging in until the last person leaves? That could be two, three, even four in the morning."

Her gaze remained on the dancers, then slowly she turned back to study his face. "Okay, you've persuaded me. Let's go."

At that moment, the busy bartender came up to her. "What can I get you?"

"Never mind." She flashed him a smile. "I've already got it."

Smug and impatient, Santos guided her to the door. Outside, the night air was pleasantly fresh against his heated skin. Gwen must be warm, too, because she carried her pretty shawl over one arm.

A few other people wandered the alleys, some stumbling and laughing loudly as if they'd had too much to drink, others wandering romantically with arms wrapped around each other. Though he wanted to put his arm around Gwen, he settled for moving closer and letting his arm slide against her bare one in a seductive brush.

"Want to go back to my cabin?" she asked.

"Of course, but . . ." He'd promised to respect Gwen's desire for secrecy. "People are likely to drift back to the ship over the next few hours. It'd be hard for me to sneak in and out without anyone seeing. Gwen, from what I've seen of Liz and Peter, I really don't think they'd care if they found out you were getting yourself a little after-hours action."

"Maybe. But professional image is still important. Other guests may be planning weddings in the future, or making recommendations to relatives and friends."

He hadn't thought of that aspect. "I see what you mean."

If not on the ship, where else could they find a little privacy? He glanced around, idly noticing that one of the shops was empty, with a sign in the window saying it was for lease. Whitewashed steps led up the side of the one-story building to a flat roof typical of Mykonos's cube-shaped buildings.

Impulsively, he grabbed Gwen's hand and tugged her toward the stairs.

"Santos, where are you going?" Flustered, she glanced around as she hurried to keep up with him.

"Don't know. Let's find out."

At the bottom of the staircase, she balked, pulling her hand from his. "This is private property."

"It's vacant, for lease. We're not going to hurt anything."

"No, but . . ."

Those pearls, nestling against the curve of her breasts, had been driving him crazy. Now he unlooped them, easing the rope of ivory beads over her head.

"What are you doing?" she demanded.

He took her shawl and small purse from her, tucked them under one arm, then went behind her. Capturing both of her hands, he drew them behind her back and wound the pearls around her wrists, binding her hands. "Taking you prisoner."

"You really are a pirate." She sounded amused.

Tugging on the end of the strand, he said, "Up the stairs, woman."

Laughing softly, she started up ahead of him, giving him a seductive view of her bare back, sweetly rounded ass, and long, shapely legs.

When they both stood on the roof, he gazed around, thinking he couldn't have chosen a prettier spot. The building they stood atop was slightly up from the waterfront, situated off one of the many narrow alleys. Around them, businesses and houses climbed the bottom of the hill, lights gleamed from a patio restaurant, and windmills added to the charm. Below, lamps lit the walkway along the waterfront and golden light poured from restaurants. In the harbor, boats of all sizes bobbed gently at the wharves or at anchor, some lit but most of them dark, and the briny scent of the ocean drifted on the breeze.

"This is beautiful," Gwen said in a hushed voice. She tilted her head up. "Look at the stars."

He did—as they were reflected in her eyes. He didn't give a damn about the stars; all he wanted was this woman. Finally, after a day of longing, he stepped closer, holding her pearl-roped hands so that his own hand rested on the tantalizing hollow at the base of her spine. When their lips touched, passion exploded in him, racing through his veins, speeding his heart, thickening his cock. He had to have her *now*.

From her soft groan and the hungry way her lips pressed back and her tongue thrust into his mouth, she felt the same way.

One side of the roof butted up against the windowless wall of an adjoining two-story building. Without breaking the kiss, he backed her up until she leaned against it. Still grasping her roped hands, he bent to place her purse and shawl on the roof, hoping it wasn't too dirty. Then he planted his free hand on the wall beside her shoulder, trapping her. "Here. Now." He ground his pelvis against her, his engorged cock telling her exactly what he meant.

Her eyes were pools of molten gold, yearning but uncertain. "We can't. Someone might see."

"Yeah. Anyone could look out a window. So what?" The idea of someone watching them was a turn-on. He glanced around, then pointed. "Look over there." Up the hill, at what looked to be a small hotel, a couple embraced on a balcony, anonymous and erotic.

Gwen stared at their entwined bodies for a long moment, then turned to him, eyes gleaming with arousal.

"Come on, take a risk." He pumped his hips against her belly.

She whimpered and her own hips twisted, grinding against him. "I want you so much. I've never felt so . . ."

"Horny?"

A soft, breathy laugh. "I'd have said aroused. You make me feel things, Santos. Things I thought I'd never feel again." She ducked her head and murmured something under her breath. It sounded like, "Things I've never felt before," but maybe he was wrong.

All the same, it reminded him that he was only her second lover, and it had been years since she'd last had sex. She deserved to be romanced, not pressured. He released her bound hands, then slipped the rope over her head in one long strand that dangled past her breasts.

He caught her chin gently between thumb and forefinger and tilted her face back up until he could look into her eyes. "Starlight in Mykonos. What more could you want?"

She gazed at him for a long moment. "Only what's right in front of me. You." She reached up with both hands, wound her fingers through his hair, and tugged his head down as she rose to meet him.

The moment the tip of her tongue touched his, he knew he was in trouble. She'd agreed to have sex and his body wanted to drive single-mindedly toward that goal. Yet he also wanted to slow down and enjoy the pale gold of her hair under the light of moon and stars, to sift its silken strands through his fingers, to savor the sweet taste of her mouth, to caress every inch of her lovely body.

He tried, he really tried to take it slow, but the moment her fingers reached for his belt buckle, he was gone. He helped her, unfastening and unzipping his pants, then letting them and his boxers drop in a *swoosh* to his feet. Erection tenting the front of his shirt, he reached beneath the hem of her sexy black dress. He found smooth, heated flesh, moist at the top of her thighs, then a narrow band of soaking-wet fabric.

Her hand circled his shaft.

Erotic sensation surged through him, making him freeze.

Tentatively at first, then more firmly, she began to stroke up and down, her touch almost enough to make him explode then and there. The soft tip of her thumb circled the head of his cock, collecting moisture and spreading it, then she pumped his shaft again, her movements growing more confident. He hadn't been circumcised and his flesh was exquisitely sensitive as she swept his foreskin up over the head of his penis, then back down again.

He gritted his teeth, forcing himself to hold back though pressure was coiling in his balls and at the base of his spine, urging him to let go.

Her other hand reached down to fondle his balls and he let out a groan. Roughly he yanked her thong down her legs. "Step out of it."

She released him and, as she obeyed, he grabbed a condom from his pants pocket and sheathed himself. Then he hooked his arms under her thighs and butt, and hoisted her up.

"Oh!" she gasped in surprise.

He heard one high-heeled sandal hit the roof, then the other one dug into his ass as she wrapped her legs around his hips and her arms came around his neck. He shifted precariously, balancing her weight, desperate to be inside her.

She leaned back against the wall, which provided more stability, then reached down to pull clothing out of the way. Her hand again closed around his shaft and tugged him where she wanted him. "You're so hot," she murmured.

No, she was. Steamy heat caressed him and the head of his cock slid against slippery flesh. She guided him back and forth, rubbing against her clit.

He needed to thrust but forced himself to hold back.

Her head was tucked down against his neck and fast, panting

breaths tickled his skin. "Now, Santos." She positioned him at the entrance to her channel.

He probably should have eased in but he was holding on to control by barely a thread, and instead he thrust hard and deep.

"Oh, God, yes!" He wasn't even sure if he'd said it, she had, or they'd both exclaimed together.

While she clung to him, he thrust again and again.

She gripped his shoulders as she hung on, riding his thrusts, moaning with passion. Her back arched and she threw her head back.

He leaned forward to rasp his teeth across the smooth curve of her neck above the chain of pearls, feeling some bizarre desire to bite her, to mark her as his, but he managed to refrain.

"Oh, Santos," she gasped. "Oh, yes!"

A primitive force surged through his loins, driving him to join with her and empty himself inside her. He let out a guttural moan, powerless to hold back any longer. As he did, she shuddered, clenched, then cried out in climax while his own orgasm roared through him.

Somehow he managed to keep them both upright even though his legs were shaking.

When he couldn't do it any longer, he gave her a quick kiss, then eased out of her. Slowly she unwound her legs and arms and kicked her other sandal off. "Let's see if I can actually stand."

When she was flat-footed on the roof, she slanted him a teasing glance. "Is this where I say, 'Oh, Santos, you're so strong'?"

He chuckled as he dealt with the condom and pulled up his underwear and pants. "I was really motivated."

"You and me both." She glanced around. "I can't believe we did that. I wonder if anyone saw."

"If they did, I hope they have a lover of their own, or else they'll be suffering from sexual frustration." He pointed. "Look, the couple on the balcony is gone."

"To a nice, comfy bed," she said in a mock grousing tone.

"You're complaining about the sex?" he teased.

Her eyes went huge and melting. "No. I'll remember this night forever."

He would, too. For a long moment, they stared into each other's eyes. Then she blinked, flicked her hair, and bent, pearls dangling, to gingerly pick her thong up off the roof. "Don't think I'll be putting this back on." She folded it and tucked it into her bag.

"You're going to walk through Mykonos with no panties?" He groaned. "Gwen, you're killing me."

The words echoed in his head. She was, in so many ways. With not only the memorable lovemaking but every other aspect of her personality: her sense of duty and loyalty, her generosity and warmheartedness, her pure enjoyment of his home country. Her core of strength as well as her occasional vulnerability. Her openness to life. Damn, but he was one lucky bastard.

For this one week, he reminded himself.

Beyond that, what Gwen wanted and deserved was a steady guy like her husband, and what Santos wanted . . .

The fact that his brain hitched was disconcerting. Always before, he'd known exactly what he wanted: the next challenging assignment, the next role to play and new place to visit, the next sexy lady to warm his bed.

But what sexy lady could measure up to Gwen Austin?

Chapter 10

THE next morning, Gwen had things easy. No new crises had arisen, and Elpida phoned to tell her Liz's aunt Esther had arrived home safely. Sarah and Andi had e-mailed to ask how things were going, and she'd replied that she had everything—work and Santos—under control, then crossed her fingers that it was true.

As the *Aphrodite* traveled from Mykonos to Paros, a lot of the guests slept in while others took beginner's Greek lessons from Santos or simply lazed around. She chose the lessons—in the interests of furthering her education, of course. Not of reliving every exciting moment on that rooftop in Mykonos. When she'd looked forward to coming to Greece, she'd anticipated a combination of challenging work, a nostalgia trip, and an adventure. Each day she felt more confident in her ability to do her job, and the sadness over not being here with Jonathan had pretty much faded. As for the adventure, it had proven to be even more exciting—and sexy—than she'd ever imagined.

As she watched Santos's lips frame syllables in Greek, she realized he'd never told her the meaning of the Greek endearments he'd used. She definitely needed a private lesson.

"Morning, everyone," a cheery female voice called out.

Gwen glanced up to see Liz's English friends Amanda and Christine, the annoying blondes who kept hanging around Santos, saunter over wearing nothing but tiny string bikinis. The bare essentials were barely contained and, as the pair strolled past, she saw naked butt cheeks. Thong bikinis. That was *way* more of Amanda and Christine than she had any desire to ever see.

Santos, damn him, was flashing his sexy white smile. "You two slept in. Did you shut the club down?"

"Close to it," Christine said, "though we missed you. Why did you leave so early?"

"You're here on holiday. But some of us are working." His gaze darted to Gwen, mischief in his eyes. "Right, Gwen?"

"Exactly," she agreed. "And speaking of which, it's time to end the lesson. We'll be anchoring shortly for a morning swim."

The guests dispersed, including the two blondes, who headed for deck chairs.

"Coming swimming this time?" Santos asked Gwen.

"I just might." Not, of course, because she didn't trust him alone with the blondes, but because she was dying to take a dip in the Aegean.

She headed to her cabin to change, then studied her reflection critically. The blue bikini showed more flesh than she'd ever flaunted in public. When she'd bought it—and gotten a bikini wax—she'd thought she was daring. Now she was afraid she looked like a granny. She huffed out a sigh, slipped on a sheer cover-up, and tossed a towel and flip-flops in a beach bag.

On deck again, she joined the passengers who were heading to the beach. When the Zodiac delivered them, some strolled along the sand, cameras in hand, while the rest dropped their gear and went into the water.

Gwen wasn't much of a swimmer, but she enjoyed paddling in the clear water. It was cool enough to be bracing but far warmer than the Pacific Ocean she'd grown up with. Tiring quickly, she headed back to shore, where she sat on her towel, alone for once, to watch the others frolic.

The two blondes were doing far too much near-naked frolicking with Santos. It ticked her off and made her anxious. They looked beautiful, the three of them: Santos's brown skin, black hair, and rugged masculinity were set off by the two curvy, lightly tanned blondes.

Santos broke away from them and, treading water, glanced around at the other swimmers and paddlers, then up at the beach. He swam toward shore.

When the water was chest high, he stopped swimming and put his feet down. As he strode toward shore, he raised both hands to slick water out of his hair, then shook his head. Droplets flew, glinting in the sunshine, and wet black curls tumbled around his face.

Muscles in his shoulders and chest rippled as he pushed against the drag of the water, a sea god emerging from his element. Water trickled down his torso, slicking the black hair scattered across his pecs, making the arrow that led down the center of his body even more pronounced.

His waist was lean. Naked. The band of his board shorts sat low on his slim hips. Wet fabric clung to him, hinting at the shape of his package.

Firm thighs emerged from the water, then strong, well-shaped legs as the ocean slowly released its grip on him, washing gently around his calves, clinging to his ankles. Then he was on the beach, striding toward her.

Arousal coursed through her as he came to a stop beside her towel. "I'm hot," she told him. "Drip on me."

"You *are* hot." He flicked a few drops from his chest to her bare skin, where she'd swear they sizzled. "You okay? You didn't stay in the water long."

"I'm not a very good swimmer, but I enjoyed it."

"I could give you lessons."

She laughed up at him. "You could give me lessons in all sorts of things." Then, unable to stop herself from sniping, she said, "But then, I'm not the only one who'd be interested. You have a couple of fans in Amanda and Christine."

"Jealous?" he teased.

"No, I . . ." She flicked her hair back. "What's up with them anyhow? It seems like they're both after you."

"Yeah, they've made that pretty clear."

"But . . . If you chose one, wouldn't the other be jealous?"

"They don't seem the jealous sort."

Humph. If they weren't jealous, it meant they didn't really care. No, wait, that couldn't be right. It suggested that if she was jealous, she must care. Well, she did, as a friend, but it would never be anything more. He was absolutely the wrong kind of man for her, and he'd made it completely clear he was unavailable for a long-term relationship. This was just a holiday fling.

Right. It was *her* fling, and she wanted Santos for the entire week, with no other women in the way.

"Though," he commented, "they'd prefer if I chose both of them. Together."

"Together?" What did that mean? "Oh! Uh, you mean . . ." Embarrassment heated her cheeks.

"A three-way."

Would he do that? It must be pretty tempting. How could she possibly compete with an offer like that?

"Gwen, Santos, guess what we spotted?" A breathless female voice made Gwen turn to see Liz's parents bustling toward them, both with binoculars around their necks.

"An icterine warbler," Mrs. Tippett announced proudly.

"I really think it was an olivaceous," her husband said. "They're far more common."

As the two debated, Gwen watched Santos stroll to the edge of the ocean. "Time to come in," he called to the swimmers, and she saw that the Zodiac was heading over from the *Aphrodite* to pick everyone up.

They'd have lunch aboard the ship as it continued its journey to the harbor at Paros. The afternoon would be busy, with a bus excursion to a popular resort, then a walking tour of the harbor town. They'd stroll from the busy waterfront to the old town, a typical Greek labyrinth, and to a Venetian fort from the thirteenth century.

The evening would be a traditional Greek night: classic dishes served at a taverna, live bouzouki music, and Greek dancing. First a belly dancer to liven things up, then folk dances done by Greeks in traditional costumes. It would be a far cry from dancing at the ritzy club in Mykonos. Hopefully, there'd be less opportunity for the blondes to get their hands on Santos.

A three-way. Good God. She must seem so "plain vanilla."

AFTER dinner, Gwen watched admiringly as a smoky-eyed belly dancer swiveled her hips, jingling the coins on the scarf tied over her filmy harem pants. She flirted harmlessly with the male guests and exchanged comments in Greek with Santos. Gwen had no idea what the two of them were saying, only that the dancer's body language was seductive and Santos certainly wasn't giving her the cold shoulder.

The penalties of a casual affair, she thought ruefully. Without the slightest bit of commitment between her and Santos, he was free to choose any other woman. Of course, she was free to see another man, but no guy on the cruise could compare to the dynamic Santos.

When the belly dancer gave one last jingling hip shimmy and disappeared behind a curtain, the same local musicians who'd played during dinner returned, this time accompanied by folk dancers. The dancers performed a couple of dances, then urged the guests to participate.

Santos was one of the first to be drawn in. Strong and graceful, he clearly knew the steps. Perhaps his grandmother—his *yiayia*—had taught him. Or, more likely, some pretty Greek girl.

She was being ridiculous, feeling jealous over a man she'd never see again after this week. It was even more foolish to wish he were a different kind of man, the kind who, like Jonathan, believed firmly in long-term commitment. Her mom had played that loser's game—of wishing a leopard would change its spots—for years with her dad.

Besides, why was she even thinking about a man for the long term? She was still trying to figure out who she was and how she wanted to live her life.

Her affair with Santos was all about enjoying the moment. And so, when he avoided the English blondes and held out his hand to Gwen, she let him draw her into the line of laughing dancers and clumsily tried to master the steps. What did it matter if she got them right, so long as her arm was linked through his?

It was wonderful to see the rest of their group having such a good time. Even Liz's mom was dancing, linked on one side to her husband, of course, and on the other, surprisingly, to Kendra, the workaholic, who Liz had pulled into the dance. Then Kendra's uncles joined in, with Flynn tagging along and—another surprise—inserting himself between Mrs. Tippett and Kendra and really getting into the spirit.

When everyone eventually tired, they trooped back to the *Aphrodite*. Hoping Santos would come to her, Gwen turned on the CD player he'd brought. When she'd asked her neighbors if her music disturbed them, they said they never heard a peep from her cabin, which was a great relief.

After getting ready for bed, she lit a couple of candles she'd bought, turned off the lights, and slipped between the sheets naked. He would come, wouldn't he? Not choose the three-way?

Disturbingly, she remembered the nights her mom had waited for her dad, when he'd said he was working late, had a business dinner, or whatever the latest excuse happened to be. She'd caught her mother sniffing his shirts and checking his pants pockets. Preparing his clothes for the dry cleaner, her mom had said when she'd realized Gwen was watching, but Gwen knew better. Her dad had been a philanderer, and they'd never been able to trust a word he said.

Her mother shouldn't have put up with it. Gwen never would. Fortunately, with Jonathan, she'd never had a moment's reason to doubt him. He'd been devoted to her, never a man to even flirt casually with other women.

Not a charmer like Santos, who had a flashing smile and a wink for everyone from Mrs. Tippett in her unflattering hat to Amanda and Catherine in their near nonexistent bikinis. But that wasn't a bad thing. The guests all loved him, the men included. The problem wasn't with Santos; it was her own insecurity, not believing she was enough woman for a guy like him.

The door opened silently and he came in, easing it shut and locking it behind him.

"You came," she said, almost surprised after all her musings.

"Of course." He glanced at the candles. "You knew I would."

No, she'd hoped. "When I saw the candles, I thought of you. Of us." Oh damn, now he'd think she was being all romantic, when this relationship was just about sex.

"Candlelight's much nicer," he said approvingly. He grasped the top edge of the sheet, his knuckles grazing her chest. "May I look?"

She felt a ridiculous shyness, but forced herself to say lightly, "Be my guest."

He flicked the sheet aside, revealing her in her nakedness. A slow grin curved his mouth. "Oh, yeah. That's an image I won't forget."

They were only words, easy flattery, yet they warmed her. She glanced down, saw the rise of an erection under his fly. Just looking at her, anticipating sex with her, turned him on.

And that turned her on. "Your turn to give me an image," she said, sitting up. "Get naked, Santos."

He did, in seconds flat, as she watched. Casually he tossed his clothes on the chair, then he stepped toward the bed.

"No, wait." She held her hands out, palms toward him. "Just stand there a moment."

He did, and she took him in, remembering how he'd looked when he'd risen from the ocean, water streaming down his virile brown body. Whoever said women didn't get turned on by looking was dead wrong. Her nerve endings had sprung to life, tingling with desire. "Hmm, wet or dry, I'm not sure which I prefer." She eyed his swollen cock, her sex clutching with need. "Naked, definitely, though."

He laughed softly, then found a condom and came to her. Sweetly, slowly, sensually, they made love without saying much. They rolled, first him on top, then her, then him again, speeding the pace, then slowing it. He brought her to climax, then again and again, until finally he let go deep inside her. And all the time, she felt so in sync with him, it amazed her.

Satiated and exhausted, she folded down to lie atop him like a blanket and gaze into his eyes, dark pools that reflected candlelight. "A perfect end to another wonderful day."

He lifted a lock of her hair, which seemed to grow lighter by the hour. "Are you enjoying it here? Greece suits you. You're glowing."

"That could be the sex." The truth was, it was Santos himself. He made her glow, from head to toe, inside and out. And it wasn't just sex. She liked him, relied on him constantly during the day, and loved the understanding way he listened when she shared her most painful memories.

The way he made her feel was scary. So far, her life had fallen into two parts: a childhood where her untrustworthy dad was the strongest influence, then a marriage that was shaped by her totally reliable husband. Right now, her goal was to figure out who she was as an independent woman. She couldn't let herself fall for Santos.

There was absolutely no reason that thought should make her heart ache, yet it did.

She slipped off him, pulled up the sheet, and curled on her side to face him as he slid an arm under her shoulders. Maybe the candles had been a mistake. It was too cozy, cuddling up like this in their warm glow.

Returning to what he'd asked, she said, "Yes, I do love it here. Nothing against Canada, but I can't believe you'd rather live in Toronto than here."

"Are you saying you'd pick a Greek island over Vancouver?"

"No, but Vancouver's nicer than Toronto. I've visited Toronto in winter, and no thanks. What I want is a home base in Vancouver and lots of opportunities to travel."

"Have you been to many countries?"

"No. Jonathan and I took a few holidays, and I went to some conferences with him, but those were short trips. Mostly, we were saving up for that big sabbatical trip." She suppressed a twinge of bitterness. "Anyhow, I love travel and it's one of the great things about my job. The more experienced I get, the more weddings I'll be handling in places like this."

"That's something I like about my job, too. I often get assignments in foreign countries because I'm willing to travel anywhere. This one, of course, was a natural for a Greek with a decent knowledge of the Cyclades."

"You really love your job?"

"Yeah, it's perfect. Exciting. Each file's a new adventure."

"Isn't there a lot of desk work, too, like research on the Internet? And boring stuff like surveilling—is that a word?—accident victims who may be faking injuries?"

"Sure. I do some of that, but the guys and gals who don't want to travel or do undercover work handle more. I specialize in undercover. It's challenging playing a role, infiltrating a company or a nonprofit. Or I'll play the new neighbor, the friendly bartender, whatever the job calls for."

"People like you and trust you. You get them talking." A natural-born charmer like her father, and all the time he was playing a role, living a lie. More efficiently than her father had.

"Gwen, is something wrong?"

She wrinkled her nose. He'd been reading her not–poker face again. "In some ways you remind me of my dad."

"You mentioned him before, but didn't elaborate."

"He was charming, too, and people trusted him. He could play roles, talk his way into getting hired for almost any job, sell"—she remembered her mom's phrase—"sell rain to Vancouverites, he was that persuasive. He liked variety, loved excitement and travel." Loved women.

"There's a *but*."

"He was also . . ." She shifted position restlessly and he stroked her shoulder gently. "He didn't stick at one job long because he got bored or screwed up. He didn't follow through on commitments. You couldn't rely on him." Quickly she caressed his shoulder. "I'm not saying you're like that. It was the other part, the charm and love of excitement." At least Santos was honest in saying he didn't want to settle down rather than marrying and then cheating on his wife.

He nodded. "It's hard growing up with a parent you can't rely on."

"Hard for Mom, too. She'd be furious, then he'd do something romantic and outrageous and . . . and *slimy*. He'd charm her all over again and she'd forgive him." Gwen had felt helpless, watching the bizarre dynamics between her parents. "It was so up and down. For me, when I hit adolescence I became cynical and wasn't as forgiving. Of either of them. That's when I got pretty wild and hung out with kids like Brad." She'd caused her mom a lot of stress, too, which in hindsight she'd always regretted.

"Yeah, I can see why you'd do that."

"It was stupid, though. After that horrible fire, I realized I was being just as much of a jerk as my dad. Chasing the next thrill, and not giving a damn who got hurt."

"You were a teenager. *Self-centered* is part of the definition."

"I guess." Remembering what he'd said, she went on. "You said 'it is hard' not 'it must have been hard' growing up with a parent you can't rely on. You know what I'm talking about, don't you?"

Now he was the one who stirred, as if the topic made him uncomfortable. "You really want to hear this?"

"Yes." They might only be together a short time, but she did want to know him. "I told you my family secrets. It's your turn."

"Fair enough." Keeping his arm under her shoulders, he rolled onto his side to face her. "My parents are self-centered and they're all about the next adventure. When they decided to have a kid, that was the next adventure. Turned out I wasn't all that exciting, just a lot of hard work. And they've never been into hard work."

"Surely at least one of them had a job."

"Not so's you'd notice. Dad's father was a shipping magnate and occasionally Dad would do some work for the company—fun things in foreign places—but mostly he's just lived off the family money. His parents are dead now and he sold the company. My mother grew up very differently. *Yiayia* Maria and *Pappou* Eugene, her parents, are salt of the earth, but Mom found Naxos boring, the way I did. She got a job crewing on a yacht, met my dad, loved that whole jet-set life."

"You said you pretty much grew up on Naxos," she remembered. "Your parents . . ."

"Dumped me there a large part of the time, so *Yiayia* and *Pappou* had to look after me. I'd just be getting settled with them, then one or both of my parents would sweep me away again for a while."

"One or both?"

"They're constantly breaking up and getting back together. And sometimes my dad's parents in Athens—the filthy rich ones—would want me with them. It was unsettling."

Being in bed, candles flickering, made for an easy intimacy. "I'm surprised you didn't end up longing for roots and stability."

"Guess I'm too much like my parents."

"You're more responsible, though."

Black eyes studied her curiously. "What makes you say that?"

"You found a job that gives you the variety, challenge, and excitement you enjoy, and you've stuck with it. You've also been a great cruise director, even though it's not your real job."

"Wish I was doing as well on my real job," he muttered.

She'd wondered how it was going, knowing she couldn't ask. Now that he'd raised the subject, she said, "To me, everyone looks pretty harmless."

He shrugged. "Most white-collar criminals do."

"Why are you undercover on this cruise and not at the suspect's workplace?"

"Sorry, I can't tell you any more."

She did understand about job responsibilities. Her own included. She sighed unhappily. "I really hope this doesn't affect the cruise or the wedding."

"I'll try not to let that happen."

Try. She hoped he tried really hard.

Chapter 11

AS soon as he rose the next morning, Santos checked and found there was Internet access, and collected e-mail. At his instruction, the intern had looked more deeply into Kavanagh's trial, and in particular Kendra Kirk's role.

He shut down his computer and drummed his fingers on the desk. The intern reported that Kendra had an excellent success rate, and if she decided to prosecute she was almost guaranteed to win a conviction. Of course, jury trials were notoriously unpredictable, and a man with Kavanagh's charm had likely swayed the jurors. Still, he had to wonder if Kendra had deliberately blown the case.

Maybe she and Kavanagh had been coconspirators before he'd stolen the five million, or perhaps the man had bribed her—or wooed her—once he'd been charged. Perhaps for her, it wasn't about the money. Kendra wouldn't be the first intelligent woman to fall in love with a criminal.

Mind humming with possibilities, Santos hurried upstairs. The cruise had started on Friday, it was Tuesday now, and on Thursday the *Aphrodite* would dock in Crete and the guests would leave to explore the island, with Liz and Peter's wedding taking place on Saturday. The cruise director would normally return with the ship on Thursday. He was running out of time, but what else could he do except observe and try to get closer to Kavanagh and Kendra?

When Santos got to the dining room, there was no sign of them, nor of Gwen, so either they hadn't arrived yet or they were outside.

He filled a plate, poured coffee, then went outside. His gaze immediately found Gwen, who was huddled with Captain Ari, studying one of her innumerable sheets of paper. She glanced up and gave him a cheerful morning smile, which he returned. The sight of her always brightened his mood, even when he had to pretend they were no more than friendly colleagues. Yet he felt a pang at the thought that they only had a short time left together.

He forced his focus back to his job. Kavanagh, from the looks of it, was charming some of the older ladies. Kendra sat with her uncles. He chose her, figuring that, as a less experienced criminal than Kavanagh, she might be more inclined to give something away.

He headed over to their table. "Mind if I join you?"

All three greeted him with smiles that seemed genuine, and he wondered about this version of Kendra. Last night, too, when she'd joined in the dancing, she'd seemed far more relaxed than usual. "You're looking cheerful this morning," he said to her. "I hope you're enjoying your holiday. It must be a change from that demanding job as a lawyer."

"It's definitely that," she said, sipping orange juice.

Santos tucked into his bacon and eggs as her uncle William commented, "We were just saying last night how good this trip is for her."

"Our Kendra works far too hard," her uncle Phil said.

"Yeah, yeah," she said with an affectionate smile. "How many times have I heard that?"

"What kind of law do you practice?" Santos asked her.

"I'm a Crown Counsel. A prosecutor."

"Ah, you put the bad guys in jail. That must be rewarding."

Her brow pinched slightly. "It is."

"Seems to me it could be frightening, too. Violent criminals, gangs. Don't you worry they might want vengeance? Even white-collar criminals can be scary, they're so damned smart. Maybe not so prone to violence, but they can hurt people in other ways."

"Believe me, we know that," William said gruffly. "Kendra's parents—"

"Uncle William," she said sharply, "I don't want to talk about that."

Her uncle reached over to squeeze her hand. "Sorry, hon."

"It's okay. Just, you know." She shrugged, then pushed back her chair. "I have a few things to do before we go ashore. See you later."

Silently, the three of them watched her walk away. Noting the change in her mood, Santos decided to have the intern research Kendra's parents.

Phil said to Santos, "Tell us about today's agenda. A swim first, then we'll be at the island of Ios for the day? And tonight it's the stag and stagette parties, right?"

As Santos provided details, he reflected on patterns and pieces, and things that didn't fit. Right now, he was having trouble making this odd assortment of puzzle pieces fall into place to reveal the full picture. But eventually, when he had enough of them, the image would come together. He just hoped he was the one who managed to reveal the truth.

And that somehow he could do it without messing things up for Gwen.

GWEN finished doing check-ins with Captain Ari and Chef Ilyas, then wandered over to the table where Santos and Peter's dads, William and Phil, were lingering over coffee. They promptly invited her to join them, which she did, glad for the opportunity to feast her eyes on her lover.

William, Peter's biological dad, said, "Gwen, you and Santos are doing an amazing job. You're giving Peter and Liz a week they'll never forget." He glanced at his husband. "Too bad we didn't have you arrange our wedding."

"I'm sure yours was lovely." She grinned mischievously. "But if you're ever thinking of renewing your vows . . ."

They all chuckled.

"Greece is the perfect place for Peter and Liz," Phil said. "It gives him a connection with his mom."

She'd noticed that the two men and their families seemed completely comfortable with the rather unusual family history. "The idea was Peter's and I agree it's brilliant. He said his mom used to tell him stories about Greece and he'd always wanted to come here."

"It's good that he remembers some things," William said. "He was only eight when Marina died. He takes after her, though. Even looks more like her than me."

Phil linked fingers with him. "We try to keep his memories of his mom alive. It's important for Peter and for William as well. You should never forget a person you loved so deeply."

"No, you shouldn't." Though she'd finally gotten rid of Jonathan's clothes and university stuff, Gwen kept a few pictures and mementos around. "It's hard," she mused, "finding the right balance. You need to move on but you don't want to forget."

"It is." William gazed at her. "You've lost someone. A parent?"

"No, they're both alive." Though they'd finally divorced ten years ago and she rarely saw her father. Nor did her mother, who had even started dating again.

"If you don't want to talk about it," Phil said.

"It's not that. Just, this is a wedding and . . ." She took a breath and glanced at Santos, who gave an understanding smile. Then she gazed at the other two men, who she'd really come to like. Not wanting to shut them out, she said, "I was married and my husband died of cancer."

After they murmured sympathies, she said, "Don't spread it around, okay? It's a gloomy subject, with Peter and Liz getting married in a few days."

"Isn't it hard for you," Phil asked, "being a wedding planner?"

"No. I'm happy for all these couples. Love's a wonderful thing. The best thing in the world. I just wish them better luck than I had. When I got married, I thought we'd have forever, but that's not how it turned out." She touched her bare ring finger.

William nodded. "Yeah. Then you get pissed off at the world and, though it's ridiculous, even at your spouse for deserting you."

"I didn't get mad at—" If she was totally honest with herself, there had been times she'd felt like shaking Jonathan and telling him to fight harder, as if it was his fault he was dying and abandoning her. "He promised me forever. It wasn't his fault he broke that promise."

William reached over to touch her hand. "The anger is normal. So's the guilt for feeling mad, and so's feeling all-around crappy."

Just as she'd done for the year after his death when she wallowed in misery. Grief, anger, guilt, fear—they'd held her back from rejoining the world.

Santos shifted casually in his seat, and under the table his sandal-clad foot came to rest against hers.

"Disappointed, resentful, pissed off," William said wryly. "But you have to let it go, Gwen. You have to forgive. Forgive your husband, and forgive yourself for having all those negative feelings."

She closed her eyes for a moment. The image of Jonathan's face filled her mind: the love in his eyes, and the sorrow when he knew the end was coming. Oh yes, she forgave Jonathan. And yes, she was human. Her feelings had been normal, perhaps inevitable.

Opening her eyes again, she smiled at the groom's dad. "Thank you. You're right, and I'm getting there. But I do know I have some issues around promises and reliability." And she should be grateful to Santos for laying everything out so clearly for her, so she didn't rely on him for something he wouldn't—couldn't—give her.

"Rightly so," Phil said. "Promises should be kept, and reliability is important. That's an attribute you definitely have, Gwen." He glanced at Santos. "You, too. You're both always there when someone needs you."

"Thank you," she said, seeing Santos's nod.

"Reliability is good," William agreed, "but you have to realize, Gwen, you can't control everything."

Ouch. Her lips twitched. "You've noticed I'm a bit of a control freak?"

"For the first couple of years after Marina died—until I met Phil, in fact—I was too controlling with Peter. I had let my wife out of my sight and she was struck by a car and killed."

"So . . . what are you saying?"

"I'm guessing that when your husband became ill, you felt like life had become uncontrollable."

"Yes." She'd had panic attacks and hidden them from Jonathan. Even now, when her carefully organized plans went awry, she'd feel the familiar rise of panic and struggle for control.

"So now, at some level, you figure that if you control everything, nothing bad will happen."

She nodded slowly.

"But you can't control everything," Phil pointed out gently. "That's what William finally understood. Yeah, it's awful when your spouse dies. It's about the worst thing you could ever imagine."

She nodded again.

"But you and William survived, Gwen. It was hard but, what, did you think it should be easy, losing the person you love most in your life? Some things in life just fucking suck, if you'll pardon my French."

Those words rang through her, clear and pure as a bell. Why hadn't she realized that before? "You're right. And no, it shouldn't be easy." The people who'd tried to cheer her up and told her she needed to get over it had been wrong. Her grief had been right, honest, and loving. And so had her eventual decision to move on, to be strong and even happy.

"But you coped. You coped with the worst thing that could happen, and look at you now, all strong and healthy and beautiful."

His words, so close to what she'd just been thinking, touched her. She reached over to squeeze his hand. "Thank you, Phil."

"In life, things will go wrong and you have to trust yourself to be able to cope."

Santos, who'd been listening quietly, nodded agreement. "Not everything on this trip has gone according to plan, and you've handled every problem that came up. Have faith in yourself, Gwen."

"Which is stronger?" Phil asked. "The oak or the willow?"

"Uh . . ."

"The willow, because it's flexible. Rigidity—too much control—makes you vulnerable. You can break. Flexibility is better because you can bend with whatever comes along." He wrapped an arm around William's shoulders. "And believe me, when you're raising a kid, there's no telling what will come along next."

"Hey, you guys talking about me?" Peter came up from behind Gwen, dressed in board shorts and carrying a towel.

Liz, in a yellow bikini, rounded the table to hug his two fathers. "Morning, Dads Two and Three. Going to come swimming with us?"

"Is it that time already?" Gwen glanced at her watch, then around the table at William, Phil, and Santos. "Thanks, guys. It was good talking to you." Keeping her tone light, she added, "You've saved me hours on a shrink's couch."

When Liz turned a curious face to her, Gwen waved her hand. "Don't ask. They just made me realize I'm carrying heavier baggage than I thought I was."

A sympathetic grin perked the bride's lips. "Why don't you toss it overboard? Then you'd be free to reinvent yourself."

Santos touched Gwen's shoulder lightly. "Don't do that. I kind of like you the way you are." The words were public ones, but the warmth in his eyes made her heart thump.

Damn, she could so easily fall for him, and that was the last thing she wanted. If she ever fell in love again, she needed another Jonathan, a man who believed in commitment and happily ever after, and would fight to his last breath to give them to her.

IT was another busy day, but as Gwen explored the island of Ios with the group and dealt with whatever issues arose, she reflected on her conversation with Santos and the two dads and came to some tentative conclusions.

Yes, it was good to be prepared. She had a detailed schedule; a tote with sunscreen and bandages hung over her shoulder; and she knew how to ask, "Where's the bathroom?" in Greek. But it was impossible to be prepared for everything, and she was actually pretty resourceful when it came to dealing with the unforeseen. The only thing that really gave her trouble, that was getting out of control, was her confusion over Santos. Much as she told herself she was being stupid, her feelings were growing beyond lust and affection. Too bad emotions didn't always fall in line with good intentions.

In the early evening, everyone gathered on deck for a drink, most choosing either Greek beer or the fruity drink called a Heat Wave that had become popular among the guests. Spirits were high as "the girls" and "the boys" anticipated heading off for Liz's stagette and Peter's stag party. Gwen watched Santos surreptitiously as he joked with Liz's dad. Her lover was casual in jeans and a light blue shirt, so much more handsome and sexy than any of the other men.

She'd told him he shouldn't come to her cabin tonight. The parties would run late and excited guests would be milling about—or at least, that was her excuse. Really, she needed a night alone to try to put their relationship in perspective.

It was Tuesday, and after a few more days, she'd likely never see him again—unless she invited him to return to Athens with her and share her last couple of days in Greece. Did she want more time with him? Time to fall even harder for him before they said good-bye?

The thing was, she didn't want to say good-bye. And yet it was inevitable.

When she'd met Jonathan, their relationship had developed slowly. When they'd become friends, she'd told herself it could never be more than that, not between a university professor and a high school student. But their friendship had warmed slowly to something deeper that felt totally right to both of them. Something strong and true but not, she had to admit, as passionate as what she felt for Santos.

"'Bye!" "Have fun but not too much fun." Male voices cut through her thoughts and she realized the guys were heading off for the stag, tossing teasing comments over their shoulders.

Determined to focus on her job, she smiled at Liz and her mom. "Well, ladies, let's go have a good time."

WEDNESDAY, Santos woke feeling grumpy. Though he'd slept well and was looking forward to a day on Santorini, he had missed spending a couple of private hours with Gwen last night. For the sex, yes, but also for the way they hugged and talked afterward. It was going to be agony waiting for tonight.

He fixed himself some yogurt and honey, added fruit and a bun, and was pouring coffee when Kavanagh came in. The man's expression said he wasn't in a good mood, and he took no food, only a cup of coffee.

Yesterday, both he and Kendra had been cheerful and relaxed, and Kavanagh had also been in good spirits at the stag. Was this just another example of the man's moodiness, or had something happened since then?

"You should have something to eat," Santos said. "We have a jam-packed day on Santorini."

"I'll get something later," he said gruffly. "Just need some caffeine to wake me up first."

"Are you having a good time on this trip? I heard you say it's your first time in Greece."

Kavanagh's smile looked forced. "Yes to both. I haven't done a lot of foreign travel."

Was it possible he planned to use this wedding cruise as an innocent-seeming excuse to get out of Canada, then head off to a country that had no extradition to enjoy his five million? "Are you heading home right after the wedding or continuing your travels?"

"Heading home."

Santos wished Insurance Assured could access flight manifests and check that fact, but those were confidential. "Need to get back to your job?"

Kavanagh frowned. "I have commitments."

"Oh?"

The man didn't respond, so Santos pushed a little. "I enjoy travel. Too bad it costs so much. A person almost needs to be a millionaire."

Kavanagh's eyes narrowed and he looked as if he was in pain. He didn't respond to Santos's comment, but instead said, with an attempt at lightness that didn't quite come off, "So it's Santorini today. That's the island you see on so many posters of Greece, right?"

Resigned, Santos accepted the diversion. "Yes, it's very dramatic with the volcanic caldera, and the town of Fira high on the cliff above."

"Caldera?"

"Cauldron. Once, there was a huge island, then a gigantic volcanic eruption occurred, the center of the island collapsed, and the sea rushed in. Some people claim it's the lost city of Atlantis. Come outside. You don't want to miss seeing the approach from the water."

Together they walked out.

Over by the rail, Kendra stood talking to some other people, looking far happier than Kavanagh. She glanced over and smiled.

Santos smiled back, but beside him, Kavanagh stopped and turned. "You're right," he said abruptly, "I should get some food." He hurried away.

Santos glanced back across the deck, to see Kendra watching with a puzzled frown.

Another oddly shaped piece for his puzzle.

IN the afternoon, as the group explored the ruins at Ancient Thira, Gwen found herself thinking about Jonathan and what William had said about his wife's death. She wandered over to a stone wall, where she sat and stared out at the ocean, reflecting.

Someone sat beside her and she glanced up. It was Kendra Kirk. Gwen gave her a smile. "Can I do something for you?"

"No, I just thought . . . wondered . . ." The other woman seemed uncomfortable, and Gwen wondered what was on her mind. "Are you okay, Gwen?"

"Fine, of course."

"You looked kind of sad."

That sure wasn't the image she wanted to portray at a wedding. "How could I be sad, here on Santorini? Are you having a good time, Kendra?"

"Yes, but look, this doesn't always have to be about us. The guests. You're allowed a moment here and there to just be you. To feel sad, if you want to."

There was sympathy, understanding, in the other woman's gray-green eyes. "If I want to." Gwen tested the words. "Actually, I guess I kind of do. I was thinking about someone I lost. And it's okay, it's normal, to be sad, isn't it?"

Kendra reflected. "Sad, or sometimes mad. Depends on how you lost them."

"That's true. And when you lose someone too young, there's probably always a reason to be a little mad."

"I think so." Something in Kendra's tone said this was personal. "You've lost someone, too."

She nodded. "A long time ago. But there's still a part of me that's mad. And sad. Maybe that never goes away."

"Maybe it doesn't." Gwen paused, not wanting to intrude. Tentatively, she asked, "Do you want to talk about it? Who it was and what happened?"

A pause, a breath. Then she said, "My father. He committed suicide when I was fifteen."

"My God, I'm so sorry." Gwen caught her hand, which lay between them on the stone wall. "That's terrible."

"It was. He and Mom lost everything they'd saved because they trusted someone they shouldn't. Dad didn't have the strength to cope. So he quit. And my mom, she fell apart."

"That's tragic." And here Gwen had thought her family situation was pretty bad. "It must have been horrible for you."

"It was. But my uncles were wonderful, and a distant relative who I barely knew became a mentor, and . . . it all worked out."

"Not the way it was supposed to, though."

"No," she said softly. "But things don't always work out the way they're supposed to."

"That's so true," Gwen said.

"Want to tell me your story? I'd be glad to listen."

This reminded her of being with Sarah and Andi. Sharing confidences, sympathizing with each other. She sensed she could trust Kendra. "Just between us?"

"Of course."

"It's nothing that dramatic. I married young and he died of cancer."

Kendra squeezed Gwen's hand. "That must have been awful. To think you've found a man to spend your life with and . . ."

"Yes. To find out that the 'till death do us part' thing would happen sooner than you'd ever imagined."

"How long ago?"

"Going on two years. I spent most of the first year pretty much destroyed," she confessed.

"I can only imagine. But look at you now." Her gaze held respect.

"Thanks. I'm a work in progress but I'm doing okay."

"Way better than my mom." Kendra patted her hand, then let go. "She was destroyed, and never pulled out of it. You've done an amazing job of getting on with your life."

Gwen smiled. Yes, she'd grieved, was still grieving, and that was normal, but she was coping and moving on. Why hadn't she realized how strong she actually was? "Thanks, Kendra. I appreciate that." She glanced at her watch. "I'm glad we had this chance to talk, but now I need to round people up. It's time to move on to the folklore museum."

Together they stood and glanced around. She saw Santos in the distance. Touching her ring finger one last time, she put the past behind her. When Santos glanced in their direction, she waved, hoping he'd realize she was not just saying it was time to head back, but letting him know she was looking forward to being alone with him tonight.

"Have you and Santos worked together before?" Kendra asked.

"No, in fact we just met on Friday."

"Well, you make a great team. You're so in sync."

"Thanks." Gwen could feel her cheeks heat. Yes, they were, for this short period of time.

Her heart might end up bruised, but that was a small price to pay and she could deal with it. When she was back in Vancouver, her nights would be lonely, so for the next while she'd stock up on memories.

Chapter 12

THAT night, sitting at a dinner table across from Kendra, Gwen thought of how lucky she was to be here on Santorini. Their dinner reservation was timed for sunset-watching from a cliff-side restaurant in Fira overlooking the spectacular caldera, an ocean-filled volcanic crater surrounded by volcanic cones.

Waiters served crisp white wine and brought platters of Greek appetizers, mostly seafood. People who'd originally been cautious were now happily eating squid and octopus.

Across the outdoor patio, a number of guests—especially the female ones—were getting their pictures taken with Santos. No wonder. He was as photogenic as the amazing view. She knew it was ridiculous of her to feel jealous when he put his arms around toned waists and let pretty young women nestle close to him. An insecure part of her wondered if last night, when she'd told him not to come to her cabin, he'd been with one of those girls. It shouldn't matter, and yet it did.

Now he glanced over and waved. "Come on, Kendra, Gwen. I want pictures with you."

Kendra shook her head, smiling, but Gwen did want a picture with him. A souvenir, as if she'd need anything to remind her of this man. Muttering, "I suppose it's something we could use on the website," she went over to join him.

He freed himself of the blondes who'd wrapped him from either side and put his arm around Gwen.

"Aren't your arms getting tired?" she muttered under her breath.

"Getting tired waiting for you to come over here," he returned, making her smile.

The camera, held by William, clicked.

Santos's arm tightened and he called, "Take a couple more, to make sure we get a good one."

While William fiddled with the camera, Santos whispered, "I'm so hungry for you, *latreia mou*. Tonight. Yes?"

"Yes. I can't wait for—"

She broke off as Kendra, accompanied by Peter with his camera, came over. Reluctantly, Gwen surrendered her place in the curve of Santos's arm and returned to her seat.

The sky shifted from blue to shades of yellow as the sun began to set, and everyone's attention turned from food, wine, and conversation to watch nature's show. Golden light warmed the white walls of the buildings, with the occasional round blue roofs providing contrast. As the sun dropped, the sky's palette ranged from deep apricot at the top through to a blinding white-gold dazzle as the sun hit the water.

Spectacular. Romantic. Something made her turn her head and she saw Santos watching her. Everyone else's eyes were glued to the sunset. He lifted his wineglass to her in a silent toast and she smiled and lifted her own. How could she feel so connected to a man who'd only be in her life for a few days?

As the sky darkened, tiny white lights brightened the patio and waiters brought candles in holders that protected them from the evening breeze. Lights came on in the other buildings of Fira, too, and the town looked magical, just like the photos of Greece Gwen had admired for years. She was living inside a picture postcard.

Lucky, so lucky to be here, and yet . . . No, she needed to stop obsessing and enjoy the moment. Later, when Santos came to her cabin, she'd enjoy every one of those moments, too.

AFTER boats from shore had returned everyone to the *Aphrodite* for their last night aboard, Santos waited impatiently on deck until the guests drifted away, either to their cabins—as both Kavanagh and Kendra did—or to the bar for a final nightcap. He hadn't been alone with Gwen, really alone, since the night before last.

He'd watched her a lot, though, as he puzzled over the way she made him feel. He had dated many women, enjoyed their company in bed and out, and when he moved on, he felt no particular regret. He hoped they didn't either. In Toronto, he had a friend with benefits, a no-strings arrangement that suited them both perfectly. He always made it clear to women that a guy like him, always looking for a new adventure, wasn't a good bet for a relationship. The last thing he wanted was some woman relying on him.

How crazy that the idea of not seeing Gwen again made him feel . . . empty. As empty as when he'd been a little kid and his parents would go away again. That was back before he realized they'd never stay, and had steeled himself to not care.

The anchor chain rattled and the engines cranked over. The *Aphrodite* was leaving Santorini. Overnight, the ship would travel to Crete. Tomorrow, the guests would disembark—and he needed to find an excuse to go with them. Unless, of course, he resolved the Kavanagh file before then, but that was unlikely, and in any case he did want a few more days with Gwen. She'd said nothing about their parting, and he hoped she'd be willing to support him in staying with the group.

Cautiously he took the stairs down to the lower level guest cabins, carrying a sheaf of papers in case anyone saw him.

As he stepped into the corridor, a man was walking quickly down the hall away from him. Auburn hair, a white shirt, jeans. It was Kavanagh. And he went into Kendra Kirk's cabin. The door closed silently behind him.

Proof positive that something was going on between them. Were they coconspirators, lovers, or both?

Insurance Assured's intern had checked into that comment William Kirk had made about Kendra's parents. Turned out her mom and dad—William's brother and his wife—had been defrauded and lost everything. Her father had committed suicide and her mom had never recovered, remaining a semi-invalid to this day. Kendra had been fifteen. After a tragedy like that, it was difficult to imagine her conspiring with a white-collar criminal, or falling for one, yet there was no denying what Santos had just seen.

He slipped quickly down the corridor and eased into Gwen's cabin.

Greek music played softly and she stepped out of the small en suite, lovely in a lacy white bra and thong.

Eagerly he went to embrace her and she hugged him tight, lifting her face to his. "I missed you."

"God, me, too." He kissed her quickly, needing to taste her, but Kavanagh had distracted him. "Kendra Kirk's in a cabin by herself, right?" He asked the question knowing the answer.

She pulled back, frowning. "Kendra? Why?" Crossing her arms across her chest, she said, "Isn't it enough you have those two blondes proposing a three-way?"

His lips curved. "You're cute when you're jealous."

She tossed her head. "If you're sleeping with someone else on the ship, I have a right to know."

"Jesus, Gwen." He generally didn't like jealous women, yet for some reason he was kind of flattered. "No, I'm not sleeping with anyone else. But if I do, you'll be the first to know."

She glared. "Talk like that's not going to get you into my bed tonight."

And now she'd distracted him from Kavanagh and Kirk. Puzzled, he asked, "What's up with you? You said you weren't into a serious relationship."

She plunked down in the desk chair, looking confused. "I . . . I'm not. It's the wrong time in my life. And you're the wrong man."

Ouch. He didn't want a serious relationship either, so why did that *wrong man* comment hurt? A little irked, he said, "Then why do you care if I sleep with someone else?"

"Because . . . it's insulting. It's like I'm not enough for you." Her chin went up but her brandy-colored eyes looked wounded.

He sighed, forgetting his annoyance, and reached down to take her hands. "You're more than enough." Since he'd met her, he hadn't felt the slightest desire for anyone else. "No, I don't want to sleep with the English blondes, nor with Kendra, nor anyone else on this ship. Okay?"

Her lips twisted in a little smile. "Yeah, I guess. But then why were you asking about Kendra?" Her eyes widened. "She's not your suspect?"

"Didn't say she was," he said firmly, letting go her hands and straightening. "But I'm curious. Flynn Kavanagh just slipped into a room down the hall. I think it's hers."

"Wow." Her eyes widened. "Kendra and Flynn?" She shook her head. "No, that can't be. They don't hang out together, barely even speak to each other."

"I know, which is why it seemed weird to me." He leaned against the wall, studying her. "Why did she get a private cabin?" So she'd have a place to meet with her lover?

"So she could work." She gave a quick head shake. "Wait, of course she's not your suspect. I'd forgotten; she prosecutes criminals."

He chuckled at her naivety. "People aren't always what they seem."

"You're saying it *is* her?" She gaped at him in disbelief. "No, that's not—"

"Gwen, stop. Stop trying to guess who it is. I'm speaking in general terms." He tugged her up and wrapped his arms around her, feeling all those soft, warm curves barely concealed by her skimpy lingerie. "Take you, for example. You pretend to be a control freak but you're really a risk-taker."

Something flickered in her eyes. "Oh yeah, being with you is a big risk." Her tone aimed for teasing but missed, and he wondered what that was all about. She freed herself from his arms and went to sit on the bed, her back against a couple of piled pillows. "Actually, I've been thinking about the control thing, after what Peter's dads said."

This night wasn't turning out the way he'd expected. Still, this seemed to be important to her. "Yeah?" He sat on the edge of the bed beside her.

She leaned forward, bringing her knees up and looping her arms around them. "Yeah. When I was a teen, that fire made me realize my life was out of control. Jonathan offered stability, reliability, maturity—as well as love, of course. It was incredibly appealing."

"I can see that." He stroked her bare leg, a soft caress up and down from knee to ankle. Where was she going with this? She knew he wasn't the guy to be giving her those things.

"I gave up the risk-taking side of myself, and other things, too. But of course," she added quickly, "Jonathan made compromises, too."

"He did?"

"Yes. He changed his work habits so we could have dinner together every night, the way I wanted." She gave a fond smile. "He was a meat and potatoes guy but he went along when I wanted to try cooking ethnic dishes, though I'm not a great cook. I got him to stop wearing stuffy old tweed jackets with elbow patches—honestly, you'd have thought he was in his sixties, not his thirties—and he got me to dress like a woman, not a teenager. Yes, we adjusted to each other, figured out how to be a couple."

Being a couple was a concept he'd never thought much about, but he guessed that made sense—as long as neither person gave up too much.

"Then he got sick," she said quietly, "and life spun out of control again."

"Must have been horrible." He circled her ankle with his fingers, feeling the fine bones and thinking how strong she'd been to stand by her husband and watch him die.

She gazed down at his hand. "This time, Jonathan couldn't rescue me. There was no solution. But I controlled everything I possibly could, and I guess I've been doing it ever since." Her gaze lifted to his face, her brown eyes troubled. "Until you came along."

No, he definitely didn't want to be controlled. He squeezed her ankle and gently teased, "You don't look so happy about that."

A quick flash of smile, there then gone. "I am. You've given me so much. But it's also . . . disconcerting. I really like you, Santos. I'm going to miss you."

"Yeah, me, too." Words he'd never said to another woman. It struck him that in his own way, he was just as organized as Gwen. He'd organized his life so he'd never have to miss anyone the way he'd missed his parents each time they dumped him in Naxos. How had this woman gotten under his skin? And what was he going to do about it? He filed those thoughts away to examine later. "Look, we're together now. Let's enjoy it."

After a moment, she gave a tentative smile, and this one reached her eyes. "Maybe that's my lesson for this trip. Relax and enjoy the moment."

He stroked his hand up her calf, over her knee, then halfway up her inner thigh. "I can help with that."

"You can." She studied him, and those golden flecks in her eyes caught fire. "Particularly if you take your clothes off."

He complied, but slowly, liking the attentive way she watched, and the flush that bloomed on her cheeks and chest. Stripping for her was enough to arouse him, and by the time he slid down his boxers, his cock was filling and rising.

"Like magic," she murmured, then she patted the bed beside her. "Lie down, Santos. I think you've kissed and licked every inch of my body, and I want to explore yours."

When he sprawled on his back, she kneeled beside him and slowly ran her fingers over his shoulders, then down to his pecs, teasing her fingers through curls of black hair and flicking gently against his nipples, making them pucker tight. When she bent to take one in her mouth, he shoved himself up on a couple of pillows so he could watch.

Her hair, drifting like pale gold silk across his skin, was so fair in comparison to his tanned brown flesh. Heated lips held him and she simultaneously sucked his nipple and swirled her tongue around it, sending hot pulses of arousal surging through him.

He ran his fingers through her soft hair. "Feels good, Gwen. So good."

She nipped lightly, a hint of pain to sharpen the pleasure, and he moaned approval.

Slowly she made her way over to his other nipple and gave it the same treatment as his cock swelled with the desire to feel that wet, heated mouth.

Taking her sweet time, she moved down his body with soft kisses, teasing licks, and nibbles. By the time she reached his groin, he was desperate enough to plead, "Suck me."

"I intend to."

But instead she stroked him experimentally. "You haven't been circumcised," she murmured.

"It's not as common in Greece." He was glad, too, because he savored every bit of sensation as her gentle fingers teased his foreskin up and down over the head of his cock.

"Let me know if I do something that hurts." She bent, but rather than taking him into her mouth, she kissed her way almost primly down his shaft in a chain of little closed-mouthed caresses that, together with the soft drift of her hair, pricked every cell to needy attention. When she reached the base, she began to lick—big, bold, swirling strokes that ignited sensation, making him moan as she made her way back up.

Watching her work his cock was almost as erotic as feeling it.

She slid his foreskin up to cover the crown, then eased it down again, her tongue replacing it. Her moist stroke circled the crown, she delicately licked up pre-come, then she flicked the tip of her tongue across the tiny eye.

Finally, when he thought he couldn't take a moment more of this erotic torture, she opened that wide, sensual mouth and took him inside.

Again, he moaned in bliss.

She moved up and down on him, only able to fit half his length in her mouth. But her fingers worked the bottom half of his shaft, pumping busily up and down.

"Harder," he grated out. "Faster."

But when she did, he could only take it for a few seconds before he thrust his hand into her hair and pulled her away. "Inside you."

She shook her head, tousled hair flicking around a flushed-cheek face. "No. I want you to come in my mouth."

He groaned, and when she lowered her head again, he didn't stop her.

Nor did he try to hold back as her hands and mouth drove him higher, as tension built almost to the point of pain, as he watched his slick, swollen shaft plunge between her sweet lips. Her fingers teased his balls as they hardened and drew up, then she worked him even harder until the pressure crested and finally broke. He couldn't hold back a shout, but managed to smother it against his forearm as he pumped his essence deep into her mouth.

Then, hungry to kiss her, to taste himself on her, he hauled her up so she sprawled awkwardly across his body and he took her mouth in slow sips and nibbles.

"Santos," she murmured, eyes glazed with passion.

Appetite whetted, he needed to taste more of her. "Up on your knees."

She gave him a puzzled look, but obeyed.

He slid down the bed under her raised body, his legs hanging off the end, until her slick, pink pussy hovered directly above him. With both hands, he gripped her hips, holding her there as he stabbed his tongue inside her.

"Oh, God, Santos," she gasped.

She writhed against him as he ate her, his tongue exploring every fold, every secret place, lingering over the swollen nub of her clit, until she shuddered and pulsed in orgasm against his lips.

When the ripples faded, she gave a satisfied sigh. "Wow." She clambered off him and they rearranged themselves on the bed so his arm was around her and her head rested on his chest.

"*Latreia mou,*" he murmured.

"What do all those Greek words mean?"

Why was it easier to whisper endearments she didn't understand? "*Latreia mou* is *my darling, glyka mou* is *my sweet. Se thelo poly* is *I want you.*"

"Mmm, nice. There was another one, about wanting to make love?"

"*Thelo na se paro.*" And he did, over and over again. "Gwen, there's something I need to talk to you about."

"Mmm hmm?" she murmured lazily.

"We dock in Crete tomorrow. Your original cruise director, Giorgos, would have gone back with the *Aphrodite.*"

Her body, which had been limp with satiation, tensed and she thrust herself to a sitting position. "Oh my God, I never thought about that. I just assumed you'd be here until after the wedding. But you're supposed to be the cruise director, so . . . Is your investigation finished? Are you leaving us tomorrow?"

Selfish bastard that he was, he liked the unhappiness in her eyes. He squeezed her hands. "My assignment's flexible. So far, I'm pulling together pieces of the puzzle, but I'm not seeing the whole picture yet." He was increasingly concerned that Kavanagh, and possibly Kendra, might not return to Vancouver but instead disappear to a country with no extradition. "I'd like to stay with the group. And with you, *glyka mou.*"

"Oh, yes." Relief softened her face, then she frowned again. "But how can we justify it?"

One way was to say they were lovers and wanted to stay together. But he knew better than to suggest that, as she'd worry about looking unprofessional. "We could say Giorgos, who I'm filling in for, has returned to work, so I'm free. On Crete." He grinned at her. "I speak Greek and you don't. I've come to feel like part of the group"—which was true—"and if I offer my services, free of charge, to Liz and Peter, and to your company, perhaps I'll be invited to stay for the wedding?"

"I'm sure you will, and my vote's a wholehearted yes." She threw herself into his arms and he hugged her close.

Chapter 13

THURSDAY morning, Santos rose determined to search Kendra's cabin before the crew went in to clean, to hunt for clues as to what she and Kavanagh had been doing.

When he came on deck, neither of them had arrived yet. Liz and Peter were there, though, talking to her parents. He went over and wished them all a good morning, then said to the bride and groom, "Could I have a moment of your time?"

"Sure." With curious expressions, they followed him over to the railing.

He gestured ashore. "Crete, the *Aphrodite*'s final stop. That means I should be leaving you."

"Oh, Santos!" Liz exclaimed. "That never occurred to me." She flung herself at him and gave him a warm hug. "Thank you so much for everything you've done. You've just *made* this cruise, you and Gwen." When she pulled back, she screwed up her mouth. "I can't believe you're going. You're so much a part of our group."

Peter stepped forward to shake his hand. "Yeah, man, I totally agree. It's going to seem strange getting married without you there."

Pleased that they'd given him an opening, Santos said, "I'd love to see the two of you get married. If you wanted to invite me."

"Of course you're invited," Liz cried. "But your job . . ."

"The man I've been relieving is coming back to work, so I'm not needed on the *Aphrodite*. And I have a week's holiday. I'd love to stay on with your group and help out. No charge, of course, just as, you know . . ."

"Our friend," Peter said.

Santos nodded. "Thanks. I can give Gwen a hand with translation, liaison with the hotels and bus company, that kind of thing."

Liz let out an excited squeal. "Brilliant! That's so generous of you."

"Yeah, really," Peter agreed. "But best to talk to Gwen before we decide. She's so organized, we don't want to mess up her plans."

"I can persuade her," Liz said confidently.

"I hope so," Santos said, tongue in cheek.

"She just came on deck," Peter said. "Let's talk to her."

The three of them went over to Gwen, and Santos suppressed a grin as Liz made her case and Gwen pretended to reflect. Then she said, "I think it's a great idea. How generous of you, Santos, to spend holiday time helping me out." When she added, humor creasing the corners of her lips, "I must find some way of thanking you," he almost laughed out loud.

"So you'll come into Chania with us?" Liz asked him. This morning's breakfast was the last meal aboard the *Aphrodite*. The guests would leave the ship to explore the town, and while they were doing it, the crew would arrange for all the luggage to be transferred to a hotel.

"I'll even play tour guide."

"You don't have to do that," Gwen said.

"I'm happy to."

"Let me just run and get you the folder with my notes on Chania."

"Sure." He surrendered to her compulsive efficiency. While she went belowdecks, he grabbed a quick bite to eat and wondered if Kavanagh and Kendra were still in bed together.

Apparently not, because when Kavanagh arrived, he wore a sour face. What was up with those two? The man had just dished out some food when Kendra walked in with her uncles. She looked tired and unhappy, and when she saw Kavanagh, she quickly glanced away.

Kavanagh did, too, and headed outside.

Kendra's uncles were trying to persuade her to eat. Santos figured he'd wait a few minutes and see if she settled down with breakfast, then he'd rush to her cabin. In the meantime, he followed Kavanagh outside. Gwen met him, handing him a thick file folder, and he muttered a rueful, "Gee, thanks."

He caught up with Kavanagh. "Good morning, Flynn. You look tired. Didn't you sleep well?"

All he got in return was a gruff, "I'm fine," then Kavanagh moved past him and took a chair over to the railing, clearly seeking privacy.

Shaking his head, Santos glanced around to find Kendra. She sat with her uncles, toying with her food.

Unobtrusively, he headed for the stairs, then hurried to her cabin. He slipped inside. Her computer sat on the desk, open but turned off. Her suitcase, filled neatly with clothing, rested on a bed that was thoroughly rumpled on both sides.

He checked the pillows. Yes! There were a couple of curly auburn hairs as well as one of Kendra's own straighter black ones. He slid a tiny camera from his shirt pocket, clicked photos, then took a small envelope from his pocket and collected the hairs.

Next, he looked in the wastebasket in the en suite. No condoms or other evidence of sex, but the hairs and rumpled bedding were highly suggestive. So, last night they'd had sex, and this morning they were at odds again. Very puzzling.

He glanced at her computer, wondering if he had time to turn it on and check her recent e-mails, and any documents she'd been working on.

The woman had looked unhappy and restless. Chances were she'd return to her cabin sooner rather than later. Santos couldn't be caught here.

As he went back up the stairs, he mentally reviewed the evidence. Flynn Kavanagh and Kendra Kirk were lovers. Neither had acknowledged any prior connection, and no one else seemed aware of one. Since the cruise had started, in public they'd alternated between ignoring each other, acting pissed off, and surreptitiously casting longing gazes. How much was real and how much an act? Money and sex were a tough combination. Add love as a possibility, and the mix became even more volatile.

When he emerged on deck, Kendra was rising, and he gave a whistle of relief that he hadn't lingered in her cabin. Kavanagh still sat alone, his back to everyone.

Gwen, who was seated amid a large group of guests, flagged him down. "Santos, everyone's so pleased you're staying on with us. Have you been to Chania before?"

"Thanks." He smiled around at the people he'd come to know and tried not to let his eyes linger on her face. "Yes, several times. You'll enjoy it."

Someone asked him a question, and as he answered, other passengers moved over to join them.

As he spoke to them, he was only half concentrating. The back of his mind toyed with the big question: Might Kavanagh and Kendra be planning to disappear?

They'd both chosen to come on this cruise. She was the groom's cousin and their family was close, but she was also a workaholic whose last holiday had, according to the intern at his office, been four years ago. Kavanagh was a friend of Liz's, but not an exceptionally close one, and he rarely traveled. Being here broke each of their normal patterns. The cruise had, however, given them an innocent excuse to get out of Canada. Together.

Five million dollars wasn't a fortune, but it would be a good starting point for two highly intelligent, motivated people. With Kavanagh's IT skills and Kendra's legal knowledge, they could easily disappear to a country where, if they ever were tracked down, extradition wasn't available.

They both had family back home, though, and seemed devoted to them. Kendra had her widowed mother, and Kavanagh had a single parent mom and a younger brother with Asperger's. Unlikely they'd abandon their families. But they could, a few weeks or months from now, bring their families to join them wherever they ended up . . .

If they disappeared, and did it on his watch, he'd be in deep shit with Insurance Assured. He'd have to keep a very close eye on them as he played tour guide.

Gwen said, "Okay, everyone, the rest of the questions will have to wait until we're ashore. Please get yourselves organized for the day and make sure your luggage is packed and locked."

He rose to help spread the message to other passengers scattered around the deck.

As soon as he and Gwen were alone, she said quietly, "You're distracted. Has something happened? Or you're expecting something to happen?"

"I can't talk about it."

Her eyes narrowed. "Tell me no one's being arrested in Chania. The wedding's in two days and everything's going so smoothly. Don't mess it up."

"I'll try not to." It was the most he could promise.

She huffed and stalked away.

He went below to change out of uniform into shorts, gather his own stuff, and skim over the notes in the file folder she'd given him. When he came back up on deck, it was to hear Kendra tell Gwen she wasn't going ashore with the group. She said she'd received e-mail from her office and needed to do some work.

Gamoto. Santos wouldn't be able to keep an eye on her. And where was Kavanagh? Most of the guests were assembled, and the man wasn't among them.

He breathed a sigh of relief when Kavanagh, looking out of breath and out of sorts, joined the group. This man was Santos's top priority. Still, after everyone had thanked Captain Ari, Santos's sound-sleeping roommate, Chef Ilyas, and the rest of the crew, Santos hung back to say to the captain, "You'll make sure Ms. Kirk gets to the hotel?"

Santos had become friends with Ari this week, but when he'd announced he wouldn't be returning with the *Aphrodite*, the captain's thick brows had risen. They did so again as Ari answered, "Of course."

"If there's any problem, any change in plans or anything, give me a call on my cell."

"And why would I do that?"

"Because we want to make sure everything goes smoothly for Gwen," Santos said. "You know how she fusses over every last detail."

That won him an understanding smile, and the captain's agreement.

The group disembarked for the final time and people exclaimed with pleasure as he led them into Chania's narrow lanes, pointing out remnants of Venetian and Turkish architecture. Gwen cast suspicious glances in his direction, and Kavanagh seemed lost in thoughts that put a dark expression on his face.

Hands in his pockets, the man barely glanced at the attractive buildings or tempting displays in shop windows. However, a couple of minutes after the group passed a travel agency, he snuck away and went through its doors. What was he up to?

Santos stopped the guests and launched into an impromptu lecture about the history of the town, glad he'd skimmed Giorgos's notes.

A few minutes later, Kavanagh came out of the travel agency, tucking his passport and something else—airline tickets?—into his pocket. Santos tensed, not knowing what he'd do if the man headed in the opposite direction, but instead he rejoined them.

Santos wound up his talk and led the group around the corner to a craft shop. "Have fun shopping for ten minutes, then we'll move on."

He rushed back to the agency. Speaking Greek to the pretty young woman behind the counter, he said, "I'm here to meet a friend, but I'm late. Has he already been here? A guy about my height with auburn hair? A Canadian?"

"Yes, he was just here."

Santos grimaced. "Damn, he'll be annoyed. Did everything go all right? He was worried no one would speak English."

She smiled sympathetically. "He did seem agitated, but yes, it was possible to change the tickets just as he wanted."

"So, he got a flight . . ."

He hoped she'd fill in the details, but instead she switched to English. "As you see, my English is fluent. There was no problem."

Gamoto. Flight manifests were confidential. There wasn't enough information for his employer to get a warrant. Still, once Santos had hurried to the tourist shop he'd sent the guests to and ensured Kavanagh was there, he went outside again and put in a quick call on his GSM cell phone to update his manager.

"Damn," Celia Jenkins said. "Kavanagh's changed his ticket, or both of theirs, and God knows what the Kirk woman's doing on the ship. Moving money to wherever they're planning to go? This is not looking good."

"Any suggestions?" He kept an eye on the shop door as they spoke.

"If they skip, we're SOL on ever recovering the money. But we don't have enough to have the Greek police detain them." She paused. "Be nice if the man misplaced his passport."

He wasn't sure if that was a broad hint. "He keeps pretty close tabs on it." He thought quickly. "If I tell everyone who he is, it'll embarrass him but won't stop him fleeing. Same if I disclose who I really am."

"What if he was accused of stealing something in Greece?"

"It might hold him a day or two, but not necessarily help us get evidence against him."

"What if the lawyer was arrested? Would he come to her rescue or keep pretending he barely knows her? It'd shake things up. Sometimes that's all it takes—a change in the dynamics."

"True." It'd shake up the wedding, too, which wouldn't be fair to Liz and Peter. Or to Gwen.

"You know I can't ask you to trump up evidence against her. But we're out five million if Kavanagh skips."

So, what was she saying? Frame a coconspirator to catch a thief? "Yeah, I—"

"Santos?" A woman bustled out of the shop. "I'm so glad I found you." It was Liz's aunt Madge.

"Gotta go," he muttered into the phone.

"Can you help me?" the aunt asked. "Am I converting this price to British pounds correctly?"

"Let's take a look."

They went into the store together and he got her sorted out, then he headed over to Kavanagh, who stood by himself, staring at a display of jewelry. If one of those expensive baubles found its way into his pocket without him knowing, and he left the store without paying . . .

"Buying a gift?" Santos asked.

The man's gaze jerked toward him, his surprise making it clear he'd been off in a world of his own. "Just looking."

"I noticed you going into a travel agency. Is there anything I can help with? Dionysus Cruises would be happy to make any arrangements you need."

"No, no, it's fine."

Santos kept his gaze on the man's face, hoping to make him uncomfortable enough he'd offer more explanation. Perhaps he did have an innocent one.

After a moment, Kavanagh said, "I just needed to confirm my return flight."

A blatant lie, which meant the flight change was anything but innocent. "Ah yes, that's always a good thing to do."

Santos glanced at the collection of gold jewelry. His training as an investigator would have made equally good training for a thief. It'd be easy to pinch a couple of those and slide them into Kavanagh's pocket without him noticing.

It would be unethical, but he'd bent the law before to aid in catching a criminal. Kavanagh would leave the store and Santos would tell the manager he thought he'd seen the guy pinch something.

Gwen's clear laugh rang out, and he glanced across the store to see her and Liz's mom chuckling over some souvenir. This wedding trip meant so much to her. How could he ruin it?

And it hit him. He cared about her. That was why the thought of them going their separate ways made him feel empty. She was different. Special. The first woman who'd been more than a fun, sexy companion and had touched his heart. He wanted to be a man she could rely on, but how could he—

"See anything you like?" a male voice asked. Startled, Santos realized Kavanagh had moved on and a jewelry salesman was smiling at him hopefully.

Santos glanced back at Gwen. "I do." Which made his life kind of wonderful, yet incredibly complicated. Impulsively, he said, "Give me a pair of gold earrings, women's earrings, with the key design. Like mine. And quickly."

As he signed the credit card slip, he wondered if he'd ever give these earrings to Gwen. If he messed up the wedding, she'd probably never speak to him again. *Gamoto.* What the hell was he going to do?

Chapter 14

FOLLOWING Santos to the charming little hotel where their group would be staying tonight, Gwen felt unsettled and anxious.

Last night, she and Santos had been so intimate, not just with their lovemaking but when she talked about her personal issues. Today, he was a different man. Though he looked casual in shorts and a short-sleeved shirt, he seemed tense and distracted.

As he'd led them around Chania, she'd kept glancing around, afraid police officers might rush toward them and make an arrest, yet unwilling to believe he'd really do that to her. A dozen times she'd thought of calling Sarah or Andi, but what could they say? This kind of situation had never arisen before at Happily Ever After. She had to deal with it herself.

Damn, Santos had her so distracted she wasn't giving the wedding party the attention they deserved either. Determinedly, she applied herself to her job as Santos collected passports, and between him, her, and two desk clerks, they got everyone checked in and matched up with their luggage.

"Don't forget," she told the guests, "we'll meet here in the lobby at eight to go for dinner."

"Gwen," Santos said rather formally, "if you have time, I'd like to discuss the plans for tomorrow, and how I can best assist."

The next day, Friday, would be full, with a bus taking them on a tour of western Crete. They'd end up in a rustic hotel close to Elafonissi, the pink sand beach where Liz and Peter had chosen to be wed. Or at least that was the plan—unless Santos ruined things. "Okay," she replied, anxiety making her heart race.

A few minutes later, they entered her second-floor room, very attractive with its windows open to the sun, one wall painted a vivid teal that reminded her of the ocean, and a miniature orange tree on a table by the window. The bed—king-sized—looked vast in comparison to the one in her cabin on the *Aphrodite*.

She pulled her gaze from it to Santos. In other circumstances, he'd have kissed her, tumbled her to the bed. Instead, he ran a hand through his hair and began to pace. "I have a problem."

Though she'd been expecting it, her knees still went weak. She perched on the side of the bed and demanded, "Tell me."

"I can't, just that I may have to take action."

"No!" Her heart thudded. She gaped at him as he strode to the window, back toward the bed, then to the window again. "You can't ruin things."

"I may have to. Look, Gwen, you have to—"

She thrust off the bed, hands fisted at her sides. "No, I don't *have to* anything, except make sure the wedding goes off without a hitch. You can't spoil that, Santos, you just can't. And stop pacing, you're driving me crazy."

"Sorry." He came to stand in front of her. "This is a mess."

"That is *not* what I want to hear."

He scrubbed his hands over his face. "Sit down."

When she again sank down on the bed, he grabbed a chair

and pulled it up so he could sit in front of her. It reminded her of the first time he'd come to her cabin. Santos, so handsome and sexy in his white uniform that she'd had trouble believing he was actually attracted to her. Over the next few days, though, he'd convinced her.

She'd believed that not only was he attracted, but more. That in his own way, he cared for her. That he was a good man and he understood how much this wedding meant to her.

She'd even . . . *Damn, that's why this hurt so much.* Despite all her logic and good intentions, she'd let herself fall for this man—as much more than a holiday fling. *Stupid, stupid, stupid.* He wasn't a man like Jonathan; he'd told her that right up front.

He reached for her hands, but she jerked them away. Trying to control her panicked breathing, her feelings of hurt and betrayal, she said grimly, "Tell me what's going on."

"You know it's confidential."

"I don't give a damn. You're planning to fuck up the wedding. I deserve to know what the hell is going on." She'd never been one to swear—not anywhere but inside her head—but now the words came bursting out of her mouth. And they were only half of what she really wanted to say. Pride wouldn't let her reveal her pain and anger over the way he'd charmed his way into her fragile heart and then stomped all over it. How could she have been taken in by a man like her dad?

Santos looked vaguely stunned. After a moment, he said. "Yeah, you do deserve to know. But Gwen, you have a lousy poker face. If I tell you, you'll give it away."

If he hadn't seen her love, then she was getting better at hiding things. "I won't. I promise." She had to shove her personal feelings aside and concentrate on the wedding, and to do that, she needed to know the truth. "Trust me," she demanded.

He sighed. "Okay."

For the next few minutes, she listened, eyes growing wider and wider. "Flynn and Kendra? Criminals? I can't believe it. He seems like a nice guy, even if he's moody. And Kendra's a good person. Santos, we had a really good talk and I felt close to her."

"Just because you talked some girl-talk, that doesn't mean she's innocent." She got the impression he'd barely managed to restrain himself from rolling his eyes.

Folding her arms tightly across her chest, she snapped, "It wasn't *girl-talk*! It was about losing people you love, and how to be strong enough to move on."

"Okay, fine, but most criminals aren't all bad. It may even be that Kavanagh and Kendra plan to use the money to help their families."

She frowned, really not wanting to believe any of this.

"The evidence is piling up," he said. "Piece by piece. All Insurance Assured cares about is getting the money back. To do that, we need to get him—them—back to Canada. And he was at the travel agent this morning, changing his tickets. My bet is that he's going someplace where there's no extradition. Maybe taking her, maybe not. They weren't on the best of terms this morning."

"Damn." She would *not* hyperventilate. "This is unbelievable." And horrible. On all counts. "Why me? Why my wedding? This is so unfair."

"I'm sorry." He took her hands again, and this time she was too upset to pull away. He squeezed them. "I know how much this wedding matters to you. I'd do anything to keep from ruining it."

That did it. She yanked away. "Having one of them arrested would definitely ruin it," she said bitterly. Everything—her love life and her career—was crashing down around her. "When you told me you were an insurance fraud investigator, my first thought was that you'd rock the boat, but I never imagined it would be this bad. You've betrayed me." Though she struggled to hold them back, tears of hurt and anger glazed her eyes.

"Gwen, I'm sorry, but be reasonable. You know my real job comes first."

She blinked back the tears. "Oh yeah, your job's so much more important than me."

"I didn't mean . . . *Gamoto*." He ran a hand through his hair. "Not more important than you. But it's the whole reason I'm here and I have a duty. Look, I tried to make everything really clear. I didn't want you doing what my grandparents did and counting on me for something I might not be able to give you."

She bit her lip to stop its trembling. "God forbid I ever count on you." To support her in her job or to care for her as a person. "Even though, that very first day, you said you wouldn't let me down."

He sighed, then reached over to cup the side of her face. When she tried to pull away, he tightened his grip, holding firmly and forcing her to look into his eyes. "I don't want to let you down. I hate to disappoint you or hurt you the way I did my grandparents. But don't ask me to betray my employer. Don't ask me to let a criminal get away." His dark eyes full of concern and frustration, he added, "Please."

What could she say? No, she couldn't ask Santos to let a criminal escape just so her first exotic wedding went perfectly. Even if he did something to disrupt it, Liz and Peter would still get married, and that was the one thing that mattered most to her.

And yes, he had been up front with her all along. She should have known what she was getting into—job-wise and emotionally—when she got involved with him. She'd been stupid, and that didn't make her bruised heart feel the tiniest bit better. "Okay," she said grudgingly, "you're right. Now, let go of me."

When he loosened his grip, she eased away. With Jonathan, the two of them had been a team. They'd set goals together and always supported each other. She and Santos were the opposite. Their goals were in direct conflict. Likely, so were their emotions. She'd been ready to give him her heart, a gift that would likely have appalled him.

Grimly, she asked, "When are you going to do it? So I can start planning damage control."

"I don't know. There's no way of finding out the date on his new tickets. Right now I have his passport, so unless he gets it back he's not going anywhere."

"What? No, the hotel took everyone's passports."

"For registration. I got them all back. They're in the safe in my room. Until he asks for it, I won't do anything."

"Really?" Should she even dare hope he meant it?

"I promise I won't do anything unless I absolutely have to." He caught her hands and squeezed them. "I really don't want to mess things up for you. You have to believe that."

The ache in her heart made her say, "Why? Why would I believe that?"

He gazed into her eyes, his own dark ones glowing with an odd light, one she hadn't seen there before. "Because I care, Gwen."

Yeah, sure. "If this is how you care for your friends, it's a wonder you have any," she sniped.

The corners of his lips twitched. "You won't cut me a break, will you?"

Something about his expression—a softness that really did look like caring—eased her pain and anger just a little. "Tell me why you deserve one," she said more mildly.

"Because . . ." He swallowed. "I need you."

"To go along with your plans, keep your secrets, and—"

"No." He tightened his grip on her hands, silencing her. "I mean *you*. Not your help, though I need that as well. But you, Gwen. When I started thinking about not seeing you again, I felt empty. I want you in my life. Not just now, but when we get back to Canada. The way I care about you . . . it's more than just as a friend or a lover."

"Oh!" It was just a squeak, one of total astonishment. And the beginning of hope. "But I thought you weren't into—" She broke off before saying *commitment*. He hadn't asked for commitment, just to keep seeing her.

"I don't know what I'm into. This is new. I've never felt this way before and . . ." He shook his head, looking baffled. "I'm confused."

A surprised laugh jolted out of her. "That makes two of us." He'd never felt this way before? She was that special to him?

"Your home is in Vancouver, I'm in Toronto, and I've no idea how we would work things out, I just know I want you in my life."

Before she could tell him she felt the same, he rose and pulled her into his arms, where his warm strength enveloped her. Familiar, comforting, sexy. "Tell me you have feelings for me," he said.

"I do. But—"

Before she could go on, he laughed exultantly and kissed her, a fiery kiss that left her breathless. It was good, so good, but there was something she needed to get straight.

"No, wait." She forced herself to pull out of his arms. "If we're going to go somewhere with these feelings, you have to know something. I told you that I'm just starting to find myself as a single woman, but there's one thing I know. If I get involved with a man, he has to be someone I can trust and rely on."

He nodded slowly. "When I make a promise, you can rely on it. I'd never betray you." Tentatively, he rested his hands on her shoulders.

His hands felt awfully good there. Warm, reassuring. A physical connection, but more than that. A deeper connection that was just as real as his strong, brown hands. He wasn't a serious, cerebral man like Jonathan, but in the ways that mattered he was the same: responsible and trustworthy. Not a man like her father.

And she didn't have to be a control freak any longer. As Peter's dad Phil had said, it wasn't the rigid oak that was strong, it was the flexible willow. She had that kind of strength.

"I believe you." She stared straight into his eyes, so he could see the truth in her own. "And I'd never betray you."

He smiled warmly. "I know that." Then he frowned slightly. "But our job responsibilities are still in conflict."

She shook her head sadly. "And there's no magic answer, is there?"

"What do you say we work on it together? Let's try to find the best solution, so a criminal doesn't escape and so that Liz and Peter get the wonderful wedding they deserve."

Together. He did see the two of them as a team, and he respected and cared about her needs and feelings. There might not be a magic answer, but she already knew that problems arose that didn't have easy, or even good, answers. She'd also learned she was strong and, whatever happened, she'd cope. She and Santos, together, would work it out. "That sounds good to me."

He slipped his hand into his pocket and pulled out a small box, which he handed her. "Then wear these, as a symbol of"—he waved a hand—"everything. Us meeting here in Greece, falling for each other. Of the future."

Their future. When she'd arrived in Greece a week ago, she'd imagined an adventure. Even in her wildest dreams, she couldn't have envisioned this moment. Eagerly, she opened the box and exclaimed with delight. "Earrings like yours. I love them."

When he bent his head to kiss her and she rose joyfully on her toes to meet his lips, she had a strong intuition that one day before long, she'd be saying the words "I love you."

Making Waves

Chapter 1

Aboard the *Aphrodite*,
sailing from Zea Marina to Cape Sounion, Greece—
Friday, May 13, 5:00 P.M.

KENDRA Kirk jumped when the GSM cell phone on the desk in her small private cabin beeped a reminder. She typed another few sentences to finish off a memo to a paralegal back in the Crown Counsel office in Vancouver, which she'd send the next time the *Aphrodite* had Internet access. Then she shut down her laptop and rose, stretching, stiff from two hours at the computer.

It was time to go up on deck for the cocktail and appetizer party that was the official start to Peter and Liz's wedding cruise. The thought of fresh air and, with any luck, sunshine, was appealing. And, though she wasn't a very social person, she was looking forward to seeing her uncles—the fathers of the groom—and her cousin Peter and his fiancée, Liz.

Besides—she gave a quick grin—Peter and her uncles would

lynch her if she missed the party in order to work. In her opinion, it was no sin to be a workaholic, especially when your job was the pursuit of justice. Still, she knew they worried about her. They always had, ever since her teens, when she'd lost her dad, and then her mom had become a semi-invalid.

She changed into olive green capris with a sleeveless top patterned in shades of green, clothes she'd bought specially for this trip. Then she brushed on a touch of eye makeup, blush, and lip gloss, liking the way the colors in the top brought out the green in her gray-green eyes. Luckily, her black hair had enough body that if she kept it short and paid for an excellent cut, she never needed to fuss with it. A flick of a comb, and she was ready.

Taking the stairs, she tried to remember the last time she'd goofed off. A few years ago, when she'd gone to a Canadian Bar Association conference in Québec City, she'd stayed a few days to explore the city and visit Montréal. And—her lips curved at the memory—lucked into a fling with another lawyer, a Québécois man who spoke English with a sexy French accent. A two-day affair that suited her perfectly; a man who didn't ask more from her than she wanted, or was able, to give. Work and family were her priorities.

Not that she was at all averse to orgasms. The occasional sex partner like Phillippe provided fuel for masturbation fantasies. Yes, most of her orgasms came from her own fingers and a couple of battery-operated toys, a system that was efficient and uncomplicated.

She emerged onto the main deck, where a bright sun, the deep blue sea, and white sails against a brighter blue sky made her smile again.

Most of the other guests had already arrived and were either sitting at small tables snacking on appetizers or leaning on the ship's railing watching the coast as it slipped by. She felt a moment's pang that her mother couldn't be here, but being with strangers made her mom anxious and travel terrified her. Oh well, there'd be lots of photos of the cruise and wedding, and Kendra would buy gifts to take home.

Kendra waved to Peter and Liz, who stood amid a circle of friends, arms around each other, looking summery and happy. Uncle William and his husband, Phil, both slender, stylish men in their late fifties, sat at a table talking to the *Aphrodite*'s cruise director, Santos, who she'd met when she came aboard. The Greek was distinctly hot, the white uniform setting off his dark, dashing good looks. If she was into another fling, Santos would definitely be fling-worthy. He even had a delicious hint of an accent.

She was due for some male hands-on sex and a source of fresh fantasies. Disconcertingly, over the past few months she'd been having particularly steamy fantasies about the last man in the world she should be attracted to. One she had only touched once, and had prosecuted for white-collar crime. She was a black-and-white thinker and her analytical brain couldn't understand how a woman could be attracted to a criminal, yet at night her body had ideas of its own. She'd be so much happier if she could replace images of Flynn Kavanagh with the sexy Santos.

Still, she wasn't about to fool around with a man right under the eyes of her family.

She walked over to the table where Greek appetizers—the food kind, not the male kind—were laid out attractively, and served herself spinach pie, mini meatballs, pita bread, and hummus. Not being the adventurous type, she steered clear of the deep-fried squid. A crew member came over and offered her a drink, and she asked for dry white wine.

"I'll bring it to you," he said with a smile.

"I'll be at the table over there." She pointed to her uncles' table. Santos was standing, apparently encouraging another couple—older, with glasses, gray hair under travel hats, and binoculars around their necks—to join her uncles.

The newcomers sat, and Santos moved off to talk to someone else.

When Kendra walked over, her uncles both rose, beaming. She'd been a child when William's wife—the mother of the groom, Peter—had died. A few years later he and Phil had gotten together, and both uncles had been there for her when her family fell apart. Surrogate fathers, almost.

The men barely let her put down her plate before smothering her with hugs and kisses. She returned the embraces warmly. "Hi, Uncle William, Uncle Phil. It's so good to see you." Usually she and her mom got together with them every couple of weeks, but she'd been working extra hard lately so it had been more than a month since she'd seen them.

"You, too, hon," William said. "Hardly recognized you in normal clothes."

She caught the other couple at the table exchanging quizzical glances. "Lawyer suits, he means," she explained. "Hi, I'm Kendra Kirk, Peter's cousin."

"John and Henrietta Tippett." The man spoke with an English accent. "Liz's parents."

"I'm so happy to meet you. But I didn't realize this was a gathering of in-laws. I don't want to intrude."

"No, no, please do," Henrietta said, looking almost relieved. Then, flustered, "I mean, not intrude, you're certainly not doing that, just that . . ."

"We're pleased to have you join us," her husband rescued her.

It was William and Phil's turn to exchange glances. Amused ones. Kendra recalled that Liz had grown up in a tiny English village, and she guessed that the cosmopolitan gay married couple might be a bit foreign to the bride's parents. Of course, the English villagers with binoculars slung around their necks wouldn't be the typical sight in downtown Vancouver either.

"Liz mentioned that you came to Greece for your anniversary one year," the gregarious Phil said to the Tippetts as Kendra dug into her plateful of food.

She savored a spicy meatball as John said, "Yes, our twenty-fifth. That was, er, how long ago, dear?"

"We're going on forty-four years now. Our Liz was an unexpected blessing rather late in our marriage," she explained. "So let me see, that would make it—"

At that moment, the crew member delivered Kendra's wine and she thanked him. Behind him, she caught sight of a man walking from the deck into the dining room. What an odd coincidence. Tall and rangy in beige pants and a short-sleeved white shirt, with auburn hair that glinted under the sun, he looked a little like Flynn Kavanagh, the man who'd starred in her recent sexual fantasies.

Taking a sip of wine, deliciously dry and tangy, she realized she'd lost the thread of the conversation. One of the Tippetts must have asked her uncles if they'd ever been to Greece before.

"No," William said, "the closest we've come was Italy, on our honeymoon."

Henrietta took a rather large swallow of red wine. "Er, your honeymoon. Italy. How delightful."

Kendra caught Phil's eyes, which were dancing. "Of course," he said, "you know William's wife was Greek, don't you?" Peter had told Kendra that his mom's family had been invited on the cruise but, coming from a small village in Crete and not knowing any of the other guests, they'd declined. They'd be at the wedding itself, and Peter and Liz would spend some time with them during their honeymoon.

"I believe we did hear that," John murmured. "Greece is such a beautiful country for a wedding. Peter and Liz's, I mean. Er, you didn't get married here, did you? I mean, the first time?"

Kendra had trouble keeping her mouth straight, and could see her uncles were having the same problem. Hurriedly she raised her wineglass to her mouth to hide her grin.

"No," William said. "The first was in Vancouver. And the second as well, because of course there aren't that many places where two men can marry."

"No, I suppose not," John said.

"Over the years," William said philosophically, "we've learned when to stand on principle and when to compromise."

Henrietta nodded thoughtfully. "Very true. This wedding, for example." She touched her husband's arm. "Of course John and I wanted Liz to get married in the church where she was christened, but the important thing is that she's found a man she loves."

"Exactly," Phil chimed in. "Love's the most important thing in life."

Something twinged in Kendra's heart. Once, she'd had girlish dreams of romance and marriage. For some couples, like the two at this table, happily ever afters were possible. But that hadn't happened for her parents, and she couldn't see trusting in such a tenuous dream. Her work was concrete and rewarding and it, along with her family, was all she needed in life.

She lifted a forkful of spanakopita to her mouth, then froze as the auburn-haired man walked back out on deck, a couple of drink glasses in his hands.

Oh my God! It *was* Kavanagh.

Automatically, she ducked her head, fork clattering down on her plate, hoping he wouldn't look her way. Unless he had a double, the man she'd been fantasizing about—the man she'd prosecuted for stealing five million dollars—was aboard the *Aphrodite*!

Warily, she gazed up from under her eyelashes, checking that he'd disappeared from her line of sight. Then she raised her head and, ignoring the uneaten bite of spanakopita, took a hearty slug of wine. What was he doing here?

He was free to go where he wanted, of course. She, who at the age of twenty-nine had the highest conviction rate in the province, had lost that particular trial though she'd prosecuted it to the best of her ability. Her boss, Dorothy Brant, had insisted she press charges despite Kendra's professional opinion that there wasn't enough evidence to convict. And Kendra had agreed, because she trusted Dorothy's judgment and also out of loyalty: The woman had been Kendra's role model and mentor since her dad died. Also, Kendra had wondered if her own judgment had been affected by her attraction to Kavanagh.

An attraction that had flared the moment she first bumped—literally—into him.

Into her mind flashed that memory. She'd been hurrying to a meeting in one of the downtown towers that housed a number of law firms, juggling her purse, briefcase, damp umbrella, and cardboard cup of freshly purchased takeout coffee. Rushing to fling herself between the closing doors of an elevator, she caught a heel and tilted forward. Straight into the arms of a tall, rangy man with auburn hair and green eyes that sparked with first surprise and then shock as her scorching hot coffee splattered all over his crisp white shirt.

Strong hands caught her forearms, no doubt to steady her, yet they had the opposite effect. Something zingy and unsettling trembled through her as she stared into dazzling green eyes framed by thick, mink brown lashes. Eyes that were staring back just as hard, as if he'd forgotten the coffee and was totally focused on her.

Behind her, the elevator door closed, caging her alone with him.

Now his eyes began to twinkle and he said, with a slight Irish lilt, "And here I was just wishing for a nice hot cup of coffee."

She forced herself to pull free from his grip and push the button for the twentieth floor. "You probably didn't want to wear it, though. I'm so sorry. Are you all right?" God, he was cute.

"Surprisingly so." Gingerly he touched the front of the sodden shirt, where it molded to a sculpted chest. "I'm thinking it's likely to be the best thing that'll happen to me all day."

A compliment? Was he flirting? Did she want him to? The instant, powerful attraction she felt was new for her.

The elevator button dinged, and she saw they'd reached her floor. He started to say something, but she cut him off. "Of course I'll pay to have your shirt cleaned." Reaching through the open elevator doors, she dumped her briefcase, umbrella, and near-empty coffee cup on the carpeted floor outside. Bracing her back against one of the sliding doors to hold it open, she reached into her purse. "Let me give you my card." Now he'd have her number. If he called, if he did flirt, she'd decide what she wanted to do.

"Sure and I was just going to ask for your number," he said with a smile. He glanced down at the card and his face tightened.

That had been her last sight of him as the doors slid shut.

A few days later, she'd been handed the file on Flynn Kavanagh, an IT consultant who was the prime suspect in the theft of five million dollars from a major law firm. She'd gazed at the photo, immediately recognizing her elevator companion and understanding the reason for his sour expression and his comment about the spilled coffee being the highlight of his day. Likely, he'd been on his way to a lawyer appointment.

Now, she took another slug of wine and forced herself to focus on the present. Why was Kavanagh here? Who had invited him? Surely he wouldn't have come if he knew she'd be on board. Damn, this could be nasty.

She went to take another drink and discovered her glass was empty. Glancing around the table, she realized the Tippetts were discoursing enthusiastically on the birds to be found in the Cyclades Islands and her uncles were politely feigning interest. "Excuse me a moment." She held up her wineglass in explanation, then hurried inside to the bar.

There, she asked for a refill and climbed up onto a bar stool to wait.

Behind her, a male voice said, "And here I am, back again. One of the ladies is wondering if you can make her a drink called a Heat Wave." The voice had the slight Irish lilt she remembered all too well.

She squared her shoulders and, with a sense of inevitability, swung around on the stool to face Flynn Kavanagh.

STUNNED, all Flynn could do was gape when he found himself face-to-face with the last woman he'd expected to see. This afternoon, Kendra Kirk was casual in a summery top and capris rather than a business suit, but no question that this was the woman who'd haunted his steamiest dreams. The one who'd spilled burning hot coffee all over him and bewitched him with luminous gray-green eyes.

No, fuck it, this was the woman who'd caused his real-life nightmares. The one who'd persecuted him. He'd come on this cruise in hopes of clearing his mind and beginning to plan the future, and now the past had confronted him.

Anger rushed through him in a red-hot tide. Grinding the words out with contempt, he said, "What the hell are you doing here?" His body felt so taut, it almost vibrated. He wanted to shake her, hit her. Dammit, he wanted to kiss the bitch. During the trial, he'd had days to ponder how a man could want to fuck a woman he hated.

She'd held all the power—the power to ruin his life—and she'd bloody well done it.

She glanced around, perhaps checking whether any guests were in earshot. "We need to talk. Let's not make a scene." A long, elegant finger pointed toward the farthest corner of the bar, deserted because all the guests were outside.

"Oh, by all means, we wouldn't want to make a scene," he said sarcastically. The woman was calm and in control. Had she known he'd be here? Had she actually come on this cruise knowing they'd see each other every day? Just how coldhearted could she be?

When she hopped off the stool, the ship lurched slightly and she almost lost her balance.

Instinctively, he grabbed her shoulders to steady her. Her bare skin, warm and soft under his fingers, sent a jolt of arousal through him. The same arousal he'd felt when she'd tripped into that elevator and he had caught her.

Arousal that was irrational and completely unwelcome. He let go as if she'd singed him, and stalked over to the table she'd indicated, though restless energy wouldn't let him sit.

When she came to stand in front of him, he demanded, "Did you know I'd be here?"

She was tall, maybe five ten, but still several inches shorter than he, so she had to tilt her head up to look at him. Her eyes, fringed in long black lashes, were greener than he remembered. Cool, a little mysterious. He hated that he found her so attractive.

"No, I didn't know," she said, her voice as cool and controlled as her face.

"You didn't look surprised when you saw me."

"I noticed you earlier, when you walked out of the bar. Believe me, I had no idea you'd be on this cruise. Who invited you?"

"I'm a friend of Liz's. Why are you here?"

"I'm Peter's cousin." She frowned. "Liz didn't know about . . ."

"The trumped-up charge? The persecution?"

"The trial," she said grimly.

"She knew, but I may not have mentioned your name." He'd referred to Kendra as "the bitch" and "my persecutor." He'd been so wrapped up in his problems that, when Liz got engaged, he'd barely registered that her fiancé's name was Peter, much less that his surname was the same as Kendra Kirk's.

He'd RSVP'd "no" to the wedding invitation, but Liz had

dragged him out for a drink and told him to stop wallowing in misery. She said a holiday would give him a fresh perspective so he could sort out what to do next. Even though the jury had acquitted him, the trial had cost him his big clients and he'd had to fold his IT consulting business. His girlfriend had deserted him, too, either doubting his innocence or not wanting to date a guy with a tainted reputation.

He gave a snort of disgust at the irony of the whole damned situation.

"What?" Kendra asked.

"Life just won't cut me a break." He sure as hell wasn't going to gain perspective with her around.

"Nor me," she muttered. "You're definitely not the person I most wanted to see." Then her dark lashes flickered downward and color stained her cheeks.

Sexual awareness, a strange zing of energy, arced between them. She felt it, too, that bizarrely inappropriate attraction. She gazed up again, eyes wide and searching, pink lips parted.

He had the odd wish that they could undo the past, all the way back to that first meeting in the elevator. He wanted her to see him for who he really was: a decent guy who'd either been framed or had the worst imaginable luck. And he wanted to see her as someone other than the lawyer who'd ruined his life.

A burst of animated voices made him glance toward the bar. The Greek cruise director and a handful of guests stood there, discussing drinks. Carefree, as people should be on holiday.

Bitterness soured his mouth. Would he ever be carefree again? "Are you going to tell everyone?" he asked roughly.

Color stained her cheeks. "Tell them . . ." She shook her head as if clearing it. "You mean about the trial?"

He scowled. What else could there be? The attraction neither of them would ever act on?

"No," she said quickly, "there's no reason to. You had a fair trial and—"

"Fair? Being charged and taken to trial wasn't fair. The way you went after me, like it was a witch hunt, wasn't fair. I didn't fucking do it, don't you get that?"

Those huge eyes searched his face. She bit her lip. "This isn't the time or place to discuss it."

Over by the bar, the cruise director—what was his name? Santos?—was eyeing them with a speculative gaze. Just what Flynn needed: everyone onboard knowing about his past. Voice low, he said, "No, it's not."

"But . . . maybe we should, if we can find an opportunity."

He deliberated. "Perhaps." Otherwise, he'd carry this load of anger, frustration, and—damn it—lust around with him for the whole cruise.

"So, should we pretend we never met before today? That way, we won't have to explain the circumstances."

"Yeah." He figured she was doing it to save embarrassment for Peter and Liz, not as a favor to him, but he was grateful all the same.

No, wait. He wouldn't be grateful to this woman. She owed him—a debt so huge it could never be repaid.

She nodded, then turned and walked away.

How many times had he seen her saunter back and forth across the courtroom with that same long-legged grace, the hint of a hip sway under the shapeless barrister's robe? Today, she seemed less sure of herself, and much more sensual. The clingy capris highlighted the enticing curves of her hips, butt, and legs. This was the first time he'd seen her bare arms, as soft and creamy as the face he'd memorized in court. The face that had haunted vividly sexual dreams that left him furious with himself for desiring a woman he hated.

The last time they'd spoken face-to-face, he'd been in the courtroom under oath and she'd been cross-examining him. She'd been the enemy.

Today, on a cruise ship in Greece, they were wedding guests. Bottom line: He was a man and she was a woman. She was as aware of that fact as he was. Not that they'd do anything about it.

Across the room, she leaned against the bar beside Santos and said something to the bartender.

Flynn's gaze fixed on the curves of her butt. He imagined her bent over the bar, bare-assed, as he took her from behind. His cock swelled.

The bartender handed her a glass of white wine. Santos, speaking quietly, said something to her.

She tossed a quick, almost scornful glance in Flynn's direction. Her voice carried clearly across the room. "No, everything's fine. I can handle him without help."

Handle him. She'd tried that once, and neither of them had come out winners.

He watched as she went out on deck with the cruise director, then went over to the bar. He'd like a double Scotch, but had learned alcohol solved nothing. Instead, he settled for a Mythos beer. The bartender handed him the bottle along with a fruity drink. "The Heat Wave you asked for earlier," he said when Flynn looked surprised.

"Right. Thanks." He was about to take a slug of beer when another male voice said, "Girlfriend troubles?"

"What?" It was Santos again. Girlfriend? In that elevator when they first met, he'd planned to call her. Until he'd read her card. "Oh, her? No, I don't even know her. Excuse me, a lady at my table's waiting for her drink."

If only it were true that he didn't know Kendra Kirk. Since he'd met her, his life had been one major fuckup, and it showed no signs of improving.

Chapter 2

IF Kendra Kirk hadn't been present, Flynn might have actually enjoyed himself that night. The ruins of the temple at Cape Sounion were spectacular, with a "time immemorial" sense that could have helped him put his own problems in perspective if the lawyer hadn't been there to keep them fresh in his mind.

He and she stayed out of each other's way, but it was impossible to ignore her. Tonight she wore white pants, as did many of the women, yet her simple white sweater, together with her elegantly cut short black hair, made her as striking as the view.

His gaze kept drifting from the sunset to Kendra, and he often caught her glancing back.

He was furious, aroused, confused, and none of that was going away until he could talk to her. He'd hoped, amid the crowd of sightseers brought in by tour buses, that there might be an opportunity, but the wedding planner kept close track of her charges. When the tourist site was closing for the night and everyone headed back down the hill, Gwen even hung back with Santos, no doubt counting heads.

Resigned, Flynn went with the group as they returned to the
Aphrodite.

Aboard, a casual dinner was served buffet style: grilled souvlaki
along with Greek-style rice, potatoes, and salad. He chose a skewer
of lamb and another of prawns, then glanced around, wondering
where to sit. Kendra was at a table with some young people he didn't
know. As if feeling his gaze on her, she glanced up, then quickly
away again.

Santos, who was sitting with a middle-aged couple and two pretty
blondes, motioned toward an empty chair beside him, but another
waving hand caught Flynn's attention. It was Liz, seated with Peter
and her parents. She popped to her feet and headed toward him.

He sent a "thanks anyhow" smile in Santos's direction, then
went to meet Liz. "Having a good time?" he asked.

"Brilliant!" Her sparkling eyes and bright smile confirmed it.
She tilted her head and said, in her English accent, "And you, Flynn?
Are you having fun?"

Evasively, he said, "A lovely place, nice people, what's not to like?"

"You *so* need a holiday. It was total crap what happened to you."

Unlike his ex-girlfriend, Liz had been on his side with no questions or doubts from the day he'd been charged. They'd only known
each other a couple of years, yet she'd believed in him. "Thanks, Liz."

"How are Ray and your mom? I'm sorry I had to stop my sessions with Ray because of the wedding. I know he gets upset when
his routines are disturbed."

Flynn and Liz had met when she, a psychology student, had volunteered at social skills coaching sessions for kids with Asperger's syndrome. Flynn's brother, Ray, thirteen at the time, had connected with
her, which was rare for him. Flynn and his mom had met her, then
asked her to do private coaching two or three times a week. Liz was
outgoing and generous, and along the way they'd all become friends.
Now she was in her master's program, doing her thesis on Asperger's.

"They're doing okay. It'll help Ray learn to be more flexible."

She grinned. "We all have our strengths and weaknesses. He may not be flexible but he's brilliant in maths." She bumped her shoulder against his. "Even smarter than his big brother. Now come on, your dinner's getting cold."

He caught her arm. "Liz, does anyone else know about the trial?"

Her expression sobered. "Well, Peter, in general terms. Like, that the police couldn't catch the real criminal so they went after you. He knows you're innocent."

"Because you said so? Thanks. How about your family and friends, or Peter's?"

"I haven't mentioned it to anyone else. Peter wouldn't either. Flynn, this week you're supposed to forget all about it. That's why I insisted you come."

Across the deck, Kendra Kirk glanced up again, then deliberately away.

No, this week there'd be no forgetting the past.

POKING at her dinner, Kendra watched Flynn looking so friendly with Liz. He'd said Peter's fiancée knew about his trial, and obviously they were still friends. Kendra didn't know Liz well, but she seemed like a nice person, and Peter had good judgment. Hard to believe her cousin would marry a woman who'd befriend a criminal.

Flynn had always maintained his innocence, and when he'd done it again a few hours ago, his voice had rung with passion and conviction. It had on the stand as well. He'd convinced the jury to acquit—but of course his testimony had been thoroughly rehearsed, no doubt every word and nuance of expression fine-tuned and practiced with his lawyer.

Yet even when she'd been building the strongest possible case against him, she'd had doubts. Among the other Crown Counsel she was known as having a sixth sense, one that helped her decide when to press charges and when not to. That instinct was largely responsible for her high conviction rate: If she charged someone with a crime, they were guilty and she could prove it. With Flynn, she hadn't felt that certainty.

Still, she had trusted her boss's experience and judgment. Dorothy Brant, the assistant deputy attorney general, was a law school classmate of one of the partners who owned the business that had been ripped off, and she wanted Flynn in jail.

After the jury acquitted, Kendra had done some atypical second-guessing. Had her attraction to Flynn swayed her judgment, or even her presentation of the case? Or was her gut instinct right, in which case refusing to stand up to Dorothy had ruined the life of a man who might be innocent? But then she'd realized she was being ridiculous. She'd done her job to the best of her ability, the jury had made its decision, and it was time to put the past behind her and move on. People who let the past weigh them down could end up like her parents.

But now, with Flynn here on the *Aphrodite*, the past had intruded into the present. They needed to decide how to deal with that so their tensions didn't ruin Peter and Liz's wedding cruise.

Most of the guests were yawning, jet-lagged and tired from long hours of travel, fresh air, and excitement, not to mention the effects of Greek wine. It was dark, with only a few lights on deck to supplement the moon and stars in the clear sky above. Though it wasn't eleven yet, a number of guests headed off to bed. A few others claimed spots at the railing to stargaze, talk quietly, or embrace. It was romantic.

Not that romance was her thing. That kind of emotion was messy. Trusting someone else was dangerous. People ended up getting hurt. She'd learned that when her father died and her mother disintegrated, and the lesson was reinforced each day as new files crossed her desk. It was much easier—safer—to stay uninvolved.

Flynn, who'd been sitting with Peter, Liz, and Liz's parents, rose and held Mrs. Tippett's chair as the woman got up. The Tippetts linked arms and, both stifling yawns, headed inside. Peter and Liz, arms around each other's waists, headed for the bow of the ship.

When Flynn gazed in Kendra's direction, she cocked her head unobtrusively in the direction of the stern. A moment later, she excused herself to the two people still left at her table, and strolled casually toward the back of the ship.

When she got there, she realized there were too many other guests scattered along the railing to allow for privacy. Sighing, she turned to retrace her steps only to find Flynn so close behind her that he had to catch her arms to keep her from crashing into him.

That was the third time she'd stumbled into him and the third that he'd caught her. Even through her sweater, she felt the shock of his touch. Almost like static electricity, but more pleasant.

She jerked back. "Sorry, I didn't know you were there." She spoke in the same hushed tone others on deck were using, but chose neutral words, knowing someone might overhear.

"Nice night, isn't it?" His tone had an artificial politeness, the anger that had been in it earlier suppressed, as he stepped past her to lean his forearms on the ship's wooden rail.

"Lovely." She did the same, careful to leave inches between their arms.

"Is that the Big Dipper?" he asked, pointing.

"Sorry, I've never been a stargazer." Then, under her breath, "We need to discuss this situation."

"Yeah," he said firmly. "But not where anyone can overhear, and that's a problem. There's no privacy on this ship. Not even in the cabins."

He assumed that she, like the other guests, shared a cabin. Instead, she'd paid extra for a private one, a place where she could work without distraction.

She bit her lip. No, she didn't believe he posed a threat—and if she raised her voice, much less screamed, her neighbors would hear.

The idea of being alone with him in that small space with a double bed was disturbing for an entirely different reason.

How ridiculous. The thing that mattered was hearing what he had to say and the two of them deciding how to act. Putting it off until tomorrow wouldn't solve anything. "I have a single cabin," she said softly, without inflection.

The night was quiet enough that she heard him swallow. In a voice barely louder than the soft ocean breeze, with that lilting accent he said, "If that's by way of being an invitation, you know what message we'll be sending to the other guests."

That they were going to have sex. Just like in her fantasies. "I don't want that," she said, a little too firmly, a little too loudly.

He continued to study the sky, and she noted how starlight etched and sharpened his strong features and burnished his hair. "Me either," he said. "I could sneak in when everyone's settled down for the night so no one thinks we're having a tryst."

"A tryst?" She cocked an eyebrow.

He gave a small, quick smile, the first she'd seen from him. Was that a dimple in his cheek, or just a shadow? "My ma's word," he said. "She's a bit of a romantic, despite everything."

What did that *everything* refer to? As best she recalled, his mother was a single parent and he had a half brother with some kind of learning disability. So, his mom had loved and lost twice?

Why should she care about his mother, his family, or how supremely hot he looked in the starlight? She just needed to resolve their current dilemma. And after that, she needed a lengthy session with the sex toy she'd packed in her cosmetic bag. It had obviously been way too long since she'd had an orgasm, or she wouldn't be feeling this edgy, achy need.

"My cabin," she said under her breath. "Bottom deck, number 3C. What about your roommate? Who is it?"

"A cousin of Liz's from England. I'll wait until he's sound asleep."

"Good. I'll leave the door unlocked and—"

A female giggle interrupted her and she turned to see a couple going at it hot and heavy. Friends of Liz's; she didn't recall their names. The young woman's leg wrapped around the man as if she was trying to climb him. "We can't," the girl said breathily. "Not here." But her tone said she wanted to.

Arousal pulsed warmly in Kendra's veins. Yeah, she could understand the appeal. A man's strong arms around you, his rigid cock exerting delicious pressure in exactly the right spot . . .

"We should leave them to it," Flynn said.

She tore her gaze away from the intertwined couple to look at him, trying to hide that she was turned on. Flynn stared down at her with an intensity that made her heart race, that made her envision him shoving her against the rail and taking her.

The temptation to sway forward, to press up against him, was nearly irresistible. She sensed he felt it, too, this irrational attraction. She cleared her throat and said dryly, "I hope the ship's railing is sturdy."

"Is that all they make you think of?"

No, the lovers made her think of stripping off her pants and underwear, unzipping his fly, and screwing his brains out. "What else?" she managed to toss off casually.

LATER, in her cabin, wearing her sleeveless green blouse and white pants, Kendra felt strangely vulnerable. She almost wished for one of her tailored pantsuits. Armor. Being a lawyer gave her certainty, position, a way of facing a chaotic world.

Strength and confidence were crucial. Her parents had lacked them. When they'd been defrauded, her dad hadn't been able to cope and had taken his own life. Her mom, his partner in work and in life, fell apart and became a semi-invalid. Kendra had been fifteen.

When Kendra talked to her mom's second cousin Dorothy Brant, then an ambitious Crown Counsel, at her dad's funeral, she found her purpose in life: bringing criminals to justice. Dorothy took her under her wing, providing a role model, mentorship, and ultimately a job when Kendra graduated top of her class from law school. The goal Kendra had set in her teens still gave her an identity, confidence, the knowledge that she was making the world a better place.

That was what she needed to hang on to, and not let herself be distracted by her silly fascination with Flynn Kavanagh.

She turned on her computer, unlocked her briefcase, and extracted a file. Yes, she was due holidays, but she'd never been a vacation person. She had disappointed Dorothy by losing the Kavanagh case and was working extra hard to make up for it. Dorothy wasn't a soft person, not the kind to bond emotionally with, but her respect and approval meant everything to Kendra. The fact that she'd told Kendra she was off her game and needed a break only made her more determined to prove herself.

Tonight, Kendra's usual ability to focus deserted her, but she still managed to be productive for more than an hour. Then the door opened and Flynn stepped inside, tall and handsome, his green eyes smoldering with emotions she couldn't read.

Too bad her cabin didn't have a window or even a porthole. She felt claustrophobic and short of breath. Hurriedly, she saved and closed the document she'd been working on, then locked the file folder in her briefcase.

When she turned back to him, he was still standing just inside the closed door, arms crossed over his chest.

"Have a seat," she offered, trying not to flush as she gestured toward the bed. The cabin only had one chair. "Let's keep our voices down so we don't wake my neighbors."

He sat, and she turned the chair to face him, sitting square in it with her shoulders back. Taking control, she said, "We need to agree on how we're going to act this week. Peter and Liz are what's important, not our . . . differences."

"Differences? You ruined my life, woman." He growled the words in a low voice. She heard anger and bitterness, but also pain, frustration, and a hint of bewilderment.

Was he as confused about her as she was about him?

Steadying herself, she said evenly, "You did that yourself, Mr. Kavanagh."

"Fuck with the *mister.* It reminds me of being in court. Call me Flynn." He raked his hair back. "And no, I did nothing of the sort."

Her attraction to him was magnified in close quarters and it was hard to keep her focus. "Whether or not we agree on that, we need to put the past behind us."

"Easy for you, I was just another *case.* For me, it's my life. My whole damned life has been ruined. Because *you* went and charged me with a crime I didn't commit."

There was no purpose to rehashing this, but it seemed he wouldn't let it go. And maybe she was curious about what he'd say. "When we spoke earlier, you said you're innocent."

"I've been saying that since the beginning. It's true."

"Then tell me about it."

He interlocked his fingers, pressing hard enough that she could see the tension in them. Then he sighed and dropped his locked hands to his lap. "You've heard the whole story, and you didn't believe me then. Why should I go through it again?"

She should let this go, yet something drove her to say, "Because I want to hear it in your own words. And I'm guessing you want to tell it, or you wouldn't be here."

He muttered something under his breath, a curse she didn't catch.

To get him going, so he wouldn't just reiterate the testimony he'd given in court, she said, "Tell me about your IT work."

Staring down at his hands, he began slowly. "I've been an IT consultant since I got my computer science degree. At first I worked for a tech firm, but I fancied being my own boss, doing things my way. I set up my firm and built my client list."

His gaze lifted to meet hers, green eyes dark in the rather dim light of the cabin. "I enjoyed the work, each day bringing a different challenge." His eyes narrowed. "Yes, I had access to everyone's private information, both business and personal. But never did I abuse that trust. I wouldn't steal paper clips from a client, much less five mil."

"Paper clips aren't worth stealing."

"Jesus, woman, d'you always interpret things so literally?" His accent made *Jesus* sound like *Jaysus*.

Her chin lifted. "I deal in black-and-white, not shades of gray." It was something Dorothy had said at the funeral all those years ago, and Kendra had loved the sense of certainty it conveyed. Bad guys should pay for their crimes. Period.

"I know all about your black-and-white. Except this time you chose the wrong color."

She made her strongest argument. "The only person aside from the partners who had access to all the passwords, access codes, and details of the security system was you. You admitted that on the stand."

He leaned forward so his face was only inches from hers, his eyes shooting sparks. "But I didn't *do* it. Maybe one of the partners did."

She shook her head. "Neither had a motive, and neither has the tech skill."

"Then someone managed, by hard work or luck, to break all the codes. Like my expert witness said on the stand, it can be done. And speaking of motive, you know I had none."

"Money's one of the strongest motives," she said with certainty. "You have a single parent mom who only works part-time and a half brother with special needs. You're the main support of the family."

"And I make—*made*—good money. Plenty to meet our needs. I'm not a criminal, Kendra."

It was the first time he'd spoken her name, and he'd done it without being invited. Even though he said it in anger, it rolled off his tongue with a touch of Irish brogue to fancy it up, and she had the odd thought, *What a pretty name that is.*

"I had no more motive than either of the firm's partners," he went on. "Less. They kept their business, and the insurance company paid out. I lost my business because many of my clients weren't sure they could trust me."

He'd lost his business. It was true that a "not guilty" verdict didn't equal "innocent" unless the real criminal was found and convicted. Even if his clients wanted to believe in him, how could they take that risk?

If he was innocent and she'd wrongly prosecuted him . . . Her mouth dry, she swallowed again. Hard.

"Yes, I have some money put by," he said, "but I have to start again. Find some other career, maybe retrain." He did look sincere, even to the uncertainty in his eyes that suggested he had no clear vision of his future.

"If you'd stolen the money, you'd have it offshore," she countered. "You'd find a way of using it. You're smart enough to figure that out."

"I am." He clipped out the two words, then stared her down.

His gaze was so intent, she sucked in a breath in anticipation of what he'd say next.

"And if I wanted to steal five million dollars, I'm smart enough to do it without having the circumstantial evidence point straight back at me."

She let the breath out slowly, between slightly parted lips. There it was, the issue that had given her the most trouble. As she'd told Dorothy, Flynn was a very bright man, highly skilled and experienced with information technology. Her boss had reminded her that most criminals got caught because they did something stupid, and said Flynn was no exception.

The police had found no other suspects, no evidence that pointed elsewhere. Dorothy had convinced Kendra he was the guilty party. "Your lawyer made the cleverness argument in court very successfully," Kendra said.

"And I was acquitted. Damn it, Kendra, I'm innocent."

She gazed into his eyes, drawing on her sixth sense, trying to read into his mind, his heart. If he spoke the truth, then, oh, God, what had she done to him? Quietly she pointed out, "The trial's over. Even if you persuaded me, it wouldn't change anything."

"It would." Startling her, he grabbed her hands and held them tightly. "You'd believe me."

The heat of his hands, the blaze in his eyes, made her tremble. "Why does that matter?"

"I don't know!"

"Shh, keep your voice down."

"I don't know why it matters, but it does."

His intensity, his closeness, the tension between them made her cheeks burn. She wanted to raise her hands to cover them, but he'd trapped both hands in his. "I don't know you, Flynn." She spoke his name for the first time. "How can I just change my mind and believe you after I spent months preparing the case, weeks in court?"

His fingers bit into her hands. "You shouldn't have prosecuted in the first place."

"I was doing my job," she said sharply.

"You honestly believed I was guilty, and you had enough evidence to convict me?"

Chapter 3

FLYNN expected a firm "yes," but instead Kendra's lashes drifted down and she studied their hands, still locked together on her lap. She'd told him she dealt in black-and-white, but now he sensed ambivalence.

Finally, she looked up. "My office made a decision. We need to be tough on white-collar crime." Her voice strengthened. "Some people think it's just money, but that's not true. People are hurt and the consequences can be horrible."

"Yeah." He released her hands and crossed his arms over his chest. "Believe me, I know that. In this case, I got hurt. It felt like you had it in for me." Begrudgingly, he added, "My lawyer said you had a rep for being tough but fair."

"It's the Crown's job to present the evidence fairly and to prosecute vigorously."

Frustrated, he rubbed his hands over his face. "I hate your job."

She gave a quick, surprised snort. Then she said, "It's a good job, an important one. Mostly, I get it right."

"And sometimes you don't." The injustice of that still burned like acid in his veins—side by side with the arousal that being this close to her sparked in him. Bizarre that those two things could coexist.

He lowered his hands and gazed into those pretty greenish gray eyes. "And now, Kendra? Do you still believe you got it right?"

In a voice so low he could barely hear, she said, "I don't know." Then she shoved her chair back and stood, not touching him. "I have to think this over. Alone."

He stood and moved closer, deliberately invading her space. "Why?" Why couldn't she trust him?

She gazed up defiantly. "It's my process. I gather information, then reflect. Is there anything else you want to tell me?"

He drew in a breath, then let it out. "Think about what my mother said on the stand. About how she raised me, and the kind of man I turned into."

"She's hardly an unbiased witness."

"She's an honest woman," he said fiercely. "I'm asking you to be the same. Be honest with yourself, and then with me."

She nodded slowly. Then her dark brows kinked. "Flynn, I still don't understand why this is so important to you."

He could smell her scent, something flowery and feminine. Her eyes were wide and earnest, her pink lips parted slightly.

Emotions swirled in an uneasy jumble, making him shift restlessly. That same crazy mix of anger and lust, laced now with hope. Hope for what, he didn't even know.

"Flynn?" That one syllable left her mouth open in a perfect position for a kiss.

Without a moment's pause or reflection, he leaned down, grabbed her face between both hands, and pressed his lips to hers with the force of all those roiling emotions.

For a moment she didn't respond, and he wondered, in some dim recess of his brain, if she was going to haul back and slap him.

Then she surged up on her toes, breasts grazing his chest, and kissed him back with just as much fire.

The passion that zapped between them gave him an instant hard-on. Plunging deep into the kiss, he let go of her face and grabbed her hips, bringing her flush up against him. His hands slid around to the curves of her butt, grasping them firmly and dragging her even tighter against him as he ground into the soft flesh of her belly.

Hungrily, demandingly, he pillaged her mouth.

She darted her tongue between his lips, hands gripping his head and holding him exactly where she wanted him.

But he wasn't giving up control to this woman. His tongue dueled with hers and chased it back into her mouth, then he nipped her lip, hard.

She moaned and ground her hips against him until he thought he'd explode from the rough, delicious pressure. "Jesus," he gasped.

She stiffened, suddenly going rigid in his arms. Her head jerked back and she stared at him with lovely, stunned eyes. "Oh, God, what am I doing?"

"Seems obvious," he growled, reaching between them to find the button at her waist.

"No!" She scrambled backward, almost tripping over the chair. "No, we can't."

"Oh yeah, we can." He went after her, reaching out to grab her shoulders. "And we're going to."

"Flynn! No!"

This time, her words actually penetrated his passion-glazed mind. She'd clenched her arms tight over her chest and her whole body was trembling.

"Fuck." He released her and took a step back. "That was . . . I have no idea what that was." Damned good, at least for him, but she was acting scared. How had he misread her so badly?

"Wrong. It was wrong. You shouldn't have done that."

"You kissed me back." She'd given all the right signals, seemed as into it as he was.

"I shouldn't have. You have to go."

He scrubbed his hands roughly over his face and tried to will his aching, rock-hard cock to subside. "Sorry." He'd come to her cabin hoping to convince her he was a good guy, and then he'd acted like a sex-crazed idiot. What a fuckup.

As he opened the door, he glanced back at her.

Those huge eyes watched him. She murmured something, so softly he barely heard her. It sounded like, "It wasn't just you."

KENDRA spent much of the night sitting atop the bed in her cabin, computer on her lap, reviewing the Kavanagh file. She'd been lucky enough to get Internet access, so had logged into her office remotely and downloaded her notes and the trial transcript to her laptop. When she read his mother's testimony, it brought back a vivid memory of the woman in the witness box. Of the emotion on her face and the way her voice had rung with sincerity.

In the dimly lit cabin where Flynn had kissed her, Kendra read the details of his life as recounted by his mom. He'd been born in Ireland, his father died when he was young, and Flynn became the focus of his mother's life. She raised him to value family, honesty, and responsibility, and he became the man of the house. When he was twelve, she married again and they moved to Vancouver with her new husband, a Canadian of Irish descent she'd met when he was studying at University College Dublin, where she worked as a secretary.

She'd made a bad choice, she admitted. When she'd had Ray and he'd proved to be a peculiar child with behavior problems, her husband couldn't handle it. She said she realized too late that the man had issues himself, and perhaps even had undiagnosed Asperger's.

Like his son.

Kendra realized her recollection had been wrong. It wasn't a learning disability Flynn's half brother had; it was Asperger's syndrome. Ray was diagnosed when he was seven and Flynn was twenty-three. Their mom said Flynn had helped her raise Ray. Not only did he help with living expenses, but as his income increased he paid for special tutors and activities. More than that, he spent much of his free time with his family, providing guidance to Ray and emotional support to his mom and helping her make decisions about Ray.

Flynn's mother had almost canonized him.

Knowing what a strong impression she'd made on the jury, Kendra, in her closing, took the tack of arguing that if Flynn was indeed the caring son and older brother his mother had portrayed, he might have seen himself as a Robin Hood. Perhaps he took money from an insured law firm so his brother could receive the care he needed. She'd thought that line of reasoning might make a guilty verdict more palatable to the jury. It hadn't.

Nor had she fully convinced herself. Now, months after the trial, as she studied the evidence and the trial transcript and remembered the witnesses on the stand, the trial came alive again for her. And she remembered how, during it, her sixth sense had nagged at her more than once. She'd gone to Dorothy, who had reminded her that a prosecutor must be strong and decisive, that self-doubt was wishy-washy and would destroy her effectiveness.

It wasn't so much that she'd believed firmly in Flynn's guilt as that she'd believed in Dorothy.

Now she had to face the truth. If it hadn't been for her boss, Kendra wouldn't have prosecuted Flynn.

Did that mean, though, that she believed him innocent? She closed her eyes and let all the images and words drift through her head, including the earnestness and frustration on his face last night. Then she called on her sixth sense.

And faced the truth. She had prosecuted an innocent man.

Kendra shoved aside the computer and turned off the light. She had chosen law because she wanted justice for victims and wanted criminals put away. But this past year, she had meted out injustice. Because of her, Flynn had lost his business, the one that not only supplied him with challenging work but provided in large part for his brother and mom.

What could she say to him? Was there any way she could fix this? Would he ever forgive her?

And how did that fiery kiss figure into things? Last night, if she hadn't come to her senses, they'd have had sex. There were at least a dozen reasons it couldn't happen. Not least that he hated her, and for a very good reason.

THE next morning, unable to sleep, Flynn rose while his roommate was still snoring, showered and dressed quietly, and went up to the top deck. What conclusions had Kendra reached about his innocence, and how did she feel about their heated kiss? Did she now think he was both a thief and a man who forced himself on women?

He didn't find out, because she never showed up for breakfast.

After the meal, he caught up with Peter and Liz as they headed to their cabin to change into bathing suits for a morning swim. Walking with them, trying to sound casual, he said, "Didn't see your cousin this morning, Peter. Hope she's okay. Does she get seasick?"

"I don't think so. She's probably in her cabin working."

"That's no good," Liz said. "We're in Greece, for heaven's sake. Why did Kendra come if she's going to spend all her time belowdecks?"

"Probably because my dads and I are always on her case about working too hard."

Liz tilted her head. "Then get on her case about coming along on today's excursions. I want everyone to have a holiday they'll always remember."

Flynn struggled to hold back an ironic grin. He'd bet Kendra wouldn't soon forget this trip.

They'd reached the door of Liz and Peter's cabin, and Liz gazed up at Flynn, a gleam in her eyes. "Kendra's lovely, don't you think?"

Warmhearted Liz loved trying to fix other people's problems. "I'm not interested."

"In her, or in dating at all? You haven't been out with anyone since Sandy."

"Yeah, and look how well that worked out." Sandy was the ex who'd dumped him when the trial began.

"You've had a rotten year for women," she agreed. "Between the bitch persecutor and your traitor ex. I wish they were both here so I could knock their heads together and throw them overboard."

"That's my sweet bride," Peter teased, putting his arm around her.

"Thanks for the thought," Flynn said. If his loyal friend ever found out Kendra was the "bitch persecutor," it wouldn't be pretty.

She flipped her hair. "Your luck's due for a change, Flynn. You know this ship's the *Aphrodite*, don't you? Do you know who Aphrodite is?"

"Some Greek goddess."

"The goddess of love and sex. In Greek terms, we're on the love boat."

"This isn't the time in my life to start a relationship."

She paused only a moment. "Okay, forget the love part. Kendra doesn't seem big on relationships either. Right, Peter?"

"Nope, she's all about her job. Almost never dates."

Interesting. Okay, she was serious and rigid, but also beautiful, bright, successful, and—as that kiss had told him—passionate. The memory of her body pressed against his, their tongues tangling together, made his blood heat.

Liz gave him a mischievous wink. "So let's call it the sex boat rather than the love boat. Why don't you and Kendra make a few waves?"

His pulse raced at the thought, but he had to get Liz off this subject. "If I was into making waves, it wouldn't be with her, and I bet she'd say the same. We met last night and . . ." He shook his head.

"Didn't click?" Liz asked.

"Right," he managed to say. In fact, their mouths, their bodies, had clicked together like interlocking jigsaw pieces, fused by fiery heat. He thrust his fists into the pockets of his shorts to conceal his growing erection.

"Well, that's too bad," she said. "I'll just have to find you someone else." She glanced at Peter. "Your cousin as well. I did catch her eyeing Santos. There's a guy who could show a girl a really fine time."

Flynn clenched his teeth at the idea of Kendra sharing her lips, her body, with any other man.

"A shipboard fling," Peter said skeptically. "That's not Kendra's style."

"You never know what a woman's capable of," she said teasingly. "Sometimes those buttoned-up, repressed types are real tigers."

One kiss had told him that was true of Kendra. And, irrational as it might be, he wanted her to be *his* tiger.

LATER in the morning when the *Aphrodite* docked at the island of Kythnos, Kendra did emerge on deck. In brown shorts and a sleeveless top patterned in black and shades of brown, with her long, sleek legs and arms, she reminded Flynn of a sexy jungle animal. A tiger indeed.

Then, across the deck, her gaze met his. His heart sank when he saw the sadness in her eyes, the strain on her face. No good news there.

She started slowly toward him, then Liz hurried over and caught her arm. "Kendra, are you all right? We missed you at breakfast."

"I'm fine. Jet lag, I guess. I couldn't get to sleep, then finally I did and I ended up sleeping in."

"The time change is tough, isn't it?"

Peter came to join them and gave Kendra a quick hug. "Hey, coz. Didn't get a chance to talk to you last night." He kept an arm around her shoulder as he caught Liz's hand and the three of them went to disembark.

Sighing, Flynn joined the other passengers as they went ashore to board a bus.

It took them inland, where they wandered around a picturesque village. For the first while, Liz and Peter kept Kendra close to them, so Flynn did his best to enjoy the scenery.

Following the wedding planner's instructions, he'd brought his camera on the cruise. It was a top-quality Nikon, and he used it for family photos and to take shots for the client websites he used to design, back when he had a business. Now he found it a good distraction. He had an eye for composition, and taking photos made him concentrate on, and appreciate, what he was seeing.

He was taking shots of old men with tiny cups of coffee who were bent over a game that resembled backgammon in the courtyard of a coffee shop when Kendra stepped up beside him.

"I want to apologize for last night," he said quietly. "The kiss. I got carried away and I should have stopped when—"

"No, that's okay. Look, last night I reviewed the trial transcript—"

"Wait." Just past her, he saw Liz eyeing the two of them with a speculative gleam. Much as he wanted to hear what Kendra had to say, this wasn't the time. "Not now."

Kendra's eyes, more gray than green today, widened, then she squeezed them closed and raised a hand to her forehead as if she had a headache. Without another word, she walked away.

Frustrated, Flynn turned away. She'd reviewed the trial transcript and she looked unhappy, so likely she'd reconfirmed her belief in his guilt. Why had he thought she might believe him? Why should he care?

He sighed, then noticed Liz's dad clicking a shot of his wife standing under an olive tree. Shaking his head—didn't the man realize he'd positioned his wife so the trunk looked like it was growing out of the top of her hat?—he went over. "How about I take a few pictures of the two of you together? Over here by the steps, and we'll get that blue pot of pink geraniums as well. And why don't you take off your hats for a moment, so your faces aren't shaded?"

As they followed his instructions, smiling with pleasure, he thought wryly that he could always start a new career as a wedding photographer.

Chapter 4

WHEN the group returned to the *Aphrodite*, Kendra hurried down to her cabin and flopped on the bed.

Facing Flynn this morning, guilt-wracked, had been one of the most difficult things she'd ever done, then he'd cut her off brusquely. He was right, they shouldn't discuss it in public, but she needed to apologize.

Words were meaningless, though. Was there any way she could make things right? She could go to the media and say she had reviewed all the evidence and believed she'd been wrong in bringing the charge against Flynn, and she now believed him to be innocent. It would cost her her job.

Fair enough, after costing him his. Still, was there any hope it would make his clients come back? What if she contacted them personally?

A knock sounded on her cabin door and Uncle William called, "Kendra? You in there, hon? It's time for dinner."

She groaned softly. Hours had passed with her just lying there castigating herself. "I'll be up in a minute."

Quickly she put on a long skirt with a T-shirt over it, a loose belt at her waist. Without bothering to check her reflection, she picked up a sweater and went up on deck.

Most of the passengers were sipping pre-dinner drinks and talking happily about the afternoon excursion she'd missed—a visit to the harbor town and a medieval town close by. She went to the bar, where the bartender said, "Try a Heat Wave. It's very refreshing."

"Sure." She waited while he poured juices and fruity alcohol over ice, then sipped the resulting concoction. "Very nice." Usually, if she drank at all, it was wine. If she hadn't felt so rotten, this drink might almost make her feel as if she was on holiday.

When she went outside, she glanced around, wondering if Flynn was there. The conversational groupings shifted and she saw him talking to Liz and a couple of her friends from England, a pair of attractive blondes.

As if he felt Kendra's gaze, his head lifted and he stared at her over the heads of the blondes. Liz glanced up, too, and smiled at her, but Flynn looked quickly away. He shifted position deliberately, so his back was to her.

Was he being discreet, or shunning her? Quickly she turned away, too, bumping into the cruise director, who stood nearby. Santos reached out quickly to steady her, his strong brown hand catching her arm. A lovely masculine hand, yet it didn't stir her blood the way Flynn's did. "Are you okay?" he asked.

She gave an artificial smile. "Great, except for being hungry."

"We'll soon solve that problem. Everyone knows Greek food is the best in the world."

He said the last words teasingly, and her spirits lightened a tiny bit. "Spoken like a loyal Greek. I admit I haven't eaten much of it."

"Do you like lamb?" When she nodded, he went on, "You must try the roast lamb tonight. Be adventurous, Kendra."

"Maybe if it just extends to roast lamb. Other than that, I'm not the adventurous type."

He winked. "Never know until you try. I heard someone say you're a lawyer?"

"True."

"Perhaps not the most adventurous career? Or is it?"

"It has its moments."

"Tell me more." He seemed attentive and interested, and he was certainly handsome and charming, yet she didn't feel any chemistry between them. Not like with Flynn, the man whose back was still turned to her. How could she make amends if he wouldn't even look at her?

"Kendra?"

She realized Santos was gazing at her, looking puzzled. "Sorry," she said, "I think Gwen's trying to get everyone organized to go for dinner."

He gave a rather frustrated sigh, followed by a wry smile. "A cruise director's job is never done. I'll look forward to talking to you again."

He went to assist Gwen, and the pair herded everyone into town for dinner at a picturesque taverna. The wedding planner used seating charts designed to get people mingling. Kendra found herself at an inside table with an aunt and uncle of Liz's and some friends of the bride and groom, while Flynn was on the outdoor patio. She couldn't see him without craning her neck, which she definitely wouldn't do.

Later, she'd find a way to talk to him. She didn't believe in putting problems off until the morning. For now, catchy Greek music was playing, the food smelled delicious, and she'd barely eaten all day. She took Santos's recommendation and enjoyed the roast lamb, drank red wine from Crete, then savored the sweet honey-nut baklava that was served for dessert. When a waiter offered everyone glasses of ouzo, she accepted. Liquid courage.

After dinner, the wedding guests formed a raggedy group as they strolled along the waterfront, heading back to the *Aphrodite*. She noticed Flynn stop to peer into a shop window and seized the opportunity. Stepping up beside him, gazing at that strong, handsome profile rather than in the window, she pointed blindly at the window and said in a public voice, "Isn't that lovely? I'd like to take one home."

He turned, startled. "Kendra?" Brow kinked in a puzzled frown he said, rather cautiously, "You would? I wouldn't have thought it was your kind of thing."

Her gaze followed the finger she'd pointed, and she realized she was staring at a religious icon—a painted wood man she assumed was Jesus. "Uh, well . . ."

"I was thinking Ma might like him. She's done her fair share of praying," he added wryly.

The words hung between them, a reminder that his mother would have prayed about her son's trial. The mellow Greek night was full of tension, an energy that pulsed between them.

Disconcertingly, she remembered being in his arms, the wet heat of his mouth, the rigid press of his erection and, despite everything, desire heated her.

She struggled to shove it aside and concentrate on what needed to be done. "Flynn, I need to talk to you," she said under her breath.

"Can't do it here," he said equally softly.

"Come to my c—" The word "cabin" got lost as a male voice called, "What are you two looking at?"

A couple from their group joined them at the window.

Flynn gave her an almost imperceptible nod then said to the other man, "I was asking advice on a gift for my mother. What do you think? Would you go with a Jesus or a Virgin Mary?"

She left them and rejoined the group.

When they'd boarded the ship, Uncle William came over. "It's a lovely night for stargazing."

She faked a yawn. "I'm sure, but the jet lag is catching up with me."

"Tell me you're not going back to that laptop."

"Not tonight. I wouldn't be able to concentrate." And that was the truth. She kissed his cheek. "Night-night. Kiss Uncle Phil for me."

Then she hurried down to her cabin to wait.

It wasn't long before Flynn opened the door. She was sitting on the bed, back against the wall, a couple of pillows behind her. When she started to move, he said, "No, stay there."

He pulled up the chair and sat facing her, so close she could almost feel his heat. Face taut with tension, he said, "Say it. Whatever you need to say."

She took a deep breath and trusted in her sixth sense. "I believe you. I was wrong." As she spoke, his face lit, almost like the glow illuminating that religious icon. "I made a horrible mistake, Flynn."

He leaned toward her as she went on. "I wish there was something I could do to—"

He grabbed her shoulders and his lips stopped her, hard and forceful like last night. So fierce she couldn't think, so irresistible she could do nothing but respond. She and Flynn kissed so hard her lips hurt and she felt a tooth cut into the soft inner flesh. His fingers bit into her and desire licked through her like wildfire.

He tore his mouth from hers. "Damn it, Kendra, you ruined my life. Why do I—"

"I know, and I hurt your mom and your half brother and I'm so sor—"

Again, he cut her off with a kiss, grinding his lips into hers as if maybe he was trying to punish her. Except, as much as it hurt, it felt that good, too. He broke the kiss again.

"I can't get it back," he gasped. "Everything I lost. I can't get it back."

"I know, but I'll do everything I can and—"

This time, she wasn't surprised he didn't let her finish. In fact, when their lips met again, she wrapped her arms around him and pulled him closer until he sprawled halfway across her. Against her thigh, through her skirt and his pants, she felt the steely brand of his erection. Crazy as it was, she wanted him desperately. Her sex was moist and aching and she wanted to rub herself, grind herself, against him. She wanted to strip off his clothes and feel him plunge into her the way his tongue was ravishing her mouth. She let out a whimper of need.

"Oh, Christ." He pulled back. "I'm hurting you."

"No, no, you're not." He was, but it didn't matter, she wanted everything he could give her. All the emotions, bad and good. She wanted to take them—him—inside her until their bodies drove each other to the shattering point.

He drew back slightly and stroked hair from her brow with surprising tenderness. "You really believe me? You believe I'm innocent?"

"Yes."

His green eyes glowed. Then, as she went on to say, "I should have seen it from the start," they darkened.

"Yeah. Fuck, yeah, you should have."

So much anger, so much pain. Wordlessly, she stared up at him.

"I shouldn't want you." His words grated out as if they hurt him.

"But you do, and I want you."

He groaned and his lips descended again in a brief, intense kiss. Then he slid away from her to grab her T-shirt and haul it roughly over her head. He didn't undo her bra, just dragged it up, the edge grazing her sensitive budded nipples, to follow her tee.

Without pausing to caress her breasts, he stripped off her skirt, then her brief panties, and she lay exposed to his gaze, her body trembling with need.

His eyes lingered for only a moment, then he yanked his shirt over his head and stripped off his pants and underwear. He moved so quickly she couldn't see him properly, could only get an impression of lean muscles, before he came down on top of her.

His lips were harsh against hers and his tongue thrust deep into her mouth. His chest crushed her breasts and his rigid penis ground against her pubic bone. She was on fire for him.

She moaned into his mouth, then her tongue thrust back against his. Tilting her hips, she raised her legs to wrap around him so the head of his shaft, blunt and hot, rubbed against her swollen clit. Sensation, so sharp and sweet it made her gasp, shot through her.

He slid back and forth, their flesh slick with her juices, and inside her the drive toward orgasm built. She needed him now, inside her, deep and hard. The past didn't matter, nothing mattered except that right now they had to fuck each other.

She reached down between their bodies, grasped him firmly, and guided him between her folds. With a deep groan, he thrust powerfully into her core.

She was tight, hadn't had intercourse in a long time, and it hurt, but in such a good way.

He pulled back, thrust again, deep and hard, holding nothing back.

It felt so good she couldn't stand it. A scream built in her throat, but no one must hear, so she managed to hold it back. Inside her, that delicious tension grew, centered, coiled.

He drove into her, panting like he was finishing a marathon. "Fuck, Kendra," he grunted.

He raised up on his arms, lifting his body higher on hers so his cock brushed her clit, and she locked her ankles behind him. As he stroked hard and fast, she pressed and rubbed against him, chasing the orgasm that was so close.

Then he shuddered, growled, and plunged into her, jerking hard in his release. So hard that her body convulsed around him in a wrenching climax. This time there was no holding back her scream, so she stifled it against her forearm.

Gradually, he collapsed down on top of her. Gasping, chests sweaty and heaving, they lay locked together. He was heavy; she couldn't breathe; her body still trembled from the blaze of passion that had swept through it, then shattered in near-violent climax.

"Jesus." His breath puffed against her neck. Finally, he forced himself up on his arms, rolled off her, and flopped on his back beside her, shoving the spare pillow under his head. "That was . . ."

She turned on her side so she could watch him. His body, now that she saw it stretched out, was wonderful. Like her, he was lean, but in his case that leanness was well muscled. When, after a few moments, he hadn't come up with a word, she supplied, "Intense?"

"Yeah." He turned his head to gaze at her. "Are you okay?" The anger had burned off from his eyes and now she saw only concern.

"I'm fine." Lazily, her gaze drifted over his nudity, from firm pecs to taut skin over six-pack abs to the sweet dip of his navel— mmm, this was the stuff of fantasies—and down to . . . Her eyes widened as, horrified, she realized, "We didn't use a condom."

"Shit." He jerked up. "I was so carried away—"

"You didn't think," she finished, heart racing, "and neither did I." How could she be so stupid? It had been more than a year since she'd had sex, a two-nighter with a visiting colleague. Though she'd always used protection, she was cautious enough to also get tested after each new lover. "Flynn, I have an IUD and I'm clean." But what about him? How could she have taken such a risk?

"Me, too." Then, as if realizing she needed more reassurance, he said, "It's been a while, and I've been tested since my last girlfriend and I split up."

A grim undertone to those last words made her wonder guiltily if he and his girlfriend had broken up because of the trial.

Suddenly she felt self-conscious lying there naked with this man. She leaned over the side of the bed to find her T-shirt and slipped it on, tugging it down to her thighs. Sitting up in bed, she folded her hands in her lap. "Flynn, there was more I wanted to say before we, uh, got carried away."

He rolled onto his side, not seeming to care in the least about his nudity, and propped his head on his hand so he could gaze up at her. "What?"

She focused on his eyes, not his distractingly appealing body. "If I could undo the whole thing, I would."

He snorted. "Believe me, so would I."

"Is there anything I can do to make it better? If I contacted the media and gave an interview, said that I'd been wrong and was now convinced of your innocence . . ."

His brows drew together. "You'd do that? Wouldn't it get you in shit at your office?"

"Maybe."

Now his brows rose.

"Yes," she amended. "Crown Counsel are supposed to do our jobs right the first time, not have second thoughts. And not cast the administration of justice into question." Dorothy would take it personally. She'd be annoyed, disappointed, and she'd have to decide whether to fire her protégée. "But that's not your concern. It's my screwup so I should bear the consequences."

"That's generous of you." He sounded surprised and pleased, but he was frowning. "But Kendra, I'm not sure it'd have much effect. I've already been acquitted, and you can't prove I'm innocent."

Somehow, she had to make this right. "I'll go see all your old clients and tell them I was wrong." The law was black-and-white: She'd been wrong; he was innocent; justice should be restored. "I'll tell them they should trust you and hire you back."

A spark of hope kindled briefly in his eyes, then faded. "It's hard to restore trust when it's lost. Besides, they've replaced me by now. It wouldn't be fair to their new consultants to fire them and hire me back."

"Damn."

"I'd put it a little more strongly." He sighed and rolled onto his back again, stacking his hands behind his head, which had the effect of making all the muscles in his torso tighten.

She shouldn't be noticing his body at a time like this.

"I've been through this so many times in my head," he said. "Trying to figure out the best-case scenario. There's only one: catching the real thief."

He was right. "It has to be one of the partners," she said. One of whom was Dorothy's law school classmate. "If the police aren't prepared to take a closer look at them, I know a great PI."

"Already did that. She didn't find anything. She's even been checking every month to see if either of them's spending a lot of money or talking about retiring to the South of France. Nothing."

"I'm sorry. What do *you* think? You must have come up with a theory."

"I'd have sworn both of them were honest." He gave a snort of disgust. "Though they obviously didn't think the same of me or they'd have testified for me. So I figured, yeah, one of them could have framed me. That makes more sense than there being some brilliant unknown hacker. Besides, the chances of tracing a hacker somewhere in the world who's living off those millions is virtually impossible."

"Damn."

He stared at her, eyes cool. "Yeah. I get it, Kendra. All of it. You were doing your job. Now you've realized you were wrong and apologized. That's all you can do." He sighed. "Maybe I should say I forgive you, but it's not that easy. I've . . . I've hated you for a long time. A weird thing to say when we're in bed together, but it's true."

Her heart clutched with pain. "I understand."

Moving heavily for such a lean, graceful man, he slid off the other side of the bed and bent to gather his clothes. He pulled them on in silence, covering up that beautiful body. A body that, she realized now, she'd likely never see again. He'd had sex with her out of the same inexplicable primitive need that had driven her, but he couldn't forgive her.

He stood and gazed down at her. "I wanted you to believe me. I don't know what I figured that would solve." He turned and walked out the door.

Kendra took the pillow his head had rested on and clutched it tightly to her chest. Never in all the time since her dad had died and her mom had fallen apart had she felt so powerless. And this time, everything that had happened was her own fault.

Chapter 5

FLYNN actually slept soundly, a rare thing in the more than a year since his troubles had started. But he woke feeling hollow. When his roommate rose and prepared for the day, Flynn pretended to still be asleep. The Englishman was too chatty and cheerful for his current mood.

When he was alone, he sat up in bed, stacking pillows behind him. Rays of morning sun came through the window to lay a path of pale gold across the white sheet.

Kendra believed him. They'd had sex senselessly, passionately, sex that was as much making war as making love. She'd given him that, surrendered her body to his need.

He wanted to do it again. More slowly, sensually. Yet a part of him still hated her. Nothing had been resolved. He was still in the same mess, one that she'd created.

Lethargically, he showered and dressed, then headed up for breakfast. Would she be there? Despite his ambivalent feelings, he craved the sight of that slim, sleek body, the body he'd plunged mindlessly into until he exploded so hard he almost passed out.

Would her eyes be green today or gray? Would they be pools of guilt and sorrow or would they blaze with passion? Or would she be royally pissed off at the way he'd stomped out last night?

If he'd thought she fascinated him before, having sex with her had only made the situation worse. He'd been out of his mind.

He gave a bitter laugh. Fuck if that wasn't the truth. Out of his mind with anger and lust. And she, probably out of guilt and lust, hadn't stopped him.

He emerged on deck, emotions in a turmoil, and glanced around. The *Aphrodite* was underway, white sails filling with a fresh breeze, morning sun glinting off the water, and people relaxing and planning a day of sightseeing. Holidays had been rare for him. When his brother Ray had been young, it had been clear he didn't do well with too much stimulation and changes to his routine, so family trips had been out. Then when Flynn had set up his own consulting firm, he'd been pretty much indispensable to his clients.

No, his *skills* had been indispensable. The clients didn't give a damn about him, or they wouldn't have turned on him.

He headed into the dining room to get breakfast from the buffet, and there was Kendra. Wearing capris, a T-shirt, and big sunglasses, she stood with a bowl of yogurt in one hand and a mug of coffee in the other, chatting with Santos and looking far too friendly.

When she glanced over and saw him, the smile on her face died. She said something quick to the cruise director, then hurried away, careful not to brush against Flynn.

Santos strolled over to Flynn. "That one doesn't seem to know the meaning of the word *holiday*."

He scowled. "Wouldn't know. I've barely met her."

"You don't seem in the best mood this morning. Anything I can do?"

Flynn shook his head. "Just need my morning coffee." What he didn't need was to chat with a Greek who the ladies, including Kendra, apparently found irresistible. "Excuse me."

He gathered coffee, bacon and eggs, toast, and fruit, then headed outside, pretty much pissed off with the world.

Liz, sunny in yellow, gave him a bright smile from where she and Peter sat with friends. Their table was already crowded so he didn't join them. Besides, he wasn't in the mood for her cheer.

His ma's face flashed into his mind, brows raised as she teased, "Sure and you're enjoying being such a gloomy Gus, aren't you, me lad?" It was what she used to say to him when, as a boy, he'd been in a sulky mood.

Here he was, at the age of thirty-one, indulging in a good sulk. Wasn't that what Liz had been pointing out, a bit more subtly, when she'd told him he could use this holiday to plan his future?

Musing on that, he went to join Liz's parents for breakfast. She had talked about them, so he knew to ask how they were enjoying the birding. And they'd clearly heard of him, too, because they inquired after his ma and Ray.

"Liz says your brother doesn't adapt well to change," Mrs. Tippett said. "It must be difficult for him, having both you and Liz away."

"It is, but Ma's there, of course. And even when I'm in Vancouver my schedule's always been erratic, so he's learned to adjust. I try to phone every morning at eight, and as long as I can manage that, he's usually fine."

"What time is that, here in Greece?" Mr. Tippett asked. "It would be, what, a nine- or ten-hour difference?"

"Ten, yes. So that's six in the evening. With my cell phone, I can call from wherever I am. And for this trip, I got a GSM with a SIM card, to make sure we could stay in touch."

"Modern technology," the other man said. "A blessing and a curse."

"Well, technology's my field"—or at least it used to be—"so mostly I count it as a blessing." The curse was that it had allowed someone to frame him. And there he went again, focusing on the past. It had become a habit. Not a healthy one.

"Are you one of these Twitterers?" Liz's mom asked. "Our daughter says we're old fogeys, but as far as I'm concerned, only birds should be tweeting."

"They probably have more interesting things to say than most of the folks on Twitter," he joked, winning a smile from her and beginning to feel better.

The three of them chatted easily for a while longer and he found himself envying the Tippetts. They'd married young, hoped for children without success, then had Liz when they'd long given up hope. They clearly loved each other and were happy with life.

"The thing we most wanted," Mrs. Tippett said, "was for Liz to find the right man, and now she has so we're on to the next thing. Grandchildren. We're not getting any younger."

"Speak for yourself," her husband put in.

"You're young at heart," Flynn said diplomatically, "and that's what counts."

"Oh, you're a charmer, you are. John, you should take lessons." She cocked her head in Flynn's direction. "You're older than Liz by a few years?" she asked. When he nodded, she said, "And still single. I imagine your mom's not so happy about that?"

"Sure and you're right about that. She has her heart set on grand-children, too."

"And you, Flynn? What do you want?"

He sighed. "I'd like to fall in love, marry, have kids. But as Ma gets older, Ray will be more and more my responsibility. That's a lot for a woman to take on." Most of the women he'd dated, including Sandy, had felt uncomfortable with his brother. Of course, Ray wasn't a comfortable person to be around. You had to really get to know him to understand that his quirks, bluntness, and lack of empathy weren't deliberate but symptoms of his Asperger's, and to appreciate his strengths, like his loyalty and sharp brain.

Mrs. Tippett tsked. "It wouldn't stop a girl like Liz."

"You're right. Any idea where I might find one just like her?" Clearly, a workaholic prosecutor who saw life in black-and-white terms wasn't that person. His body might lust after Kendra, but his brain had more sense.

"She'll come along when the time is right," Mrs. Tippett said.

Mr. Tippett, who'd been listening in silence, said, "If I'd sat back and waited, Charlie Carpenter would have married my Henrietta."

She batted his arm. "Never. You know I was just dating him to light a fire under you so you'd get off your arse and come after me."

Her husband laughed, then said to Flynn, "There you go, boy. Sitting back waiting isn't the way to go after what you want."

No, but you had to know what you wanted. It seemed Liz and her parents were both delivering the same message: It was time to get off his arse, stop feeling sorry for himself, and figure out his future.

And that he could do. He was powerless to change the past, but he had power to create a future.

Feeling more energetic and optimistic than he had in a very long time, he turned his head as a cry went up from passengers standing along the railing, saying Mykonos was in sight.

As he and the Tippetts headed over to join them, he glanced around. No Kendra. Did her determination to spend so much time in that windowless cabin have something to do with him?

He watched the coastline of Mykonos and hoped she'd make an appearance today. He needed to tell her to let things go.

After they'd docked, people streamed to their cabins to prepare for a shore excursion. He caught Liz as she passed him heading up the stairs, and smiled at her. "Hey, you were right."

She'd been looking a little distracted, but focused on him and grinned. "Hi, Flynn. You want me to matchmake you? With Kendra?"

She wouldn't be suggesting that if she had any idea who Kendra really was. "No, that's not what I meant. I've finally come to grips with not being able to change or fix the past. I need to move on and figure out the future."

She beamed and threw her arms around him. "I'm so glad. You're such a great guy, you could do anything. You just need to think about open doors, not closed ones."

Which kind of door was Kendra Kirk?

"Are you all right?" he asked, belatedly focusing on Liz rather than himself. "You looked a little distracted, and why weren't you out on deck while we docked?"

"Long story. Auntie Esther has a small emergency back home—nothing serious—and she has to fly back. Gwen's got it all under control."

"I'm sorry. It's too bad your aunt will miss the wedding."

"It is. She was having such a good time, too." She tilted her head and stared up at him. "You know what? I'm not going to settle for anyone having less than a stellar time this week."

Her adamancy made him grin. "Stellar? That's asking a lot, but I'll do my best."

"And so will Kendra Kirk," she said, "if I have anything to say about it."

A knock sounded on Kendra's door. "Kendra, are you in there?" It was Liz's voice.

Kendra, sitting at her laptop, called, "I'm working." Not so much because she had to, but because it was better than facing the man whose life she'd destroyed. The man she'd slept with, who still hated her.

The door opened and Liz stepped in. "This is Mykonos, you have to come ashore and—" She broke off at the sight of Kendra's face, eyes no longer hidden by sunglasses. "What's wrong?"

Liz gave her the same forced smile she'd given Santos and a few of the guests when she'd emerged briefly to collect breakfast. Stress and sleepless nights had given her bloodshot eyes with bags under them. "Must be allergies," she lied. "Greece seems to be bad for me."

"You've never suffered from allergies." Uncle William stepped into the room, with Uncle Phil close behind. The tiny cabin was crowded now, and she felt ganged up on.

"I brought reinforcements," Liz said unapologetically.

"I've never been in Greece before," Kendra snapped. "I must be allergic to something here."

"We'll take you to a pharmacy and get antihistamines," Uncle William said.

"No need," Uncle Phil said. "I brought some with me. I'll run and get them."

"I have vitamin C and echinacea," Liz said. "They're wonderful for anything that ails you."

The two of them scurried off, leaving Uncle William. He said, "You're the healthiest person I've ever met. What's wrong?"

The sympathy in his eyes made her sigh. "Nothing I can talk about. It's my own damn fault and I'll have to sort it out myself."

"Ah. Something to do with work. Poor baby." He bent down to kiss her cheek. "But how is staying down here helping you sort it out? You're in Greece. Enjoy, recharge your batteries, then you'll be able to tackle the problem."

She couldn't spend the rest of the week refusing to face Flynn. He would always hate her, and with good reason. She deserved the pain that caused her, and she'd just have to deal with it. No more shutting herself in her cabin the way her mom shut herself off from life.

Squaring her shoulders, she rose. "You're right." She gave him a quick hug. "Thanks, Uncle William. Now go away and let me get ready. Oh, and tell Uncle Phil he can skip the allergy meds."

When Liz brought vitamin C and echinacea, she took them; her immune system could use the boost. Then she changed into a khaki skirt and a white short-sleeved shirt, applied sunscreen, slid her sunglasses into place, and went up on deck.

Most of the other guests had already gathered. Flynn was by the railing, his back to her as he talked to those pretty blond friends of Liz's.

Gwen hurried up. "Liz tells me you're suffering from allergies. Is there anything I can do?"

Guiltily, she said, "Thanks, but I've taken some stuff. I'm sure I'll be fine."

"I hope so. We have such a wonderful day planned, exploring Mykonos Town, taking an island tour, then going over to Delos, the sacred island."

"Sounds like fun." If she hadn't felt so shitty, it actually might.

Santos called out, "Okay, everyone's here. Let's go see Mykonos."

Several people cheered and followed him off the ship, Liz and Peter in the lead. "You go ahead," Gwen said. "I'll bring up the rear."

Kendra took a few steps, wondering if she should catch up with her uncles or maybe join Liz's parents, who seemed like a sweet pair. A few other relatives were here as well and she hadn't spent much time with them, but she didn't want to go through the whole allergy thing again. She made a rotten liar.

Flynn came up to her, an unexpected smile on his face. "Good morning."

Her pulse quickened at his nearness and her eyes widened in surprise at the smile. "Good morning," she returned cautiously.

"I've been doing a lot of thinking," he said quietly as other passengers, eager to disembark, jostled them. "Can we talk?"

Her heart gave a skip. Maybe he didn't hate her after all. "Yes, of course. When—"

"Hey, Kendra." Annie, a second cousin, touched her arm, "it's good to see you doing something other than work." She winked. "I promise not to tell Dorothy."

"Thanks, but she said I was due a holiday."

As Annie strolled away, Kendra said to Flynn, "Maybe we can find an opportunity today?" She didn't want anyone getting the impression they were lovers, but it was normal for cruise guests to chat with each other.

"Hope so." His gaze lingered on her face a long moment, then someone bumped him and he stepped away.

Hope. That was the operative word. For the first time since he'd left her cabin last night, she felt the awakening of hope.

She fell in step beside Liz's parents, and Mr. Tippett said, "Kendra, tell my wife there was no reason for her to go back to England."

"What? Why would you?"

Brow furrowed, Mrs. Tippett said, "My sister Esther's flying home to care for a friend who's had an accident. Maybe I should have gone with her."

"She's a perfectly capable woman," her husband said as they stepped down to the dock and strolled toward dry land. "And your daughter's getting married. Here."

"I could fly home and come back for the wedding."

"But then you'd miss the whole cruise," Kendra said. "Liz and Peter would be so disappointed, and your poor husband, too."

"There," Mr. Tippett said. "Listen to the girl. And besides, you'd miss the birds."

"Are the islands good for bird-watching?" Kendra asked.

"Oh, yes," Mrs. Tippett said, face brightening. "They're on a number of migratory bird paths."

"There are some rare species, too," her husband said. "Aren't there, dear? Tell her about Crete."

Distracted from her concern about her sister, his wife said, "We're staying on Crete a few days after the wedding in hopes of seeing a bearded vulture and an Eleonora's falcon."

"Really?" A bearded vulture? Seriously? That didn't sound the least bit appealing. Still, she almost envied the elderly couple, sharing a hobby they were passionate about. For her, since her dad died, life had been serious. Her R & R consisted of hanging out with her mom and uncles, sharing the occasional drink and lawyer talk with colleagues, and enjoying a rare quickie fling with a man she'd never be serious about.

Her life would have been so different if her dad hadn't committed suicide. If her mom hadn't fallen apart.

Not that Kendra ever planned on having children, but if she did, she'd damned well be there for them.

Glancing ahead, her gaze lit on Flynn. She thought of his mom, a strong woman who'd built a good life for her kids when her first husband died and her second deserted her and the boys. Flynn had taken responsibility, too, helping raise and support his special needs half brother.

He'd make a good husband and father. Staring at his broad shoulders under an olive green tee, she had a sudden vision of him holding a laughing baby securely in his strong arms.

"He's a fine young man," Mrs. Tippett said.

"What? Uh, who?"

"Flynn Kavanagh."

"I'm sure he is, though I barely know him."

"Liz speaks highly of him, and we had a good talk with him." The elderly woman eyed her shrewdly. "He deserves a special woman."

She nodded. Yes, he did. A woman who supported and loved him, not one who messed up his life.

"Oh, look at the pelicans," Mrs. Tippett cried excitedly.

For the first time, Kendra really looked around her, taking in the attractive white, cubist architecture with touches of vivid blue here and there, flowers overflowing pots and draping balconies, and the pair of pelicans strolling the narrow cobblestone street like a couple of tourists.

Smiling with pleasure, she remembered the disposable camera Liz had given her and pulled it from her bag. Her mom would love these pictures. Glancing around, she noted windmills up the hill and hoped Santos would lead them in that direction.

This was all so new to her, this climate and scenery: the blaze of sun so raw and bright, the rickety multicolored chairs on an outdoor patio, tiny lizards sunning themselves. It was picturesque and charming, and she regretted that yesterday she'd been so self-absorbed she'd barely noticed her surroundings. Somehow, the Greek sun and the charm of this town gave her strength and hope.

Glancing down another alley, she saw a golden cat stretching luxuriously beside a chipped green pot that held bright pinkish purple bougainvillea, and stepped forward to frame it in her camera lens.

As if her thoughts had summoned Flynn, he came to stand beside her. Hooking his sunglasses in the neck of his T-shirt, he raised his own camera. "Mind if I take some shots, too?"

Her heart raced simply from having him beside her. "Please do. That cat's begging to have his picture taken."

Camera raised to his eye, he said, "Kendra, I need to move on."

A quick glance around assured her no one had followed them into this alley. "I want to help. However I can. Talk to your old clients or—"

"That's not what I meant." He lowered his camera and turned

to her, expression intent. "I need to leave the past behind. I've been dwelling on the negatives, the injustice—" When she winced, he said, "Sorry."

"No, it's me who's sorry. You have every reason to hate me, but"—she took a breath, tilted her chin—"I hope you don't."

He gazed into her eyes. "I don't. Not anymore. You made a mistake. A bad one, and I know you're sorry."

Relief washed through her. "Thank you."

"I need to think about the future and be positive."

Thinking of her parents, she nodded vigorously. "It's hard to let go of something so terrible. But until you do, it can poison your life."

"It was, and I don't want that." He studied her. "You look tired."

"I haven't slept much the last couple of nights. I've been feeling rotten about what I did."

One corner of his mouth lifted. "Have to say, I don't mind hearing that."

"Yeah, I'm sure."

And now he smiled, really smiled, and said, "But let it go now. Okay?"

Flynn, smiling at her. Oh my, he really did have a dimple, and wasn't it a killer? She had to smile back and say, "I'll try." Already, she felt the stress and tiredness lifting.

"So I'm thinking we have a decision to make," he said with that charming hint of an Irish lilt. "What are we going to do about this . . . thing between us?" The sexy gleam in his eyes left no doubt what he was talking about.

Sex.

Lust hit her, hot and hard, a rush of adrenaline that left her breathless. That was what she wanted, yet the idea was crazy. "I don't know."

He glanced past her, and she did, too, ensuring no one was coming their way. "Liz told me you and I should get together and make a few sexy waves," he said.

Surprise and the beginning of a smile touched her face, but disappeared when he went on. "If she had a clue who you really are . . ."

She winced. "Yes, I hate to think. And the same with my boss. She's a distant relative. She'll see cruise photos, hear people talk."

"And because you prosecuted me, she'd think . . . what?"

"That I'm sleeping with the enemy. Look, if you want me to go to the media and tell them I was wrong, I will. If it costs me my job, that's only fair. But if not, I don't want to lose my job over a holiday fling."

"She'd fire you if you slept with someone who'd been acquitted?"

"She already thinks I screwed up the case. If she hears we're involved, she'll figure I did it deliberately because you were my lover."

"But we just met."

"In the justice system, appearances can be as important as reality."

He frowned. "I really don't like your job. I hate all the black-and-whites. Reminds me of my brother, Ray."

Startled, she said, "Your brother?"

"He has Asperger's and he's a literal thinker. Life's about rules, everything's black-and-white. What's wrong with a little flexibility?" A twinkle lit in his green eyes. "What do your rules say about us being secret lovers?"

Her pulse fluttered in her throat, making it hard to breathe. "That it wouldn't be wise . . ."

"But you want it, too." He stepped closer, so the fronts of their bodies almost touched. "Do you always have to do the *wise* thing, Kendra? Can't you ever just do what you want?"

Another pulse throbbed, swollen and achy, between her legs. She could have him inside her again. The idea was irresistible. "We'll have to be careful." Hard to do, when right now all she wanted was to plaster her body against his and kiss him until they were both senseless.

"We can do that." The expression in his eyes told her he, too, was imagining sex.

She lowered her gaze, saw an erection press against the fly of his shorts, and fought to suppress a whimper of need. "We can't do this. Talk like this. We'll give it away."

"God, how am I going to wait for tonight?"

Chapter 6

KENDRA drew on all of her willpower and steered clear of Flynn all day. With the knowledge that he'd forgiven her and the promise of sex singing in her veins, she threw herself into the holiday spirit. She took photos, bought souvenirs for her mom and a few people in the office, and picked out a purple sundress for herself. At lunch, she sipped retsina, which made her feel adventurous even if she wasn't crazy about it. She tried calamari for the first time in her life and pronounced it delicious. Being relaxed—or maybe it was the retsina—helped her overcome her usual social awkwardness and chat easily with the other guests.

Still, when the group took a boat excursion to the sacred island of Delos, she preferred to explore the ruins alone. Birds sang, tiny flowers bloomed in the grass, lizards skittered out of her way, and she could almost feel the raw edges of guilt knit together. A sense of peace sank into her soul. She wished she could bottle this experience and take it home to her mom.

From Delos, they returned to the *Aphrodite* so everyone could

have a short rest and get changed. The night's agenda called for dinner on the rooftop patio of an upscale restaurant, then, for whoever
wanted, a visit to Mykonos's famed nightclubs.

She'd never been the nightclub sort, and no way could she risk
dancing with Flynn. Surely he'd skip the club scene, too, and come
to her cabin. To ensure it, she chose a figure-hugging wrap dress
that was sleeveless and revealed a lot of cleavage and leg. The fabric
was a silky silver-gray, and a black shawl and wedge sandals added
nice accents. In this outfit, her eyes were a luminous gray, and a
touch of makeup made them more dramatic. Though she'd slathered
herself with sunscreen all day, her cheeks were flushed from sun and
anticipation.

When she came up on deck, Flynn's eyes widened appreciatively
at the sight of her. Heat moved through her as she took him in.
He always looked great, but tonight, like most of the guests, he'd
dressed up a bit more than usual. Slim-cut black pants were topped
with a sage green shirt of loosely woven cotton, the arms rolled
partway up his forearms. Casual yet elegant. Definitely sexy.

Full of high spirits, the group strolled together as Santos led
them to one of the many white, cube-shaped buildings. They went
up a flight of outside stairs to find an elegantly decorated rooftop
restaurant with a large patio.

As if to test her and Flynn's resolve, the wedding planner's seating chart, for the first time, put them at the same table. Flynn's
cheek dimpled as he waited for Kendra to seat herself, then he took
the seat beside Liz's aunt, who was directly across from her.

Santos, seated at one end of the table, asked them to go around
the table quickly and introduce themselves. They all did so, adding
labels such as "a friend of Liz's" in Flynn's case, and "Peter's cousin"
in Kendra's.

"As I'm sure you all know by now," Santos said when everyone had finished, "I'm Santos Michaelides, cruise director on the *Aphrodite*."

Liz's aunt said, "What a perfect job."

He chuckled. "It has its benefits." He glanced around the table. "How about everyone else? What do you do back home?"

The woman to his left said she was an interior decorator. Santos asked if Greece was inspiring her, and she enthused for a few minutes. Then Liz's uncle said he was an accountant, but was looking forward to retirement. Santos asked what he planned to do once he was retired, and he mentioned golf.

His wife, across from Kendra, said, "And gardening. He's going to help me in the garden. That's my passion, along with my job as an elementary school teacher."

Next, Santos turned to Flynn, and Kendra held her breath, wondering what he'd say.

"Computer programming. I won't bore you with the details." His voice was flat.

"Programming's intriguing," Santos said, "and I imagine it pays well, doesn't it?"

Flynn shrugged. "Decently."

"Do you build software or video games?" the cruise director asked. "Or programs for clients who need specialized applications?"

Flynn shifted uncomfortably. "Er, actually at the moment—"

Hating this, Kendra broke in. "Sorry, and no offense, Flynn"—she shot him a cool gaze and saw gratitude in his eyes—"but here we are on a lovely night in Mykonos. We want to leave our boring jobs behind." Quickly she searched for a change of topic. "Santos, tell us about the nightclubs. Where are you going to take us?" She leaned forward, feigning interest.

The cruise director gazed at her consideringly. Okay, fine, he thought she was rude. But why didn't he answer her? "Santos?"

"Sorry, just doing a mental review of my notes." He went on to describe options for after dinner.

Kendra settled in to enjoy the evening, though even as she relished the lovely food and admired the stunning sunset, a part of her couldn't wait for it all to be over. Last night when she and Flynn had had sex, he'd taken her roughly and she'd felt his anger. Now that he was no longer angry, what would it be like between them?

Watching him across the table while pretending not to watch, acting as if she barely knew him and didn't much care for him, heightened every sense. It was like exquisitely subtle foreplay. She knew he was just as aware of—as aroused by—her as she was him.

Would they make love fiercely or slowly? Or maybe both?

HAVING dinner with, but not with, Kendra was frustrating. He wanted to grab her, haul her off, and screw their brains out. A part of him resented the hell out of the need for secrecy.

Yet he understood. She shouldn't jeopardize her job over a holiday fling, and he didn't want anything to disturb Liz and Peter's wedding celebration. If his loyal friend found out Kendra was the person who'd messed up his life, she'd be outraged. Trying to explain how he and Kendra had gone from enemies to lovers would be too damned complicated.

For him, somehow, it had been amazingly easy. Once he'd made the decision to stop obsessing about the past, his gloomy mood had lifted, his anger had dissolved, and he could look at Kendra and see a sexy woman, not his persecutor.

Impatiently, he waited while the sun set—spectacularly, he had to admit—and everyone finished eating and drained their last cups of coffee. Santos said, "What has everyone decided?" He glanced at Kendra. "Kendra, did any of those clubs sound good to you?"

Her own gaze flicked momentarily to Flynn's, then focused on the cruise director. "They did, but I'm pretty tired. Jet lag, allergies, maybe just fresh air and good food. I think I'll head back to the *Aphrodite*."

Several people enthused about the clubs, but others said they'd wander back to the ship and maybe get a drink along the way. Flynn casually said he'd do the same. Then, finally, they were all on their feet, heading for the stairs.

Everyone gathered in the cobblestone alley, under the gleam of a golden streetlight.

Kendra looked fantastic tonight. In Greece, where almost everyone had naturally dark skin or a tan, she was elegant and exotic with her pale skin and black hair. Her silver dress was made of a silky fabric that clung and shifted seductively. It wrapped at the front, one side over the other, fastening with a bow looped at her waist. The V-neck revealed cleavage, and when she walked, her long, shapely legs were exposed briefly, almost to midthigh. Flynn studied the bow, imagining giving it a tug. Was it the only thing that held the dress together? He couldn't wait to find out.

Fidgeting, he listened while Santos gave directions to a few nightclubs, as well as back to the harbor.

Flynn had a different location in mind, though for now he and Kendra tagged along with the group heading in the direction of the harbor. She no doubt assumed they'd meet in her cabin.

He hoped she liked the surprise he'd lined up. Now, if he could just find a way of separating her from a couple of relatives she was chatting with.

As the guests straggled along, a few dropped off to explore quaint alleys or pop into a bar for a drink, but not Kendra's relatives. Finally, as the remnants of their group strolled along the harbor, a woman named Annie, a cousin or something of Kendra's, said, "Look at that adorable bar. Let's stop for a nightcap."

Kendra pleaded tiredness, but thankfully the rest chose the bar.

The moment her relatives had disappeared inside, he touched her arm and unobtrusively drew her around a corner into an alley.

"Couldn't wait for a kiss?" she teased, gazing up expectantly.

He wasn't about to turn down that offer. Drawing her deeper into the shadow of a recessed doorway, he wrapped his arms around her. Through the clingy, silky fabric, he cupped the sweet curves of her ass and felt her muscles tighten as she raised up to press her body against his. Lust, too long repressed, raced through him, tightening his own body and swelling his cock.

When he touched his lips to hers, primal instinct urged him to fuck her right here, standing up in a doorway.

The way her mouth meshed with his, hot and greedy, told him she wouldn't refuse.

But this wasn't the way he wanted it.

He forced himself to loosen his grip on her backside, to gentle the kiss and then ease his mouth from hers. "Kendra, not like this."

Her eyes, liquid silver glazed with passion, stared up at him. Then she blinked, gave her head a shake, and freed herself from his arms. "No. Let's get back to the ship. We should separate. I'll go first." She hiked the fringed shawl more tightly around her shoulders.

"No," he said. "Not the ship. Tonight, there's something better."

"What do you mean?"

"I'll show you." Taking her hand, he led her to the far end of the alley and they peered out cautiously. The coast was clear, so he led her back up the hill, choosing a different route from the one they'd just followed, in the hope they wouldn't bump into any fellow passengers.

"A moonlight stroll?" she asked, squeezing his hand. "It is lovely, isn't it?"

"Yeah." He was aware of the moon and stars in an indigo sky, the mellow light seeping from doors and windows, the scent of orange blossoms, the call of a bird that the Tippetts would no doubt be able to identify. But mostly, he was intent on weaving his way through the narrow streets and among cubist buildings that all looked pretty similar to a stranger. Fortunately, he had a good sense of direction, and he was highly motivated to be alone with Kendra.

It must have been three-quarters of an hour or more since they'd left the restaurant when they reached the attractive little hotel he'd discovered earlier. He pulled out an old-fashioned metal key.

"Flynn?"

"Thought it would be nicer than your cabin."

She glanced from him to the hotel—the typical white and blue, bedecked with bougainvillea—then back again. "It's charming, but we can't spend the night off the *Aphrodite*. If we go back in the morning, especially wearing evening clothes, everyone will know what we've been up to."

He put a hand on her lower back and urged her toward the steps. "We won't stay out all night. Santos said people will be dancing until three or four in the morning, scattered among several different clubs and bars."

She'd gone up three steps as he was talking, but now stopped to look at him. "Still, if we go back together . . ."

He kept his hand on her back, wishing he could touch the bare skin beneath her dress. "Then we won't. Once we get near the dock, you can go aboard first. I'll hang back and follow."

When she bit her lip uncertainly, he said, "We'll have hours together. It's a pretty room, I saw it earlier. A big bed with a canopy kind of thing and a balcony with an ocean view. We can open the doors to the sky and ocean air."

"Tempting . . ."

"The longer we stand here on the hotel steps, the more chance someone we know will come by."

He grinned as she hurriedly scrambled up the steps.

The small lobby was deserted, a bell set prominently on the

desk. Flynn led Kendra to the steps and they went up two flights then down a hall, and he unlocked the door.

When he flicked the light switch, she stepped forward eagerly. "How pretty."

The room was simple, with white walls, tile floors, and wooden furniture, but there were picturesque touches like the turquoise trim around the mirror and balcony doors and the raspberry pink hibiscus plant. Best of all was the king-sized bed, with gauzy white draperies hanging from the ceiling that could be pulled, *Arabian Nights* style, to enclose the bed. Small shaded lamps on either side of the bed shed golden light.

"Oh my God, what an incredible bed," she exclaimed. Still, rather than stopping at it, she went past to step out onto the large balcony.

He followed her.

Staring at the panoramic view of the waterfront, a smile on her face, Kendra slipped her arm around him and he did the same, holding her close to his side.

"A starlit night in Mykonos," she said. "You and me together. Never in my wildest dreams . . ." She broke off and turned in the half circle of his arm, eyes glowing. "Thank you."

Her face was even prettier than the view. He stole a kiss. "Better than a cramped cabin without even a porthole?"

"A million times. You'll spoil me." She said it as if it was an unusual thing.

He touched her cheek and repeated words he'd heard since he was a boy. "Every woman deserves a little spoiling now and then."

"Some woman has taught you well."

"Ah now, that'd be my ma. She said life's rough and women work hard and too often get taken for granted."

"True, and we take ourselves for granted. I'm so busy I rarely treat myself to anything more than an extra sprinkle of shaved chocolate on my morning latte. But now"—her lips curved and her silvery eyes sparkled—"I think I'll treat myself to Flynn Kavanagh."

He held his arms open wide. "Help yourself. Start anywhere."

She glanced around like she was checking whether anyone could see them. Their balcony was pretty secluded. Her eyes widened. "Look down there!"

He glanced down and across, gaze landing on a roof where— "They have the right idea." A couple was backed up against a wall, bodies twined in a passionate embrace.

"If we can see them, they can see us," she breathed. "And so can anyone else who looks up."

"But no one would recognize us. The pair down there could be anyone, even people off the *Aphrodite* for all we know. It's anonymity, in public. Sexy, isn't it?"

"Sexy?" she repeated doubtfully. And then, "You're right. I should be more adventurous." Her lips curved and she reached for the top button of his shirt. "A naked man in the starlight," she said with relish. "Now that's the stuff of fantasies."

His own fantasies usually pretty much stopped with the woman being naked; the setting didn't matter. But tonight, he had to admit a balcony by the Aegean was pretty damned fine, and that "anonymity in public" idea was titillating.

As were Kendra's soft fingertips, brushing the smooth skin of his chest as she undid button after button. Each graze, as she made her way down the center of his body, had almost the same effect as if she'd been caressing his cock. He hoped she'd get to his pants soon. They were uncomfortably tight.

He hadn't tucked his shirt in, so she didn't have to tug it free from his pants. He wore no belt, and she went directly to the button at his waist. As she wrestled with it, she said, voice breathy and impatient, "Take your shirt off."

He let it slide down his arms and tossed it onto a deck chair. The slight coolness in the air felt good on his overheated skin. Not that he'd be cooling down anytime soon, because she was sliding down his zipper. Fabric parted, releasing some of the pressure on his erection, barely confined inside light boxer briefs.

Not bothering to pull his pants past his hips, she cupped her hand over him, humming wordless approval. Then she said, "Pants. Off."

Somehow, as she caressed him through his underwear, he managed to get out of his sandals and pants. He hooked his fingers in the sides of his briefs. "On or off?"

"Off." It was only a breath of air.

He obliged gladly and his erect cock sprang free.

She took a step back and just stood looking. "You're gorgeous," she whispered. "So lean, so strong. You look like a dancer."

"A dancer? Give me a break."

Humor kinked her lips. "You're too macho to be a dancer? That's not fair. They're strong, athletic, agile, coordinated—"

"Why are we talking about dancers? It's your turn to get naked." He ran a finger along the V of the neckline, over the soft, curving edge of one breast, and into the hollow between it and the other one. "I like this dress. Does that tie at the waist undo the whole thing?"

"You really want me to tell you?"

He shook his head and yanked on the bow. The outer layer of fabric fell free and he saw more glimpses of breast and thigh, but the inner part of the dress stayed in place, secured somehow.

"There's a tie inside, too."

Accepting the invitation, he slid his hand across the smooth, warm skin of her waist and found another bow, which he undid as well.

The dress fell away from her body and for a moment he thought she was naked under it. But as she gently tugged the dress from his nerveless fingers and put it on the chair, he realized she did wear a bra and panties. They were flesh-colored, barely there. Through them he could see the dark shadows of her areolas, the hard buds of her nipples, and the small triangle of black curls at the apex of her thighs. "Sexy," he muttered approvingly. "But sexier off." He wanted to touch every inch of her, taste her, do everything with her.

Mostly, he wanted to bury himself inside her until they both cried out in release.

When he tried to unfasten the front clasp of her bra, he realized his body was so tight with need that his hands actually shook. He managed to get the clasp undone and stripped off her bra. Her breasts were small, high, each the perfect size to fit his palm.

Eager to see her totally nude, he tugged off her panties.

In the dim light, Kendra was dramatically beautiful: black hair, creamy skin, eyes glinting like silver. Almost like a black-and-white photograph. A little mysterious and remote, stunning and almost untouchable. "Sure and you take my breath away."

A brow quirked, breaking the illusion of remoteness, as did the teasing note in her voice. "There's that Kavanagh charm."

He shook his head. "Nope. The literal truth." He put his arms around her and drew her close, her sleek curves smooth and soft against his bigger, harder body. Their bellies sandwiched his rigid cock between them and he ached to be inside her. In the night air, her skin was a little cool, or maybe that was only the contrast with his own, which was blazing hot.

Her lips were sultry, though, and offered without a second of hesitation. She gave generously in that kiss, and took demandingly, as if it was her right to possess his mouth. And maybe it was. He sure as hell wasn't going to protest. She could possess his whole damned body and he'd die a happy man.

Flynn ran his hands up and down her back, feeling slim, tensile strength, petal-soft skin, the firm cheeks of her ass. One finger tracked the line of her butt crack and she squirmed and pressed closer against him, wriggling her pelvis against his erection.

Her hands explored his back, too, molding and testing his muscles. She made soft, hungry sounds as they kissed, and his male ego swelled along with his cock at the knowledge that she wanted him as badly as he wanted her.

Chapter 7

NEED urged Flynn to take her, here and now, but he found enough self-control to hoist her in his arms. "Let's try out that bed." Leaving the balcony doors open, he carried her inside. An armful of naked woman. What a turn-on.

When he lowered her to the bed, she pulled back the bedspread and top sheet. He laid her on the bottom one, crisp and white, not much lighter a color than her delicate skin, then followed her down.

She tugged on something, and the drapes tumbled all around the bed, creating a see-through tent. "Our private world," she murmured, "like an *Arabian Nights* fantasy."

His own fantasy came true when she spread her legs in invitation. He lay between them, his weight resting lightly on her. He meant to stay there only a moment, to give her a quick kiss on the lips then begin exploring her body with his hands and mouth.

But her arms wrapped around his back, one gripping his ass. Her lips trapped him, her tongue seduced him, the kiss drugged him so he lost track of everything but the need to merge with her. His tongue and hers twined, danced, mated. And now, as she lifted her hips and he felt her hot, slick center, he thrust deep into her core, his hardness gripped and caressed by plush feminine softness.

"So good," he muttered, sliding out and plunging back, again and again, a day of anticipation and arousal giving him a powerful need to drive toward climax.

He forced himself to slow down. Last night he'd been driven by a potent mix of emotion, and the sex had been so raw it was almost painful, physically and emotionally. Tonight he wanted to really feel and appreciate Kendra, and to take care of her needs. His enemy had become his lover, and he found something intimate and rare in the way they trusted each other enough to not use protection.

"Hang on." He rolled them so she was on top.

Now he could caress the long line of her back, squeeze the firm curves of her arse, and his thrusts were slower, more controlled. If she wanted, she could set the pace.

"Mmm." She thrust back, wriggling her hips, then lifted her upper body slightly and brushed her breasts back and forth across his chest.

He slid a hand between their bodies and captured one breast, soft and pliant. He cupped, kneaded gently, flicked the pad of his thumb against the budded nipple. "Sit up. I want to see you."

She nipped his lower lip, then pushed up on her hands until she was sitting astride him, his shaft buried deep. The breeze from the balcony door fluttered the sheer drapery behind her.

At first she didn't move, just gazed down at him. "Nice view, mister."

"You can say that again." He'd dated thin women and voluptuous ones, women with different skin and hair colors, and always found them sexy. But Kendra . . . The stunning black-and-white photo had come to life: black hair a little mussed, ivory skin glowing golden in the lamplight, a flush on her cheeks and chest, pink lips slightly swollen, and nipples rosy and tight. No, this woman wasn't remote, she was seriously hot—and he was lodged firmly in her core.

He pumped his hips, reminding her of that fact. He had put her on top so she could set the pace, but a complete halt wasn't acceptable.

Taking the hint, she began to rise and fall on him, the kiss of her sheath tight and clingy, slick and warm, giving his cock exactly what it craved. He groaned with pleasure as throbbing arousal built inside him.

When he raised his hands to caress her breasts, she leaned forward slightly so they swung neatly into the curves of his palms. She rested her own hands on his chest, bracing herself, and their bodies telegraphed a dynamic tension as she moved back and forth, up and down on him.

He played with the soft, supple flesh in his hands and teased her nipples, rubbing them gently between thumbs and index fingers.

Her chest rose and fell quickly, her breath coming in soft pants that made him realize he was gasping, too, and much less subtly.

When her hips began to rotate so she swirled around his shaft as she rode him, he groaned again, the sensations so incredible he knew he couldn't last long. "Jesus, Kendra, this is good."

"So good."

His body tightened with the achy pressure that told him he'd almost reached the point of no return. He slid one hand down to where their bodies joined and found her swollen clit. He brushed it lightly with his thumb and was rewarded with a moan of pleasure.

She speeded her pace, adjusting her angle so her engorged bud pressed harder against his thumb and he took the hint, firming his touch a little.

"Oh, Flynn, yes."

God, yes. He was about to burst wide open, and he needed to take her with him.

He squeezed her clit gently, rubbing it between his thumb and finger the way he'd done with her nipples, and she cried out. Spasms of orgasm surged through her, rocking against him.

With a hoarse cry, he let his own orgasm rip through him and into her.

Lost in sensation, he eventually realized her body was softening, relaxing, and he steadied her as she climbed off him and collapsed on the bed beside him, flat on her back.

She raised a hand and smoothed a few damp wisps of hair off her forehead, then let her hand flop against his arm as if she didn't have the energy to hold it up. "Wow. That was wonderful."

"Oh, yeah. Worth waiting for." He stroked her hand.

With her other hand, she reached out to touch the drapery that enclosed them. "Love this bed." She gazed at him, eyes warm. "Thanks for getting this amazing room."

"My pleasure."

"I bet there's even a real bathroom." With an anticipatory smile she edged over to the other side of the bed and slipped out.

Sitting up to enjoy the view of her naked back, especially that sweet little arse, he said, "Want to share a bath?"

"In a tub? A real tub?" She glanced over her shoulder, then speeded her pace and went into the bathroom. "Lovely."

Did she mean the bathroom or the idea of sharing a bath? With any luck, both. "Is that a yes?"

Body framed in the open doorway, she turned. "Definitely. Just give me a minute."

When the door closed behind her, he lay back in postorgasmic bliss. He hadn't felt this good in . . . well, definitely not since he'd been charged with theft.

Damn, he wasn't supposed to be thinking about the past, but it was a difficult habit to break. Especially when he was with the woman who'd been responsible for his troubles.

The bathroom door opened and he realized water was running in the tub. Kendra stood in the doorway. "Coming?"

He could revisit his old grudge, or bathe naked with a sexy woman. No contest. As he walked across the room, he tried to let go of the tension that had crept into his body and mind.

KENDRA watched Flynn walk toward her, gloriously naked. His body really was that of a dancer, or a soccer or tennis player, strong and lean and agile. She'd only had a few lovers, and had never felt so powerfully attracted to a man before. It was wonderful to finally be able to give in to the sexual pull she'd felt from the moment she first met him.

After these few nights, she'd have a wonderful stock of masturbation fantasies when she returned to her normal life. That was how things had always worked in the past. She had flings, not relationships. She'd always liked the word *fling*. It suggested something casual and fun that was easily tossed away afterward.

Now a disquieting thought crossed her mind. Would it be as easy to relegate Flynn to the realm of sexy fantasies?

She brushed away the thought. Why would she have a problem, when she never had before?

As Flynn stepped into the bathroom, her gaze cruised his body: broad shoulders, a chest bare of hair so his ripped muscles were even more apparent, six-pack abs, impressive package, and strong, well-shaped legs. When she finally focused on his face, she caught the flicker of something in his green eyes. Hesitation? No, it must have been a trick of lighting, because now it was gone.

"I used lemon verbena in the bath," she said, enjoying the tang in the steamy air. "They have rose, too, but I figured that wasn't your scent."

"Good call." He glanced at the tub and cocked an eyebrow. "Bubbles? Seriously?"

"I'm a woman. What do you expect?" It was so rare for her to have the time to luxuriate in a bath, she was going to take full advantage. "This bathtub is decadent." The tub, made of peach-colored marble, was oval shaped and set into a rectangular frame so it was surrounded by ledges. On one corner sat an orange hibiscus plant; another held fluffy, cream-colored towels; the other two had baskets with luxurious bath products. The bronze taps were located on the side rather than at one end.

There were candles, too, and she lit them, then clicked off the overhead light. Bubbles massed on the surface of the water, glistening and glinting in the flickering golden light. Oh yes, that was more . . . No, not romantic, she wasn't into romance. More sensual.

She dipped her foot in to check the temperature, then with a purr of satisfaction slid in and sank back against one end of the tub until bubbles covered her chest. "Come on in. The water's fine."

"Bubbles." He stirred them gingerly with one big masculine foot.

She chuckled. "They won't bite. And I promise I'll still think you're macho."

He snorted a laugh. "Okay, okay." Tentatively, he stepped in and eased down to sprawl at the opposite end of the tub, his legs brushing the outsides of hers.

"Doesn't it feel wonderful?"

"Feels okay, but you're all hidden under those damned bubbles. I'm in a bath with a naked woman and can't even see her."

"Then you'll have to operate by touch." She bent her knee and slid the sole of one foot along the outside of his leg. Later, she'd go for the inside, but right now she wanted to mellow out after that wonderful orgasm.

He rested his hand atop her foot.

Her head fell back against the edge of the tub and she closed her eyes, the better to savor all the sensations: silky warm water against her skin, a whisper of cooler air on her face from the open balcony door, and the scent of a country garden. Flynn's hand caressing her foot.

"Pretty lady. How come you're still single?"

She gave her standard response. "Married to my work."

"No man can compare?"

"Not so far." Then, in the interests of honesty, she added, "Not that I've been looking. When it comes to my job, I'm quite driven."

"The pursuit of justice."

She heard the edge in his voice and tilted her head to gaze at him. "In your case I got it wrong. But yes, I want to get criminals off the street, put them where they can't hurt people."

"It's a good goal, but . . ."

"What?" It was hard to read his expression in the candlelight.

"It sounds like it's more than a job. Like it's personal."

"It is."

His hand rubbed circles on the top of her foot. When she didn't go on, he said, "I'd like to hear about it."

This wasn't something she talked about with her colleagues. The family rarely discussed it either because it had happened so long ago. For some reason, sitting in a bubble bath in Mykonos with a man she'd once done her best to convict, she felt the urge to share.

"I was fifteen. Mom and Dad were both real estate agents, saving to open their own agency. Some guy offered them a supposedly great investment opportunity. It was a scam. He ripped off a bunch of investors and skipped the country. My parents not only lost their savings, they'd put a second mortgage on the house and invested my college fund. Everything was gone."

"White-collar crime. I can see why you . . ."

Went after Flynn so hard. Had that played into her willingness to go along with Dorothy? "My dad was shattered," she said softly. "Couldn't function. He . . ." She swallowed.

He gripped her foot warmly. "Kendra? What happened?"

"He went to the garage, locked the doors, and started the car engine. My mom was out doing errands. When she came back, she found him. It broke her, too. She might have survived the loss of their business, their savings, their hopes. But when he abandoned her, she fell apart. She never worked again, despite meds and counseling. She still has trouble functioning in the world."

"I'm sorry."

"Neither of them was strong. But I met someone who was, at Dad's funeral. Mom had a distant cousin I'd only seen a time or two before, a Crown Counsel."

He reflected. "After a criminal destroyed your family, she gave you a goal, a purpose."

He got it. "Yes. She was my inspiration and my mentor." Not a soft, affectionate woman like her mom, but a goal-driven, black-and-white one. A twinge of guilt passed through her. Dorothy would be pissed off if she saw Kendra now. "And now she's my boss. Yes, I'm married to my job. It's important work."

Flynn was only a temporary distraction, as was this holiday. She'd enjoy the diversion, then throw herself back into her job when she returned to Vancouver.

"Even so, everyone needs a personal life."

She shrugged. "I see my mom a lot. She's a sweet person and she needs help with some things." Like paying bills, grocery shopping, getting to medical appointments. Fortunately, between Kendra, her family, and a college student who helped out a couple of times a week, her mom could live in her own house. "She likes having me there, even if I'm working while she watches TV. Uncle William and Uncle Phil are a big part of our lives, and Peter."

"What about friends, hobbies?"

"I get together with colleagues occasionally. That's all I have time for. All I want."

"Really?"

She'd thought so. "How about you? I know you have a single parent mom and a half brother."

"You've been reading my file." Again there was an edge.

She swiped a few sweaty bits of hair back from her face and gazed at him, uncertain. "Flynn, I . . ."

He let go of her foot, heaved a sigh, then stretched back, both his arms extended along the sides of the tub. "We can't erase the past."

"And things I say remind you of it."

"Yeah." He closed his eyes and tilted his head back.

"Maybe this isn't going to work. Or . . . we could just have sex. Not talk."

He didn't open his eyes but one corner of his mouth curled. "Every guy's idea of a perfect relationship."

She'd never been great at social chat anyhow—and the sex was terrific—so why should she feel disappointed? "So do you—"

"Kidding." He held up a hand and his eyes opened. "No, it's good when we talk. Kind of like lancing a sore to get the poison out."

"Ouch. I don't want to—"

"Hey, I'm a tough guy." He lowered his hand under the water again and recaptured her foot. "It's good for me. I really want to move past the crap and put things in perspective. Ask away."

She stroked her other foot against the outside of his hip. "Okay, tough guy soaking in bubbles. You spend a lot of time with your family, don't you?"

"Yeah, there's just the three of us, and Ray needs special care. You know about Liz, right?"

"Uh, what about her? That she's a friend?"

"Also, she does social skills coaching with Ray. That's how we met."

"Social skills coaching?"

"Kids with Asperger's tend to be deficient in that area. They're literal, don't pick up on subtleties or nonverbal cues, can come across as self-centered, stupid, or even mean."

"They don't play well with others?"

"In a nutshell."

She smiled sympathetically. "I'm kind of like that. I'm goal-focused and not so great at social skills."

"Exaggerate that a thousand times and you've got Ray. Don't get me wrong, he's a good kid. Loyal to Mom and me. Bright, even genius level when it comes to maths. Just not the easiest person to be around. Like if you said, 'Hi, Ray, how are you?' you'd get a recitation of everything from his temperature to his bowel movements."

She chuckled and bubbles shifted on her chest, tickling. "Well, it *is* a stupid, time-wasting question."

"Sure, but it's a social nicety. He has neurological issues that mean he doesn't understand such things. Liz teaches him, role-plays with him so he can practice."

"Must be tough for all of you." Quietly, she asked, "His dad bailed?"

"Uh-huh. My own father was a good guy, and when he died in an accident on a construction site, it was just Ma and me. She was young and things were tough. She worked as a secretary at University College Dublin and that's where she met Ray's dad, a graduate student from Canada. They got married and he brought her back to Vancouver. It didn't work out so well. She's outgoing and demonstrative and he wasn't. Later, Ma and I figured maybe he had Asperger's."

"It's hereditary?"

"There can be a hereditary component."

"You'd think that would have given him sympathy for Ray."

"Empathy and relating to people's feelings can be hard for people with Asperger's. He said it was too much for him, he couldn't cope. He moved away and last we heard he lived alone."

She frowned. "When people get married and have kids, they should commit for the long term."

"Sometimes they aren't capable of it."

Like her parents. "I know. And that's sad." She gazed at him across a field of glinting bubbles. "You've never been married?"

"No, but I remember what it was like when my father was alive, and I'd like that for myself."

Before her dad died, Kendra had thought the same. Then her world fell apart. She'd learned that happy families don't necessarily last, whereas her work would always be there to give her an identity and purpose. "But you haven't met the right woman?"

"No, and it's complicated. Ray is high functioning and he'll end up living independently and supporting himself. But in a way he's like your mom. He'll need someone looking in, making sure he's doing okay."

"That's not so complicated. Family should do that for each other anyway. What does that have to do with you marrying and having kids?" She was pretty sure Flynn would make a great dad and probably a really good husband, too.

"Women have trouble getting along with Ray and understanding his place in my life."

"He's your brother," she said indignantly. "You don't just . . . ditch your family because they're different or because things get difficult."

"No, you don't," he said firmly. "Not everyone understands that." A note of humor entered his voice. "Liz's mom says I need to find a woman like Liz."

"I guess you do." And why did that thought make her feel a little sad?

"And now to get back to you," he said.

"Me?"

"Before you changed the subject, we—"

"What?" She sat up, soapy water sliding down her skin. "I didn't change the subject."

"And now you're trying to distract me by flashing your breasts."

She glanced down and saw the tops of her areolas peeping through melting bubbles.

"We were talking about your personal life," he said, "and you neatly switched it to mine."

She shook her head and slid an inch or two lower. "I told you all there was to tell."

"I don't think so. You may be married to your job, but you must date, don't you?"

"Not really. I have flings now and then. Like this." Though this one was different in so many ways. "I dated when I was younger, but it distracted me from work, and the truth is, I suck at it."

He gave a surprised laugh. "I doubt that."

"You said Ray is literal. Well, I'm pretty direct. Dating's often a bunch of silly game-playing." She crossed her arms over her chest. "If you want to have sex, then have sex. If you want to get married, then say so up front so the other person knows where things stand. Be yourself, don't play a role so someone will like you—because then it's not you they like anyhow. It's a waste of time."

"You're doing the black-and-white thing again. You kind of have a point, but . . . Okay, let's try this out. Say you and I just met and I ask you out. Am I really supposed to say, 'Hi, I'm Flynn and I think you're hot and I'd like to have sex with you. Down the road, I want to get married so I'll also be checking you out for that role. And by the way, I have a younger brother with Asperger's who might talk about bowel movements or quantum physics at dinner. How are you liking me so far?' "

Chapter 8

LAUGHTER bubbled out of Kendra. "Actually, you're sweeping me off my feet. But that's me, and admittedly I'm weird."

Flynn's warm laugh echoed hers, and in the candlelight his dimple flashed. He snapped his fingers. "So that's been my problem. I haven't been dating the weird girls."

"Glad I could help you out." Lazily she swirled warm, silky water up over her shoulders.

"But seriously, do you figure you'll ever get married? Have kids?"

Her hand stilled. Slowly, she shook her head. "I do better alone."

"That sounds lonely. I know you work like a demon, but when it's the middle of the night and you're alone in bed, is your job really all you need?"

She had her sexual fantasies, but those were only about physical release. When it came to emotional fulfillment, masturbation didn't cut it. But love, marriage, they took so much trust. Trust that your partner would be there for the long haul, that he'd be strong and loving enough not to bail when the going got rough.

She shrugged, feeling soap-slippery water ripple around her upper arms. "No one has everything. My life is rewarding." Hearing the defensive tone in her voice, she wondered if she was trying to convince him or herself.

He nodded slowly. "True. So, just to be totally up front about things, for you this is just a fling, right? When we go back to Vancouver . . ."

"It'll be over." Had she said that too firmly?

"You can't risk your job. And if I told Ma I was dating the woman who'd . . . you know."

Ruined things for Flynn, as well as hurt his mother and Ray. "She'd never forgive me. Never understand."

"She's very protective of her family."

"I respect that. I respect her. When things went wrong for her, she didn't fall apart. She looked after her family and moved ahead." She shook her head quickly. "I'm not dumping on my mom, just saying you're lucky yours is so strong."

"I am."

He gazed at her for a long moment. "I know I said talking was good, but this is getting . . ."

"A little heavy? Yeah, I never talk about things like this." She frowned in puzzlement. "And to do it naked in the bath with a seriously hot guy . . ."

He slid farther down in the bath and wormed his feet behind her lower back. "Enough talk. Come here." His feet exerted pressure, urging her toward him while his eyes gleamed with sexy mischief. "You need a good wash."

Happy to go with the change in mood, she scooted forward, lifting her legs over his until she was sitting in the V of his legs, her legs wrapped around his sides. "Because I'm a very"—she paused, drawing each word out—"dirty . . . girl?"

He threw his head back and laughed. "Something like that. Or

I'm a dirty boy who wants to get his hands all over you." They were close enough now that she could see his dimple and the gleam in his eyes.

"Hands are good, but . . ." She reached for a frilly mesh bath sponge that sat on the side of the tub. After dipping it in the water and slicking a little soap over it, she ran it lightly, teasingly, over his shoulders and chest, making sure to flick his nipples. Such a nice body. She almost wished for brighter light and clear water so she could see it.

"Hey, that's nice. Sexy. Now I see why women use those things."

Normally she took a morning shower, scrubbing a sponge briskly over her skin to invigorate herself. But on the rare occasions she made time for a bath before bed, it was accompanied by scented bubbles, a sexy fantasy, and slow, teasing caresses of a bath sponge. Now she had a fantasy come to life, and arousal stirred her body from relaxed to tingly and aware. She toyed with his nipples awhile longer, knowing he must be wondering when she'd take that sponge lower down.

Anticipating the feel of him in her hand, she could wait no longer. She slid the sponge down until her hand nudged his erect cock. "What have we here?" With her free hand she held it gently while she smoothed the sponge over his flesh, hoping the mesh surface would provide sexy stimulation. She worked the sponge up and down and all around his shaft.

He moaned and shifted restlessly. "Man, that feels good."

With one hand pumping his cock slowly, she took the sponge to his sac, circling and stroking, letting the frilly mesh edges tease the base of his shaft and his perineum.

"Jesus, yeah." His hips jerked.

God, it was so sexy touching him this way under the water, feeling his response. She was almost as turned on as he was. Her fingers tightened on his shaft and slid faster up and down as she focused the sponge on his perineum.

"Shit, Kendra, I'm gonna come."

His hips thrust again, his cock jerking in her hand as he cried out. She felt his come, hotter than the bathwater, gush over her hand.

Her body clenched, wanting to come, too, eager for his touch to make it happen. But for now, she eased off, still holding him as he finished climaxing.

When he heaved out a giant sigh and the tension slipped from his body, she let go. He flopped against the back of the tub, eyes closed, and for a few minutes didn't move. Then he raised his head, opened his eyes, and said, "Okay, I may live." He leaned forward to give her a kiss. "Thanks for the best bath I've ever had."

"My pleasure."

The dimple flashed. "Speaking of your pleasure . . . Move back so you can relax against the edge of the tub."

"Relax? I don't think that's going to happen. That was a real turn-on."

"This will be, too. Lie back."

She did, resting her arms along the sides of the tub, body humming with arousal. When he touched the sponge tentatively to the delicate skin of her upper chest, she shivered at the sensation—a combination of very gentle massage and erotic stimulation.

"Tell me what feels good," he said.

"Like that. Not too hard. Circles, flicks."

"Show me."

Her eyes had been half closed but now flew open to meet his intent gaze. She dropped her hand to rest it on his and together they stroked her breast: over the top, under the bottom curve, around in circles, then flicking across the nipple, moving away only when the sensation grew too intense. "Oh yes, Flynn, that feels wonderful."

His fingers lifted, capturing hers and intertwining with them. She guided his hand and the sponge to her other breast, luxuriating in the feeling that there was all the time in the world to take care of her needs slowly, enticingly, and thoroughly—and one very sexy man who seemed committed to doing it exactly the way she wanted it.

Tingles rippled outward and down to her pussy and she squeezed her thighs together, savoring the sweet, needy ache between them. If Flynn had closed his lips on her nipple and sucked, she might have come. If he rubbed her clit, she would for sure.

Instead she guided him to less sensitive territory, swirling the sponge over her rib cage, giving her body a chance to unwind. Oh no, she didn't want to climax yet. She wanted the tension to build until she was ready to scream with the need for release.

"Wish I could see you under all those bubbles," he said, his voice husky.

"I'll help you find your way." She slid his hand across her stomach in wide circles that flirted with the top of her pubis, the edge of the sponge a sexy tickle that made her crave more.

She spread her legs and indulged in a slow dip between them with the sponge, its frills softly stroking her sensitive folds. Steering Flynn's hand, she glided the sponge back and forth, giving herself exactly the pressure and speed she needed to drive her closer to the edge but not tip her over. Though she didn't focus on her clit, the edge of the sponge gave it teasing brushes.

It was so sexy, the two of them doing this together, fingers interlocked, his hand warm and hard under hers. Flynn was so sexy, auburn hair tousled and damp, green eyes dark and intense in the flickering candlelight, taking such good care of her.

With each stroke, her body tightened. She whimpered with pleasure. Sometimes she thought these moments were the best, the ones where she was so close, tension coiling and anticipation building, pleasure mounting until she could hardly bear it.

Finally, so needy she couldn't stand it any longer, she guided

Flynn's big hand and that soft sponge to focus on her clit, brushing it lightly. "Oh, God," she gasped. She stared into his eyes. "Make me come, Flynn."

Again the sponge brushed her nub, and again. She panted for air and realized she was gasping, "Yes, yes, oh yes."

One more caress and that was it, she broke, crying out as orgasm splintered through her, sharp and strong. She rode the incredible sensations, then, just as they were beginning to ebb, Flynn dropped the sponge, spread her open, and thrust a finger inside her.

Arousal jolted through her again. "Oh my God, yes!"

Another finger joined it, spreading her, pumping in and out and swirling deep inside her.

The sensations that had been fading began to build again, fast and hard.

His thumb pressed her clit and a sensation so intense she couldn't name it blasted through her, and again she shattered, her body spasming hard around his fingers.

He stayed there, palm warm and firm against her pussy as she came apart.

JESUS, she was something. Stunning, responsive, inventive, and man, was she gorgeous when she climaxed.

He waited until the final tremors had faded away, then eased his fingers out of her body.

She lolled back, sinking into the tub until the water reached her chin. "That was unreal." She didn't open her eyes but her mouth kinked slightly. "The bubbles inspired you."

He snorted. "Now let's go to bed and do things the old-fashioned way." Despite two orgasms, his cock was rock hard again.

One eye opened. "The old-fashioned way?"

"Try it, you'll like it."

"I'm boneless. I don't think I can move."

He stood, water and bubbles cascading down his body. "I'm definitely not boneless."

The other eye opened and she stared up at his hard-on. "Very true. And pretty impressive."

He held out a hand.

When she reached up to take it, he hauled her to her feet. Bubbles slid down her skin, revealing her sleek, flushed body. If he'd been sensible, he'd have dried them both off. Instead, he hoisted her into his arms and again carried her to bed.

When he bent to lay her down, she kept her arms around his neck. "This is the old-fashioned way?" she teased. "Wet?"

"Definitely wet. I like you wet."

"You make me wet." She released his neck and lay back.

He sank down beside her, wanting to kiss every inch the sponge had caressed, this time seeing and tasting her. He bent to tongue the soft, damp flesh of her chest, nipping and sucking but not enough to leave marks. Then the amazingly soft underside of her breasts. Her puckered areola. When he finally took her beaded nipple gently between his teeth and sucked hard, she shuddered and gave a soft cry.

Slowly, he worked his way down her body until he was kissing the tender area at the very top of the inside of her thigh. Her skin was dewy from arousal and her sweet musky smell, mingling with the herbal one of the bubble bath, intoxicated him. He eased off the bottom of the bed, the tile cool and hard under his knees. "Toss me a pillow and slide down the bed."

She obeyed, her face rosy and hair tousled. "Flynn?"

He slipped the pillow under his knees. "Lie back and let me taste you."

Without another word, she did. He caught her by the hips and lifted her pussy to his mouth. Rosy folds, slick with her juices. "So pretty." He lapped gently, testing her response, then firming his tongue as she squirmed against him.

When he dipped his tongue inside, she trembled around him. God, she was sweet, and he was so horny his whole body ached. Wanting to know her even more intimately, to go deeper than he could reach with his tongue, he used his fingers to explore her mysterious, unseen center. Ah, there it was, the spot that made her whole body clench.

He tapped it again, that secret, hidden spot, stroked against it, then held her as she exploded.

Fingers still inside her, he laved her pussy with his tongue, then turned his attention to her clit. His tongue swirled figure eights around it, and again she climaxed, with a deep moan.

"Flynn," she gasped a minute or two later, "if this is the old-fashioned way, I guess I'm an old-fashioned woman. But now I really want you inside me."

That was exactly where he wanted to be. He released her hips and she squirmed up the bed, then he lay between her legs and took her mouth in a deep, sensual kiss, both of them sharing her intimate flavor. When she tilted her hips, he slid inside with a groan of satisfaction.

Wanting to see her spread out beneath him, he carefully rose up on his knees, raising her hips. Her shoulders remained on the bed and her back arched, her bent knees on either side of his hips. He gripped her thighs, holding her there as he stroked deep inside her.

She slid her hands under her butt cheeks, adding support, finding the angle that worked for her. Her firm little breasts thrust upward, nipples pink and hard.

In this position, he could watch himself plunge in and out of her, see her slippery cream coat his shaft. Watch the way her head twisted on the pillow and see her pink lips part to let out sighs and whimpers. Heat coiled inside him, urging him to lose control and go for it, but this time he wouldn't give in. He kept his thrusts slow and steady until Kendra's hips began to writhe and she muttered, "Oh, God, oh yes."

Her pussy ground against him, rubbing her clit against his shaft so he felt that hard little nub. He speeded his pace, trying to hit the G-spot he'd found earlier with his fingers, while his own orgasm built toward inevitability.

Kendra cried his name on a high note and he felt the pulsing waves of her climax, and finally he could let go.

With a groan of relief and joy, he pumped hard and long inside her.

Now this, this was perfect.

THE next day, during a lazy morning of late rising and a swim, then an afternoon touring the island of Paros, Flynn reflected on his future.

Through photography, he was rediscovering his joy in design. His IT business had involved some creativity, but he'd like even more. That thought was on his mind when, at six o'clock that afternoon, he stood on the bow of the *Aphrodite*, a Heat Wave in one hand, and phoned his ma.

After they shared the highlights of their days over a sketchy cell connection, she said, "You sound better, Flynn. Like you're really on holiday."

He gazed at the scenic harbor in Paros and sipped the fruity, summery drink. "I feel better. I'm managing to put the past behind me."

"That's grand." He knew she wouldn't elaborate because Ray was with her in the kitchen. Flynn and his mother hadn't told his brother about the criminal charge and trial, nor the loss of Flynn's business. It would have been too much for him to deal with, an unnecessary stressor when there was nothing he could do to help.

Her voice went on, broken by static. "Tell Liz I bless her for twisting your arm and getting you to go."

"I will." Of course, part of his good mood had to do with Kendra. Last night had been— He gripped the cell tighter as he realized something. It had been the best night of his life. Now there was a mind-blowing thought, and he hadn't the faintest idea what to do about it.

"Flynn? Are you there? Can you hear me?"

"Sorry, Ma. Yes, but I missed that. What did you say?"

"Last night I got up to go to the bathroom and"—cell static interrupted for a moment, then he heard her voice again—"at three in the morning, bed not even slept in, working on something. An iPhone app, isn't that what you said, Ray?"

Usually Ray, who lived by routines, went to bed at the same time every night. But he was prone to obsessions and occasionally he'd get so caught up in something that he could be at it for hours without coming up for air. "I'll have a word with him about it and—"

He heard his brother's voice in the background. "It's 8:05, Ma. I talk to Flynn at 8:05."

"Okay, Ma, love you. Now pass the phone to Ray."

When he heard his brother say, "Hello, Flynn," he responded, "Hi, bro, what's this I hear about an iPhone app? You couldn't wait until I got home so we could do it together?" They'd often spend hours together, enjoying working on a project like this.

Ray went off into technical detail about an app that would track investments, put in automatic buy and sell orders, and transfer funds to and from different accounts. It was pretty impressive, from what Flynn could make out between bursts of static.

"Where did you get the idea?" he asked. Ray wasn't exactly an innovative guy.

His brother said something about a website—Flynn thought he caught the phrase "hacker challenges"—but the static was getting crazy. Maybe he should drop their mother an e-mail and get her to check it out. Chances were, it was legit and ethical, but he didn't want Ray getting himself into any kind of trouble.

Since Ray was seven, he'd been smart enough to get around any controls Flynn might put in place to restrict his Internet access. Nor did it work to make him use the computer at the kitchen table where Ma could keep an eye on him. He'd only sneak down in the middle of the night when she was asleep. And then there were all those computers at Ray's school . . . No, they'd relied on giving him rules about what he could and couldn't do, explaining why, and periodically checking up on him. Sounded as if it was time for another check.

Hoping Ray could hear better on his end, Flynn delivered the requisite lecture about getting enough sleep, then said, "Have a good day, Ray. Talk to you tomorrow morning."

"Yes, at 8:05. Oh, I forgot to ask how you are."

Flynn grinned. People with Asperger's tended to be self-centered and, as he'd told Kendra, deficient in social skills. But, thanks to Liz's coaching, and Flynn's and his mother's reinforcement, Ray was learning. "I'm having a great time, Ray. Thanks for asking."

As he closed the phone, he gazed away from the harbor and out at the ocean, still smiling. There were times back when Ray was young that Flynn had resented him for being so weird and always requiring their ma's attention. But once his brother had been diagnosed, Flynn had realized that blaming Ray would be like blaming a baby who'd been born deaf or blind. Neurologically, Ray wasn't typical. But, as Liz always said, everyone had their strengths and weaknesses; each human being was unique and special.

Ray was his brother and he loved him. They'd always found things they enjoyed doing together, especially since they were both interested in technology. As Ray got older, they'd played around with video games and apps, Flynn's creativity, visual skill, and training complemented by Ray's near-genius math brain and dogged persistence and attention to detail.

Hmm. It might be fun to start his own business creating games and apps. He could use a course or two to fine-tune his skills, but he was damned good at animation and the creative side. As a bonus, the business might provide employment for Ray—perhaps a part-time job now, working into full-time when he finished his education.

Now, this was an idea Flynn could get behind. The future was actually looking bright. At least on the work side.

He rested his arms on the ship's rail. On the personal side . . . There hadn't been one for nearly a year, and now there was Kendra. When they got off the *Aphrodite*, would they really head in separate directions and never see each other again? The necessity had seemed obvious, yet he'd just spent the best night of his life with her.

Making sexy waves was all well and good, but Aphrodite was also the goddess of love, and he had a feeling the goddess wasn't going to settle for just sex.

As for Kendra—how she felt and what she wanted—the woman was confusing. She wasn't superficial, and she'd shared deeply personal things with him. Was her devotion to her work really so single-minded she couldn't contemplate making room in her life for love? For, down the road, a husband and family? Or had her family's tragedy made her wary about loving, about commitment, about planning a future with someone?

He had to find out.

Except, his emotions had taken such a battering this past year. Kendra wasn't a cruel woman, yet due to her mistake, she'd destroyed his career. Was he an utter fool to get in any deeper with her?

Chapter 9

A few hours later, Flynn watched with pleasure and lust as Kendra, looking summery and casual in a purple sundress, let Liz drag her into the line of laughing people who were trying out the steps to a Greek folk dance.

Her uncle William, sitting beside him at one end of their dinner table, turned to his husband, who was seated on his other side. "How great is that? It's a sight I never thought I'd see."

"She's a different woman than the one who boarded the *Aphrodite*," Phil agreed, smiling.

Flynn eavesdropped shamelessly as William said, "Get her out of the business suit and gradually some of the emotional armor comes off. I hope she'll learn from this and not revert when she gets back home."

Emotional armor. It seemed her uncles also believed Kendra was afraid to let herself care.

"She's always been too influenced by Dorothy," Phil said.

Dorothy must be the role model Kendra had talked about. Her boss, and one of her reasons for keeping their affair secret.

"With the way her mom was," William said, "she needed a role model."

"Too bad she picked one who thinks she's better than the rest of the world," Phil sniped.

"I'm not sure that's true. Dorothy just doesn't like people."

"Because she thinks she's better than them."

William chuckled. "Whatever. But Kendra's not like that. There's a warm heart under that armor. Look how she is with her mom, and how she helped us after your surgery."

"She should take that warm heart and fall in love. Have children. I want grandnieces and nephews as well as the grandkids Peter and Liz are going to give us."

Flynn tended to agree about Kendra, yet the idea of her doing it with another man hurt. With him, though . . . Yeah, maybe he could envision that, like something in a dream. In reality, so many things stood in their way.

"Come on, love," Phil said to his husband, "let's join the dancers." They rose and started to leave the table, then he glanced back at Flynn. "Hey, man, d'you have two left feet? Aren't you going to dance?"

Yeah, he was. In fact, he strode with determination to the weaving line of dancers. Kendra was beside Liz's mom, their arms around each other's waists. "Ladies," he said above the catchy music, "my ma taught me it's supposed to go girl, boy, girl, boy."

"Right you are," Mrs. Tippett said, and a moment later he was snugging one arm around her sturdy waist and another around Kendra's slender one.

"Show me what to do," he said to them, and soon the three were bumping hips and laughing their heads off. He liked this playful, carefree side of Kendra. But feeling her muscles flex under his arm, rubbing his hip against her soft one, seeing her long, bare legs kick back and forth gave him a growing hard-on he had to fight to control.

Fortunately, the music stopped. Mrs. Tippett let go of his waist and fanned herself. "And here I thought I was in good shape from all the birding hikes we take."

Kendra let go on the other side and said breathlessly, "I know what you mean. I spend half an hour a day on a treadmill, but it's not the same."

Flynn, who'd always run, swum, and played tennis, and had done so almost compulsively in the months he'd been unemployed, was breathless only because of her nearness and his anticipation. Gratefully, he saw Gwen and Santos rounding people up.

Mr. Tippett, who'd been dancing on his wife's other side, took her hand. "I'm ready to call it a night. Maybe on the way back to the ship, we'll hear a Scops owl."

"In town, dear? Do you really think so?"

"One lives in hope."

Flynn smiled at that. One did indeed.

William and Phil, also holding hands, strolled past. "Night, everyone," Phil said. "Sleep tight."

"Night, uncles," Kendra said, and Flynn and the Tippetts added their good nights.

When the gay couple had moved on, Mrs. Tippett said to Kendra, "I didn't know quite what to make of your uncles at first, but they're nice, aren't they?"

"Very."

"So different from us," her husband said. "Absolutely no interest in birds."

Flynn stifled a grin and caught Kendra doing the same.

"Not so different," his wife said. "We all want grandchildren as soon as possible." She tugged her husband's hand. "Let's go listen for an owl."

When they'd gone, Flynn leaned close to Kendra. "Shall we skip the owls and meet in your cabin?" Much as he'd have liked to get a hotel room again, tonight everyone was heading back to the *Aphrodite* together and it would be obvious if he and Kendra snuck off.

She reached into her purse. "Bring this with you. It guarantees admission." After glancing around to check that no one was watching, she slipped something into his pants pocket.

He caught a glimpse of a small, rose pink tube. "Lipstick?" What was this new game?

"Take a closer look." Her cheeks were pinker than the dance warranted. "When you're alone." She turned on her heel and sauntered away, hips swinging in that skimpy sundress.

Casually, he slipped his hand into his pocket and palmed the tube. His thumb brushed something. A switch? He pressed it, and the object in his pocket hummed and began to throb, startling him so he barely found the presence of mind to turn it off.

Well, damn, it was a vibrator. She wanted them to play with a vibrator. Immediately, his cock thickened.

WHEN Kendra saw the door begin to open, she jumped off the bed to meet Flynn with a kiss.

He met it fast and hard, then pulled back, resting his hands on her shoulders. "Seriously? That thing's tiny."

She chuckled. "What a guy. You think size is all that matters. Believe me, my toy gets the job done. And I figured if my luggage was inspected, no one would think twice about seeing that in my cosmetic bag along with a couple of lipsticks."

"Good point." His lips kinked.

She wondered what he was imagining. An airport official holding up a giant phallic-shaped dildo in the middle of a crowded airport? "Want to try that kiss again?"

Flynn accepted the invitation, tossing the vibrator on the bed and pulling her into his arms. This kiss was long and slow, hot and wet.

He stepped back and tugged one skinny strap off her shoulder. "I like the dress."

She did, too. The purple brought out the green in her eyes and made her pale skin look even creamier. He probably liked it because it was skimpy.

His next comment supported that theory. "What are you wearing under it?" He traced the front of the fitted top. "I'm not seeing bra straps."

"That'd be because I'm not wearing a bra," she purred.

He ran his hands down the back of the dress to where he could feel the curves of her bottom through the soft cotton. "I'm not feeling panty lines."

"A thong."

He eased the hem up until he could curve his hands around both bare cheeks. "God, you feel good."

She rubbed her pelvis against his erection. "You, too." Her hands got busy with the buttons of his shirt.

He unzipped the back of her sundress, then they moved apart to pull off clothes. For her, it was just a matter of letting the dress slide down, then slipping out of it and draping it over the chair. She left her thong on, a tiny black one, just one scrap of clothing to tantalize him.

She lay back on the white sheet and ran her fingers up and down the small, slim vibrator. When Flynn was naked, she tossed the toy to him. "Take it for a test run."

He sat on the bed, studying her with a gleam in his eye.

She slid a pillow under her hips as he flicked the switch on the vibrator, then he pressed the tip against his palm.

"That's not generally where I use it," she teased.

Mischief sparked in his eyes. "Oh, yeah? Where, then?"

"Use your imagination."

He bent over her and ran it down the side of her neck to her shoulder. "How about here?" To her surprise, it sent erotic twinges through her.

"Not bad, but not my favorite place."

With a light touch, he drew throbbing circles around her breast, moving toward the center, then tweaking her nipple between finger and thumb.

"Getting warmer." Her sex was already pulsing in anticipation.

When he pressed the head of the vibrator over the front of her thong and followed the narrow strip of fabric between her legs, she gave a sigh of pleasure and spread her legs wide. The vibrator hummed gently but insistently, pressing the silk against her tender skin, drawing teasing circles that barely brushed her clit.

"I want to see you," he said, and tugged the thong down her legs. "I want to watch your body respond."

She felt so exposed, open for him like this as he positioned himself between her legs, but the heated glitter in his eyes was a turn-on. And so was the humming toy, dwarfed in his big hand as he traced it over her labia, her own moisture making it slide easily. If it really had been lipstick, he'd have been drawing a colored mouth around her opening. As it was, the touch sent warm shivers of arousal through her.

He varied his touch, sometimes lighter and sometimes firmer, and switched from straight strokes to circles and back again. The toy dipped inside her channel. Not knowing what he'd do next, her body tightened and quivered in anticipation. She loved how Flynn made a sexy game of this, teasing her toward climax, building the sensations slowly and inevitably.

Finally, he applied the tip lightly to her clitoris, and she moaned. "Yes."

"Harder? I don't want to hurt you."

"A little harder. Firm pressure just . . . oh yes, right there." Body tensing as she neared the edge, she focused on that steady pulsing, a beat that throbbed both inside and outside her body.

He eased back and she groaned in frustration, but a moment later two fingers slipped inside her, opening her, beginning to pump. Her internal muscles gripped him and her whole body shook as he gently rubbed her G-spot.

The vibrator pressed her clit exactly the way she'd taught him, her body tightened, and . . . he slid the toy away again. She moaned with need.

Flushed and intent, he stared down at his hands playing with her.

Her gaze tracked down his body, saw his thick erection rising up his belly. She wanted him inside her, but not yet, not until he relented and gave her that first orgasm, the one he seemed so intent on withholding—on building until she was ready to scream for it.

"Flynn," she gasped, tightening her muscles around his fingers. "Please. I need . . . oh, yes."

He'd stroked the humming toy back to press firmly against her clit, moving in the tiniest, most intense circles. "Don't go," she panted, closing her eyes and writhing against it, and this time he didn't. Inside her, his fingers stroked that magic spot, and all the arousal that had been gathering surged together in a giant wave that crested and roared through her.

She pressed her hand over his, holding the vibrator just where she needed it to prolong her climax. When the shudders finally subsided, she eased him away.

He slid his fingers gently out of her. "You're so beautiful when you come."

Opening her eyes, she saw him staring down raptly, the fingers that had been inside her now wrapped around his erect cock.

"I need to be inside you," he said.

She sat up and took the sex toy from his hand. "Don't you want to know what this feels like?"

"Jesus."

"I take it that's a yes?" She shoved at his chest with her free hand. "Lie down."

He sprawled back on the bed, so totally masculine and gorgeous, legs slightly spread.

She kneeled beside him, tempted to just bend down and suck that huge, luscious cock into her mouth. But she was curious about the vibrator. She clicked it on. "I've never done this before so you'll have to tell me what feels good." Tentatively, she ran it along the base of his shaft.

He twitched. "That's . . . interesting."

"Interesting good?"

"It's getting there. Oh yeah, that's nice," he said as she buzzed it up his shaft and teased the underside of his crown.

Pre-come glistened in the eye of his penis and she dipped her head to lick it, then couldn't resist lapping all around the head of his penis. Sliding the toy down his shaft, she closed her lips over him and took him in.

Licking and sucking, she fumbled blindly with the vibrator, stroking his balls, then pressing it behind them.

His hips jerked, then his hand came down to cover hers, holding it there. "That's hot. That thing throbbing while you're sucking me off."

He could say that again. She slid the fingers of her free hand up and down his shaft, below where her mouth could reach, his skin slippery with her saliva. Faster she worked him, feeling his body go rigid with tension. So was hers, but this was about his pleasure.

His hand pressed hers with the vibrator harder against his perineum, then he groaned, a feral sound deep in his throat, and his come jetted into her mouth, hot and salty.

She swallowed as he continued to pulse, aware that he'd pulled the vibrator away from his body. Its low humming was like the buzz of a persistent insect until her thumb found the switch and turned it off.

His erection began to subside, but when she started to lift her head, his hand came down to hold her there. "Suck me, Kendra. Slow and easy."

She did, gently at first, then, as he hardened again, more firmly.

His fingers grabbed a handful of hair and tugged. "Now let's do this together."

Lifting her head, she saw him smiling at her. "An excellent idea." She swung her body atop his, trapping his rigid length between her thighs for a moment, then lifting so he could slide inside her.

They both sighed with satisfaction. "Come here," he said, tugging her down to lie atop him as he pumped slowly, gliding on the cream of her arousal. He circled her with his arms and rolled their bodies so she was underneath.

When she reached up to adjust the pillow under her head, he caught her wrists with one big hand and held them above her head. His eyes were a deep forest green as he smiled down at her. "You're really something."

"You, too," she breathed, and when she left her lips parted, he kissed her in a deep, sensual kiss that went on and on.

Slowly, very slowly, their bodies wove together in tiny movements, not a fiery drive to orgasm but little licks of flame, crackling through their nerve endings, sizzling through their veins.

He was by far the best lover she'd ever had. The way he made her feel was incredible, and it wasn't just physical. When he pulsed deep inside her, when his tongue stroked the inside of her mouth, the sensations went beyond sex to something she'd never felt before. Sex was about joining, but in the past it had always been two separate bodies giving and taking pleasure, not two human beings merging.

Was it because of her and Flynn's history? For them, nothing could be impersonal. Was that why the sex felt so intimate, and she felt an emotional connection she'd never experienced?

She couldn't tell where her body left off and his began. She couldn't tell if his cock was hitting her G-spot, or whether his shaft or pubic bone was brushing her clit, because all the sensations merged together in a warm, glowing, pulsing . . . "Oh!" Orgasm snuck up on her, rippled through her, and the ripples kept coming and coming.

Flynn was climaxing, too, the spasms of his orgasm blending with hers, prolonging it.

When both their bodies finally stilled, she wondered fancifully if they'd actually melted together so they could never be pried apart.

But eventually, he pressed a kiss against her neck and began to raise himself. "I'm too heavy."

She hadn't noticed, and in fact her body felt vulnerable and exposed when he heaved himself off to lie on his back. A moment later, though, he put an arm around her and tugged her close so she was curled against his side, one arm and one leg thrown over his body. She rested contentedly, coasting on endorphins.

After a few minutes, his hand caressed her shoulder. "Kendra, I've been thinking about what I want to do next."

"You're ready for another round already?" she asked disbelievingly. She felt so satiated and exhausted, she might never move again.

He chuckled. "No, I mean thinking about the future. I have an idea for another company I might start."

"Really? Tell me." If he did and it was a big success, she might feel a tiny bit less guilty.

"I will, but there's something else I want to talk to you about."

"Is there some way I can help? I'd do anything."

"Anything?" he queried suggestively. Then his voice sobered. "What are your dreams? When you think ahead, is all you see your job and your family?"

"I don't look ahead much. I mean yes, of course my job and family. They're . . ."

"What?"

Very softly, she finished the thought. "Everything I have. Everything that matters."

"You could have more. Don't you want more? Love? Maybe children?"

She'd avoided romance and emotion. They were dangerous. People could get hurt. It had always been easy to stay safe and uninvolved because she'd never had strong feelings for any of her lovers. Until now. Lying wrapped up with Flynn, how could she not want more? But that wasn't her path in life. "I'm not a relationship kind of woman."

"I think you are. If you weren't, you wouldn't be so devoted to your mom, your uncles."

"That's different."

"How is it different than loving a man and having kids?"

Why was he asking this? Did he have feelings for her? The idea was . . . exciting, amazing, but terrifying. She shifted uneasily. "My uncles have never let me down, and Mom, she's . . . she's all she's capable of being. To get involved with a man, to commit and trust, trust that he'd be there, that he'd be strong enough to hang in there no matter what happened . . ." She shook her head. "That's big."

"It scares you."

"Yes," she admitted, just a soft breath against his shoulder.

"Your dad let you down."

Perceptive man. "Your family experience wasn't much better. Your dad died, then your mom remarried and that guy abandoned your family." So how had Flynn turned out so much better adjusted—so much braver—than she had?

"You talked about role models, and your boss. My role model was Ma. She held things together and made Ray and me believe we were the best things that ever happened to her." He covered her hand where it lay across his chest and squeezed it. "It's rough about your dad. He must have been shattered to do something like that, but he's only one man. Look at William and Phil. Neither's ever going to quit on the other, or on Peter, you, or your mom. Right?"

"No. They wouldn't."

"So it's possible, Kendra. But you have to be strong, too. Strong enough to trust."

How had this man who'd known her only a few days come to know her so intimately? "Where are you going with this, Flynn?"

"You said people should skip the silly games and be straight-forward. So, here it is. When we get back to Vancouver, I want to keep seeing you. And you already know that, down the road, I'm looking for marriage. For a woman who'll become part of my family."

Her heart lifted. Oh yes, this man was sweeping her off her feet. Much as she might tell herself it was crazy, that she wasn't a relation-ship kind of woman, she hated the thought of losing Flynn. He was sexy, smart, sweet, and if there was ever a man she could trust, one who'd proved he stood by people when the going got tough, he was that person. And yet there were so many reasons against it. "I could lose my job, and your mother would never accept me."

"You're saying it's easier to quit than fight for what you want? Just like your dad?"

Her mouth fell open. No, she wasn't like her dad. Was she?

"These last months," Flynn said, "I got stuck, feeling bitter and sorry for myself. Now I'm figuring out what I want, and I'm going for it. How about you?"

She had no idea what to say, but he went on anyway. "You know what your uncles said? You're a different woman than the one back home, and they're thrilled. They like this Kendra, and so do I. The one who's happy, dancing Greek folk dances, making love with a man who cares about her. Don't leave that woman behind in Greece."

No, she didn't want to. Flynn was telling her she didn't have to. All she had to do was say, "All right. I do care for you, Flynn, and I want to keep seeing you when we—"

His lips captured the last syllable.

Chapter 10

BY the end of the next day, Flynn was thinking that a guy could get used to this life. A leisurely breakfast, a morning swim, playing tourist in an interesting Greek town—this time on the island of Ios—then a delicious dinner by the ocean, and lots of laughs at Peter's stag party.

The only thing that would make this better was if he and Kendra could acknowledge their relationship. They'd decided not to until they got back to Vancouver, spent more time together, and figured out how serious they were about each other. If they were going to tell her boss and his ma, it had to be done in person.

So he waited impatiently as people hung out in the hallways, comparing notes about the stag and stagette. Finally, everyone had gone to their cabins and his roommate was asleep. He snuck out to Kendra's cabin, wondering if she'd even still be awake.

When he slipped inside, she was in bed, a sheet covering her. Sleeping. He would wake her; he knew she'd want that. But for a moment, he enjoyed standing there watching.

She'd loosened up so much in the last few days, and even her cabin showed it. Yes, her closed computer still sat on the desk, but a colorful scarf lay across it. A small painting of a Greek town sat propped against the wall, candles flickered, and a pair of rope-soled sandals almost tripped him when he moved toward the bed.

She stirred and her eyes fluttered open. "Hey, I'd almost given up on you."

He stroked soft wisps of black hair off her cheek. "You know what? I like you."

Her eyes glowed. "I like you, too." Then they sparked and she said, "Take your clothes off and show me how much."

And so he did.

FLYNN woke in his own bed the next morning, smiling. The future was brighter than the Greek sky outside his cabin window. As his roommate babbled on about Santorini, today's island, all Flynn could think was that he'd see Kendra.

Last night, they'd not only made sweet, slow love, but they'd talked for ages. She was a complicated woman, wounded by her past but strong and determined. A woman to care about. And he did. More than he'd ever cared for a woman before. She felt the same, she'd confessed, for the first time in her life. The road ahead had some definite bumps, but he and Kendra could handle them as long as they stuck together.

Finally, his roommate left and, whistling, Flynn showered and dressed in shorts and a tee. Ready to go up for breakfast, he picked up his cell from the table by the bed where he'd tossed it before going to Kendra's cabin last night. He'd turned it off then, and now when he turned it back on, there was a message.

He heard his mother's voice, sounding stressed. "Call me as soon as you get this."

Damn, why hadn't he turned his phone on last night? He punched speed dial, heart racing. What time would it be there? Late evening? When she answered on the second ring, he said, "Ma, what's wrong?"

"Flynn, thank God."

"What is it? Are you sick? Is it Ray?"

"Wait a minute."

For agonizing minutes he held on, then he heard her say, "Ray's in his room and I've gone into my bedroom and closed the door."

"Ma!"

"No one's sick, it's nothing like that. It's— Oh, Flynn, I don't even know how to say this."

His heart slowed and he sat on the edge of his bed. No one was sick or injured, so it couldn't be too awful. "Start at the beginning." The connection was better this morning, with only a little static.

"After Ray went to school this morning, I got your e-mail about checking what websites he'd been visiting, to see if I could find something about hacker challenges."

Shit. He scrubbed his hand over his face. "What's he been doing?"

"I found the site where he got the idea for the investment application. It's password protected but I tried all the passwords you said he might use, and one worked." She drew a long breath. "This site is really, really obscure. I doubt many people would find it. God knows how Ray did, but that's our Ray, isn't it?"

"Yeah. So, what's the site?"

"It isn't good. What he did wasn't the real challenge, it was just the beginning. The challenge is, well, I think it's identity theft. To get someone else's investment information and passwords and pretend to be them, managing their accounts and . . ." Her voice trailed off.

"Ma!"

"And to transfer the proceeds of sale to numbered accounts."

"What? That's theft." A horrible suspicion dawned on him but he brushed it aside. "Ray wouldn't do that. He's no thief."

She didn't answer.

"Ma!" he said for the third time.

"No, he isn't, because he knows it's wrong. That's black-and-white; it's a rule. But you know he has trouble with concepts, Flynn. I doubt it would dawn on him that this was stealing. He'd just be obsessed with figuring out all the steps in the puzzle."

The suspicion settled in his gut, heavy and vile. "You don't think . . ."

"Oh, Flynn." Now he heard tears in her voice. "Yes. Yes, he did. I went back through the challenges and I found it. It was . . . This is so beyond me. I don't really get this technology stuff. But the challenge was about identifying a big litigation firm, and accessing client trust accounts. That's what happened, isn't it?"

Flynn groaned. "Yeah."

"You've said enough things about your clients, he'd know you represent one of Canada's most famous litigation firms. He must have figured out your access codes, logged on to your client's site, and he'd know how to make it all untraceable."

Cold sweat broke out on Flynn's skin and nausea gripped his stomach. Light-headed, he lowered his head between his knees. "Ray did it? He stole the five million?"

"Don't say *stole*, he wouldn't mean to steal."

No, he wouldn't. Which meant Flynn couldn't even be furious with him. He fisted his free hand and punched the hard mattress on his bed. "Where's the money?"

"I don't know. I haven't talked to him; I wanted to discuss it with you first. Flynn, you know he'd never have meant to hurt you."

How often had he and his mother, Liz, and Ray's teachers tried to make Ray understand that actions had complicated and far-reaching

consequences, ones that went beyond the immediate ones Ray saw?
"I know," he said heavily. "And we didn't tell him about the trial
so he'd have had no way of knowing. Jesus, whoever's behind that
hacker website probably has the fucking five million."

Normally, his ma would ream him out for swearing, but today
she was silent.

A little static crackled on the phone line.

Finally, she said, "What are we going to do? Your brother can't
go to juvenile detention."

"Of course not." Even Flynn, who loved and looked after Ray,
got annoyed by some of his habits. His brother, with the smart-
ass way he came across, his literal thinking, the way he'd only wear
certain colors and then only on certain days, and a hundred other
quirks, wouldn't survive being in custody. Besides, he wouldn't have
taken the money if he'd realized it was stealing.

Flynn could clear his name, but at his brother's expense, which
made it impossible.

But this hacker challenge thing wasn't just about Ray. In all
likelihood, it was run by a criminal who was siphoning funds from
a bunch of computer geeks like Ray—many of whom likely had
Asperger's—who he'd deluded into thinking they were only doing
tech challenges.

"You have to talk to Ray, Ma. Find out what he did with the
money."

"What should I tell him about you and the criminal charge?"

He considered. "Nothing for now. Just find out about the money.
When I'm home, you and I can decide how to handle the rest."
Maybe he should fly back now, but that would raise questions aboard
the *Aphrodite*. He didn't need people—Liz, and especially Kendra—
looking too closely into his personal life. Oh shit. Kendra.

"I'll talk to him right now," his mother said. "Will you be there
if I call back?"

"I'll be right here." He tossed his phone on the bed. Outside the porthole, the Greek morning sun was still shining. One deck up, people would be eating, talking, having fun. Kendra might be there. When he'd risen, the thing he most wanted was to see her face.

Now it was the last thing. What could he possibly say to her? If he told her, there was only one way a black-and-white thinker like her would react. He couldn't do that to Ray.

If he kept it secret . . . His ma had taught him that sins of omission were as bad as sins of commission. Secrets and lies were no foundation for a relationship.

Cursing, he lay back on the bed, scrubbing his hands across his face in frustration. It was perhaps fifteen minutes before his cell rang.

He grabbed it and sat up, praying his roommate didn't return. "Ma?"

"The money's in an offshore account. I made Ray show me. It's untouched, even earning interest."

Relief swept through him. Maybe this could be fixed. "What did he plan to do with it?"

"Nothing. He said there was more to the hacker challenge, about transferring it to some numbered Swiss account, but that didn't present any additional challenge so he didn't do it."

There really was a criminal mastermind behind the hacker challenge. Probably the investment one as well. Maybe all the challenges on that website. He got up and paced between the two beds. That criminal needed to be caught. But how, without involving Ray?

His mother's voice broke into his thoughts. "Flynn, we have to give the money back."

"I know."

"How can we do it so that your name is cleared, but Ray doesn't get in trouble?"

"Let me think about it."

"I've always taught you boys to confess your sins and take the consequences, and we have to make sure there are consequences for Ray. We have to make him understand he did something wrong. But, son, he can't go to trial. That whole process—you know how terrible it is."

"Sure do," he said grimly.

"Ray couldn't handle it, and it wouldn't even be fair. It's not like he understood what he was doing."

"I know." Another fear suddenly gripped him. "Did he do any of the other challenges?"

"I asked. He said no, they were too easy."

He gave a ragged laugh. "Thank God. And you'll make him stop with the investment app?"

"I already did. Oh, Flynn, I feel so terrible. I should have kept a closer eye on him."

"So should I. But that's the thing with Ray, isn't it? Our brains don't work the way his does, so we never know what we should be watching for."

"He's a good lad, for all that."

He smiled sadly. "I know he is. We'll work this all out."

"You'll call as usual tomorrow morning?"

"Eight your time, on the dot," he confirmed. He'd talk five minutes with her, casual chat that Ray could overhear. Then she'd turn him over to Ray, who didn't have a clue how much trouble he'd caused. "'Bye for now. Try to get some sleep. I love you."

Feet dragging, he went up on deck. Having lost his appetite, he took only coffee from the breakfast buffet. Santos said, "You should have something to eat. We have a jam-packed day on Santorini."

"I'll get something later. Just need some caffeine to wake me up first."

"Are you having a good time on this trip? I heard you say it's your first time in Greece."

He forced a polite smile. "Yes to both. I haven't done a lot of foreign travel."

"Are you heading home right after the wedding, or continuing your travels?"

"Heading home."

"Have to get back to your job?"

Flynn liked Santos, except that sometimes his casual questions were hard to answer. Now a headache began to pulse behind his temples. A year ago, he wouldn't have taken time off because his clients depended on him. Now he needed to hurry home to deal with the situation Ray had created. "I have commitments."

"Oh?"

When Flynn didn't elaborate, Santos said, "I enjoy travel. Too bad it costs so much. A person almost needs to be a millionaire."

The cruise director's aimless chatter was cutting too close to home. "So it's Santorini today," Flynn said, to turn the conversation in a neutral direction. "That's the island you see on so many posters of Greece, right?"

"Yes, it's very dramatic with the volcanic caldera, and the town of Fira high on the cliff above."

"Caldera?"

Santos explained about a volcano and said something about the lost city of Atlantis, then told Flynn he had to see the approach from the water.

Together, they headed out on deck.

Kendra stood by the rail, this morning in sage green capris and a green and white top, talking to a couple of Liz and Peter's friends. He could see only her profile, glowing and animated. As if she felt his gaze, she glanced around. Seeing him, a smile touched her lips.

He couldn't smile back. Couldn't face her. Abruptly, he turned away, saying to Santos, "You're right, I should get some food."

As he hurried inside again, headache pounding now, he felt the burn of two curious gazes on his back. Bypassing the buffet, he went straight to his cabin, hoping Kendra wouldn't follow.

WHEN the *Aphrodite* had anchored in the incredible caldera at Santorini, the guests gathered their things to go ashore. Kendra, ready and waiting on deck, was worried about Flynn. Should she find some pretext for wandering by his cabin? Perhaps he was ill. He'd appeared on deck for only a moment at breakfast, and looked uncomfortable.

Ah, there he was, with his roommate. The roommate went to join friends. Flynn's gaze passed over her almost as if he didn't see her, then, raising his camera, he headed over to the ship's railing.

The blissful glow she'd woken with was but a memory now. They'd confessed they were falling for each other, so how could he ignore her now? Yes, they'd agreed to keep their relationship a secret, but couldn't he meet her eyes or give a quick smile?

Puzzled, still concerned he might not be feeling well, she pulled out her own camera and drifted over to stand beside him. In a casual voice designed to be overheard, she said, "It's a photographer's paradise, isn't it?"

"I'm sure there's no picture that hasn't been taken a million times before," he said, also in a public, impersonal voice, not even glancing at her. "This is one of the most photographed scenes in Greece."

She lowered her voice. "Flynn, are you all right?"

"A bit of a headache." Then, slowly, he lowered the camera and turned to her. "We agreed not to let anyone know about us."

"Yes, but you're taking it to an extreme. It's like you can hardly bear to look at me."

"Oh, Kendra." His green gaze softened, then his eyes clouded. "Everything's so complicated."

Last night he'd sounded optimistic. Now it seemed he was having second thoughts. This was *exactly* why she avoided relationships. "Well," she said snippily, "we certainly wouldn't want to deal with anything *complicated*, would we?"

He winced. "Sorry, it's not that I don't care, but . . . Hell. I wish we could wipe out the last year."

So much for leaving the past behind and moving forward, for fighting for the things you wanted. Maybe he really couldn't let go of his anger. Trying to figure out what to say, she realized her uncles were heading toward them. "Hi, uncles," she called out, adding under her breath to Flynn, "We'll talk tonight?"

"Yes," he said, almost reluctantly. Then he turned to greet her uncles, raising his camera. "Want a picture of the three of you with Santorini as a backdrop?"

He got them to pose and Kendra tried to smile. The past nights with Flynn, their emotions, new and tender as they were, had felt genuine to her. Had she been so wrong? What had he said just now? *"It's not that I don't care."* Which meant he did care, didn't it?

Uncle Phil took her arm. "Come on, the boats are here to take us to shore." At the other islands, they had docked and guests could simply climb down from the *Aphrodite*. Here, they'd anchored in the bay and small boats were taking them in.

"And then we'll have a big decision," Uncle William said. "How to get up the hill to Fira. Donkey or cable car?"

Santos had told them they had their choice of transportation from the harbor up to the capital of Fira atop the steep hill: donkey, cable car, or the more prosaic buses or taxis. "Donkey," she said firmly. "That sounds like fun."

As their boat scooted across the bay, she thought that whatever was going on with Flynn, he sure didn't look happy. She wasn't thrilled to bits herself, but she was damned if she'd turn into the kind of woman who let a man control her happiness. He could mull over the complications and tonight they'd talk. Between now and then, she'd enjoy Santorini.

Once ashore, she looped her arms through her uncles' and, leaving Flynn behind, they went to join Liz and Peter and the other guests who'd opted for a donkey ride. Laughter rang out and camera shutters clicked as the donkeys wound up the switchback to the top, arriving at another of Greece's lovely white and blue cubist towns.

Santos and Gwen gathered everyone together to board a charter bus, and they toured the island with stops to photograph a lighthouse, eat lunch at a black sand beach, and taste wine at two different wineries.

For the most part Flynn wandered around alone, taking pictures. Either he was really getting into photography or, for some reason, he was using that camera as a barrier. Either way, he didn't look like he was having fun. Kendra tried not to worry about him, about them, and to concentrate on all the great activities Gwen and Santos had lined up.

As she wandered the ruins at Ancient Thira, she came upon the wedding planner sitting on a stone wall and gazing out to sea, lost in thought. Kendra's first instinct was to leave her alone, but she looked sad, which was uncharacteristic. It dawned on Kendra how much Gwen had given them all this week, and how she was always upbeat as well as efficient.

Quietly, she took a seat beside her.

Gwen glanced up, then smiled. An upbeat smile. "Can I do something for you?"

"No, I just thought . . . wondered . . ." She really did suck at social stuff. "Are you okay?"

"Fine, of course."

"You looked kind of sad."

"How could I be sad, here on Santorini? Are you having a good time, Kendra?"

"Yes, but look, this doesn't always have to be about us. The guests. You're allowed a moment here and there to just be you. To feel sad, if you want to."

After a pause, Gwen said slowly, "If I want to. Actually, I guess I kind of do. I was thinking about someone I lost. And it's okay, it's normal, to be sad, isn't it?"

Kendra pondered that, thinking of her father. "Sad, or sometimes mad. Depends on how you lost them."

The other woman's eyes widened a little. "That's true. And when you lose someone too young, there's probably always a reason to be a little mad."

"I think so."

Gwen tilted her head and studied Kendra's face. "You've lost someone, too."

She nodded. "A long time ago. But there's still a part of me that's mad. And sad. Maybe that never goes away."

"Maybe it doesn't." She hesitated a moment then said, "Do you want to talk about it? Who it was and what happened?"

For years, she'd barely mentioned her father, yet this week she'd told Flynn and now she felt the strange urge to tell Gwen. Somehow, she thought this woman would understand. "My father. He committed suicide when I was fifteen."

Gwen grasped her hand. "My God, I'm so sorry. That's terrible."

"It was. He and Mom lost everything they'd saved because they trusted someone they shouldn't." She shook her head. "Dad didn't have the strength to cope. So he quit. And my mom, she fell apart."

"That's tragic. It must have been horrible for you."

"It was. But my uncles were wonderful, and a distant relative who I barely knew became a mentor, and . . . it all worked out."

"Not the way it was supposed to, though." Gwen still held her hand, a reassuring warmth.

"No." That was exactly right. Kendra had built a meaningful

life, but nothing had worked out the way it was supposed to. She should have had parents who looked after her, a loving home. It shouldn't have been her, at fifteen, looking out for her mom. "But things don't always work out the way they're supposed to."

Gwen shook her head. "That's so true."

"Want to tell me your story? I'd be glad to listen."

"Just between us?"

"Of course."

"It's nothing that dramatic. I married young and he died of cancer."

Their hands were still clasped, and Kendra squeezed Gwen's. "That must have been awful. To think you've found a man to spend your life with and . . ." She had just begun to consider that possibility herself—at least until Flynn started acting so strange.

"Yes. To find out that the 'till death do us part' thing would happen sooner than you'd ever imagined."

"How long ago?" Kendra asked softly.

"Going on two years. I spent most of the first year pretty much destroyed."

"I can only imagine. But look at you now," she said admiringly.

"Thanks. I'm a work in progress but I'm doing okay." Gwen sounded almost surprised.

"Way better than my mom." She gave the wedding planner's hand a pat, then released it. "She was destroyed, and never pulled out of it. I think you've done an amazing job of getting on with your life."

"Thanks, Kendra." Gwen smiled at her. "I appreciate that." Then she glanced at her watch. "I'm glad we had this chance to talk, but now I need to round people up. It's time to move on to the folklore museum."

They both stood. Kendra noticed Santos in the distance, glancing their way. Gwen raised a hand and waved, likely signaling him to start gathering the guests.

"Have you and Santos worked together before?" Kendra asked as the two women walked toward him.

"No, in fact we just met on Friday."

"Well, you make a great team. You're so in sync."

For some reason, Gwen blushed as she said, "Thanks."

In the middle of the afternoon, the group returned to Fira, which Santos said was known for jewelry and art, to shop. Kendra bought gifts for her mom and the college student who helped out with her care.

As she browsed the jewelry, she noted a number of pieces that looked like stylized blue eyes and asked about them. A salesgirl said, "Oh yes, everyone should have one. They're a charm to protect you from the evil eye." Feeling whimsical and a little foolish, Kendra bought herself one.

Nor could she resist a corset-style top in blue-green silk that made her think of the shifting colors of the ocean and a swirly skirt to match. Flynn could eat his heart out when he saw her tonight in a top that unhooked all the way down the front.

Of course, if he decided he was man enough to deal with a few *complications*, she just might let him unfasten her hooks.

SITTING in a patio restaurant watching the sun set over the caldera that evening, wearing her new outfit and her charm against the evil eye, Kendra nibbled on squid and octopus, foods she wouldn't have dared try a week ago. A number of guests were getting their pictures taken against the spectacular backdrop, many of the women with Santos's arm around them. The man certainly enhanced the view, but her taste ran more to auburn-haired Irishmen.

Flynn, who'd been seated a couple of tables away from her, had risen from his chair to take pictures—not of Santos and the other guests, but of the sunset. After giving her an appreciative look when he first saw her, he'd kept his distance.

In a few hours, they'd talk. Until then, there was no point worrying.

Beside her at her table, Liz and Peter fed each other rings of squid sautéed in white wine and herbs. Across from her, Gwen gazed across the patio with an unusually sour expression.

When Kendra followed her gaze, she saw Santos, this time with two of Liz's friends draped all over him. The pair of English blondes were flirtatious and a little outrageous, and to Kendra it looked as if they were making a serious play for the cruise director. Whether he was interested, she couldn't tell. He spread his charm evenly. In fact, catching her and Gwen watching, he beckoned. "Come on, Kendra, Gwen. I want pictures with you."

Smiling, Kendra shook her head. Gwen paused, then muttered, "I suppose it's something we could use on the website," and walked over to join him. Santos seemed quite happy to nudge the blondes aside to put his arm around Gwen.

Peter, sitting beside Kendra, popped up with his camera. "Come on, coz. Let me take a picture of you with Santos. You can stick it on your desk at the office and tell everyone it's your Greek lover. It'll do wonders for your reputation."

A photo of her with Flynn would ruin it—though, from the way he was behaving, there wasn't much chance that picture would ever happen.

She let Peter pull her up. When they went over to Santos, Gwen moved out of the curve of his arm and Kendra took her place.

When she glanced in the direction of her lover, he still had his camera up and seemed oblivious to her. She smiled into Peter's camera lens while he took a couple of shots. Then she collected her own camera and moved to the far end of the restaurant to lean against the patio railing and take a few pictures. This truly was a lovely spot. She lowered the camera and just stared out at the view.

She'd never before envied Peter and Liz, but now she almost did. How wonderful to be sharing this with a person you loved. One you planned to spend the rest of your life with.

A soft click made her turn.

Flynn, standing only a few feet away, lowered his camera. For the first time today, she saw naked emotion on his face: the same yearning she felt. Well, how about that. Despite all the complications, he really did care for her.

But would those complications be too hard to overcome?

Their gazes held for a long moment, then he gave a rueful smile, a nod, and turned away.

She realized entrées were being served, and returned to her own table to dine on mussels in ouzo, tomatoes, and fresh herbs, to drink white wine, and to wait for the evening to be over so she could be alone with Flynn. Uncertainty didn't suit her. She'd rather tackle problems head-on.

At long last, the group was ready to go. As they left the restaurant, the white town and the harbor below sparkled with hundreds of lights like a fairyland.

She fingered the charm around her neck. Would it bring her and Flynn luck?

Chapter 11

WHEN Flynn entered her cabin silently, Kendra rose slowly from the chair. "So you came, despite all those *complications*. What on earth is going—"

He caught her face between his hands, bent down to her, and silenced her with his lips.

She could protest, demand that he talk rather than distract her with . . . Oh my. His kiss wasn't rough, but it was fierce, passionate, almost . . . desperate?

She had to kiss him back.

His tongue delved insistently into her mouth, swirling around hers, thrusting deep, making her imagine his erection—which was rigid against her belly—doing the same inside her. Arousal rushed through her, tightening her nipples and pulsing in her sex. She trapped his tongue between her lips and sucked it the way she'd like to suck his cock.

Complications be damned. At least for now.

He groaned into her mouth, his hips pumped, and she wanted to strip off the expensive clothes she'd bought that afternoon and get down and dirty with him.

As he'd said this morning, things would be so much easier if the whole last year hadn't happened. But if it hadn't, she'd never have met him. She wouldn't have known this passion.

Her fingers fumbled with his shirt buttons.

"Damn, Kendra, when I'm with you—" He broke off.

"What?"

"I want to forget everything else."

The past, and the complications, he must mean. "Then do." She shoved the sides of his shirt back, revealing his sculpted torso. "There's only now. Only us." With time, as intimacy and emotion grew between them, they'd find ways of dealing with everything else.

He let the shirt drop to the floor, then fingered the neckline of her corset-style top, dipping his fingers into her cleavage. "This is so sexy."

"I bought it today. For you."

"Take off your skirt." His voice was rough.

She slid it off, and stood there in the corset top and a black thong. "Turn around."

Slowly, she rotated. When her back was to him, he groaned, "Jesus," then grabbed her by the hips and held her still. He pressed against her, erection between her butt cheeks. "Do you ever go commando?"

"When just seeing you makes me wet?"

He ground fiercely into her, then growled, "Bend over. Lean on the bed."

Talk about wet. Moisture escaped the thong to slick the tops of her thighs as she obeyed, forearms on the bed, butt tilted toward him. His zipper rasped, clothes rustled, and her body quivered in anticipation. His hands cupped her butt cheeks and squeezed hard, then his cock prodded the drenched strip of silk between her thighs. He slid back and forth over the fabric, pressing it against the sensitive folds beneath.

He reached around to fumble with the top hooks of the corset, undoing enough so her breasts swung free. He squeezed them, too—fingers urgent and a little rough but his touch was so good—then pinched her nipples. Leaning forward, he kissed her nape, then nipped.

Pure, sharp arousal shot through her. She moaned, thrusting her breasts into his hands, pushing her sex against his cock. "Oh, Flynn, now. I want you now."

Capturing both breasts in one hand, he reached his other hand down and yanked aside the crotch of her thong. As she tilted to meet him, the head of his cock probed her folds, found her opening, and then he slid inside, hard and deep.

So good. She whimpered with pleasure. "Yes, give me more."

With one hand fondling her breasts, smushing them together, tweaking her nipples, he thrust in and out, pace rapidly increasing. She pressed back against him, twisting her hips to find exactly the right angle.

"Shit, Kendra," he gasped. "I shouldn't want you this much."

"Why not?"

He didn't answer, just released her breasts and, straightening a little, grabbed her hips and held them tight as he drove harder and harder into her. "Touch yourself," he said.

Taking her weight on one forearm, she reached between her legs. Capturing her own moisture, she swirled her thumb around her clit as her fingers stroked the slippery base of his shaft. She wanted more, wanted to touch everything all at once, so she shifted her weight to free her other arm, too.

Now, she could stroke his balls, already drawn up tight. Feel the tension in his thigh muscles. Rub her clit in exactly the way that felt best. The musky scent of sex was ripe in the air, an aphrodisiac.

Her muscles clenched tight with arousal, spiraling so high she couldn't stand it. She squeezed his balls gently. "Now, Flynn. Come now."

He groaned something she didn't catch and his hips jerked wildly as she gave her clit firmer pressure to take herself over the edge and join him in orgasm, smothering her cry against the bed.

As their bodies gradually stopped spasming, he let go of her hips and leaned over her so his chest curved against her back. She could feel his heart pumping and his breath rasping against her neck. One arm came around her waist, holding her close.

When he eased out of her, he didn't let go, just maneuvered their bodies up the bed until they were lying on their sides, him spooning her. He undid the rest of the corset hooks and cupped one breast in his hand. "Can't believe what you do to me," he muttered, not sounding entirely pleased.

All right, it was definitely time to talk.

She lifted his arm and rolled over to face him, peeling off the corset along the way. His face on the pillow beside hers was so appealing, familiar now in superficial ways, yet he held so much inside. Her gaze skimmed over his features: the high forehead with damp auburn curls stuck to it, the nicely shaped brows and thick eyelashes a couple of shades darker than his hair, the perfectly straight nose and strong cheekbones, a sensual mouth that could kiss passionately or smile contagiously. It was doing neither, though. If she hadn't known he had a dimple, she'd never have guessed from his face right now. His green eyes were shadowed with confusion and maybe sorrow. "What's wrong?"

He closed his eyes. "Nothing. Or, you know, just the same old stuff."

"You said we should fight for what we want. And now, what? It's all too overwhelming for you?"

Eyes still closed, he said, "Something like that."

Exasperated, she said, "Don't shut me out. And look at me."

His jaw tightened and he opened his eyes to shoot her a steady, almost steely look. "If you can't let me have some privacy, things will never work between us."

She flinched automatically, then reflected. "You didn't want privacy before. Something's changed."

Restlessly, he shifted onto his back, hands stacked behind his head. "Maybe I've had second thoughts. We're too different. You see the world—justice—in terms of black-and-white. I don't."

Puzzled, she said, "But you believe in justice, don't you?"

"Of course. But in shades of gray."

"How do you mean? You're not talking about your case, are you? I mean, you're innocent and I was wrong. There's no gray about that."

"No, that's not what . . ." He paused for a long moment. "What if someone you knew, a decent person, broke the law unintentionally. Like, uh, they were shopping and stuck an item in their bag, then walked out?"

"Unintentionally? Well, shoplifting is theft, a crime of intent. If they didn't intend to take it without paying, they just forgot it was in their bag, they might not even be charged if they were credible."

"What if they did intend to take it, but didn't think of it as shoplifting?"

She cocked her head. "If they knew it was someone else's property—the store's—and they intended to deprive the store of it and not pay for it, that's theft. That seems black-and-white to me."

He gave a sigh of frustration. "It's not a good example."

Puzzled, she said, "Okay, but even if you find one and we disagree, is that a big deal? Both people in a relationship don't need to have identical views. Isn't it good to share different perspectives and learn from each other?" She touched his shoulder tentatively. "I care about you, Flynn. We won't always agree, but I'll listen and respect your opinion."

He gazed down at her hand, then into her eyes. "What if the shoplifter was a friend? Would you turn him in?"

Her friends wouldn't shoplift, but she tried to imagine the situation. "I'd try to convince him to turn himself in. I'd find him an excellent defense lawyer."

"Because justice depends on the quality of your lawyer. Fine system you work for, Kendra," he said bitterly.

"It's flawed. Is that what you want me to say? But it's the best we've got, and one of the best in the world. Flynn, I feel like we're on opposite sides again. I thought we'd gotten past that. I told you I believe you're innocent, I've apologized, I've offered to make things right in any way I can. What more can I do?"

"This isn't about me."

"Then what's it about?"

"Just . . . different philosophies."

She shook her head. "It's more than that. There's something you're not telling me. Do you still not trust me?"

His lips opened, but no words came out. And that was her answer.

The ache of loss filled her heart. She sat up, pulling the sheet to cover herself and crossing her arms over her chest to hold it there. "If there's no trust, there can be no relationship." Though she tried to keep her voice even, a quiver of hurt crept in.

"I should go," he said heavily.

"Yes."

He shoved himself off the other side of the bed. After putting on his boxer briefs, he looked at her. "I meant what I said. I care about you."

"I meant what I said, too." If she hadn't, saying good-bye would have been easy. Instead, it felt like her heart was ripping apart. Tears burned behind her eyes. She'd never felt this way about a man before, and now he was just walking away. This, *this* was why she shouldn't have let herself care.

Wait. She wouldn't be a quitter like her dad. Swallowing her pride, she said, "Flynn, I care, and I trust you. What do you want from me? To give up my job?"

"No, I know how much it means to you." He sat on the side of the bed, his back to her, and buried his face in his hands. "It's all so fucking messed up."

"What is?" Letting the sheet drop, she kneeled behind him and wrapped her arms around his bare torso. "What's so messed up? Why can't we fix it together?"

KENDRA'S arms encircled his chest, warm and firm, and her voice was pleading.

Ray had cost him his business. Was he also prepared to sacrifice this relationship, with all its potential? Kendra might understand.

And if she didn't, if she did her black-and-white thing, then he had no future with her. In which case, he'd damned well return the money himself, making it traceable to him rather than his brother. A man couldn't be tried twice for the same crime.

He put his arms over hers and hugged them briefly. "I'll tell you if you make me a promise." He let go and stood, so her arms fell away. The shawl she'd been wearing that evening lay on the desk and he picked it up.

When he turned, she was kneeling on the bed, naked but for her thong, eyes wide with concern. "What promise?"

"Put something on." He tossed her the shawl.

She sat back against the head of the bed, draping the shawl around her upper body and tugging the sheet up to cover her lap.

He transferred a bundle of their discarded clothing from the chair to the desk, and turned the chair so the back was to her. Sitting straddling it, he rested his arms on its back and stared at her over them. "I want to consult you as a lawyer."

"What?"

"I want legal advice. And I want lawyer-client privilege."

Her head began to shake. "If this is about a crime, I can't do that. I'm a prosecutor. It would be a conflict of interest."

"Shit." He thumped a fist on the chair.

Slowly, she said, "Maybe, if you told me as a friend . . . I can't promise confidentiality but I'll try to help. If we're ever going to have a relationship, we have to be able to talk and trust each other."

"You're right." Nerves jangled through him and he took a deep breath, filling his lungs and steadying himself. How would she react? So much hung in the balance. His future, Ray's, their mother's. "That shoplifting thing, it's kind of like the situation with . . . Ray."

Her body tensed and her eyes widened. "Ray? Your brother's a shoplifter?"

"No, not exactly." He ran a hand over his face. "He's the one who took the five million."

"Oh my God!" Those gray eyes were enormous now and her mouth hung open in shock.

"He didn't mean it. I mean I'm sure he didn't see it as theft. He knows not to steal. It was a hacker challenge." Flynn explained about the website. "For him, it was numbers and technology. He didn't think of it as real money, real people getting hurt."

Her eyes narrowed. "You knew this when I pressed charges against you? You were protecting him?"

"No, I didn't have a clue. I only found out—"

"Last night," she breathed, leaning forward. "After you left my cabin."

"Actually, this morning. Ma found out and called."

"That's why you've been acting so strange."

"He's my brother, Kendra." Unable to sit still, he stood, shoved the chair aside, and paced the few steps the small cabin would allow. "He's a good kid and he didn't intend to steal. The money's still there, in an offshore account." He dropped to the side of the bed, took her hands, and gripped them tightly. "We'll pay it back, with interest. No one has to know what Ray did."

"But . . ." She shook her head, looking baffled. "You could clear your name."

"Not at my brother's expense."

She tugged her hands free. "He can't just get away with it. And Flynn, he let you go to trial for his crime."

"He didn't know. We didn't tell him. As for getting away with it, Ma and I will make sure there are consequences, and that he understands what he did."

She crossed her arms over her chest. "If he's capable of understanding, then he should have understood in the first place."

"His brain doesn't make the same connections ours do."

"Okay," she said slowly. "But he's smart, right? And he knows not to steal. But . . . if he didn't actually realize he was stealing . . ." She was musing to herself now, frowning, still hugging her arms around her body. "How can a person take five million from someone and not know it's stealing? Then there's the question of whether he'd be mentally competent to stand trial . . ." She trailed off, her frown indicating that inside her brain she was still assessing the case.

He kept quiet, wondering if she'd come up with some magical answer.

She dropped her arms. "What was he planning to do with the money?"

"He never cared about it. The challenge was figuring out all the codes—including my access ones, and damn it, I had excellent security measures in place—and making everything happen in a way that was untraceable." He sighed, then told her the rest. "There was another step, but he didn't bother with it. Once the money hit the offshore account, for Ray the challenge was over."

"What was the final step?"

"To transfer the funds on to another account, one in Switzerland that he'd been given the number for."

Her jaw dropped as the implications sank in.

He said it for her. "There's a criminal behind this."

Her eyes flashed. "And that case *is* black-and-white."

"Could you go after them without bringing Ray into it?"

"We'd need the information he could provide." She raised her hands and rubbed them over her face. "Damn, Flynn, this is tough."

"You're telling me."

"Let me think." Hands still over her face, she muttered, "Diminished capacity? Mental defect?"

Flynn winced. His brother's brain was different, not defective.

"He's high functioning," she went on, "but his brain's not normal."

"Not neurotypical," he said automatically.

Her hands dropped. "What?"

"That's the term used in the autism community for people like us. People like Ray with Asperger's are on the autism spectrum, they're not *abnormal* or *defective*. We're not *normal*, we're *neurotypical*."

She nodded. "Sorry, I didn't mean to be offensive."

"I know."

"I'm just running some possibilities. Fitness to stand trial, possible defenses. Leniency if Ray helped us convict the criminal."

"My brother gets upset if I'm five minutes late phoning home, or if it's Monday and all his green shirts are in the laundry."

She gazed at him steadily. "You're saying any kind of legal proceeding would be difficult for him. I'm sorry, but that doesn't excuse what he did."

Frustrated, he said, "Have a little compassion."

"I do. But Flynn, people who . . . aren't neurotypical can't just go around committing crimes and getting away with it."

He groaned. "I agree, but this is my brother."

Her eyes narrowed. "Why didn't you supervise his computer use?"

"It never occurred to me that he'd—" He broke off with a bitter laugh. "That's life with Ray. Until the first time something happens, it never occurs to you that it would. Like, who'd have thought when you told your six-year-old brother to get lost, he'd disappear for the entire night then come back in the morning saying it was impossible for him to get lost because his brain was as accurate as a GPS?"

"I can't even imagine." She sighed. "Go back to your room, Flynn. I need to do some research."

He stood and began to pull on the rest of his clothes. "E-mail or call me if you find anything. Please?"

She nodded.

"You won't turn Ray in." He made it a statement, not a question.

"No. We'll talk when I have more information."

Exhausted and depressed, he realized the ship's engines were running. "We're on our way to Crete. This is our last night on the *Aphrodite*."

"It doesn't feel like it's been six days. In another few days we'll all head home." Her troubled eyes met his.

What would happen in the next few days, and would they go back to Vancouver as lovers or as enemies?

Chapter 12

FLYNN spent a restless night. In the morning, there was one message on his cell: Kendra, telling him to check e-mail. The moment his roommate left the cabin, he did so.

Kendra had sent a message at three A.M.

> I've done some reading and I have a better understanding of Asperger's. It seems to me that in a number of juvenile cases, referral to a community program would be appropriate, and it wouldn't even go to youth court.

Flynn blew out air in a whistle of relief. Any dealings with the law would be upsetting to Ray, but far less so than going to court. He read on.

> But here, there's so much money involved, and my boss is particularly interested in this case. I can almost guarantee she'd insist it goes to Youth Justice Court.

"Shit."

I've checked case law and it's not too helpful. Asperger's has been argued as a defense for collecting porn and hacking into government computers, saying the accused had repetitive, obsessive behavior that compelled them to keep repeating after the first time. But that doesn't excuse the first time. And you said Ray quits when he's no longer challenged.

Ray was repetitive and compulsive about some things, but what she'd said was true.

One of my classmates is prosecuting an Asperger's man on multiple charges of credit card theft. I e-mailed him; he'll be up to date on the law. And no, I didn't say why I was asking.
    The argument has also been made that if an adult with Asperger's is convicted, they shouldn't be incarcerated if the experience would be too stressful. But it's highly unlikely Ray would receive a custodial sentence anyhow. More likely it would be supervised community service.

Which might not be so awful in itself. Not like the trial. Flynn well knew how complicated and stressful the trial process could be.

Ray will need a really good lawyer, one who understands about Asperger's and how Ray's personality won't be sympathetic to a judge.
    I'm going to get a few hours' sleep. We'll talk, Flynn.

He stared at the screen. She was being all lawyer, totally impersonal. Discouraged and pissed off, he realized he should be grateful.
She'd stayed up until three working on this. She hadn't turned his
brother in. Finally, he began to type.

**Thanks for looking into this, Kendra. I wish things sounded
better. I hope your classmate gets back to you and has
something useful to offer.**

Frustrated, he clicked Send.

He was an idiot. He'd betrayed his brother and put Kendra in
an untenable position. He never should have told her. Never should
have believed they could work this out when their respective duties
put them on opposite sides.

Mad at himself, her, Ray, and the world in general, he went up
to get breakfast. Tired as he was, he needed food to keep his brain
functioning.

He didn't see Kendra but, as he finished putting scrambled eggs,
fruit, and a bun on his plate, she came in with her uncles. She paused
for a moment when she saw him, her face tired and stressed, then
glanced away and he did the same.

Not feeling sociable, he headed outside to look for a quiet corner. Santos, holding a stuffed file folder, came over and said, "Good
morning, Flynn. You look tired. Didn't you sleep well?"

"I'm fine." He headed on his way, taking a chair with him and
staking out a spot where he could sit by the railing and gaze ashore
at Crete while he ate. The plan for the day was a guided tour of the
town of Chania, then the guests would be taken to the hotel where
they'd stay tonight. He needed to pack. The *Aphrodite*'s crew would
transfer luggage to the hotel.

How could he spend the day playing tourist when Ray's fate
rested in Kendra's hands?

He forced a few mouthfuls of food down his throat, then put the plate aside and turned to survey the ship's deck. Kendra was with her uncles, poking at her breakfast. Gwen chatted with a group of guests, gesturing with animation, and there was no sign of Santos.

The latter fact was surprising, and he realized how often, when he looked up, the cruise director was watching him. And now that he thought about it, did the man's questions go beyond interest into nosiness?

Flynn snorted at his paranoia. For many months, he'd constantly looked over his shoulder, wondering if a cop, a media person, or an insurance fraud investigator was watching his every move. Santos was none of those, merely a friendly cruise director—a man that, under normal circumstances, Flynn would have liked.

The cell in his pocket vibrated, startling him. When he saw that the number was his mother's house, he checked that no one was nearby, noting that Kendra was no longer on deck. Voice low, he said, "Ma?"

"Ray transferred the money back to the accounts he took it from."

"What? I said to wait until I got home so we could decide what was best."

"I know. But I told him what he'd done was wrong, that it was theft. In his mind, that meant he had to give it back."

"Jesus." He lowered his voice even further. "Please tell me it can't be traced to him."

"That's what he says. Apparently he worked on it all last night, then he took his laptop to school, said he needed time in the quiet room, and worked on it there. All the old access codes and passwords had changed, so he had to figure all that out."

So much for Flynn's fallback position of transferring the money himself, making it traceable to him, and confessing to the theft. Ray was so damned single-minded when he got an idea in his head.

"Flynn? This is good, though, isn't it? They've got the money back and you and I will explain it to Ray, and give him consequences like—I don't know, banning computer use for a month? We'll make him understand he can't do anything like this again. Then it'll all be over."

No, it wouldn't. Because Flynn had told a Crown prosecutor. Fuck.

Besides, there was still the person who'd masterminded the hacker challenge. He or she was the real criminal and should be brought to justice. "We'll talk about it when I get home." This was Thursday and his flight from Crete was Monday morning. "Try to keep Ray out of trouble. Take his computer away now, okay?"

"I will."

When he hung up, he saw Santos and Gwen shooing the passengers belowdecks. He still needed to pack. He had just stood up when his cell rang again. This time it was Kendra. "Flynn, can you talk?"

"I'm on deck with no one in earshot." Should he tell her about Ray returning the money? No, at this point he wasn't going to share any more information.

"My colleague just forwarded me a brief laying out the case law. I'll stay here on the ship to read it and do some more research. I'll tell Gwen something came through from my office that I need to deal with."

"Thanks," he forced himself to say. She was giving up holiday time. Which she wouldn't have to do if she'd just agree that Ray should be kept out of the system entirely.

This whole mess was his fault. He knew Ray's tech skills were amazing, yet it hadn't occurred to him that his brother might use them for illegal hacking. He knew Kendra's work was the most important thing in her life, yet he'd spilled secrets and asked her to put him and his family first. How the hell could he make things right?

"Hey, Flynn," a male voice called.

He spun on his heel to see his roommate approaching.

"You need to pack your shit," the guy said. "We're going ashore in a few minutes."

"Thanks." Into the cell, he said, "Have to go. Call me if . . . you know."

"I'll call if I find anything hopeful. Otherwise, I'll see you at the hotel later. Flynn, don't hang up yet."

"Okay," he said cautiously, aware of his roommate leaning on the railing nearby.

"You need to make an appointment with a good defense counsel. Not the one you used before, because there's a conflict between your interests and Ray's. I can give you some names."

A conflict between his interests and Ray's. That wasn't how it was supposed to be. He loved Ray and he'd always looked after him. He knew that Ray, to the best of his own understanding and abilities, did the same for him. They were family, the two of them and Ma. What had he been thinking, giving Kendra power over them?

He moved away from his roommate and said, quietly and bitterly, into the phone. "Opt into the legal system? Because that worked so fucking well the last time? Can't you stop being a lawyer for one bloody moment?"

There was a moment's silence on the other end, and he felt kind of bad, but it was her fault for having that damned black-and-white thinking. In her own way, she was just as narrow and literal as Ray—and she didn't have the excuse of Asperger's.

"I'm trying to help," she said, sounding pissed. "Don't you get that? Don't you trust me?"

"How can I? You're the prosecutor."

Flynn snapped the phone closed and, thoughts in a turmoil, hurried belowdecks to toss his clothes and toiletries into his bag along with the souvenirs he'd bought for his mother and brother, and the friends who, like Liz, had stood by him. He squeezed his computer case in there, too, but took his camera and passport with him when he went to join the others, who were saying good-bye to the captain and crew.

To his surprise, Santos, dressed in shorts, disembarked with the passengers. Flynn caught up to Liz. "Santos is still with us?"

"He has some holiday time," she explained, "and Peter and I invited him to the wedding. He feels like part of our group, don't you think?"

He might, if Flynn wasn't feeling paranoid. He muttered something noncommittal.

"And he offered to help Gwen with tour guiding and liaison," she went on. "He's the sweetest man."

She was probably right. At the moment, Flynn wasn't inclined to trust anyone.

As he trailed around the town of Chania with the group, he thought how picturesque it was. The architecture was much more varied than the white cubist style typical of the Cyclades. Vaguely, he was aware of Santos talking about the town's history: Minoan, Hellenistic, Roman, Byzantine, Venetian, Turkish. He'd have been interested if he wasn't so worried.

But all he could focus on was his family's problem.

Where would Kendra's drive to see justice done lead? She'd promised to talk to him before she took action, but from what she'd said this morning, she felt compelled to turn Ray in. Once she did, her boss would insist that his brother be put on trial, and Kendra knew it.

They were enemies again, and if he let himself reflect on that, it could break his heart. Just when he'd started to feel optimistic about life, things had gotten even worse. But this wasn't the time to wallow in misery or regret. He needed to figure out how best to help his brother, and make up for his own stupidity in revealing family secrets—and then in pissing off Kendra.

If Flynn confessed to the crime himself, he could circumvent her. If she tried to say it was really Ray, Flynn would deny everything he'd told her. But first, he had to get every single detail from his brother so he could make an accurate confession and give the police the evidence to hunt down the mastermind behind the scheme.

Suddenly, his path became clear. He had to go home. Now. He'd sneak away from the group and phone the airline. A copy of his e-ticket was folded in his wallet.

Glancing around, he realized that, as well as attractive tourist shops, cute little restaurants, and a money exchange, there was a travel agency across the street. Even better. Surreptitiously, he slipped inside.

A pretty young Greek woman smiled from behind a desk. "*Kalimera.*"

"*Kalimera.* Do you speak English?"

"Of course. How may I help you?"

He unfolded his e-ticket and handed it to her, along with his passport. "I need to change flights. I have to get back to Vancouver, Canada, as soon as possible."

"Let me see what I can do. You wish to leave this afternoon?"

"Yes, I—" Kendra had promised she wouldn't do anything without first discussing it with him. Now here he was, planning to leave without talking to her.

She was his enemy.

But she was also his lover. The woman he cared for.

"Mr. Kava . . . ?" His name gave her enough trouble she didn't even attempt it.

"Kavanagh. Sorry. No, tomorrow morning."

After some busy key-clicking, she said, "You will depart Chania airport at seven A.M. With stopovers in Athens and Toronto, you will travel for almost twenty-four hours, but because of the time zones you will arrive at eight thirty in the evening."

"I leave Friday and arrive Friday?" Tomorrow, Liz and Peter and their guests, including Kendra, would be traveling across Crete to the southwest where the wedding would be held on Saturday. And he'd be flying home to spend the weekend preparing his confession to a crime he hadn't committed.

"Yes, sir," she said brightly. "You know that there will be a change fee?"

"Yes, yes. Whatever. Go ahead and book it." He gave her a credit card. His business had been lucrative but he and his family were quickly running through the money he'd saved. He needed to get his butt in gear and get something else going. He only hoped his confession wouldn't be widely publicized—and that he was right that the double jeopardy rule meant he couldn't be prosecuted again.

The agent printed out tickets and his itinerary and tucked them in a travel agency folder. The process took far too long for his peace of mind, though in fact it was probably no more than a minute or two.

He grabbed the folder from her. "Thanks."

Her "Have a good day" rang in the air behind him as he hurried toward the door.

Yeah. As if.

Chapter 13

KENDRA packed up her computer when the *Aphrodite* crew came to collect everyone's luggage.

"You come to hotel with us," a young, smiling crew member in the standard white uniform said in accented English. "There is Internet and everything. You can work some more."

But when, an hour later, she was ensconced in a bright, airy room that looked out over a charming town and scenic harbor, she didn't turn on her computer. Her classmate's brief had been exhaustive and though she'd followed up on the precedents and arguments he'd mentioned, she'd found nothing definitive to assist Flynn's brother.

Flynn was mad at her, and she wasn't thrilled with him either. Had she ever said a single thing to lead him to believe she'd shirk her duty as a prosecutor? Why the hell had he told her about his brother if he expected her to sweep the truth about a crime under the carpet?

Still, despite her annoyance and hurt, she'd put herself in the position of defense counsel and tried to figure out every angle that could possibly benefit his brother. At the moment, her best legal advice would be that Ray turn himself in and give evidence to help identify and convict the person behind the hacker challenge. That would count in his favor when it came to sentencing. Defense strategy would be up to Ray's lawyer, though.

Even if Ray did get a lenient sentence, legal proceedings would be horrible for a boy with Asperger's, and for his mom and brother. And Flynn would likely hate her.

Was there any way she could persuade her boss that the matter could be settled without taking Ray to court? No, she couldn't see it. Why did Ray have to pick a colleague of Dorothy's, and why did he have to steal such a huge sum of money?

Down below her, brightly dressed people strolled narrow streets and cobblestone alleys as if they didn't have a care in the world. Her stomach growled, reminding her she'd only poked at breakfast.

She glanced over at the queen-sized bed, a reminder that she and Flynn had gone from enemies to lovers and, it seemed, back to enemies again.

Hanging around this room wasn't doing any good, so she applied a layer of sunscreen, picked up her purse, and headed out. She'd find a shaded restaurant where she could eat outside, then take a stroll through the town and along the harbor. With any luck, she wouldn't run into Flynn or any of the other wedding guests. She needed time alone to reflect.

Half an hour later, she sat at a brightly painted but rickety table in a quiet alley, sipping white wine and eating a Greek salad. The food was good, the setting idyllic, and she felt like shit.

She'd come to care for Flynn, experiencing emotions she'd never felt for another man, and she believed he'd felt the same way. She knew he was a good man and she'd begun to overcome her fear of trusting, of loving.

If she told him his brother must turn himself in, very probably she'd destroy that fragile beginning. But if she covered up Ray's crime, and even more so if she let the major criminal behind it escape justice, she'd betray her office as Crown Counsel.

She respected the way Flynn always stood by his family. If her dad and mom had had that same strength, her own life would be very different.

Suppressing a frustrated groan, she drained the glass of wine and thought about ordering another. A part of her wanted to sit here in the shady heat and drink chilled white wine all afternoon, yet she knew that would make her feel worse, not better. Forcing herself to her feet, she decided to sightsee until the other guests were due back at the hotel and she and Flynn could have a private chat.

LATE that afternoon, sitting by the open window of her hotel room, she saw the group arrive, Flynn one of the stragglers. Santos, who, surprisingly, had stayed on with the group rather than returning on the *Aphrodite*, stood by the hotel door. Though he was now with them on a purely voluntary basis, he acted as if he was still on duty, looking as if he was unobtrusively counting heads as people went inside.

Downstairs, hotel staff would be getting everyone registered. Not wanting to call attention to Flynn by phoning him, she texted him her room number and "Come when you can."

Shortly after, she heard voices and thumping in the hallway as people found their rooms, then things settled down again. Her door opened to admit Flynn.

She rose, thinking that his casual shorts and tee didn't match up with the solemn expression on his face. Her own face no doubt bore a similar expression.

He came over to her and stopped a couple of feet away. No kiss, no smile, not even a hello. All he said was, "No good news, I take it?"

Knowing he wouldn't see it as good news, she said, "If Ray turns himself in and helps identify the person behind the scheme, he has an excellent chance of being sentenced to community service." Sitting again and gesturing him to the other chair, she gave a quick summary of her reasoning, then said, "I'll e-mail you the names of a few excellent defense lawyers."

He nodded, not like he agreed but more as if she'd confirmed something for him. "All your research was based on Ray turning himself in."

She gazed steadily back. "You can't cover up a crime."

"What if it was your mom? You said she's not functioning so well. What if she took something from a store? Would you turn her in?"

His question startled her and made her think. The year after Dad died, her mom had thrown bills in the garbage unpaid and written checks that bounced. It wasn't intentional; she was distracted by grief. Even now, Kendra handled her finances for her.

Her mom had never shoplifted, as far as Kendra knew. If she had . . . Kendra would have gone to the store, paid for the items, explained the situation, and begged them not to call the police. She wouldn't cover up her mom's unintentional crime. And yet, if the store did press charges, it would be horrible for her mother. Kendra would feel as if she'd betrayed her. So, would she really take the risk of notifying the store?

Flynn was right. This kind of situation wasn't black-and-white.

Her mom's and her relationship wasn't the typical parent-child one. Kendra had an extra responsibility, resulting from her mother's mental instability. Same with Flynn, because of Ray's Asperger's. She squeezed her eyes shut briefly. Some things truly were black-

and-white, like family loyalty. Others . . . Yes, she understood what he meant about shades of gray.

When she opened her eyes, she said words she'd never expected to hear herself utter. "If it was just Ray, and you swore you'd make sure he understood, suffered reasonable consequences, and would never do it again then . . . maybe I'd agree with you." If she did, perhaps they could salvage their relationship.

But at what cost?

Sadly, she shook her head. "But there's a real criminal behind this. It could be huge, Flynn. How many of these hacker challenges is he masterminding? How many people are gullible enough to think it's legitimate, that it's just a game? How many people with Asperger's is he manipulating and exploiting?"

When he started to speak, she raised a hand to stop him. "I've been reading about computer geeks, hackers, and people with Asperger's and high-functioning autism. Neurotypical people like you and me wouldn't get sucked in by a scheme like this, but people like them easily could. Ray proves that. And I bet there'll be other hackers who do catch on to the schemes and use them to steal money for themselves."

She tilted her chin up and gazed across at him, both sad and defiant. Even if it cost her a man—the only man—she might have loved, she had to convince him to do the right thing.

The words he spoke took her by surprise. "I know."

"You do? Then you'll take him to see a lawyer?"

He shook his head. "I'll take myself to a lawyer." Shifting in the chair, he reached into his pocket and pulled something out. When he unfolded it, she saw it was a travel agency folder. "I'm flying home tomorrow. I'm going to confess that I stole the money."

"What?" She leaped out of the chair and grabbed him by the shoulders, startling him so that he dropped the folder. "You can't do that!"

He shook off her hands. "I can and will."

"But you didn't steal it."

He slanted her an enigmatic glance. "What if I did? What if everything I've told you was a big lie? Just to get back at the lawyer who persecuted me."

For a moment, she actually considered it. Then her sixth sense kicked in. She fisted her hands on her hips. "What a load of crap."

He gave a surprised laugh. "Okay, yeah, I wouldn't do that to you."

She glared down at him. "But you'd decide to confess without even talking to me?" She'd spent hours and hours doing research and analyzing the situation, agonizing over it, and he'd made such a huge, ridiculous decision without even consulting her?

"After we talked this morning, I saw that it was the only option. You're right about nabbing the criminal behind this, and I'm sure as hell not going to trust Ray to the justice system that fucked me over." His green eyes blazed like sharp, cold emeralds.

"But to confess yourself, that's—"

"I can't be tried again for it, right? Double jeopardy?"

"Oh, God," she groaned, bending to stare into his eyes. "Yes, that's true, but your acquittal could be appealed. The limitation period hasn't expired. An appeal court doesn't usually hear new evidence, but they can if it's highly significant. A confession's pretty damned significant. You can't do it." Flynn could be convicted, go to jail. She couldn't bear the thought of him in jail.

"Fuck." He sprang to his feet, scowling, and she took a step back.

Pacing over to the window, he said, "The money's been returned. With interest."

"You—Ray?—someone returned the money?"

He turned to face her. "He did. As soon as Ma told him it was theft, he gave the money back."

"That's good. Restitution is really good. But then . . . What are you intending to say in this confession?"

He leaned his butt against the frame of the open window. "I'll spend the weekend with Ray, going through everything he did. He'll remember every detail. Then I'll see my lawyer and confess. I'll give him every bit of evidence that could lead to the person behind all this."

She strode toward him, scared and furious. "You could go to jail. You'd do that for your brother?" Of course he would; he didn't see any other choice. She hadn't given him another choice.

"Yeah. And to put away the scumbag who's using people like him." He grabbed her hands and gripped them so hard her bones crunched painfully together. "And you're going to let me do it. You won't tell them it was really Ray. Not if you care about me at all."

Of course she did. If she didn't, why did it break her heart to think of him with a criminal conviction, spending time in jail?

She could tell the police about Ray. Surely their cyber-crime geeks could find evidence against him. But if she did, it would hurt Flynn even more badly than going to jail would. Neither option was . . . an option.

"Let go. You're hurting my hands." When he did, she shook them, wincing, then rested her elbows on the windowsill and stared out, past the town and harbor to the ocean beyond, dotted with a few white sails. "Let me think for a moment."

"What more is there to think about?"

She drew in a deep breath of air scented by tangy ocean and the sweetness of the rosebushes blooming outside the hotel. It cleared her lungs, her brain, gave her a fresh perspective. And now, suddenly, the course seemed clear. Not right, in the black-and-white terms Dorothy had taught her, but just. For everyone involved. "This." She turned to face him.

"Don't go back tomorrow," she said. "Have you already told Liz and Peter, or your mother?"

He shook his head, glanced at his watch. "I call home at six o'clock. That's in half an hour. As for Liz, I hadn't gotten up the nerve. She'll be pissed." He bent to pick up the folder with his new ticket. "Santos saw me go into the travel agency, but I told him I was confirming my flight home." He cocked his head. "Does that guy seem a little off to you?"

"Off? What on earth do you mean? He's great. Efficient, friendly, charming. Flynn, are you paying attention?"

"Sorry. You were saying I shouldn't go back tomorrow. But Kendra, I—"

"Would you shut up and listen? Call the airline and switch your tickets back to the original flights. When you get home, gather every bit of information from Ray that could help identify the person behind the hacker challenge. When you've got it, I'll arrange for you to meet with an RCMP officer I know pretty well and—"

Frowning, he interrupted. "I thought you didn't want me to confess."

"Let me finish. You'll be a confidential informant. Your identity will be protected. If you think it wouldn't be too upsetting for Ray, the officer could meet with him, too. But then there's the risk Ray might tell someone about it."

"He might, might not. Yeah, it wouldn't be worth the risk." His face was brightening. "You're saying you wouldn't turn Ray in?"

She shook her head. "I'm learning about shades of gray."

His lips curved slightly.

"With the money returned and the RCMP on the trail of the criminal, with any luck your name will be cleared, Flynn."

"Oh, man. A confidential informant. That's a great idea, Kendra. You'd really do that for me? For Ray?"

She searched her heart to make certain. "Yes."

He stepped closer. "Thank you. I know this isn't easy for you."

It wasn't, but she cared about him.

"So, if I'm cleared," he said, taking another step closer so the front of his body almost touched hers, "your boss couldn't get too pissed off if you dated me."

Her heart leaped with hope. "That's a side benefit I hadn't thought of."

His smile widened, and the dimple she hadn't seen in two days winked. "A benefit? I take it that's a yes."

"Oh, Flynn." A few moments ago, she'd feared their fragile relationship had no chance. "Yes, it is." She reached up to put her arms around his neck and rose on her toes so her lips were an inch from his. "It is most definitely a yes."

Relief tasted sweet when her lips met his in a tender kiss. He caught her waist and pulled her close, his growing erection pressing against her, and his tongue slipped between her lips. Passion licked through her.

She kissed him back with need, relief, hope, and maybe even love. When she gazed into his eyes, their green depths were clear and sparkling.

Easing back in the circle of his arms, which had the added benefit of pressing her pelvis closer to his, she marveled, "I think everything's going to work out."

He grinned, again flashing that dimple. "Kendra, I'm thinking that if we've survived the last few days, we can survive anything together."

She nodded.

"Sure and it's time to reap the rewards." He bent and scooped her into his arms, then walked over to the bed and tossed her down. Gazing at her with hungry eyes, he said, "I want to make love with you for hours, and then I want to start all over again."

She smiled up at him.

"Any objection, counselor?"

"Yes. You're not naked."

His dimple flashed. "Now, that can be easily fixed."

Epilogue

DURING a light breakfast in the hotel dining room, Gwen had trouble keeping her eyes off Santos. Her emotions were so confused. She was thrilled they were lovers, that he cared about her, and that their relationship was . . . well, a *relationship*. At the same time, she was so worried about the wedding.

She and Santos had agreed that this morning he'd sit at Flynn's table and she'd sit at Kendra's. Flattered that he'd trusted her—her, with the not–poker face—she'd done her best to act normal, though nerves had made it next to impossible to eat anything.

For about the tenth time she checked her watch and saw with relief that it was time to call an end to breakfast.

She went over to Santos, thinking how attractive he looked in shorts and a casual summer shirt, no longer needing to wear the Dionysus Cruises uniform. Indulging herself, she rested a hand on his shoulder, making it look casual, but loving the flow of warmth between their bodies. "Time to do our thing," she murmured.

The suggestive grin he slanted up to her said he, too, was thinking of all the things they'd done in her luxurious king-sized bed. An entire night together—it had been pure bliss, from the many bouts of lovemaking to falling asleep tangled together and waking the same way.

Wonderful memories, but right now anxiety prickled through her. The big test was coming.

Last night, she and Santos had come up with a plan, or at least the beginning of one. Normally, she'd have made sure each guest got their passport back, but not this morning. Santos would hold on to them all and see if Flynn or Kendra asked for theirs. If so, it would be an indicator they might be heading to the airport, and Santos wouldn't let them out of his sight.

Moving to the front of the room beside him, Gwen whispered, "Kendra's in a good mood and not acting the least bit suspicious."

"Kavanagh, too. His Irish charm was showing and he seemed relaxed, even happy, when we talked about today's plans and the wedding tomorrow."

"So the two of them really have resolved whatever was bothering them yesterday morning." That had been her and Santos's impression last night when the group dined on the outside patio of one of the many restaurants strung like colorful beads along Chania's scenic harbor. Gwen had shuffled her seating chart, putting the secret lovers at the same table together with Santos so he could see how the earlier tension between them played out. Later, he'd reported that they'd been surreptitiously exchanging romantic glances.

Gwen took a breath and tried to sound calm as she called, "May I have everyone's attention?" When people turned toward her, she announced, "We'll be boarding our buses in half an hour, so please get yourselves organized for the day. Your luggage must be ready in fifteen minutes so the hotel staff can bring it down to the buses." Today, two buses would take the guests on a scenic drive west from Chania down to Paleochora on the south coast, to the small, picturesque hotel they'd be staying in.

Santos held up a zippered case that contained the passports. "I have your passports, to facilitate registration at the hotel tonight in Paleochora. If anyone needs theirs to cash a traveler's check or exchange money, come and get it from me now."

Heart racing, Gwen sucked in a breath, trying not to be obvious about watching Flynn. This half hour was the obvious window of opportunity. Chania had an airport, whereas Paleochora was a remote village.

The guests rose and started toward their rooms. Several headed over to Santos and Gwen. Flynn took his time rising, and sauntered past Kendra. His arm brushed hers and he leaned close to murmur something to her.

Gwen tensed, keeping an eye on them as she reassured a couple of older women that the buses did have toilets, and listened to Liz's dad asking Santos for his passport.

Kendra gave Flynn a smile, lingering and intimate. Were they ready to make a run for it, lovers and criminals with a cool five million? No, apparently not. She headed for the elevator and he joined up with his roommate and took the stairs.

Gwen let out a breath she hadn't realized she was holding and felt her pounding heart begin to settle.

As the rest of the guests trailed away, Santos moved closer to her. They were both packed and ready to go, nothing to do but wait for the guests to return. "Neither of our fish nibbled at the bait," he commented. "Relieved?"

She whisked a hand across her forehead. "Am I ever." She blew out another breath. "Seems like they're planning to stay for the wedding. Maybe the ticket change was completely innocent. Maybe Flynn's completely innocent. He was acquitted, after all."

"It's possible, though their behavior this week has been suspicious. I'll watch and wait. And hope the wedding goes off without a hitch." He smiled down at her, dark eyes warming intimately. Voice husky and suggestive, he said, "So, Gwen, how are you this morning?"

Sexy tingles rippled through her as she smiled back. "Great. I needed last night. The sex, the talk, the cuddling. It'll help me get through the day." She drew in another breath and let it out noisily. "I'm so relieved Flynn and Kendra didn't get their passports. I can relax a bit."

With that concern shoved to a corner of her mind, new ones surfaced. Brow creasing, she said, "Now all I need to worry about is the wedding rehearsal, then the wedding. I was crazy to show Liz and Peter photos of Elafonissi." The islet, near the southwestern tip of Crete, was stunningly beautiful. Crushed shells turned the beaches a romantic pink, which was accented by the tranquil blue-green ocean. "I suggested it as a place to visit on their honeymoon, but once she saw the pink sand, she wouldn't consider getting married anywhere else." The bride had even chosen shades of pink for her wedding colors.

Unfortunately, Elafonissi had no hotels, so they'd had to book accommodation—and this evening's wedding rehearsal and dinner—at the nearby town of Paleochora.

"The beach is beautiful," Santos said, "but yeah, remote. It'll be fun, though, bringing everyone in by boat from Paleochora."

She poked an elbow into his side. "Oh sure, fun. Easy for you to say." He had no idea how much work had gone on in preparation.

"Let me know if there's anything I can do to help."

"Just try not to have anyone arrested," she said dryly.

"I'll do my best."

She trusted him to do that. But she knew that even his best might throw a monkey wrench into all her intricate plans. If so, she'd figure out how to deal with it. No more panic attacks.

"As for you," he said, "I'm guessing tonight the wedding planner could use a little de-stressing. Maybe a massage. I'm not bad with my hands"—he flexed them, brown and strong with a purely masculine grace—"if I say so myself."

Just the sight of his hands, the memory of the way he touched her, made her quiver. "Mmm, how about a tiny sample right now?" She turned her back to him in invitation.

Warm and firm, his hands rested at the base of her neck for a moment, then his fingers caressed her skin and traced the neckline of her pale yellow top. His thumbs pressed firmly into the muscles of her neck, making her realize how tight they were. She let out a sound that was almost a purr.

Slowly, deftly, he worked up and down her neck, then out to her shoulders. It was healing and erotic at the same time. Her body warmed, melted, her knees grew weak. "Oh my, Santos, you're good at that."

"And that surprises you?"

"Not one bit. I bet you're good at pretty much anything you choose to do."

"Just try me," he murmured, bending to brush a kiss against her ear.

"I have every intention of doing exactly that. Starting with, mmm, maybe a full body massage, and then—"

From the stairwell, cheerful voices and the clatter of shoes on tile interrupted her, and reluctantly she stepped away from Santos.

LATE that afternoon, Santos stood in a shady corner of the Paleochora hotel courtyard watching the wedding rehearsal. Liz and

Peter and the rest of the wedding party were casual in shorts, and a couple of cats squalled as they fought over a scrap of food, but the mock ceremony went off with only a couple of minor glitches.

He studied Liz and Peter, who were smiling joyfully. They made a good couple. Santos believed in the institution of marriage—for those who really bought into it and honored it the way his *yiayia* and *pappou* and Peter's and Liz's parents did. People like his own parents, though, dishonored it.

His gaze turned, as it so often did, to Gwen. Rather than gazing dreamily at the bride and groom, she scribbled notes busily on a clipboard. He knew without having to ask that she was determined to fine-tune everything so that, tomorrow afternoon on the pink beach at Elafonissi, the wedding would be perfect. Her plans might or might not work out, but if there were screwups, she'd handle them with efficiency, grace, and humor.

He had figured he'd never marry, that he was too adventuresome and irresponsible. That he took after his parents. Now a fascinating blond widow had made him take a closer look deep inside himself, at the man he was and the man he wanted to be. A man who would deserve a woman like her.

The cell in his pocket vibrated. He pulled it out to take a look and, when he saw it was from the manager of Insurance Assured, answered quickly. "Hold on a minute," he said under his breath, hurrying from the courtyard to the street outside the hotel. "Okay, now I can talk. What's up?" Please, let it not be something that messed up the wedding.

"The money's back," Celia Jenkins said excitedly.

He shook his head, not understanding. "'Scuse me?"

"The five million, plus interest. It's back in the accounts."

Dumbfounded, all he could manage was, "What?"

"We're all baffled. But thrilled. We got a call from our client, first thing in the morning Vancouver time. The accountant was in early, checking something online with one of the trust accounts. She saw there'd been a huge online deposit. She checked the other accounts. On Wednesday, money was transferred back into all the accounts that were robbed."

"You're kidding. Where did it come from?"

"We can't tell. Anyhow, Santos, I called you right away because this changes things."

Trying to process this turn of events, he said, "It means it wasn't Kavanagh. Doesn't it? I mean, why would he steal the money, then return it?"

"Why would anyone?"

"That's the million—five million—dollar question, isn't it?"

"Yes, but it's not our question," she said gleefully. "All we care about is that the money's back. The client will refund our claim payout."

"This is incredible news." The ramifications were beginning to sink in. Not just those for his employer and their client, but for him and Gwen. "You're calling off the investigation?"

"Exactly."

Tension he hadn't even been aware of eased from his shoulders. Whatever was going on with Kavanagh and Kendra Kirk—whether they'd stolen the money and returned it, or been innocent all along—it was no longer any of his business.

"My next call is to the RCMP," Celia said. "They'll want to get their white-collar crimes people on this right away."

"I wonder if it'll be as untraceable as the original theft?"

"I really don't care," she said giddily. "I'm drinking champagne tonight."

He laughed, imagining Gwen's face when he told her the news. "I just might do that, too. Let me know if you hear any more."

"Will do." Then she chuckled. "Hey, I just realized something. You got an all expense paid holiday in Greece that was completely unnecessary."

Oh, but it had been necessary. Without it, he wouldn't have met Gwen Austin. "A working holiday," he reminded her, "not that I'm complaining. Oh, and Celia, I'm staying a few more days for a real holiday. At my own expense." He was going to take Gwen sightseeing in Athens, then she'd persuaded him to visit his grandparents on Naxos.

"Enjoy."

"Count on it."

He ended the call and hurried back to the hotel courtyard, bursting with the need to tell Gwen.

There she was, sitting at a red-painted wooden table with Liz, their heads bent over her clipboard. Only for something as momentous as this news would he interrupt. He strode over and touched her shoulder. "Gwen, I need a moment of your time."

"Santos," she glanced up warily, "we're in the middle of something."

"It's important."

She gave a small gasp and her eyes widened in a wordless question. He realized she must assume the worst, so he urged her over to a deserted corner of the courtyard where, under the shade of a lemon tree, he said, "The money that was stolen's been returned."

Her mouth fell open. A few sounds came out, but no words.

"My employer's satisfied, so the investigation is off."

Her expressive face shifted from shock and disbelief to excitement. "Seriously?" She grabbed his hands, squeezing hard. "Oh my God, that's wonderful. But who? How?"

"By electronic transfer, same way it was stolen. No idea who did it. I'm sure the police will look into it."

"You don't think it was Flynn?"

"Why would he? But if he wasn't the thief, then what's up with him and Kendra?"

She shook her head. "I'm so curious. Are you going to tell him about the money?"

"That would mean revealing that I'm an insurance fraud investigator. He'll find out from his lawyer." He reflected. "Though maybe not until next week."

"If he is innocent, it will be such a relief." She stared up at him. "I don't think it's really sunk in yet. It's just so unbelievable."

"Believe it. And think about this, *latreia mou*. As of now, I'm off the assignment and at your complete disposal. If you need an assistant, a translator, a masseur"—he winked—"or a lover, I'm here for you."

"All of the above," she said promptly, eyes sparkling.

THE next afternoon, Gwen set the barefoot bride, accompanied by her teary-eyed dad, on her journey down the pink sand aisle strewn with petals, then stepped back.

She stood behind and slightly apart from the family and friends who would witness the ceremony, and Santos came to stand beside her, his bare forearm brushing hers in a sensual caress. She wondered if the scene intimidated him. Single guys could feel panicky at weddings. If he was uncomfortable, he showed no outward sign of it.

Liz was so beautiful in a lacy sleeveless dress in a delicate shade of pink, carrying a bouquet of bougainvillea in half a dozen shades of pink and purple. Peter was handsome in white cotton pants and a loose-weave white shirt with a bougainvillea boutonniere, both his dads standing beside him—also a little sniffly—as best men.

The setting was perfect: sunshine, hot but not overwhelming, the gentle ocean breeze, the shifting blues and greens of the ocean, and that incredible pink sand. Greek photographers moved unobtrusively to shoot the wedding video as well as still photos.

Liz's dad gave her away, then went to stand with his wife, their arms around each other. There were no chairs, just the petal-strewn beach, and everyone was barefoot.

"Kendra and Kavanagh are looking cozy," Santos said softly.

The pair stood side by side, shoulders pressing together just the way Gwen's and Santos's arms were doing. "I really am dying of curiosity," she said. "I'd love to know their story."

"I think, after the job you've done this week, you deserve whatever you want." He leaned down, his breath a sexy tickle against her ear. "And I'm going to give it to you."

"Today I feel like I have everything I could possibly want." To have brought this wedding to fruition, and be sharing the moment with a man she truly cared for, was a wonderful experience.

"You've given Liz and Peter a unique, memorable day."

"A wedding always should be," she murmured, flattered and pleased. "A day full of love and joy." She had the best job in the world, making days like this happen.

"And honesty and commitment."

His words surprised her, and she turned to gaze up at him. "Commitment?"

He nodded, his dark eyes solemn. "Those vows are meant to be taken seriously. I think Liz and Peter know that."

"They do." She was sure of it.

"Unlike my parents," he said with a touch of bitterness.

She studied the strong face she'd come to know so well. "You're not like them."

His expression lightened and his eyes warmed. "I know that now, thanks to you." He swallowed, and seemed like he was hunting for words. "I've fallen for you, Gwen. Hard."

To hear those words—and hear them in the middle of a wedding—stunned her. In the very best way. "I feel the same."

They gazed into each other's eyes for a moment that seemed to go on and on.

Then a hushed ripple of sound made her glance toward the wedding. "They're doing the vows."

Together they turned, and Santos took her hand as Liz and Peter recited the vows they'd written themselves. Misty-eyed, she watched as two people she'd come to consider friends merged their lives and hearts.

A week ago, her goal in life had been to find herself, to enjoy herself, as a single woman. She'd figured it would be many, many years before she'd contemplate again joining her life with a man's.

Now, though . . . She squeezed Santos's hand.

He squeezed back.

DUSK had fallen and Kendra watched stars appear in the night sky of Paleochora. After a simple but delicious wedding dinner of fresh seafood and roasted lamb in the hotel courtyard, local musicians had set up in one corner. Their catchy music, combined with quantities of pink champagne and shots of ouzo, had brought most of the wedding guests to their feet to dance in a circle around the laughing bride and groom.

Kendra had been right there, with Gwen on one side and her uncle William on the other, then, somehow, it was all too much. Too wonderful. She was out of breath—from dancing, happiness, a sense of a whole new life out there waiting for her. So she'd stepped out of the line of dancers and gone to lean against a whitewashed wall, smiling as she watched the others.

Flynn separated himself from the line, too, as she'd known he would.

When he came to join her, she smiled. "Liz and Peter look so happy. What a wonderful day. And week. For all of us."

He leaned against the wall so his shoulder touched hers, bare above the corset-style top she wore with a short, flirty skirt. Around her neck was the blue eye charm that was supposed to protect against the evil eye. "It has been," he agreed. "I left Vancouver bitter and depressed. Now, though there are issues to deal with, life's full of opportunity."

"It is." And many of those opportunities involved the two of them, together.

She'd learned so much this week. Yes, her mentor Dorothy deserved loyalty, but loyalty didn't mean letting Dorothy overrule her own judgment, and it did require honesty. As soon as she got home, she'd tell her mentor boss that she was dating Flynn, and that he was innocent. And he'd tell his mother about Kendra—and that she'd made a mistake. She was human. Mistakes happened, and now she was doing everything she could to help his family.

She turned away from the dancers and stepped in front of Flynn, looking him straight in the eyes. "It's going to be tough for a while, once we get back home. Lots of stuff to deal with."

He nodded, green eyes bright and optimistic. "Yeah, but it all needs to be done, and we'll get through it. I want you to meet my mom, and Ray of course, too."

"Your mother is wonderful. I love how loyal she is to you, and I hope she'll come to accept me. As for Ray, he and I just might get along. Neither of us is great on the social conventions." She smiled up at him. "I want you to meet my mom, too. When she knows you're special to me, she'll be so happy." Then she chuckled. "Oh my God. My uncles, and Peter and Liz! They'll be blown away."

He laughed, too. "I like them. Hope they—"

He broke off, and she realized Santos and Gwen were coming over.

"Gwen, congratulations," Kendra said, returning to her position leaning against the wall beside Flynn. "You've done a fantastic job this week."

Gwen's smile held a hint of mischief. "Keep that in mind when your big day comes."

Before she'd come to Greece, Kendra had figured she'd never marry, probably not even have a serious relationship. Now there was Flynn, and anything was possible. Hoping the light was dim enough to hide her flush, she said, "Who else?" And it was true. She felt a real connection with Gwen, as well as admired her efficiency. She smiled at the other woman, noting idly that Gwen had bought gold earrings that were very similar to Santos's.

Santos said, "It's interesting, all the little dramas that have played out behind the scenes, with most of the guests completely unaware."

Beside her, she sensed Flynn's body tensing. Gwen's head cocked toward Santos, her expression curious.

Warily, Kendra studied the Greek man. "I suppose every wedding has that kind of thing."

"How often, though, do the guests include a man acquitted of white-collar crime and the woman who prosecuted him?"

She gasped, and heard Flynn suck in a breath. Gwen's eyes widened.

Santos went on. "Or an insurance fraud investigator who's trying to find proof of his guilt and track down the money?"

Her jaw dropped. What was going on?

"What?" Flynn said. "What the hell . . . you? Are you saying . . . ?"

"I'm not really a cruise director. I work for Insurance Assured."

An insurance fraud investigator? Kendra's heart leaped into her throat. He'd been watching Flynn all week? Maybe watching her, too? Every time she'd exchanged casual comments with Santos, had he been pumping her for information?

"Damn it," Flynn said, glaring at the man. Then, eyes narrowed, he shifted his focus to Gwen. "Did you know this?"

She nodded. "Not until I got to Greece, but yes, he told me right away. Though I didn't know who he was investigating until a couple of days ago."

Heart racing, Kendra was still processing the news, unsure how to react, when Santos went on. "Lots of dramas and secrets. For example, did you know the stolen money's been returned?"

So, Santos knew. Well, of course he did, if he worked for the insurance company. Did he have a clue of Flynn's involvement? Keeping her face expressionless, a trick she'd practiced in her legal career, Kendra studied Santos as, for one very long moment, no one said a word.

Then Flynn said roughly, "That's good news. But I didn't take it, so how could I know it was returned?"

"Thought your lawyer might have notified you," Santos said, watching him closely.

Flynn scrutinized him just as intently. "Not yet. When did this happen?"

"On Wednesday, then the accountant discovered it yesterday. It's possible no one's notified your lawyer yet."

Flynn nodded. Swallowed. "Well, that's . . . wonderful."

"I thought you'd like to know." Santos paused. "It's odd, though, isn't it? Why would someone steal it, then return it?"

They all stared at each other for another long moment. Gwen said quietly, "Maybe they needed it for some reason. They borrowed it, always hoping or intending to pay it back." Then her pretty golden brown eyes narrowed. "But how terrible, to let Flynn go to trial for a crime he didn't commit."

"Heartless," Santos agreed. "Though perhaps they were relying on the justice system, figuring an innocent man wouldn't be convicted. And you weren't, in the end."

"All the same," Gwen said, "it must have been horrible. I can't even imagine what it did to your life, your career, your family."

Flynn swallowed, audibly.

"I shouldn't have prosecuted," Kendra admitted. "I know now that Flynn's innocent."

"Well, it's over now," Gwen said. "Flynn, your name will be cleared." She turned to Kendra. "Won't it?"

She nodded and said forcefully, "If I have anything to say about it." Then she turned to Flynn and gazed steadily into his eyes, reaffirming her promise to him.

His face softened and his eyes lit. Yes, that was what she loved to see. A warm, dancing sparkle in their green depths.

Santos spoke again, drawing everyone's attention. "There are a couple of things I still don't understand. You two are a couple, though—"

"What do you mean?" Kendra demanded. How closely had he been watching? What had he seen?

Santos gave an amused smile. "Don't deny it. I know."

She didn't want to deny it. Not any longer. She turned to Flynn again and saw that he was gazing down at her, a question in his eyes. She moved closer to him and deliberately brushed her arm against his, trying to tell him without words that she wanted to acknowledge their relationship. Asking if it was okay with him.

He took her hand and their fingers intertwined. Joined together, they stared silently at Santos.

The Greek huffed out a breath. "Here I suspected you were co-conspirators, and really you were just secret lovers. I should have realized that." He tilted his head, studying them. "When did it start?"

"Here," she said. "On the *Aphrodite*."

Gwen gave a quick, bubbling laugh. "The love boat."

"What?" Kendra asked.

"Aphrodite. The goddess of love, sex, and beauty."

"All of that," Flynn said quietly but surely.

Kendra gave his hand a thank-you squeeze. "We had a lot of reasons to keep it secret. Including my boss, because I knew it could cost me my job if she found out. She's a distant cousin and is bound to see the cruise photos."

"If Flynn's name is cleared, that problem will be solved, won't it?" Gwen asked, sounding sympathetic.

"Hopefully. And if my boss is unreasonable . . ." Today, seeing Liz and Peter's wedding, the pureness and beauty of their love, she'd realized the truth. She smiled up at Flynn and said, simply and honestly, "Our relationship's more important than my job."

He lifted their clasped hands and pressed a kiss to the back of hers.

The wedding planner nodded approvingly.

Flynn turned to Santos. "Okay, what's the second thing? You said there were two things you didn't understand."

"Right. You went into a travel agent and changed your flight. What was that all about?"

Oh my God. Flynn's hand tightened on hers and Kendra's anxiety level ratcheted up again.

Flynn gazed coolly at the Greek. "I told you I was confirming my flight."

"The agent said you changed your ticket."

Santos had talked to the agent. But surely she wouldn't have revealed the details of the change; that information was supposed to be confidential. Heart racing, Kendra gazed at Flynn.

After a pause, he slipped his free hand in his pocket. "Want to see the tickets? Rather than go home right after the wedding, Kendra and I are staying on Crete together for a few days."

It was an excellent answer—a true one, framed in a lovely shade of gray. And it would work, if the travel agent hadn't blabbed information she shouldn't have.

"Ah," Santos said, "so that was it. And you wanted to keep that a secret."

Relief surged through her. "We did. But no longer. We're

tired of sneaking around. We want to be together, honestly and openly."

"We do." Flynn released her hand and put his arm firmly around her shoulders, drawing her against him as her arm went around his lean waist.

Santos studied them and grinned. "Makes sense to me." He turned to the wedding planner. "Gwen, what do you think?"

"I can relate to that." She smiled up at him with an expression that . . . Hmm. It looked a lot like the one Kendra figured was on her face when she gazed at Flynn.

Gwen and Santos were secret lovers, too?

The thought had just crossed her mind when Santos held out his hand and Gwen placed hers in it, then they leaned toward each other and their lips touched in a tender, loving kiss.

Kendra gaped at them, then said to Flynn, "I didn't see that coming."

He shook his head, lips beginning to curve. "How about this? Do you see this coming?" He stepped forward to face her and, taking all the time in the world, reached out with his free hand, caressed the side of her face, then lowered his head to hers.

"A mile away," she said with satisfaction, going up on her toes to meet his lips.

A moment later, chanting from the group of revelers across the courtyard interrupted her reverie. She realized the dancing had stopped and everyone was urging Liz to toss her bridal bouquet.

Santos and Gwen had turned to look, too. He, eyes sparkling, said, "Want to go see if you catch it, Gwen?"

Flynn said, "Kendra, how about you? You're tall, you could beat the others out."

Kendra laughed. Yes, she was tall, and she could be damned assertive when it suited her. "No, I'll give it a pass. I have everything I want right here."

Gwen gave her a smile of perfect accord. "I know exactly what you mean."

And, as Liz wound up to make her toss, Gwen turned back to her sexy Greek and Kendra rested her hands on Flynn's shoulders. "Yes, everything I could possibly want."

ABOUT THE AUTHOR

Susan Lyons writes sexy contemporary romance that's intense, passionate, heartwarming, and fun. Her books have won Booksellers Best, Aspen Gold, Golden Quill, and More than Magic awards, and have been nominated for the Romantic Times Reviewers' Choice award. She lives in Vancouver, British Columbia. She has law and psychology degrees, and has also studied anthropology, sociology, and counseling. Her careers have been varied, including perennial student, grad-school dropout, job creation project administrator, computer consultant, and legal editor. Fiction writer is by far her favorite career. Writing gives her a perfect outlet to demonstrate her belief in the power of love, friendship, and a sense of humor.

Visit Susan's website at www.susanlyons.ca for excerpts, discussion questions, writing-process notes, articles, and giveaways. Susan can be contacted at susan@susanlyons.ca.